D0240061

PROVENANCE

PROVENANCE

ANN LECKIE

www.orbitbooks.net

ORBIT

First published in Great Britain in 2017 by Orbit

1 3 5 7 9 10 8 6 4 2

Copyright © 2017 by Ann Leckie

The moral right of the author has been asserted.

All characters and events in this publication, other than
those clearly in the public domain, are fictitious
and any resemblance to real persons,
living or dead, is purely coincidental.

All rights reserved.
No part of this publication may be reproduced, stored in a
retrieval system, or transmitted, in any form or by any means,
without the prior permission in writing of the publisher, nor be
otherwise circulated in any form of binding or cover other than
that in which it is published and without a similar condition including
this condition being imposed on the subsequent purchaser.

A CIP catalogue record for this book
is available from the British Library.

HB ISBN 978-0-356-50695-1
C format 978-0-356-50696-8

Printed and bound in Great Britain by
Clays Ltd, St Ives plc

Papers used by Orbit are from well-managed forests
and other responsible sources.

MIX
Paper from
responsible sources
FSC® C104740

Orbit
An imprint of
Little, Brown Book Group
Carmelite House
50 Victoria Embankment
London EC4Y 0DZ

An Hachette UK Company
www.hachette.co.uk

www.orbitbooks.net

1

"There were unexpected difficulties," said the dark gray blur. That blur sat in a pale blue cushioned chair, no more than a meter away from where Ingray herself sat, facing, in an identical chair.

Or apparently so, anyway. Ingray knew that if she reached much more than a meter past her knees, she would touch smooth, solid wall. The same to her left, where apparently the Facilitator sat, bony frame draped in brown, gold, and purple silk, hair braided sleekly back, dark eyes expressionless, watching the conversation. Listening. Only the beige walls behind and to the right of Ingray were really as they appeared. The table beside Ingray's chair with the gilded decanter of scrbat and the delicate glass tray of tiny rose-petaled cakes was certainly real—the Facilitator had invited her to try them. She had been too nervous to even consider eating one.

"Unexpected difficulties," continued the dark gray blur, "that led to unanticipated expenses. We will require a larger payment than previously agreed."

That other anonymous party could not see Ingray where she sat—saw her as the same sort of dark gray blur she herself faced. Sat in an identical small room, somewhere else on this station. Could not see Ingray's expression, if she let her dismay and despair show itself on her face. But the Facilitator could see them both. E wouldn't betray having seen even Ingray's smallest reaction, she was sure. Still. "Unexpected difficulties are not my concern," she said, calmly and smoothly as she could manage. "The price was agreed beforehand." The price was everything she owned, not counting the clothes she wore, or passage home—already paid.

"The unexpected expenses were considerable, and must be met somehow," said the dark gray blur. "The package will not be delivered unless the payment is increased."

"Then do not deliver it," replied Ingray, trying to sound careless. Holding her hands very still in her lap. She wanted to clutch the green and blue silk of her full skirts, to have some feeling that she could hold on to something solid and safe, a childish habit she thought she'd lost years ago. "You will not receive any payment at all, as a result. Certainly your expenses must be met regardless, but that is no concern of mine."

She waited. The Facilitator said nothing. Ingray reminded herself that the gray blur had more to lose than she did if this deal didn't happen. She could take what was left of the payment she'd brought, after the Facilitator's commission—payable no matter what happened, at this stage. She could go home, back to Hwae. She'd have a good deal less than she'd started with, true, and maybe she would have to settle for that, invest what she had left. If she lost her job she could probably use what connections remained to her to find another one. She imagined her foster-mother's cold disappointment; Netano Aughskold did not waste time or energy on unambitious or unsuccessful children.

And Ingray imagined her foster-brother Danach's smug triumph. Even if all Ingray's plans succeeded, she would never replace Danach as Netano's favorite, but she could walk away from the Aughskolds knowing she'd humiliated her arrogant brother, and made all of them, Netano included, take notice. And plenty of other people with power and influence would take notice as well. If this deal didn't go through, she wouldn't have that, wouldn't have even the smallest of victories over her brother.

Silence still from the gray blur, from the Facilitator. The spicy smell of the serbat from the decanter turned her stomach. It wasn't going to happen.

And maybe that would be all right. What was she trying to do anyway? This plan was ridiculous. It was impossible. The chances of her succeeding, even if this trade went ahead, were next to nothing. What was she even doing here? For an instant she felt as though she had stepped off the edge of a precipice, and this was that barest moment before she plunged downward.

Ingray could end it now. Announce that the deal was off, give the Facilitator eir fee, and go home with what she had left.

The blur across from Ingray gave a dissatisfied sigh. "Very well, then. The deal goes forward. But now we know what to think of the much-vaunted impartiality and equitable practice of the Tyr."

"The terms were plain from the start," said the Facilitator in an even tone. "The payment was accurately described to you, and if you did not consider it adequate, you had only to demand more at the time of the offer, or refuse the sale outright. This is our inflexible rule in order to prevent misunderstandings and acrimony at just this stage of the proceedings. I explained this to you at the time. Had you not expressed your understanding of and agreement to that policy, I would not have allowed the exchange to go forward. To do otherwise would damage our reputation for impartiality and fair dealing." The gray blur did not reply. "I have examined the payment and the merchandise," said the Facilitator, still calm and even. "They are both as promised."

Now was Ingray's chance. She should escape this while she still could. She opened her mouth. "Very well," she said.

Oh, almighty powers, what had she just done?

The assigned pickup location was a small room walled in orchids growing on what looked like a maze of tree roots. A woman in a brown-and-purple jacket and sarong stood beside a scuffed gray shipping crate two meters long and one high, jarringly out of place in such carefully tended, soft-colored luxury. "There is some misunderstanding, excellency," Ingray suggested. "This is supposed to be a person." Looking at the size and the shape of the crate, it occurred to her that it might hold a body.

Utter failure. The dread Ingray had felt since the gray blur had demanded extra payment intensified.

Not moving from her place at the far end of the crate, not looking at it, not even blinking, the woman said, primly, "We do not involve ourselves in kidnappings or in slave trading, excellency."

Ingray blinked. Took a breath, unsure of how to continue. "May I open the crate?" she asked, finally.

"It is yours," said the woman. "You may do whatever you wish with it." She did not otherwise move.

It took Ingray a few moments to find all the latches on the crate lid. Each came apart with a dull snap, and she carefully shoved over one end of the heavy lid, wary of sending it crashing over the back of the crate. Light glinted off something smooth and dark inside. A suspension pod. She pushed the lid a few centimeters farther over. Reached in to pull back the cover over the pod's indicator panel. Blue and green lights on the panel told her the pod was in operation, and its occupant alive. She could not help a very small exhalation of relief.

And maybe it was better this way. She could delay any awkward explanations, could bring this person to the ship she'd booked passage on without anyone knowing what she was doing. She pushed and tugged the crate lid back into place, relatched it.

"Your pardon," she said to the woman in the brown-and-purple sarong. "I didn't anticipate that...my purchase would arrive packaged this way. I don't think I can move this on my own. Is there a cart I can borrow?" How she would get it onto a cart by herself, she didn't know. And if they charged for the cart's use, well, she had nothing left to pay for that. She might have to open that pod, right here and now, and hope its occupant was willing and able to walk. "Or can it be delivered to my ship?"

With no change of expression, the woman touched the side of the crate, and there was a click and it shifted toward Ingray, just a bit. "Once you have claimed your purchase," the woman said, "it is no longer in our custody and we will not take any responsibility for it. This may occasionally seem inconvenient, but we find it prevents misunderstandings. You should be able to move this on your own. When you are clear of our premises and have reenabled your communications you'll be shown the most efficient passable route for objects of this size."

There must have been some kind of assist on the crate, because although it had to be quite heavy it slid easily, though it swung wildly until Ingray got the trick of moving it forward without also sending it sideways. And she almost lost control of it entirely when, coming out of a nondescript doorway into a broad, brightly lit black-and-red-tiled corridor, she blinked her communications back on and a long list of alerts and news items suddenly appeared in her vision. A surprising lot of news items, when Ingray had set her feed to winnow out local news, all but the most urgent. Though the largest and brightest of them—large enough that she couldn't help reading it even as she desperately swung the shipping crate away from crashing into a wall—was definitely of more than local interest. GECK DIPLOMATIC MISSION ARRIVES IN TYR, it read, and smaller, beneath that, TYR SIILAS COUNCIL APPROVES REQUEST FOR PROVISIONS, FUEL, AND REPAIRS. Well, of course they had approved it. The Geck were signatories to the treaty with the dangerous and enigmatic Presger, and whatever anyone felt about who had made that treaty and how, no one was fool enough to want to break it.

Her attention to the headline brought up a cloud of more detailed information, and opinion pieces. CONCLAVE A BLATANT RADCHAAI POWER GRAB shouted one, and CONSCIOUS AI MAKES ITS MOVE AT LAST—IS THIS THE BEGINNING OF THE END FOR HUMANITY? asked another. A quiet voice whispered in her ear that a noodle shop she'd eaten at six times since she'd arrived here was open and nearby, with a relatively short queue—a personal alert Ingray had set days ago and forgotten to turn off. She hadn't eaten breakfast, or the cakes the Facilitator had offered her. But suddenly noodles sounded very good.

There wasn't time. The ship she'd bought passage on departed in three hours, which meant she had to be aboard in less time than that. And even if she'd had time—and any money at all—she could hardly queue for noodles with this body-size crate in tow that she could barely steer. She thought away every message except the route to her ship, and kept going. She could eat on board.

The route she'd been given kept her mostly out of the station's busiest areas, though on Tyr Siilas "less busy" was still quite crowded. At first she was self-conscious, afraid she'd attract unwelcome curiosity pushing a suspension-pod-size crate through the station's thoroughfares, but the crowds split and streamed around her without contact or comment. And she was hardly the only person pushing an awkward load. She had to swerve carefully around a stack of crates full of onions, apparently trundling along under its own power, and then found herself stuck for a few frustrating seconds behind what at first she took to be a puzzlingly tall mech, but when it finally moved she realized it was actually a human in an environmental support suit, someone from a low-gravity habitat, to judge from their height and need to wear the suit.

At one point she had to wait a half hour for a freight lift, and then spent the ride pinned against the lift's grimy back wall. She regretted wearing her stiff, formal sandals and the silk jacket and long, full skirts that she'd kept when she'd sold the rest of her clothes, with the intention of looking as seriously businesslike as possible. Very probably pointless—the Facilitator likely didn't care so long as her money was good, and whoever was on the other side of the deal she'd made couldn't see her anyway.

As soon as she was off the lift she girded up her skirts, and took off her sandals and set them on the crate along with the small bag that held everything else she owned now—her identity tabula and a few small toiletries— and then set out on the long stop-and-start trek through the docks, swerving around inattentive travelers when she could, the time display in her vision reassuring her, at least, that she still had plenty of time to reach her ship, which was, predictably, in the section of the docks farthest from where she'd entered.

She arrived at the bay tired, frustrated, and anxious. The bay was much smaller than she'd expected, but then she had only ever taken the big passenger liners between systems. Had taken one here, but she could not afford even the cheapest available return fare home on such a ship. She'd known this ship was small, a cargo ship with a few extra berths for passengers, known that her trip home would be cramped and unluxurious, but she hadn't stopped to consider what that would mean now that she was bringing this crate with her. If this had been a passenger liner, there would have been someone here she could turn the crate over to, who would make sure it got to Ingray's berth, or to cargo. But the bay was empty. And she didn't think she could get both herself and the crate into the airlock.

While she stood thinking, a man came out of the airlock. Short and solid-bodied, and there was something undefinably odd about his squarish face—something off about the shape of his nose, or the size of his mouth. His hair was pulled back behind his head, to hang behind him in dozens of tiny braids. He wore a gray-and-green-striped lungi and a dark gray jacket, and he was barefoot—less formal than what nearly everyone here wore for business dealings or important meetings, but still perfectly respectable. "You are Ingray Aughskold?"

"You must be Captain Uisine." Ingray had booked this berth through the Tyr Siilas dock office, days ago, before this ship had arrived here. "Or is it Captain Tic?" Somewhere like this, where you met people from all over, it was difficult to know what order anyone's name was in, or which one they preferred to be addressed by.

"Either one," said Captain Uisine. "You didn't say anything about oversize luggage, excellency."

"No," Ingray said. "I didn't. I wasn't expecting it myself."

Captain Uisine was silent a moment. Waiting, Ingray supposed. Then, "It's too large for the passenger compartments, excellency. It will need to be loaded into cargo. That's accessed on the lower level. But it's sealed up at the moment. And I'm not opening it before I see a duly registered Statement of Contents."

She didn't even know there was such a thing, or that she might need it. Then again, she'd never expected to have to deal with cargo at all. "I can't..." She really ought to have eaten something that morning. "I can't leave it behind. Is there time to open the cargo access?" She thought she was standing quite still, but she must have moved the hand that rested on the crate, because now it slid forward. She grabbed for it.

Captain Uisine laid a hand on it to stop and steady it. "Plenty of time. Departure's delayed. Have you not checked your notifications? We're here another two days."

"Two days!" It didn't seem possible. She summoned her notifications to her vision, and saw what she would have seen immediately if she'd checked her personal messages—a brief, bare note about the delay, from

Captain Tic Uisine. *Unavoidable delay*, the note called it, *due to current events.*

Current events. Of course. Ingray pulled up the news, looked closer at the information about the Geck diplomatic mission. Which mentioned, quite clearly but further in than she'd bothered to look, that arrivals and departures were being rearranged to fit the Geck in as quickly and safely as possible.

There was no arguing with that, no recourse. Even if Ingray had been traveling with Netano Aughskold, who had herself not infrequently demanded (and received) such priority, it wouldn't have done any good, and not just because this wasn't Netano's home system. The Geck were aliens, not human. They almost never left their homeworld, or so Ingray understood, and had done so now only to attend to urgent matters regarding the treaty with the alien Presger. Before the treaty, the Presger would tear apart human ships and stations—and their passengers and residents—seemingly at a whim. Nothing could stop them, nothing except the treaty, which the Radchaai ruler Anaander Mianaai had signed in the name of all humanity; the Presger apparently did not understand or care about whether there might be different sorts of humans, with different authorities. But no matter how anyone felt about the Radchaai taking on that authority, no one wanted the Presger to start killing people again.

Eventually the Geck had also become signatories, and much more recently the Rrrrr. And now there was a potential third new nonhuman signatory to the treaty, and a conclave, called by the Presger, to decide the issue. Probably everyone anywhere in the unthinkably vast reaches of human-inhabited space was aware of it, had opinions, wanted to know more, wanted to know how this conclave would affect their futures.

Ingray couldn't bring herself to care just now. "I can't wait two days," she said. Captain Uisine said nothing, didn't make the obvious comment—there was no avoiding the wait, and he had no control over it. Didn't take his hand off the end of the crate. Probably wise—Ingray didn't know how to turn off the assist. "I just can't."

"Why not?" he asked. Serious, but not, it seemed, terribly invested in Ingray's particular problems.

Ingray closed her eyes. She would not cry. Opened her eyes again, took a breath, and said, "I spent everything I had settling up at my lodgings this morning."

"You're broke." Captain Uisine's eyes flicked to Ingray's bag and jacket and sandals still perched on top of the crate.

"I can't not eat for two days." She should have had breakfast that morning. She should have eaten some cakes, when she was dealing with the Facilitator.

"Well, you can," said Captain Uisine. "As long as you have water. But what about your friend?"

Ingray frowned. "My friend?"

"The person you're traveling with. Can they help you out?"

"Um."

Captain Uisine waited, still noncommittal. It occurred to Ingray that even if Captain Uisine charged for carrying the crate in cargo, it would likely be less than a passenger fare. Maybe she'd have enough to at least buy a meal or two between now and when the ship finally left. "And while you're thinking about that," the captain added before Ingray could speak, "you can show me the Statement of Contents for the crate."

For a panicked moment, Ingray tried to think of some way to argue that she shouldn't have to show one. Then she remembered that so far the Facilitator seemed to have anticipated what she would need to bring the crate away with her. She pulled her personal messages into her vision again, and there it was. "I've just sent it to you," she said.

Captain Uisine blinked, and gazed off into the distance. "Miscellaneous biologicals," he said after a few moments, focusing again on Ingray. "In a crate this size and shape? I'm sorry, excellency, but I didn't hatch this morning. I'll be exercising my right to examine the contents myself, as outlined in the fare agreement. Otherwise that crate is not coming aboard."

Damn. "So," said Ingray, "the person I'm traveling with is in here."

"In the crate?" He seemed entirely unsurprised.

"In a suspension pod in the crate, yes," Ingray replied. "I didn't expect em to come this way, I thought I would just, you know, meet em and bring em here, and..." She trailed off, at a loss how to explain any further.

"Do you have authorizations permitting you to remove this person from Tyr Siilas? And before you mention it, I am aware that such authorizations aren't always legally necessary here. I, however, do always require them."

13

"An authorization to take someone on your ship?" Ingray frowned, bewildered. "You didn't need one for me. You didn't ask me for one, for ... my friend."

Still not changing expression, Captain Uisine said, "I don't transport anyone against their will. I say that specifically in the fare agreement." Which Ingray had read, of course; she was no fool. But obviously she hadn't remembered that. Hadn't thought, at that point, that it would be an issue. "I can ask you right now, do you want to leave Tyr Siilas and go to Hwae ..."

"I do!" Ingray interjected.

"... and you can tell me that." His voice was still serious and even. "This person cannot tell me if e wants to go where you are taking em. I don't doubt there's some very compelling reason you are bringing em aboard in a suspension pod. I would like to be sure that compelling reason is eirs, and not just yours."

"But..." But he'd already said that this wasn't a matter of Tyr Siilas law. And if he refunded her money, she might be able to find another ship for the same fare, but if she went through the dock office again she'd have to pay another fee, which she didn't have. She might be able to find passage on her own, but that would take time. Maybe a lot of time. She sighed. "I don't know why e's in a suspension pod." Well, actually, she had some idea. But that wasn't going to help her cause with Captain Uisine, plainly. "I went to pick em up, and this is how I found em."

"Is there some medical reason this person is traveling in a suspension pod?"

"Not that I know of," she said, quite honestly.

"E didn't leave you any message, or any instruction?"

"No."

"Well, excellency," said Captain Uisine after a few moments, "I suggest we open the pod and ask em. We can always put em back in if e prefers that."

"What, right here?" The bay wasn't really closed off, not at the moment, and coming out of a suspension pod was uncomfortable and undignified. Or so Ingray understood. And in the time it had taken to push the crate here, she had decided that maybe she preferred things this way, preferred to delay introducing herself to this person and explaining just why she'd brought em here.

"I don't have oversize luggage regulations for amusement's sake. The only way that crate is coming on board is through cargo access. And for what I hope are obvious reasons I'm not going to agree to that happening."

If Ingray's mother Netano were doing this, she'd have somehow obtained whatever authorizations she would need to satisfy this ship captain. Or she'd have bought passage on some ship where the captain or other crew owed her favors, or were in her power for some reason. Danach—Ingray's foster-brother Danach would probably find some way to threaten Captain Uisine, or charm or bribe him into doing what he wanted. Maybe she could bluff her way through this. Maybe tears would do it; they would certainly be easy to produce right now. But judging from the captain's reaction on hearing that she wouldn't be able to afford to eat for two days, she didn't think that would work.

She had to do something. She had to get herself—and the person in this suspension pod—onto that ship. She had no other option, no other available course, beyond staying on this station, broke and starving, for the rest of her life.

She was *not* going to cry. "Look," she said, "I need to explain." Captain Uisine had already put the worst possible construction on the situation. It wasn't going to look any better once the suspension pod was opened. She looked behind her, through the entrance to the bay, but no one was passing in the corridor beyond. Looked back at Captain Uisine. Sighed again. "I paid to have this person brought out of Compassionate Removal." No glimmer of recognition on Captain Uisine's face. She'd used the name most Bantia speakers would have used, on Hwae; maybe he didn't recognize that. She tried to think what the word might be in Yiir, which she had been using here, had used in all her brief dealings with Captain Uisine so far. She didn't think there was one—here on Tyr Siilas nearly every crime was punishable by a fine. All the language lessons and news items she'd run across discussed crime and its consequences in those terms. She called up a dictionary, tried searching through it, without success. "You know, when someone breaks a law, and either they've done it over and over again and you know they're just going to keep doing it, or what they did was so terrible they're not going to get another chance to do it again. So they get sent to Compassionate Removal."

"You're talking about a prison," said Captain Uisine.

In the corner of Ingray's vision, her dictionary confirmed and defined the word. "No, it's not a *prison*! We don't have prisons. It's a *place*. Where they can be away from regular people. They can do whatever they want, go wherever they like, you know, so long as they stay there. And they have to stay there. Once you go in you don't come out. You're legally dead. It's just, it would be wrong to *kill* them."

"So you paid everything you had—which to judge from the clothes you're wearing, and your manner, was quite a lot—to have your friend broken out of a high-security prison with a name that sounds like a euphemism for killing vermin. What did e do?"

"E's not my friend! I've never even met em. Well, I was at an event e was at once. A couple of times. But we never met in person."

"What did e do?" Captain Uisine asked again.

"This is Pahlad Budrakim." Winced, after she said it. Had she really done this? But there hadn't been any other choice.

After an endless moment, Captain Uisine said, "Am I supposed to recognize the name?"

"You don't?" asked Ingray, surprised. "Not at all?"

"Not at all."

"Pahlad's father, Ethiat Budrakim, is Prolocutor of the Third Assembly, on Hwae." No reaction from Captain Uisine. "A prolocutor is..."

"Yes," put in Captain Uisine, evenly. "A prolocutor presides over an Assembly, and represents that Assembly to the Overassembly. I've been to Hwae Station

17

quite a few times, and I pay attention to station news. I know who Prolocutor Dicat is, e's Prolocutor of the First Assembly. Eir name is on all sorts of regulations I have to follow when I'm docked there. But I don't know anything about the Third Assembly."

That made sense. Hwae Station and the several Hwaean outstations—and the intersystem gates, for that matter—were all under the authority of the First Assembly. It made sense that Captain Uisine would pay attention to First Assembly affairs and not to the Assemblies based on Hwae itself. Ingray blinked. Took a breath. "Well, Prolocutor Budrakim has held his seat for decades. There was an election just a few years ago. It was very dramatic. He almost lost. Which is how... Pahlad is...well, *was* one of his foster-children. Ethiat Budrakim is part Garseddai."

"Him and a billion other people who think it's tragic and romantic to be Garseddai." Captain Uisine's voice was disdainful. "It's only the most notorious out of a long list of Radchaai atrocities. The only system to resist invasion so effectively that the Radchaai destroyed every last one of them for it and left the entire system burned and lifeless. People like your Prolocutor Budrakim can claim ancestors who are either especially valorous or especially deserving of sympathy, whichever suits them better at the moment. Lucky for them there's no way to prove it one way or the other. Let me guess; he's descended from an Elector who managed to secretly flee the system before the Radchaai burned everything."

"But he is!" insisted Ingray. "He has proof. He's got

part of a panel from inside the shuttle his ancestor fled in, and a shirt with blood on it. And a lot of other things, jewelry and a half dozen of those little pentagonal tokens stamped with flowers that I think were from some kind of game. Or, he used to have those things. They were stolen. You really didn't hear about this?"

"I really didn't." Captain Uisine sounded half sarcastic, as though the idea that he might have heard about something that had consumed the attention of everyone Ingray had known, and pretty much every major news service in Hwae System, struck him as ridiculous.

"It was an inside job. Pahlad had grown up in Ethiat Budrakim's household, and e had been given a post overseeing the lareum where the Garseddai vestiges were kept." There had been a lot of comment about how, while it was of course generous of prominent citizens to raise foster-children from less advantaged circumstances, or even the public crèches, it had been foolish of Ethiat Budrakim to trust Pahlad so implicitly. No one was as close or loyal as your own acknowledged heirs, everyone knew that. Thinking of it still made Ingray, herself a foster-child out of a public crèche, cringe unhappily. "Nobody could have done it except Pahlad."

"And for this e is cast permanently into an inescapable prison, what did you call it, Compassionate Removal? And declared dead?" He took his hand off the crate. Put it back, when the crate shifted again, even though Ingray still held her end.

"E had betrayed eir parent! It was a huge scandal. And e showed no signs of remorse at what e had done. The whole thing had been very elaborate and cold-blooded. E managed to make copies of the things and put them in the lareum in place of the real ones, and there was Prolocutor Budrakim showing people around, you know, thinking they were the real ones, and no one knowing they were fake the whole time. And his foster-child Pahlad standing right there nearly every time, just as cool as anything, as though nothing was wrong." And after all, it wasn't as though e was being executed. "The copies were nearly perfect."

Captain Uisine thought about that a moment. "And your interest in this?"

"They never found the originals," Ingray said. "Pahlad wouldn't say what had happened to them. E insisted e had stolen nothing, and done nothing wrong. But of course e must have done it, no one else could have. So e must know where they are."

"Ah." Captain Uisine seemed to relax, and leaned back against the airlock frame, folded his arms. "You think this Pahlad Budrakim can lead you to the originals, which you can then, what, sell? Hold hostage? Restore heroically to their proper place?"

Any of them would serve Ingray's purpose, really. But what she wanted more than anything was to be able to bring them to Netano. "My mother is a district representative in the Third Assembly. She wants to be Third Prolocutor—she tried, last election, but in the end the votes tipped Budrakim's way." And Netano had never been friendly with Ethiat Budrakim, an enmity that couldn't be explained by differences of faction. After all, plenty of other Assembly representatives managed to get along quite amicably whatever their differing positions on tariffs or fishing limits. "Right now I'm one of three..." Not three. Vaor had gone last year. Gone because e'd wanted to, e'd insisted, not because Netano had sent em away, but e had wept the whole time e'd packed, wept walking out the door, and e hadn't answered any of Ingray's messages since. "Two foster-children in my mother's household. One of us will get to be Netano eventually."

"And this is how you intend to distinguish yourself in your mother's eyes," Captain Uisine guessed.

"I didn't expect Pahlad to come all packaged up like this!" She couldn't resist the impulse anymore—she grabbed a handful of soft silk skirt. "I went to, you know, the usual sort of broker here, and made an offer, to whoever could discreetly bring Pahlad Budrakim out of Compassionate Removal." Honestly, she hadn't really expected that anyone would take that offer up. The plan had been desperate from the start.

"Slavery and human trafficking are among the very few things that aren't legal here," Captain Uisine observed. "Technically, anyway. Of *course* they would deliver this person to you all packaged up. It gives them deniability. And I must say, excellency, the fact that that didn't occur to you, or that you weren't at least prepared for the possibility, suggests to me that you're not best suited to follow in the footsteps of your apparently political mother." Ingray frowned. She was *not* going to cry. Captain Uisine continued speaking. "I mean no offense. We all have our particular talents. What happens if you aren't selected to be your mother's heir?"

Possibly not much. Possibly she would just continue in her job, in the family, as she had. But Netano had always said that in anything worth doing, the stakes were all or nothing. Most families on Hwae had sent one or more children out for fosterage, or were fostering children from other households, some in temporary arrangements, some in permanent adoptions. Danach, for instance, was a foster from one of Netano's supporters. But there were always some children in every district whose parents were unwilling or unable to care for them, and had no one willing or able to foster them, who ended up as wards of the state in one of the district's public crèches. Ingray, like Pahlad Budrakim, had been one of these. "I don't really have a chance to be Mama's heir. I never really did." But if she left the Aughskold household, or was sent away, she had no other family to turn to. She would be entirely on her own. "Mama likes it when we take initiative, and she likes schemes, but she doesn't like it when we fail. If I fail badly enough I'll probably have to leave the household. Worse, I'll be in debt. I borrowed against my future allowance, to get enough for the payment. So even if I don't lose my job—which I probably will—I'll be broke. For years." For decades. "I know it wasn't exactly a prudent use of my resources," she admitted. Willed herself to open her hand, raised it to lay on the crate but instead clasped it with her other hand, a perfectly acceptable pose with no danger of anxiously clutching at things. "If I was going to borrow like that, I ought to have just invested it somewhere safe. Then if Netano sent me away, I'd have at least had enough to keep myself with. I just..." She just couldn't stand the thought of Danach sneering openly at her. Of losing any chance at all of Netano Aughskold's regard.

Captain Uisine stared at her over the crate. "I am on the very edge," he said, finally, "of refunding your passage—both of the berths you've paid for—and asking you to leave this bay. I haven't made up my mind yet. But I'll tell you one thing, there's no way you're bringing that person—Pahlad Budrakim, you said?—aboard my ship still in that suspension pod. And considering you expected to meet em awake and unfrozen, you won't have any objection to thawing em out now, I presume?"

"Will you take us aboard then?"

"I'll *consider* taking *you* aboard then. Pahlad Budrakim can do as e likes." A moment's thought. "If e doesn't want to come aboard, I'll refund you eir fare."

It could have been worse, Ingray supposed. It was *some* sort of chance, anyway. Captain Uisine put his other hand on the crate. "Step back, excellency, you don't want your foot caught under this." Ingray stepped back and the crate settled to the floor with a *thunk*. "Do you know if this person has ever been in suspension before?"

Ingray picked up her jacket and bag and sandals off the crate lid. "No, why?"

Captain Uisine touched the crate's latches and carefully slid the lid aside. "E might panic if e doesn't know what to expect. A little help would be nice."

Ingray dropped her sandals and bag, pulled her jacket on, and then helped brace the lid as Captain Uisine tilted it and let it slide down to rest against the crate.

Captain Uisine looked for a moment at the smooth, black surface of the pod, then slid open the pod's control panel. "Everything looks good," he said, as a giant black spider scuttled out of the airlock, nearly a meter high, a rolled-up blanket clutched in one hairy appendage. Weirdly, disturbingly graceful, it skittered up to Captain Uisine and stopped, turned one of its far too many stalked eyes toward Ingray. No, it wasn't a spider. It was...something else.

"Um," said Ingray. "That's...is that a spider?" She didn't know why the back of her neck was prickling. She didn't mind spiders. But this...thing was so unsettling. Its legs were jointed wrong, she realized, and its eyestalks sprouted right out of its blob of a body. There was no waist, no head. And something else was wrong, though she couldn't quite say what.

"Of course it's not a spider," replied Captain Uisine, still frowning at the suspension pod. "You don't get spiders with half-meter bodies, or two-meter leg spans. Or, you know, not unaugmented ones. But this isn't a spider." He looked up. "But it's *kind* of like a spider, I'll grant you that. Do you have a problem with spiders, excellency?" The not-spider's body trembled gelatinously, stretched to become oblong rather than round, and four extra legs slid out to touch the bay floor. "Does that help?"

Seeing the thing change shape was somehow even more disturbing, but she refused to step back, even though she wanted to. "Not really. And I don't mind spiders at all. It's just, this looks so...so organic." Except in a wrong, squishy, itchy sort of way.

"Well, yes," said Captain Uisine, standing square and stolid by the open crate. Entirely unbothered by the spidery thing beside him. "A lot of it is. Some people find it unsettling, and apparently you're one of them, but it's just a bio mech. You'll get used to it after a few days, or if you don't I'll keep it out of your way." He touched the control panel and the smooth surface of the pod broke open with a click and slid aside. For just an instant Ingray saw a person lying naked and motionless, submerged in a pool of blue fluid, unevenly cut hair a tangled mass over half of eir sharp-featured face, thin—thinner than she remembered pictures of Pahlad Budrakim—the long welt of a scar along eir right flank.

Then the smooth, glassy surface of the preserving medium rippled and billowed as the person opened eir eyes and sat convulsively up, choking, one outthrust arm smacking hard into Ingray. Captain Uisine grabbed eir other arm. "It's all right," he said, voice still calm and serious. The person continued to choke as blue fluid poured out of eir mouth and nose, sheeted away from eir body back into the pod. "It's all right. Everything's fine. You're all right."

The last of the fluid drained away from the person's mouth and nose, and e gave a breathy, shaking moan.

"First time?" asked Captain Uisine, reaching down for the blanket the spider mech still proffered.

The naked person in the pod closed eir eyes. Gasped a few times, and then eir breathing settled.

"Are you all right?" asked Ingray. In Bantia this time, the most commonly spoken language in Hwae System, though she was fairly sure Pahlad Budrakim would have understood Yiir, which Captain Uisine had used.

Captain Uisine shook the blanket out and laid it around the naked person's shoulders.

"Where am I?" e asked, in Bantia, voice rough with cold or fear or something else.

"We're on Tyr Siilas Station, in Tyr System," said Ingray, and then, to Captain Uisine, "E asked where e is, and I told em we are on Tyr Siilas."

"How did I get here?" asked the person sitting in the suspension pod, in Bantia. By now the blue fluid had all drained away to some reservoir in the pod itself.

"I paid someone to bring you out," said Ingray. "I'm Ingray Aughskold."

The person opened eir eyes then. "Who?"

Well, Ingray had never really met Pahlad Budrakim in person. And e was ten or more years older than she was, and not likely to have noticed a very young Aughskold foster-daughter, not likely to have known her name when she had still been a child, let alone her adult name, which she'd taken only months before e'd gone into Compassionate Removal. "I'm one of Netano Aughskold's children," said Ingray.

"Why," e asked, eir voice gaining strength, "would one of Representative Aughskold's children bring me anywhere?"

Ingray tried to think of a simple way to explain, and settled, finally, for, "You're Pahlad Budrakim."

26

E gave a little shake of eir head, a frown. "Who?"

Ingray suppressed a start as another spider mech came skittering out of the airlock. This one held a large cup of steaming liquid, which it passed to Captain Uisine before it spun and returned to the ship. "Here, excellency," he said, in Yiir, offering it to the person still sitting in the pod. "Can you hold this?"

"Here," said the first spider mech, in a thin, thready voice, in Bantia. "Can you hold this?"

"Aren't you Pahlad Budrakim?" asked Ingray, feeling strangely numb, except maybe for an unpleasant sensation in her gut, as though she was not capable of feeling any more despair or fear than she already had today. The Facilitator had said this was Pahlad. No, e'd said e'd examined the payment and the merchandise and both were what they should have been. But surely that was the same thing.

"No," said the person sitting in the suspension pod. "I don't even know who that is." E noticed the cup Captain Uisine was proffering. "Thank you," e said, and took it, cupped it in eir hands as Captain Uisine stopped the blanket from sliding off eir shoulders.

"Drink some," said Captain Uisine, still in Yiir. "It's serbat—it'll do you good."

"Drink it," said the spider mech, in Bantia. "It's serbat—it's good and nutritious."

What if there had been a mistake? This person looked like Pahlad Budrakim. But also, in a way, e didn't. E was thinner, certainly, and Ingray had only seen em in person once or twice, and that was years ago. "You're not Pahlad Budrakim?"

"No," said the person who was not Pahlad Budrakim. "I already said that." E took a drink of the serbat. "Oh, that's good."

Really, it didn't matter. Even if this person was Pahlad, if e was lying to her, it made no difference. She couldn't compel em to go with her back to Hwae, and not just because Captain Uisine would refuse to take em unless e wanted to go. Her plan had always depended on Pahlad being willing to go along. "You look a lot like Pahlad Budrakim," Ingray said. Still hoping.

"Do I?" e asked, and took another drink of serbat. "I guess someone made a mistake." E looked straight at Ingray then, and said, "So, when a Budrakim goes to Compassionate Removal it's only for show, is it? They send someone to fish them out, behind the scenes?" Eir expression didn't change, but eir voice was bitter.

Ingray drew breath to say, indignantly, *No of course not*, but found herself struck speechless by the fact that she had herself gotten a Budrakim out of Compassionate Removal. "No," she managed, finally. "No, I...you're really not Pahlad Budrakim?"

"I'm really not," e said.

"Then who are you?" asked the spider mech, though Captain Uisine hadn't said anything aloud.

The person sitting in the suspension pod took another drink of serbat, then said, "You said we're on Tyr Siilas?"

"Yes," said the spider mech. Ingray found she couldn't speak at all.

"I think I'd rather not tell you who I am." E looked around, at the suspension pod e sat in, the crate still surrounding it, at Captain Uisine, at the spider mech beside the captain, around at the bay. "I think I'd like to visit the Incomers Office."

"Why?" asked Ingray, almost a cry, unable to keep her confusion and her despair out of her voice.

"Unless you have financial resources we're unaware of," said the spider mech, "you won't be able to do more than apply for an indenture. You may or may not get one, and unless you have contacts here you very probably won't like what you get if you do."

"I'll like it better than Compassionate Removal." E drained the last of eir beverage.

"Look on the bright side," Captain Uisine said himself, to Ingray, in Yiir, as he took the cup from not-Pahlad. "I'll refund you eir passage, and you'll be able to eat actual food for the next couple of days."

2

Ingray leaned against the once-again closed crate, crying. Once not-Pahlad had walked out of the bay, barefoot, Captain Uisine's blanket wrapped around em, not
even looking at Ingray, she had been unable to keep the
tears back.

"Did you go through a reputable broker?" asked Captain Uisine.

"Yes." She sniffed, and wiped her eyes with the back
of her hand. "If they couldn't verify eir identity, the deal
wasn't supposed to go through. It was part of the contract." And e might really have been Pahlad, but the
more she thought about it the less sure she was that the
broker had brought her the right person. *So, when a
Budrakim goes to Compassionate Removal it's only for
show, is it?* e'd asked, with real bitterness. That hadn't
been an act.

"Did they have a good DNA sample to work with? If that was from the wrong person, or contaminated in a way they couldn't compensate for ... but they'd have told you, surely, if the sample wasn't suitable."

"I couldn't get one."

"Ah. That'll have been the problem, then. And even through a good broker, deals are always *to the best of our ability*," said Captain Uisine. "They'd have had to go by how e looked or depended on someone else to say that yes, this was really Pahlad Budrakim. You said yourself e looked like em."

"Yes." She wiped her eyes again. Did not look at Captain Uisine. Obviously she couldn't hide the fact that she was crying, but still. "Yes, e did look like em." E might well actually be Pahlad, but there was nothing Ingray could do about that. A green glass-tipped hairpin dropped onto her shoulder and then the floor. Damn. She had never been good at putting up her own hair.

And even if the person who'd just left the bay really wasn't Pahlad, even if she could prove somehow that anyone along the way had known that, she couldn't make the accusation. She couldn't afford to stay here and press charges through the Infringement Bureau, and she certainly couldn't afford to hire an advocate to do it for her. Never mind the fact that the deal had been illegal in quite a few different ways to begin with. And it wouldn't make any difference in the end—she was still left with nothing.

"Who did you deal with?" asked the captain. "Gold Orchid?" Ingray gestured affirmative. "They're a dependable firm. They won't have cheated you. Not on purpose, anyway. For whatever reason, they'll have been convinced they were delivering Pahlad Budrakim to you." A moment of silence. Then, "Or, now I think of it. Maybe they're protecting someone else's deal. Maybe the real Pahlad Budrakim isn't in prison anymore, but if they told you they couldn't produce em, you might wonder why that was, and they don't want that."

Ingray turned her head, saw Captain Uisine standing short and stolid at the end of the crate, a huge black spider mech still beside him. "What? You mean, like Pah..." No. Better to assume it wasn't really Pahlad. "Like that person said, Pahlad never went to Compassionate Removal to begin with? Or was fetched out right away? Because e's a Budrakim? Do you think so?"

"Not really," said Captain Uisine. Quietly, calmly serious. "It strikes me as needlessly complicated—brokers like Gold Orchid refuse commissions all the time, for all sorts of reasons. They might have just told you they don't buy or sell people and that would have been the end of it, I imagine. And after all, once you opened the pod and discovered it wasn't really Pahlad Budrakim, you'd be asking all of those same questions."

Ingray didn't reply, looked down at her feet again. Thought about bending over to pick up the hairpin on the floor, but given her luck right now, if she leaned forward to pick this one up three more would fall out.

Captain Uisine continued. "If you lose your job, can't you just go to the public registry in Hwae System and put your name in for employment? How bad could that be? You probably had an excellent education, you'll have met people.

You probably have the sort of skills that get someone a nice office job, at the very least. I bet if you sent a few messages, you'd have something lined up pretty quickly."

"Maybe." Without a family to help her, without contacts to speak up for her, her prospects would be limited. And it was entirely possible that if Ingray disappointed Netano sufficiently and was sent away, any office might refuse to hire her just to avoid offending Netano Aughskold.

Captain Uisine continued. "And, excellency, I know this is a delicate subject for quite a lot of people, but it seems to me that if your mother is going to turn you out of the house for not impressing her sufficiently, well, maybe you're better off on your own."

"You don't understand," said Ingray.

"Doubtless I don't," replied Captain Uisine, evenly. "In the meantime, I'll send out for some supper. My treat this once, you've had a difficult day. You can sleep aboard if you like. Why don't you stow your things, and I'll send the crate to the cargo entrance."

"I don't care about the crate," said Ingray, leaning over to pick up her sandals and her bag, and the errant hairpin. Another one dropped to the floor beside her foot.

"It's a perfectly good crate," said Captain Uisine. "And the suspension pod looks new. You can sell them when you get home. Every little bit helps."

Ingray straightened, and hurried into the airlock without answering, hoping he wouldn't see her fresh spate of tears.

There were two passenger cabins, each with two shelf-like bunks, one on top of the other. And actually "cabin" was being generous—they were little more than niches in the wall of the ship's narrow main corridor. Dismayingly cramped, and the single narrow corridor was a scuffed and dingy gray. On the other hand, the air didn't seem to have that half-stale, recycled smell that sometimes even the big passenger liners could have. Captain Uisine must have invested in a very good air recirculation system, and not cared much about the way the ship looked inside. And at least the bunk seemed clean and comfortable, and the one above was high enough that she could sit up straight. She stowed her bag under a lower bunk, ungirded her skirts, and sat down. Considered putting her sandals on, but found she didn't want to. She stowed her sandals and began to pull the remaining pins from her hair.

She'd done her best. It wasn't her fault—or, apparently, anyone else's—that she'd failed. And maybe Captain Uisine was right, and she'd be better off without Netano, without any of the Aughskolds. Netano had always been outwardly kind and generous to all her children—all of them adopted. But Ingray had known from the day she'd joined the household that her future well-being depended on not disappointing her foster-mother. All of them, including Danach, who everyone knew was Netano's favorite, were there to support Netano's political ambitions. At the very least, to be a happy, well-behaved, and well-dressed family for the news services, and ultimately for the voters. But that was the very least. Netano wanted all of her children to be extraordinary. They had, after all, been specially chosen to join her family. Fail Netano's expectations, and you were out. It had never been said aloud, not by Netano, not by anyone in the household, but even Danach knew it, and maybe that was part of why Danach was Danach.

Ingray had always felt like she didn't belong, as though at any moment her foster-mother would discover this fact, that Ingray never would have the kind of daring brilliance Netano Aughskold prized. Oh, sure, she was competent. She could remember who was who in the districts of the Third Assembly, who held what influence, who was likely to donate to a reelection fund and why, knew the pet concerns of various influential supporters, knew what to say and what not to say depending on who was listening. Ingray was one of several people in Netano's Arsamol District office who spoke directly to district residents who had complaints or concerns or requests, and these days Nuncle Lak, Netano's chief of staff, trusted her to help organize events and meetings with district residents, and she hadn't made any disastrous mistakes, not even during her first terrifying inexperienced year at the job. But competent was not brilliant. Brilliant was taking all that knowledge and those contacts and finding a way to use it to advantage. To come up with a plan, a scheme, to bring Netano more influence, more support, or really any sort of political advantage. Ingray would never be able to do that, no matter how hard she tried.

Danach certainly hadn't been deceived. He'd known from the time they were both children, and never tired of telling her that. It was a wonder Netano hadn't discovered Ingray's fraud yet.

She laid her handful of green-tipped pins on the bunk beside her, and counted them. One missing, probably fallen out on the trip from Gold Orchid to the docks.

If only. If only she really was what she had been trying so hard to be all this time. If only it hadn't been so disastrously expensive to bring Pahlad Budrakim out of Compassionate Removal. She was increasingly convinced that it wasn't Pahlad who'd walked out of the bay. Increasingly convinced by eir bitterness, and that steady conviction as e'd said that e didn't even know who Pahlad was.

Well. There was nothing she could do about that now. Best consider the future. She did have skills, and connections. She could support herself, she could pay her debt off, even if it took decades. She just had to get through the next few weeks—to face admitting her failure to Netano, and face Danach's contempt. If only there was some way to avoid that. Or better yet, to strike preemptively at Danach, to humiliate him the way he constantly tried, time and again, to humiliate her.

But wait. What if she could do exactly that?

She gathered her hair and shoved a few pins in to hold it. Got out of the bunk and went down the corridor to the ship's tiny galley. The table was folded out from the wall, and Captain Uisine sat watching the doorway, as though he had been waiting for her.

"Captain," she said, from the corridor, "I wonder if you could delay processing the refund of . . . of my friend's fare. Until I've had a chance to talk to em again."

"Had an idea, have you?" Since she had first met him,

not two hours ago, his dark, square face had shown nothing but calm seriousness. That didn't change now, but something about his manner seemed edged. Tense. "I'll delay if you like. But maybe you should eat first. Our supper should be here soon. Though I must warn you, I'm in a difficult mood just now."

"I'm…sorry to hear that, Captain." Ingray wasn't certain what else there was to say. It probably wasn't wise to ask what the problem was.

"Do you," he asked after a long, awkward silence, "have opinions to share, regarding current events?"

"About the Geck, you mean?" From that brief glimpse of news and opinion pieces she'd seen earlier, Ingray knew that the arrival of the Geck treaty delegation had brought out into the open any number of old conspiracy theories about the Geck, and about Radchaai involvement in the treaty. Ingray remembered hearing whispers, once or twice, to the effect that the Geck didn't actually exist. They seemed never to leave their homeworld, and as far as Ingray knew they only ever appeared in images in the person of human representatives. Maybe, these whispers suggested, the Geck were an invention devised to give the Radchaai extra influence on the treaty. And that wasn't the most unhinged of the rumors about the Geck she'd heard—or seen hinted at during her short sampling of recent news. But she wasn't sure why Captain Uisine would care about any of them. "No, I don't have any opinions about the Geck." Or about the business with the treaty—she'd been too busy with other things.

"If you discover any," said Captain Uisine, "please don't share them with me."

She wasn't quite sure how to respond to that, or if she should respond at all. A movement caught her eye—a spider mech, two brown cartons of what Ingray supposed was supper held above its body, jointed legs squeezed together in the narrow space of the corridor, stepping delicately toward the galley. She suppressed a shiver. She had seen mechs before, of course; everyone had, they were all over. Quite a few of them were designed in imitation of insect models. But she had never been so close to one that was so...so buglike in such a disturbing way. It made the back of her neck itch, made her want to frantically brush herself off.

She backed down the corridor to make way for the spider mech, managed to keep absolutely still as it squeezed through the galley doorway and set the cartons on the table, and then backed into the corridor and scurried off. "They're just mechs, excellency," said Captain Uisine as she came back to the galley doorway.

"You're... they're not alive?" They *seemed* alive.

"That depends on what you mean by *alive*. There is...a larger biological component than you're probably used to. But they're just mechs. They can't think for themselves. Can't think at all, really. They can perform a number of automated functions, just like any other mech, but I promise you there's no conscious AI here."

And that, Ingray realized, was what had been troubling her about the spider mechs. Their fluid, graceful movement reminded her of artificially intelligent villains in a popular entertainment. "Who controls them?" Ingray hadn't seen anyone else, or any signs of anyone else. Anything beyond the very basics of mech-piloting took a lot of attention, and some of the jobs a mech would be used for on a ship required specialized skills. Most ships Ingray had traveled on had one or more mech-pilots as part of the crew. The way these moved, so quick and unhesitating, each hairy leg placed so precisely right every time—didn't seem very mechlike. It must be that whoever was piloting them was very, very good.

"I do." Captain Uisine opened one carton. "Don't worry—I've had a lot of practice." Steam wafted up from the open carton, and the smell of spiced noodles. "Eat. Your friend is probably sitting in a waiting room. Will be for hours yet. The only way to avoid a long wait at the Incomers Office is to be very obviously rich, or well connected. You've got plenty of time to have supper."

She didn't go into the galley. Though the food smelled wonderful and it had been far too long since she'd eaten. "Why are you being so nice?" He hadn't seemed to care when she'd said she was too broke to eat for two days. Had shown no sign of caring about her at all.

"I'm an owner-operator with a small cargo ship," he said, perfectly calmly, as though the question had been an entirely ordinary one. "I've been doing this run for five years or so. The thing about small independently owned cargo ships is, lots of people think you're for sale, or easily stolen from, or available for smuggling or illicit trade. I'm not any of those things, and I've had run-ins with bad passengers before. I don't think you're a bad passenger—you could have behaved very differently when I refused to open cargo for that suspension pod. Or when the person inside that pod refused to go with you." He picked up his carton of supper. "But don't think I make a habit of this."

"Of course not, Captain." He was right. There was no rush to find the person who'd come out of that suspension pod—e was probably only just now reaching the Incomers Office, and e'd have a long, long wait ahead of em. She stepped into the tiny galley and sat down. "Thank you for the supper."

Ingray found the person who (she had decided) wasn't Pahlad Budrakim on a bench in the lobby of the Incomers Office, right where the unpadded bench met the corner of the room. Eir head leaning against the notices actually written in stark black on the white wall—presumably so that incomers who didn't yet have access to system communications, and thus couldn't see any overlays, couldn't claim ignorance of rules or regulations. Captain Uisine's blanket—a standard extruded one, dull orange-brown without even stripes or a pattern on the edges—was wrapped around em, like a lungi or a sarong. Eir arms crossed, eir eyes closed. Eir hacked-off-looking hair half over cir face. Asleep, Ingray thought. No one else was in the room—most incomers to Tyr Siilas probably had somewhere to go, once they'd managed to get a place in the queue. This person had nothing, no money, no friends, no place to stay. From what Captain Uisine had said, a wait could take days.

Ingray hadn't made a sound, she was sure, but e opened eir eyes. Looked unsmiling, unmoving, at Ingray. "Netano Aughskold's daughter," e said. "What do you want?"

"I..." She moved to sit beside em, but something about the way e was looking at her, the way eir voice sounded, stopped her. "I'd like to talk to you. May I sit here?"

"I don't imagine you need my permission." Eir tone was...not casual. Not angry or resentful or sarcastic, either. But on the edge of that. Certainly it wasn't inviting.

Ingray didn't sit. "You look an awful lot like Pahlad Budrakim."

"Apparently so," e said, still unsmiling. "Is there anything else I can do for you?"

"You could *be* Pahlad Budrakim," said Ingray. Some tiny impulse crossed eir face, some trace of a thought or a reaction, but e didn't say anything. "You really look a lot like em."

"And you went to quite a lot of trouble to get em out of Compassionate Removal."

"I did," Ingray admitted. "I wanted em to do something for me." And there had been, really, no guarantee e would have done it. "It was something only Pahlad could have done, you can't do it for me. But maybe you can do something else." She took a breath. Here it was again, that feeling that she was on the edge of a cliff, that if she backed up fast, right now, this instant, she might save herself. "Pahlad stole nearly all of the most famous Budrakim family vestiges. Ethiat Budrakim must have been beside himself when he realized they were gone, and who had done it. But Pahlad never admitted the theft, and e never said what e'd done with the things e stole."

"You were hoping this Pahlad would tell you where these vestiges were," e guessed. "You were hoping to sell the things back to Ethiat Budrakim. Or hold them hostage; he and your mother have never been friends. But now you can't do either one. So I imagine you're thinking I could pretend to be Pahlad well enough for you to leverage some money out of someone."

Ingray opened her mouth to say *my brother Danach*, but having had some food, and a bit of rest and time to think, she found herself in a much less confessional mood than earlier. She regretted as much as she'd told Captain Uisine, but still couldn't see how she could have avoided it. Doubtless her mother Netano would have found a more dignified, graceful way to tell the captain what he needed to know, without revealing more than she wanted, or coming so close to bursting into tears.

She sat down on the hard bench, half a meter away from the person who wasn't Pahlad. It was uncomfortably hard—Tyr Siilas apparently didn't want to encourage the sort of incomer who had to wait here for very long. Ingray herself had never even visited the Incomers Office before; she had always been automatically cleared before she got off whatever ship she'd arrived on. "I have..." She stopped at the sound of voices. Turned her head to see a man come into the lobby. Omkem, to judge by his sober brown-and-beige tunic and trousers, and his height. He strode to the wall opposite the door, touched it. "This is ridiculous," he said, before the acknowledgment tone could sound, as the image of a functionary of the Incomers Office appeared on the wall. "I have always been preadmitted before. I have done business here for years. For decades. Why has my ship been denied docking? I had to find a shuttle to bring me here, and now dock authorities won't let me go any farther into the station. This is outrageous!"

"Your pardon, excellency," said the functionary. Ingray could not see them clearly from where she sat, not without very obviously turning her head and staring. She didn't know what expression they might have on their face, but their voice was calm and dispassionate. "A moment. Ah, your ship is carrying cargo, and there appear to be difficulties with the manifest as it's been reported to us. As soon as an inspector is available to verify..."

"An inspector!" fumed the Omkem man. "My ship has never needed inspection before. Customs at Hwae passed it, you'd think that would mean something."

"Your pardon, excellency. We are on Tyr Siilas, and your ship must meet the requirements of Tyr law, not Hwaean. I do regret any inconvenience."

"I demand to speak to your superior!"

"Of course, excellency," replied the functionary, voice still calm. "My superior will be available in approximately six hours. If you will be so good as to return to this office at that time, or make yourself comfortable in the lobby."

Ingray, looking studiously away from the Omkem man, still saw the wall turn blank again out of the corner of her vision. For a moment she was afraid he would sit on a bench and wait, and make continuing her conversation with not-Pahlad impossible, but the Omkem man turned and strode out of the room.

"Hwae," said the person who wasn't Pahlad. "Why did he come through Hwae? It's two gates from Omkem to Hwae, and then another to Tyr. It's much more convenient to go through Byeit. That's why the Omkem are holding on to Byeit so hard to begin with, isn't it? They don't like the extra trip, and they don't like paying fees at Hwae, or submitting to inspections. Makes everything more expensive, and reminds them they're not just naturally in charge of everything everywhere."

For a moment Ingray was astonished. "The Omkem/ Byeit gate's been down for ten years."

Not-Pahlad frowned in what Ingray was sure was real surprise. Not Pahlad for certain, then. E had only been gone a few years; e would certainly have known about this. "How did that happen?" e asked.

"Byeit rebels took it down," Ingray told em. "They deposed the Omkem puppet government that controlled the gates and destroyed the gate to Omkem. Now if the Omkem want to come to Tyr they have to go through Hwae." Or if they wanted to get to Byeit, for that matter. Though the Byeit weren't allowing any Omkem through the Hwae/Byeit gate.

"They took down the gate?" Still surprised. "That's drastic."

"Yes," agreed Ingray. And then remembered what she had come here for. Looked around to be sure no one else would be coming into the room. "Look, I have a false identity already made up that was meant for Pahlad. You could use that, and we could go back to Hwae. You're legally dead, whoever you are, so your records aren't active and your return shouldn't set off any alarms. I'll give you half of whatever I get from this plan"—though at the moment there was barely anything like a plan— "and you can take that and do anything you want, go wherever you'd like."

"And then what will happen to me? Pahlad was a Budrakim, yes? And e ended up sent to Compassionate Removal. For what, for theft? You don't get sent to Compassionate Removal for a single theft, certainly not if you're rich and well connected. But if e had done much more than that, you wouldn't have ever done this. So it seems to me that Prolocutor Budrakim—one of the most powerful people in Hwae—really hates this Pahlad, or at the very least doesn't care if e lives or dies. What happens when he thinks Pahlad is back? Or is that who you plan to leverage money out of?"

"He's not, but I bet we could, if that happened." E didn't reply. "If we play the game right. But we don't have to do that. The ship I bought passage on isn't that fast; we'd have weeks to go over the details."

"Weeks alone with an escaped, legally dead convict. You don't even know what I did."

Ingray had already thought about that. Couldn't have avoided thinking about it. "If you did anything to

Captain Uisine while we were in the gate, I don't think you could pilot the ship." E probably wouldn't have to do any piloting at all while the ship was still in the gate, of course, but e would definitely have to know what e was doing once e came out into Hwae System and had to slow down, and deal with traffic, and dock. "And your identity won't match the ship's ownership documents, and while you just peacefully arriving and going about your business won't raise any suspicions, well, turning up in a ship you don't own and can't pilot, with the captain and the other declared passenger dead or missing, that will set off quite a few alarms. I imagine you'd end up back in Compassionate Removal." Nothing, not even the flick of an eyelid. Just a long silence. "Indenture contracts here are terrible."

"They're better than Compassionate Removal."

"The ship leaves in a day and a half. Almost two days, really."

"I have a better idea: you give me that identity that isn't doing you any good, but will be very helpful to me, and then you walk away from here and leave me alone."

"How is that better?" E didn't bother to answer that. Obviously it would be better for em, and not good at all for Ingray. That identity had cost her money. And it was the only potential inducement she had that might convince em to do what she was asking em to do. She couldn't just hand it over.

But what was she going to do with it, then? What possible good would it do her to hold on to it? True, the vesicle was empty, because as she'd told Captain Uisine, she hadn't been able to get hold of Pahlad's DNA. Instead she'd gotten a kit that would, she'd been promised, take a sample from whoever she wished and insert it into the documents. She'd already considered using it for herself, but the description was Pahlad's, and Ingray didn't think she could pass as a neman. Not for long, anyway. She sighed. "You're right, the identity is no use to me now. You might as well have it. Come with me to the ship, and I'll hand it over." Silence. "You don't need to worry that I'll force you to come along with me. Captain Uisine refuses to take any passengers against their will. It's the whole reason we thawed you out in the bay like that; he wouldn't let me bring you aboard unless you were awake to say you wanted to go. So you'll be able to leave again." E did not answer. The silence stretched out. "Suit yourself," she said finally, as calmly as she could, and rose and left.

Early the next morning a spider mech tapped its unsettling claw quietly on the doorframe of Ingray's tiny cabin. "Excellency," it said in its thready voice. "You have a visitor."

There was, she was quite sure, only one person likely to visit her here, and now. "Thank you," she said, and got out of bed, quickly pulled on her skirts and shirt, and twisted her hair up and stuck a few pins in—that would have to hold for the moment. She pulled her bag out from under the bunk, fished out the nondescript brown box that held the tabula and the vesicle kit, and headed down the narrow corridor.

Captain Uisine sat in the galley, eating a bowl of

rehydrated noodles and fish. "Your visitor is in the bay, excellency," he said. "It's who you think it is. And I remind you that I will not take anyone aboard who doesn't want to be aboard."

"Yes. Thank you, Captain."

The person who wasn't Pahlad Budrakim stood a few meters away from the airlock, at an angle that let em also see through the wide door into the outer corridor. Wearing nothing, still, but the orange-brown blanket Captain Uisine had wrapped around eir shoulders the day before, eir unruly, unevenly cut hair pushed back but threatening to fall over into eir eyes. Ingray wondered where e had slept last night, or if e had eaten anything. "Good morning," she said, and hefted the brown box. "You're here for this, I think." People variously dressed in lungis or trousers and tunics passed by in the corridor outside—a ship at a nearby bay must have come in recently, or one was nearing departure. And while lots of things were legal in Tyr that weren't elsewhere, and the occupants of Tyr Siilas in particular were famous for minding their own business, she didn't want anyone seeing that vesicle kit and guessing what it was. "Will you come inside?"

The person who wasn't Pahlad hesitated, just a moment, and then said, "Can't you give that to me out here?" E seemed unconcerned about the people passing in the corridor.

"I suppose." She stepped forward and handed em the box. "You'll want to put that under your...under your clothes, and find somewhere private to fill the vesicle. I think there's a lavatory just down the corridor. Or you could still come aboard and do it. I know you don't want to, I'm just telling you that's an option."

"Thank you, Ingray Aughskold," e said. Garal Ket said, if e was going to be the person the tabula said e was. Which Ingray supposed had been the whole point of eir coming here.

"You're welcome, Garal Ket."

E almost smiled. Or seemed to, though it was just the slightest twitch of eir mouth. E inclined eir head, just a bit. Tucked the brown box under the end of eir blanket and turned to leave.

E took only three steps toward the corridor before a person in the red and yellow of an Enforcement official came into the bay, two patrollers behind em in yellow jackets, their red lungis girded up, stun sticks on their hips. "Your pardon, excellencies," said the Enforcement official. "This bay, and this ship, are under interdict. No one is to enter or leave under any circumstances whatsoever. And I'll see your identification."

"We'll have to go aboard to get our tabulas, excellency," said Ingray, hoping her voice was steady despite the way her heart pounded with startlement and, she had to admit, fear. "I suppose Garal will have to make eir errand later." She gestured the newly named Garal Ket toward the airlock. "Does Captain Uisine know about this?"

"He will when I tell him," said the Enforcement official. Behind em, in the corridor beyond the bay entrance, a half dozen people walked by, looking at the Enforcement official and then quickly away as they passed.

"We'll just let the captain know you're here," said Ingray, smoothly, with her blandest smile. Garal followed her aboard without a word or any change of expression.

Captain Uisine was finishing his breakfast. "Captain," said Ingray, "there's an Enforcement official and two patrollers in the bay. The official says your ship is under interdict, and no one can come or go."

He slurped the last of the noodles and drank the broth off. And then said, "I'd better speak to this official, then."

"You don't seem surprised," said Garal, behind Ingray in the corridor.

"I didn't expect this," said Captain Uisine. "But now that it's happened, you're right, I'm not surprised." He rose. "I imagine you'll both need to produce your identification."

"Yes," said Ingray. "We're just fetching it now."

"And you don't seem worried, either," observed Garal.

"I'm not," replied Captain Uisine. "But I can't get to my own tabulas until you move farther down the corridor, excellencies."

"Of course." Ingray continued down the narrow corridor, Garal behind her, to her tiny cabin. She sat on the bunk and pulled her own tabula out of her bag. "Do you know how to use the vesicle kit? It has instructions in it."

"Yes." Still standing in the corridor, e opened the kit's top edge and peered at the contents. Removed the tiny sampler and thumbed it. Snapped the sampler back into its slot. Fifteen seconds later the brown box made a click and the hard, blue strip of an identity tabula slid out. E handed the now-useless brown box back to Ingray, who stowed it in her bag. "Do you have any idea," e asked, "what this interdict is about?"

"None whatever," she said. "Let's go see what we can find out."

3

Out in the bay, the two patrollers had taken up positions on either side of the doorway into the dock corridor. The Enforcement official stood inside the bay, where Ingray and Garal had left em, and Captain Uisine was speaking calmly to em, to all appearances not the least bit alarmed. "The ship is mine. The purchase was registered here at Tyr Siilas. I have all the documentation—the history is all in the tabula, every transfer of ownership since it came from the shipyard. I own it free and clear. I am also a citizen of Tyr, with registered residency on Tyr Siilas."

E looked over Captain Uisine's shoulder, to where Ingray and Garal approached. A quick flash of some expression when e realized Garal was wearing nothing but a blanket, quickly gone. Tyr officials were famously uninquisitive about anything that wasn't a potential breach of Tyr law. "These are your passengers?"

"Yes, excellency," said Captain Uisine. "Booked through the dock office, you'll find. I don't do any business that isn't aboveboard."

"No doubt, Captain. Excellencies." That last addressed to Ingray and Garal. "Your identifications, please." And, having examined them and handed them back, "Thank you. This is unfortunately beyond my control, Captain. Your documents are all in order, but there's really nothing I can do. The Geck delegation insists that you be placed under arrest until they can examine you and your ship for themselves, and they won't be able to do that for the next several hours, at the very least. It may well be longer than that."

"It appears," said Captain Uisine, to Ingray and Garal, "that the Geck delegation saw my ship as they were coming in, and think it's one that was stolen from them."

"It's ridiculous, I know," said the Enforcement official, "and treaty or no treaty, they don't have the right to demand the arrest of a citizen in good standing. We've told them so."

"But nobody wants to even come close to violating the treaty," Ingray guessed. The prospect of the Presger freed from the constraints of the treaty was horrifying. Even ordinarily an alien delegation would be treated with extreme care and caution, and this was not an ordinary time. "And everyone's on edge about this conclave."

"Just so," agreed the Enforcement official. "The ship is clearly your property, Captain, and once we can show the evidence of that to the Geck delegation, we expect you can be on your way. In the meantime, we've promised we won't let anyone enter or leave this bay. The Geck worry you might flee, or *orchestrate some sort of trick*, were I to believe the ambassador's exact words. This is why I didn't warn you I was coming, and why I must insist you and your passengers remain here without communicating with anyone else until the ambassador arrives. I'm sure you understand that it's in your best interest to allay the ambassador's suspicions as much as we can. Do you have sufficient food and water? Sanitary facilities functioning properly? No medical issues that might require outside resources?"

"Yes to the first two, and none that I know of to the last." Captain Uisine looked a mild inquiry over his shoulder at Ingray and Garal.

"No, Captain, we're fine. Right, Garal?"

"Just fine," e agreed.

Back aboard, Ingray said, "I don't have any extra clothes for you, but I didn't want to say that in front of the Enforcement official. Maybe Captain Uisine has something you could wear. Is the top bunk all right?"

"If no one is occupying this cabin"—e tapped the doorframe of the set of bunks on the other side of the narrow corridor—"I would prefer that."

"Of course," replied Ingray. A bit relieved, truth to tell.

E turned, looked down the otherwise empty corridor. "I wonder how you manage to steal a ship from the Geck."

"You don't think he stole it, do you? He's apparently got all the documentation."

"This is Tyr Siilas," said Garal. "And if the captain could afford a citizenship buy-in, it's not a far stretch to imagine he could also afford some well-forged documentation." E said nothing about the identification tabula still in eir left hand, which had just passed Enforcement's examination without so much as the suggestion of suspicion.

Ingray considered this a moment. "If he really did steal it from the Geck—I can't even imagine that. I mean, they don't leave their homeworld, right? Why would they even have a ship to steal? But if it's true, what's going to happen when they get here?"

"I have no idea," said Garal. "But that's hours from now. At the moment, I would like to have something to eat."

E swallowed down a bowl of rehydrated noodles in what seemed like a single gulp. "Did you eat anything yesterday?" Ingray asked, sitting across from em at the galley's tiny table. And then she realized e couldn't possibly have, not unless e'd managed to steal something. E'd left the bay with no money, no credit account, not even any identity, and carrying nothing besides the blanket Captain Uisine had given em. Where would e have gotten food?

"Is that really what you wanted to ask me?" E leaned back and pushed the bowl into the recycle chute.

"I wanted to ask it, or I wouldn't have." She picked

up her own utensil full of noodles, and then amended, "I guess it was kind of a stupid question." E just looked at Ingray, eir thin, sharp-featured face nearly expressionless. She put the noodles in her mouth, chewed and swallowed them. "What did you do? To get you sent to Compassionate Removal, I mean." E gave a brief, tiny nod, as though e had been waiting for the question, but didn't answer right away. Ingray continued. "You don't seem like a murderer."

"Quite a few murderers don't," Garal said. Calmly, as though it were an entirely normal topic of conversation. As though e had casual, personal experience with murderers—and of course, Ingray realized, e probably did have exactly that. Garal crossed eir arms and leaned back against the galley wall. "I have an educated accent and vocabulary, so you're having trouble thinking of me as a criminal. Or at least, the sort of irredeemable or dangerous criminal who gets sent to Compassionate Removal. It's a mistake I would have made, before. But most people in Compassionate Removal with my education and accent are so vicious their families or contacts have no desire to look the other way or shunt them out of the system before they get to that point. Not that a public crèche accent is a guarantee you're safe with someone. Not at all. But your chances are far worse with someone urbane, with all the right manners."

"You don't seem terribly vicious to me."

Garal blinked. "Have you been listening to what I've been saying?"

"I have," said Ingray, "and it seems odd to me that you're trying so hard to tell me how dangerous you might be. Do you have some kind of stake in my being afraid of you?"

"I never could pull it off," said Garal, and uncrossed eir arms and pushed eir unevenly cut hair out of eir face. It flopped back down again. "I was a forger. You know how much money you can get for the right sort of vestige, I'm sure. The most important ones, the mementos of the biggest events or the most widely revered dead, those may have some kind of theoretical value attached to them, but they can't be had for any price. The wealthiest, most important families and citizens own them all, and they're all carefully cataloged. There's no point forging them, you'd be found out within minutes. But if you go one level down—say, a couple of handwritten invitation sheets from a Founder's nephew's majority dinner or"—e frowned, just a bit—"that sort of thing. Those can go for quite a lot, if you just happen to find a couple in a storage unit somewhere."

"Because it's the only way to collect vestiges," agreed Ingray. "I don't, but my brother does." Thinking of Danach ruined her appetite. Or else it was the way Garal seemed to be staring at her noodles as she ate them.

"Does he." There was no hint of a question in Garal's tone. "Yes, if you're new money, with a new name, or just on the edges of old money, it's how you manage to look well connected. And, of course, there's the benefit of having those vestiges near, in your possession. Imagine the vitality that must suffuse those invitation sheets, or maybe the strips of wall hanging that were in the presence of that Founder's insignificant relative. Perhaps the great one emself was in that room! Even the smallest trace of that would be precious. And maybe, if family fortunes shift enough in the future, that nephew will retroactively become so much more important. Perhaps you—or excuse me, you said you don't collect—perhaps your brother would spend quite a lot of money for that. And he would take it very, very badly to discover he'd been cheated."

"How many vestiges did you forge?"

"Quite a lot. I specialized in invitation sheets—you find stacks of them in storage units, or just thrown away when someone dies with no heirs, so it's easy to find paper the right age. The rest is just altering them, and choosing your subject carefully. I was good at it. I sold hundreds of the things, to dozens of hopeful collectors like your brother. So when I was caught I was a repeat offender quite a few times over, and quite a few wealthy citizens wanted me gone."

Could that be true? Ingray half recalled hearing something like that, the capture and conviction of a vestige forger. It had been a very long time ago, she'd still had her child-name, had only overheard adults talking about it. Had the forger been someone who looked quite a lot like Pahlad Budrakim? It was possible. There was no way to check, they were cut off from Tyr's communication systems, but even if they weren't they were too far from Hwae for Ingray to access that sort of information without paying for it.

It might well be true. It wouldn't explain everything, but it would explain quite a lot. "So," said Ingray, slowly, setting down her utensil, looking warily at the edges of the idea that had just occurred to her, "you could make copies of the Budrakim Garseddai vestiges..."

"No no no." Ingray couldn't tell if Garal was appalled or amused. "There's no percentage in making copies of something that already exists. Particularly something *famous* that already exists. It's too easy to get caught. No, the thing to do is to make new things that plausibly *might* exist. Far fewer questions that way, far less obvious. I can do you any number of Eighth Century invitation sheets, or even personal notes if you can get me linen or paper that's the right age. Or I can do other things, but I'm best at those. But even then"—e raised both hands, palms up—"it wouldn't be exactly foolproof or safe. Besides, I haven't said I'm going anywhere with you."

"That's true." She thought for a moment. Picked up her utensil and snagged another tangle of noodles. "You must have done a lot of genealogical research. Knew who was who in lots of important families."

"Yes," Garal agreed equably.

"So you're lying about never having heard of Pahlad Budrakim. E's not just a member of an important family, e's the caretaker of a particularly famous set of vestiges. Even if you went to Compassionate Removal before e got that job, you'd have known e existed."

"Good catch." That very tiny twitch of eir mouth, barely a suggestion of a smile. "But I had no idea e was sent to Compassionate Removal. And honestly, I'm having trouble believing the story you've told me. From what I know of Pahlad Budrakim, e wouldn't have been stupid enough to do something like that. Why in the world would e ever steal eir father's most treasured and valuable vestiges? What would it get em? It's not like e would have been able to sell them to anyone."

"Did you ever meet em?" It would be so helpful if Garal had personal knowledge of Pahlad Budrakim, so that...but Garal had not, as e had already pointed out, agreed to go back to Hwae with Ingray.

"No. Did you?"

"Not exactly. I was at a couple of events where e was, or where e probably was, anyway. The opening of an Assembly session, once. I was pretty small at the time."

"I hope you saved the entry card. That's exactly the sort of thing I'd go after, if I were still in business. If I did contemporary vestiges. A minor vestige of a vaguely important but routine event, that someone would have tucked away somewhere and forgotten, nothing anyone would bother to hoard or catalog until it suddenly has a connection with something famous—or infamous."

"I sold it to my brother, actually." And that money was now gone, paid to Gold Orchid as part of her scheme to get Pahlad Budrakim out of Compassionate Removal.

"I hope you got a good price for it. Do the sleeping cabin doors lock?"

It took Ingray a few moments to process the sudden

shift of topic. "More or less. I'm sure Captain Uisine can open them no matter what, though."

"Will you knock, please, if I'm not awake at the next mealtime?"

"Of course," Ingray agreed. "I might as well take a nap myself once I'm done eating." It wasn't as though there was much else to do, stuck here on this ship with all the news and information feeds cut off. Though it might be a good idea to go over the fare agreement again—hopefully if this didn't turn out in Captain Uisine's favor, she would still be legally due a refund of her and Garal's fares. But there was plenty of time for that. Ingray was used to government officials; it might be some time before the Geck ambassador turned up, and even longer before she—he? E? It?—no, the Enforcement official had said *she*—decided to do whatever it was she was going to do.

As it happened, Ingray severely underestimated the interest the Geck ambassador took in Captain Uisine's ship. Ingray, Garal, and Captain Uisine were eating supper that evening in the tiny galley—the captain had shared out meals from the ship's store without any comment. Garal had, once again, seemingly swallowed eir rehydrated stew in a few quick gulps. Captain Uisine said, calmly, "Would you like more, excellency?"

"Thank you, Captain, no," Garal replied, just as evenly.

Halfway through the sentence Captain Uisine sat

straighter and stared ahead. Set his bowl on the table. A swishing and clicking came from the corridor, and four spider mechs rushed skittering by.

"Excuse me, excellencies," said Captain Uisine, still staring ahead. "It seems the Geck ambassador has just come into the bay. And it certainly wouldn't do to keep her waiting."

"It wouldn't," agreed Ingray, hastily pulling up the fare agreement in her vision and rising so that Captain Uisine could get past her.

"They can't have been docked for long," observed Garal.

"I don't imagine so," agreed Captain Uisine, as he brushed past.

Ingray looked at the captain's retreating back, and then at Garal. "Have you ever seen a Geck? Even pictures?"

"No."

Captain Uisine's voice came from down the corridor. "Come if you're curious, but there's nothing much to see."

For a moment, Ingray wondered how he could know that. Then she remembered the spider mechs scurrying past. Of course, he'd seen through one or more of their stalked eyes. Had probably set one at the airlock to watch the bay. And once she and Garal came through the open airlock, she understood better why he'd said what he'd said. And also realized, quite clearly, that she was fortunate that the fare agreement did seem to indicate that she would be due a refund if the Geck confiscated this ship, because no matter how genuine Captain Uisine's title to it looked, he had almost certainly stolen it.

The Enforcement official from earlier stood in the bay, and beside em a woman in a silver-and-green sarong and jacket that managed to look both subdued and luxurious, every fold and tuck, every drape of fabric, in perfect place. Her face was teasingly familiar, until Ingray realized she'd seen that face on a public newscast two days ago. This was the Chief Executive of Tyr Siilas. And beside her squatted a disturbingly gelatinous-bodied, hairy-appendaged, many-legged, and many-eyed bio mech, very nearly identical to the ones Ingray had just seen scuttling to the back of the ship. A little larger, maybe, and as Ingray and Garal came up behind Captain Uisine, it took a step forward, heavy and deliberate where the ship's mechs were unsettlingly delicate and graceful. There was no one else in the bay, and the captain had said the Geck ambassador was here, so this had to be her. Or, this had to be her mech she was piloting at any rate.

"I've presented my documents, excellencies," Captain Uisine was saying. The Enforcement official once again held the captain's tabula in eir hand. "I bought this ship five years ago, and I own it free of any lien or hold."

The Chief Executive gave Captain Uisine a sharp look. "Ownership was transferred here at Tyr Siilas, it says."

"Yes, Executive. In a witnessed contract, in the station registry office. Where there should be a recording of the transaction."

"It is fortunate," said the Chief Executive, "that you went to such pains to ensure the sale was verifiably legal and valid."

"It is my invariable habit, Executive. A moment of trouble saves a month of tears."

"Indeed." The Chief Executive turned, looked down at the spider mech, which had turned all its eyes toward Captain Uisine. "Ambassador, I'm afraid Excellency Tic Uisine's title to this ship is quite clear. The transfer was entirely legal, and the ship has a clear chain of ownership back to the shipyard. And Excellency Uisine himself is a citizen of Tyr Siilas. I examined all the records myself, this afternoon. We cannot hold him without cause, and we certainly cannot impound his possessions without good legal reason."

"Not citizen," asserted the spider mech in a whispery, whistling voice. "Not possible."

"He paid the fee," said the Chief Executive. "He has met all his obligations as a citizen since then, and he has broken no laws. He has not been served with even the smallest fine since that day."

"Money does not make a citizen," whispered the spider mech, its forest of stalked eyes still fixed on Captain Uisine.

"It does here, Ambassador," replied the Chief Executive. "Or it can. In this case it does."

Captain Uisine spoke then, his voice unbelievably calm and smooth. "What makes a citizen of the Geck, Ambassador?"

The spider mech's body trembled, and it lifted one of its claws and set it back down again with a thunk. It did not otherwise reply.

"I'm sure you'll understand, Ambassador," said the Chief Executive, "why Tyr cannot just hand one of its citizens over to you. I am quite sure that if we demanded the arrest of one of your own citizens, you would not wish to hand them over without sufficient evidence of wrongdoing."

"Not your citizen," whispered the spider mech.

"Are you," asked Captain Uisine, voice still silky, "claiming I'm one of yours?"

The trembling of the spider mech's body increased. It struck the floor twice more. "This is why," it whispered. "You did not understand why. You asked and asked. This is why."

Captain Uisine said, in reply, "I can only apologize to the ambassador for whatever misunderstanding has brought her here. I am of course pleased to be of service to the Geck ambassador to the Presger, insofar as I am able. But I am a citizen of Tyr, and the most excellent ambassador does not have the right to interfere in my affairs. I have no doubt that if she examines the treaty, she will discover this is true."

"Impudent child," whispered the spider mech. "I know the terms of the treaty better than you know yourself. You are no citizen of Tyr. And that ship, you stole. Where are the others?"

"I am a citizen of Tyr," repeated Captain Uisine. "And my title to my ship is clear."

The spider mech turned, laboriously, one leg at a time, as though it was thinking carefully about where to put each claw, and then stepped away, toward the hallway beyond the bay entrance. "Ambassador!" cried the Enforcement official, and followed.

The Chief Executive said to Captain Uisine, "A moment's trouble, as you say, excellency, prevents a month of tears. It's a very good thing you have been so conscientious about your document registration, or you might have had quite a lot of difficulty today."

"As you say, Executive," replied Captain Uisine.

"Although I rarely deal with such matters directly," the Chief Executive continued, "it is one of the duties of my office to guard the legal and contracted rights of our citizens. Conscientiousness like yours makes my job easier, so I thank you for it. But I strongly advise you not to come to my attention again anytime soon."

"I won't if I can help it, Executive," replied Captain Uisine.

"Good," said the Chief Executive, and turned and left the bay, the two patrollers turning to follow her. A quiet whisper in Ingray's ear told her that the noodle shop she liked was open. Her access to the station's information feeds had been restored.

Captain Uisine turned around. "What are you two staring at?" he asked.

"You said we could come see," said Garal.

"I did, didn't I." Silence. And then, "I've got a bottle of very good arrack on board, and I intend to open it tonight. Feel like a drink? Because I definitely do." And without waiting for an answer, he walked around them and into the airlock.

In the tiny galley, Captain Uisine set out three large, white, handled serbat cups and poured a slosh of arrack into each. Drank his own at a single gulp and poured himself another.

"So," said Garal, not touching eir cup or even looking at it, "you did steal the ship. You stole it and used it to flee the Geck home system, apparently."

"I suppose there's no point denying it now, considering," said Captain Uisine. "I stole *three* ships. Once I sold the other two I had enough for citizenship here and a *very* good set of documents legitimizing my owner- ship of this one." He drank off his second cup of arrack. "And a refit."

Ingray sipped her own. It was very strong and, as the captain had promised, very good, sweet and stinging. "How do you steal three ships?"

A spider mech scuttled into the galley doorway from the corridor. As Ingray leaned aside, suppressing a star- tled cry, it grabbed the edge of the table, levered itself up with two of its legs, and waved another one. Then it picked up the bottle and poured a fresh slug of arrack into Captain Uisine's cup, set the bottle down, and scur- ried away again.

"You're Geck," guessed Ingray, willing her heart to settle, just managing not to stand and brush herself off. "I mean, you're one of the humans who live with the Geck. So how can you be a citizen of Tyr?"

"I'm not Geck," said Captain Uisine. "The Geck were accepted into the existing treaty largely because of their close association with humans." He gave a small breathy laugh. "But that presents a problem. Do those closely associated humans count as humans or as Geck, under the treaty? And the Geck aren't the only ones to have that problem. The way the treaty deals with it is incredibly weird and complicated—it was drafted by the Presger translators, after all—but in my particular case the upshot is, if I voluntarily take citizenship with a human polity, then I am human for the purposes of the treaty."

"Which means the Geck have no right to interfere with you at all, unless it somehow touches on the treaty," Garal said. Captain Uisine made a small, still-seated bow in eir direction.

"Wait." Ingray was more bewildered by the answer, not less. "So anyone can just declare that they're human or Geck or Rrrrr or whatever?"

"Not just anyone," said Captain Uisine. "I told you it was complicated." He turned to Garal. "You should let me cut your hair. It looks like you hacked it off yourself with a dull knife."

"I thought even the humans who lived with the Geck didn't like leaving their homeworld," observed Garal, as though the captain had said nothing at all about eir hair.

"They don't," agreed Captain Uisine. "It's very stressful for them."

"That was a mech, right?" asked Ingray. "Not the ambassador herself?"

"That was a mech," Captain Uisine agreed. "The ambassador herself is . . . very different."

"So what happened?" asked Ingray, after a short silence and another sip of her arrack.

The captain picked up his cup. Took only a sip this time, and set it back down. "My gills never developed. Don't look at me like that, it's a very big deal there. Without gills you can't swim down. And if you can't swim down by a certain age, you can't stay on the planet." Ingray considered asking what he meant by *swim down* but decided any answer would probably just puzzle her more.

"You could walk into a mod shop and lay down your money today and walk out with perfectly good gills," Garal said.

"Too right," Captain Uisine agreed. "Although it's not actually as simple as buying gills. You'd need a few other changes to accommodate them. Still, you're right, I could do that. But where I come from, if they don't come in on their own, that's a sign you never belonged in the first place, so there's no point. Or so we're always told. Once I got to orbit I learned that actually, there's some room to maneuver. Some people who need a little helping along will get it. Not me, though."

"Why not?" asked Ingray, and then remembered the ambassador's whispered *You did not understand why. You asked and asked.*

"It was suggested to me in orbit that I was too good a mech-pilot to keep onworld. Pretty much every intra-system ship there is remotely piloted, and while they do like to have access to trade and to system resources, even looking through a bio mech is upsetting, when it's off-world. They'll do it if they have to, but otherwise they leave it to the exiles in orbit."

"So why steal a ship?" asked Ingray. "You could have just left. A good mech-pilot can always get a job."

"Partly because it's not actually that easy to get passage out of that system, if you're from there," said Captain Uisine. "But mostly because *fuck them*, that's why."

"So, is…" Ingray hesitated, not sure asking questions was a terribly good idea. But the captain seemed so much more talkative than he had been so far, and the whole situation was so bizarre. He and the ambassador so obviously knew each other. *Impudent child*, the ambassador had said. Ingray wanted to ask, *So is the ambassador your mother?* But they had only seen a mech—maybe the ambassador herself wasn't human. "The ambassador has gills? Is she in a tank of water? Is that why she used the mech just now?"

"She might be in a tank. Probably is. But she can breathe air, too, if she needs to. She'll have used the mech because she couldn't bear to get off her ship. Oh, shit."

"What?" asked Ingray.

"We've got a departure time, and it's just a few hours from now. I'd better get ready. And I'd better stop drinking. Excellency"—this directed toward Garal—"I'll be closing the airlock in a few minutes. Are you coming with Excellency Aughskold, or are you going to sleep on a bench at the Indenture Office for the next three weeks and then end up in some horrible situation that's probably as bad as what you just got out of?"

71

"Nothing is as bad as what I just got out of," said Garal. And then, "The fare's paid? And it includes food and a place to sleep?"

"It is and it does," Captain Uisine confirmed. "And a haircut. Tomorrow. When I'm sober."

"Can I think about the haircut?" asked Garal.

Captain Uisine grinned, startling when he'd been so serious all the short time Ingray had known him. "I like you, Garal Ket. I don't know why, and I probably shouldn't, but I do. And you, Ingray Aughskold, once you get home you should steal whatever you can from your mother and get the hell away from her for good. You'll never make a politician."

Before Ingray could muster up any sort of reply to that, indignant or not, Garal asked, "Do you drink very often, Captain?"

"Almost never," confessed Captain Uisine. "But don't worry. We'll get into the gate just fine." He rose and squeezed past Ingray into the corridor, followed closely by another spider mech that had apparently been lurking just outside the door. And which didn't seem the slightest bit unsteady or awkward.

"It's not getting into the gate that worries me," said Ingray, once the captain and his mech had moved out of earshot.

"No," agreed Garal, "we've got bigger problems. Or we will, once we get to Hwae. In the meantime, I think the captain actually gave you some good advice. You said you had some sort of plan?"

"I hadn't worked out the details yet, because I didn't know if you would agree to come with me."

"Well," said Garal, as the floor and table shivered with the *thunk* of the airlock closing, "I'd say it's time to start working them out."

4

A week into the trip to Hwae, Ingray found Garal sitting at the table in the ship's tiny galley, a spider mech behind em cutting eir hair. No tools, just snipping Garal's hair with one of its claws. "Almost done," it whispered in its thin voice as Ingray stopped in the doorway. "Sorry for the delay, excellency."

"It's all right." The galley doubled as the ship's very limited gym—a necessity on a ship so small, on a long trip—so exercise times were more or less tightly scheduled. But a few minutes now wouldn't cause any serious problems, with only two passengers aboard.

"There," said the spider mech, and ran four of its claws through Garal's now quite short hair, leaving it neatly brushed. "Much better. If you'll step out into the corridor, excellency, while I clean up."

Ingray backed up so that Garal could come out of

the galley. "It actually looks nice," she said. Sincerely, although the short hair was also oddly incongruous—on Hwae, it was mostly children who kept their hair short, but Garal did not otherwise look the least bit childlike. "I'm not sure I'd let one of those spiders touch me."

"They are disquieting, aren't they."

She found she couldn't quite bring herself to say they looked like they might be alive and thinking. She thought of the news from Radch space, the whole reason the Geck ambassador had left her homeworld to begin with—Radchaai artificial intelligences declaring themselves independent, and potential signatories of the treaty with the Presger. But, she reminded herself, that was very far away.

"All yours, excellency!" said the spider mech, and scuttled away down the corridor.

Ingray looked into the galley. The table and chairs had been folded back, and the little bit of exercise equipment pulled out, the floor over the treadmill pulled up. "I wish there were more room to really walk," she sighed. And then hoped the spider mech hadn't heard her. She had, after all, bought passage on this ship quite voluntarily, and so far everything had been calm, clean (if cramped and dingy), and just generally well run, and Captain Uisine had been unfailingly pleasant and courteous. And while she didn't think he spoke Bantia, she knew the spider mechs could translate it. But then, he was probably used to passengers' irritation at some point in a trip.

"I like it," said Garal. "It's safe."

"Safe?"

"It's small enough that I know exactly who's here and where we all are. There's food. Outside there's just kilometers of empty space." E closed eir mouth on that, abruptly, as though e had been about to say more but suddenly changed eir mind. "So, this brother of yours, who you sold your vestige of Pahlad Budrakim to. Would that be Danach Aughskold?"

For a moment Ingray was astonished, but then she remembered that eir business as a forger of vestiges of course meant that e kept track of important families. She'd said as much herself already. "It would." She stepped into the galley and onto the belt and started it moving. "Supposedly Netano will choose the most promising of her children to take her place, and it could be either of us and we should be working hard to be chosen, but everyone knows she's giving her name to Danach."

"So why encourage competition, then?" asked Garal.

"I think she intends the threat to keep him sharp. If he always knows he's going to inherit there's no reason for him to work at anything, right?"

"Hm," said Garal, as though e disagreed, but e didn't expand on it. "I take it he's who you're hoping to con, with my help."

Ingray had been turning plans over in her mind for the past week but had not settled on any of them, let alone said anything more to Garal Ket about her thoughts. She wasn't quite sure how to answer em now.

"I've never met Danach Aughskold, but I know his reputation. I don't imagine you like him very much."

And then, into Ingray's continued silence, "We've got another two weeks of travel. I'm trying to imagine what I'll do after that."

"I suppose you could do whatever you liked. You don't have to go back to wherever you came from, or go anywhere the Budrakims are likely to see you. You could go to the public registry, and probably find pretty decent work."

"I suppose I could," said Garal. E didn't sound enthusiastic about the prospect, but then, e had never sounded terribly enthusiastic about anything in the week or so that Ingray had known em. "I'd like to know all my options, though."

Ingray stepped for a few moments in silence. She'd rarely come out and said anything about her various plans. And she had never quite gotten to the point with this plan where it seemed to make perfect, brilliant sense. "Danach," she said finally, "is a serious collector. Or he considers himself to be one. He's always on the lookout for exactly the sort of thing you said you did—vestiges that seem insignificant now, so they go for cheap, but they'll turn out to be valuable later. He considers it an investment."

"Why worry about an investment when he's going to inherit Netano's not inconsiderable wealth, as well as her vestiges?"

"He wants to add to that. And every time he buys some trinket for cheap that turns out to be worth a lot, he gets a thrill out of the idea that he's cheated someone out of a treasure. He's said as much."

"Delightful." E had to be speaking sarcastically, but there was no trace of it in eir voice or on eir face.

"So," said Ingray, and then hesitated, feeling an unaccustomed sense of uncertainty. Her last big plan had failed completely, and she was entirely out of resources. "So," she said again, "what if we turned up and you told Danach that you knew where the Budrakim Garseddai vestiges were? That you'd give him that information in exchange for a sufficiently high payment. I know he can't sell them, or display them. He'd probably want to give them to Mama."

"It has the virtue of being very straightforward," Garal commented after a moment's consideration. "There is the difficulty that I don't know where the Garseddai vestiges are, and when your brother goes to retrieve them he will find nothing, and there we'll be."

"Yes. But if we ask him for enough, we can buy a new set of identities and then go back to Tyr Siilas and buy citizenship." Silence. Unsurprisingly—it was the part of the plan that was the most impractical, the blankest in Ingray's mind. "And if we choose the spot right, we can convince him the vestiges are somewhere really inconvenient or expensive to get to. Or, you know, somewhere he can get into a lot of trouble if he's caught poking around for stolen goods."

Garal Ket stood silent in the corridor, apparently thinking for a good ten seconds. Then e said, "Let's talk some more about that."

Ingray waited until they left the ship at Hwae Station to access the public news and data feeds. She could have looked sooner—could probably have had access while the ship was still in the Tyr/Hwae gate—but hadn't wanted to know if any of her family had tried (or not tried) to contact her. Now as she stepped through the airlock, a flood of messages scrolled past in her vision. None of them looked urgent, or even particularly interesting, and she blinked them away.

"How do I have messages?" asked Garal, behind her.

She turned. E wore a dark blue coverall that Captain Uisine had given em, and over eir shoulder e carried a large velvety-looking black bag Ingray supposed was from the same source, though what Garal needed with a bag when e didn't have any other possessions at all Ingray wasn't sure. "I had it set up that way," she said. It had cost extra, but it was too easy to spot a fake identity when they had no personal data anywhere in the system. "Your travel history says you've been away from Hwae for a while." She looked around for directions and saw a path to the left marked INCOMING TRAVELERS on the dull green floor.

"Not that way," said Garal. "We're on the other side of the station from where the passenger ships usually dock. That exit comes out a long way from anywhere we want to be. If we go the other way we'll be just a short distance from the System Lareum and the Assembly Chambers."

And it was a direct tram ride from the System Lareum to the elevator shuttle, where they were headed. Ingray pulled a map into her vision. "You're right," she said. "We'll spend half our time backtracking if we go that way." She frowned. "But it looks like we'll have to walk the whole way?"

"There should be a freight transport, it has room for passengers. Or, it did last time I was here. You send a request to…"

"Ah, thanks, I found it." She sent the request and turned right into the scuffed gray corridor beyond the bay. After passing a few more bays she said, "So, we have enough money to take transport the rest of the way home, but then we can't afford to eat. If we eat, we'll have enough for probably one night's lodging as well." If Captain Uisine had not bought the crate and suspension pod from her, sparing her the trouble of pushing it around and trying to sell it herself, she would still be completely broke. "Well, you can probably get yourself on the public allotment list, if you like. I can't. And if I call home and ask for a ride, someone will probably help us."

"But you'd rather not do that," guessed Garal. "I can't say I blame you, and besides I think you'll be in a better position if you arrive home without having to ask for help to get there."

Ingray waited a moment for em to say more, but e didn't. "All right," she said finally. "I'll claim us seats on the next elevator shuttle."

A walk, a tram ride, and several minutes in a lift took them to the freight transport, which took them on a slow, rumbling ride through tunnels Ingray had never imagined existed to another stretch of dingy corridor with two doors at the end. They walked past the line at the door marked NON-HWAE CITIZENS, to where the floor changed from dull gray to brass-bordered blue tiles and a bored-looking guard sat staring. "Identity tabulas, please," e said dully as Ingray and Garal approached. Ingray had already begun to pull hers out of her jacket. She held it up as she walked past the guard. Tried to keep her breathing even, her steps no more hurried than any other tired traveler. This was a moment when Garal's identity would be under extra scrutiny. *Just walk*, she told herself.

She didn't dare turn to look for Garal until they were well away from the door, down another corridor and through a much larger entrance into one of the station's main thoroughfares, a broad avenue that led to a wide, open space in front of the System Lareum, where, finally, surrounded by people passing, files of crèche children streaming toward the lareum entrance, under cover of the noise and chatter, she stopped to look at em. E looked calmly back at her, eir tabula already tucked away again. "All right?" she asked.

"Just fine," e said.

"Let's go, then." Though it was a nonsensical thing to say; they were already walking toward the tram that would take them to the elevator shuttle.

But she was brought up short by someone calling, "Ingray! Ingray Aughskold!"

Damn. She knew that voice. She put a smile on her face, though she feared it wasn't a convincing one. She was tired, and she'd been wearing the same clothes for just short of a month, though they were as clean as the ship's laundry facilities allowed. She'd done her best to put her hair up with the few pins she had left, but her best wasn't very good and she very obviously had no luggage beyond her shoulder bag. And while this person was nominally her friend, Ingray knew he was much more sympathetic to Danach. "Oro," she said, "what a surprise."

"I haven't seen you in months!" exclaimed Oro happily. "Where have you been?"

"Oh, traveling." She didn't look around for Garal. "Glad to be home."

"Where are you coming from?"

She considered lying, but there would be no point, really. "Tyr Siilas." And braced for questions about what she'd been doing there.

But instead Oro asked, "So did you see the Geck?"

Ingray blinked. Tried to look as though the question hadn't startled her. "How could I have? They arrived just hours before my ship left, actually." A little surprised at how easily the lie that wasn't technically a lie had come into her mouth.

"Well"—he leaned closer—"if you aren't going down the elevator right away, maybe you can see them when they get here."

"What?" There was no concealing her surprise at that. "I thought they were going on to Ildrad. That's what the news said at Tyr Siilas."

"They changed their mind for some reason. They'll be coming out of the Tyr Siilas gate sometime tomorrow, and it won't hit the newsfeeds for a few hours yet.

Nobody's sure why they decided to change their itinerary, though there are lots of theories. System Safety is putting together a plan for handling the change in traffic and making sure nothing untoward happens, and once they have that in place they'll announce. I had it from my nuncle. In fact, I'm running an errand for em right now. If you want, I can get you in on the greeting party." He glanced briefly at Ingray's rumpled jacket and skirt, her hair half falling out of its chignon. "It'll probably be very late tomorrow, or even the next day. I have no idea if you'll see any actual Geck, but it's worth the chance."

She smiled again, hoping it looked vaguely sincere. "It's awfully nice of you to offer, but I've been away so long and I'm eager to be home. Catch up next time you're onworld? You can tell me all about the Geck."

"Sure, sure." And after a few platitudes he was gone, off into the crowd.

Ingray looked around again for Garal. Didn't see em. Closed her eyes and took a breath. Garal couldn't have gone far. Or if e had, well, there was nothing she could do about that. She opened her eyes again.

Garal stood beside her. "You're going to have to show me how you did that," she said. E gave a small quirk of eir mouth, the closest Ingray had seen to an actual smile, but e didn't reply. Ingray said, "We need to warn Captain Uisine. The Geck are coming here." She knew the captain intended to stay longer in Hwae System than he'd previously planned, so that he could be sure to avoid the Geck ship.

"I heard," said Garal. "I've already sent the message."

Eir face was as blandly expressionless as ever. "He says thanks."

"Why would they come here? Don't they have to be at the Conclave?"

"From what I can tell," said Garal, "it's going to take years for everyone to get to that conclave, and probably a few more years before the first meeting even happens. The question of who's representing humans there is still unsettled. Radchaai involvement in this business has left a lot of people with a very bad feeling. Depend on it, there are going to be arguments all through human-inhabited space about who should and shouldn't be at that conclave. We'll be lucky if there are no actual wars over it." And then, in response to Ingray's open astonishment, e said, "There wasn't much to do for three weeks. I caught up on the news."

Well. That made sense. "It's not our problem, I guess. Let's go to the elevator shuttle lobby and find someplace to sit down." It was getting to be late at night, on the schedule Ingray and Garal had kept for weeks.

By the time they reached the lobby and found seats, Ingray had lost all but two of her remaining hairpins and was glad to sit down again. She was sorely tempted just to lie down on the bench. She thought that even in the noise and chaos of the lobby she'd be able to get at least a little bit of sleep.

The lobby was crowded with travelers from every part of Hwae, and even some from outsystem—mostly tourists from Omkem, who were fascinated enough by the ruin glass on the planet that they traveled through two gates to visit, even though relations between Hwae and the Omkem Federacy had been tense ever since the Omkem/Byeit gate had gone down, and Hwae had become their only route to Byeit, which they badly wanted back. But most of the people here were Hwaean. A few aisles of benches away from Ingray and Garal sat two dozen Hwaean adolescents in identical blue shirts and lungis, carrying identical small shoulder bags. Or they mostly sat. Some stood in clusters, talking or giggling. A fair number sat looking at handhelds, another few staring off into space. Looking at a news or entertainment feed, maybe, though the uniforms looked like these children were from a public crèche and very possibly might not be able to afford the implants yet. If ever. Maybe they were enthralled by the shifting historical images cast on the walls of the lobby—right now it was the Archprolocutor of the Assemblies of Hwae presenting the final payment for construction of the Tyr/Hwae gate to the collected Tyr Executory. In the picture the archprolocutor presented the payment in a gilded and inlaid box, though of course no physical currency had changed hands on the occasion, or any other in the centuries-long course of the debt. Behind the archprolocutor stood the prolocutors of the four Assemblies of Hwae, ready to unroll the length of linen they held and reveal the *Rejection of Further Obligations* and officially declare themselves the government of an independent Hwae. Then again, maybe the children were just tired and bored. At the end of one bench, two of them slept, huddled together.

Longing suddenly seized Ingray. She had come from a public crèche but had gone to Netano Aughskold's house when she was still quite young. If she had stayed, she would certainly have had very little luxury in her life, but would she have had crèchemates like this, to lean on so comfortably? Ingray had been a ward of the district, one of a number of children whose parents were unwilling or unable to care for them. Her life was so different now, because Netano had adopted her. And if she left the Aughskolds she would have no family at all, and no way to go back to what she had been, no way to find a place where she'd have naturally belonged if Netano had chosen some other child. No way to find even a shred of the comfortable companionship she saw here.

She couldn't imagine snuggling up against Danach like that. Not even during the times they got along. And there had been times like that, every now and then, particularly when the family's interests were at stake for some reason.

Then again, neither she nor Danach had ever had to sleep in a lobby. Every time they'd been to the station, Ingray had had a room with a bed, where she could wait until just before the shuttle boarded.

She looked at the cost of a train ride from the elevator base to the city where Netano's house was, and compared that with how much money she had left from the sale of the suspension pod. Sighed. "Well, we've got enough for all our transport anyway. Or most of it. We'll have to walk from the district transport terminal to the house, and it's quite a distance."

"That'll be a nice change, anyway," Garal said. "You did say you wanted to be able to walk more just last week."

Ingray made a small breathy laugh. "And supposedly a person can go weeks without eating." They'd both claimed a half-day water allowance on the way to the lobby, so at least they had that.

Garal swung eir bag onto eir lap and opened the latch. Showed Ingray what was inside: foil-wrapped, spongy blocks of nutrients. Ingray stared at them, then looked up at Garal's sharp-featured face. "What, did you skip lunch every day?" She tried to remember if she'd ever seen em eating a nutrient block on the ship. She herself had gotten heartily sick of them.

"Every other day." E did not visibly react at all to her surprise. "I'd have saved some of the noodles, except those aren't very good to eat if you don't have access to hot water."

It had never occurred to Ingray to save some of her food. Why would she? Apart from the last day or so of her stay on Tyr Siilas, she had never once worried that she might not be able to eat in the future. "Well, that's... good thinking."

Garal pulled a nutrient block out of the bag and handed it to her. Pulled another one out for emself and latched the bag shut again. "I suppose the Aughskolds didn't go on crèche trips." Not looking directly at the children ahead of them, but clearly referring to them.

"No, we had tutors, and went on family trips. We did

come to see the System Lareum, though." Of course. Everyone came who could. It was the one place to find vestiges of the system settlement and founding, vestiges of nearly every important event in the history of Hwae. Every citizen should have an opportunity to see them in person, to be in their presence. Which was why politicians like Netano Aughskold often made a point of helping children in their districts do exactly that, and no doubt why those blue-uniformed adolescents were even now noisily waiting for the shuttle back home.

Garal chewed and swallowed a bite of nutrient bar. "What must that be like," e said, "to see things your own family gave to the lareum?"

There were some Aughskold vestiges there. But Ingray hardly knew how to answer. She had been proud to see them, of course, but at the same time they hadn't quite felt like they had anything specifically to do with her. "Complicated," she said. "You already know, I'm sure, that the couple of most famous Aughskold vestiges here originally belonged to other families."

"Ah," said Garal, "is that still an issue? It's been, what, a hundred years?"

"And surely, no matter who really owns them, it's better for everyone that they're in the System Lareum," Ingray agreed.

Garal made a quick, skeptical *hah* sound. "I guess I'm not surprised. Though, knowing what I know now, I wonder how much of what's in the lareum is fake to begin with."

"What, you think there are forgeries in the Hwae System Lareum? But you said yourself, before, that it's too risky to fake famous vestiges. Or do you mean maybe Pahlad stole those, too? I'm not sure e would ever have had the opportunity." She frowned. It had never occurred to her before, the possibility that anything in the System Lareum might not be what it was supposed to be. That any of it might be *copies*. What would be the point of that? How a vestige looked, what it was made of—none of that really mattered. What mattered was, it had been touched by certain people, actually, physically been there when pivotal, system-shaking events had happened. Events that had led to the founding of Hwae, that had made all of them who they were today. What good would copies be, of something like that? Why bother to come to the station to see them? You might as well just look at pictures. "That would be *terrible*."

"That's not quite what I meant," said Garal, and took another bite of eir nutrient block.

"And what would be the point of stealing such famous vestiges? You couldn't sell them. You could never let anyone else see them. You'd have to, what, keep them locked up, forever."

"Indeed," said Garal.

Ingray wrinkled her nose at her own nutrient bar. "Who comes up with these flavors? Stewed chicken with pickled cabbage? It's not like they're fooling anyone. It's a block of yeast."

"I have some of the curried fish ones, if you'd rather."

"Ugh, no." She tore the foil open, took a bite. "I don't

mean to sound ungrateful. I'm very glad you have these, and very glad you're sharing with me." She thought of saying *But whoever makes these must hate humanity*, and then remembered Garal swallowing an entire meal at a single gulp, when e'd first come to the ship, and the fact that e felt it necessary to hoard food for the future, and ate her food in silence.

5

Of course the day that Ingray and Garal had to walk the nine kilometers from the city transport terminal to the Aughskold house would be gray and rainy. A mild, steady rain, but within an hour of starting out Ingray's jacket and skirts had been soaked through, her hair plastered to her head and back, her bag dripping. Garal looked similarly soaked but did not complain, did not say anything, just walked, shoulders hunched, staring down at the ground, as though e meant to disappear into the rain. They passed several mechs stepping through the wet streets on unguessable errands, but not many people, not once they'd started out on the pedestrian courses and left the transport hub behind. Everyone else had sense enough to stay inside today, or take the city trams if they had to go out. Even the black-paved plaza in front of the Arsamol District Planetary Safety Headquarters, usually full of people passing, was silent and empty but for the pattering of rain, and a boxy gray-green mech stepping stiffly along the cracks between the paving stones looking for any sign of incipient weeds. Here and there a doorway would open on light and dry warmth as someone would dash from indoors to a groundcar. By the time Ingray and Garal approached Netano's house Ingray had lost any convincing memory of being dry.

The front of the house, like the other houses on the street, was high and broad, and the entrance opened right onto the public walkway. Unlike its neighbors, it was built of the ruin glass that the first human settlers had found scattered all over the planet, one- and two- and even three-meter carefully placed, irregularly shaped chunks of it, blue and green and one streak of intense red slashing down, not quite in the center of the wall. Each block was shot through with twisting, convoluted shadows, some sort of inclusion maybe, but on the rare occasions someone had managed to break a block or (more frequently but still difficult) grind it down, there had been nothing but glass. At night the lights inside would shine through the wall, making the front of the house glow. Even in daylight the colors seemed luminous, particularly on gray, rainy days like this one.

Seeing the bright house-front, Ingray felt its utter familiarity, and a yearning to be finally inside and at home. At the same time she had a disconcerting sense of strangeness, as though the house she'd grown up in had become something foreign to her. Or something she was foreign to. Was the house different, the colors faded, the twisting shadows, perhaps, changed in shape, as Ingray and her siblings had believed they did, when they were small? Or was it that it seemed forbidding to her now, returning as she was with no money at all and only the most forlorn hope of making anything of herself, of being able to remain an Aughskold much longer? She was too wet and tired to ponder for very long. The door swung open at her touch, and they stepped into the entrance hall.

Silence, except for the sound of the rain outside and the intermittent patter of water dripping onto the amber-tiled floor. Netano kept many of her most important vestiges here, a practice that older names like Ethiat Budrakim considered showy and vulgar. There was no question, though, that visitors knew whose house they were in from the moment they entered. If they had to wait, there was a bench by the stairs from which they could contemplate the wall, bordered with red, blue, and green triangles near the ceiling but otherwise plain white, the better to show off the vestiges that hung there: entrance tickets from Assembly sessions and receptions decades and centuries in the past, all of them elaborate black script on stiff, brown-bordered paper; a scattering of invitation sheets in blue and yellow and pink and pale purple, bearing the names and dates of previous Netanos, or their illustrious friends and relations; a small grouping of black linen rectangles, with names painted in white, each one from the hand of the person named, flowing script or awkward dabbing, depending on the ability or inclination of the writer.

"Well, well," murmured Garal, beside her. "My own work in the Aughskold lareum. That's an achievement."

"What?" Ingray turned to em, startled. Frowned at em. "Your own...is it one of the black linen ones?" That had been a very popular sort of vestige about two hundred years ago, very distinctive, and it was an easy way to make an entertainment set during that time look authentic. It would be quite easy to forge if you had the right materials and knew what names and styles of writing to use. She would never have thought of that, if she hadn't met Garal.

"No, not those. Though some of those may be fakes, too. I'd have to look closer to be sure."

"Then which..." She stopped. They shouldn't be having this conversation in the foyer. And besides, it didn't matter. They should both go straight upstairs to her room. There was a bath there, and dry clothes. Ingray was only about average height, and thickly built, so none of her clothes would fit tall, thin Garal particularly well, but it would be better than nothing. They would leave a long, wet trail across the foyer, up the stairs, and down the hallway to Ingray's room. A mech would clean it up—one came stepping stiffly into the hall as Ingray thought of it, small and gray and moving straight toward the growing puddle they stood in—but Ingray didn't like even the fact of it, the evidence of their long, miserable walk from the transport hub being laid out on the floor for anyone to read. Of course the door opening would have alerted the staff to her arrival, and any moment now...

A servant came into the hall. Cast an outwardly impassive eye on the puddle where Ingray and Garal stood, the mech stepping toward it. "Miss Ingray. Your mother is in the front reception room."

Damn. That was not a neutral piece of information. It was very possibly a direct order from Netano herself. She suppressed a sigh. "Thank you." She turned to look at Garal, silent, slouching, staring floorward. She had not anticipated having to show Garal to Netano, not just yet. But if she sent em to her room, or had em stand out in the hallway while she went in, that would probably attract even more attention, and curiosity. "We need to speak to Mama. Hopefully it won't take long." She wished she could say, out loud, *Be careful, be inconspicuous.* Because if Netano noticed Garal and started asking questions, well, that would be the end of everything.

Garal said nothing, didn't make even the smallest gesture in response, but e followed when she moved toward the reception room door.

The front wall of the reception room was blue and green ruin glass, but the wall opposite the door where Ingray and Garal came in was all broad windows, plain and clear, looking out onto the rain-washed garden, moss-lined stones and silver-wet willows, three stone benches, swaths of flowers bent by the rain, their colors faded-looking in the gray light. The other walls were hung with slubbed silk, rough-woven in waving bands of red and yellow and green. Netano Aughskold, nearly as tall as Garal and imposingly solid, sat on a low-backed cushioned bench, her hair—thick and dark, the sort of hair that hairpins didn't fall out of, that would stay once it was twisted or braided—was pulled back with a bright yellow headband, to fan out behind her head. If Ingray ever wished she'd been Netano's biological child, it was because of that hair.

Netano was talking to two visitors Ingray had never seen before, a man and a woman in perfectly ordinary loose trousers and tunics but whose pale skin, blunt features, and accent—and gaunt height—said they came from Omkem, two gates away. Ingray thought of the man in the Tyr Siilas Incomers Office—but beyond looking like Omkem these two didn't really look like him once Ingray thought about it. The woman sat on a bench, the man on a cushion on the floor.

And of course her brother Danach was there to see her discomfiture, half lying in a broad armchair. Danach had always been the best-looking of Netano's children, tall and wide-bodied, his face broad-featured; his hair, which easily grew long, was thick and dark and tightly curled. He always carried himself with a sort of insolent ease that his good looks somehow made charming to everyone but Ingray.

"Ingray!" exclaimed Netano. "Where have you been all these weeks? Your nuncle has been asking after you."

"Just traveling, Mama." Danach gave a short laugh but didn't say anything more. Ingray hoped her anxiety over Garal standing behind her would only show as embarrassment at being seen like this, dripping wet in front of guests in the formal reception room.

"On a wander, eh?" asked the Omkem woman. "I

remember my own wander! What an adventure that was. I was much younger then, of course, and thought nothing of sleeping in whatever corner I could find, or taking any sort of horrible odd job for a week or two to earn my fare on some tiny cargo ship. These days I fear it wouldn't be half so charming." She smiled. "But I'm so glad I did, even if it took me a month or more to recover afterward. But so much worth it, yes! I went all the way to Nilt, you know. I was determined to see the famous bridges! They are even more astonishing in person than in recordings. I'll never forget it, as long as I live. That was the one place I brought something back from—*you* know, my dear, how lightly one travels on a wander! But the nomads there, who follow the bov herds, they make the most beautiful patterned rugs and blankets, all hand-spun and hand-woven, in the most delicate colors. I couldn't resist buying one, even though it meant working an extra week to get passage away."

Her companion, at her feet, seemed to look vaguely off into the middle distance. As the woman spoke, his gaze changed focus to somewhere immediately in front of himself, and he blinked but said nothing. He must have been some relation to the woman—some of the Omkem had some strange ideas about families, and couldn't speak the names of certain relatives, or even address them directly. The Omkem Federacy was a multisystem power—or they had been until recently—and sometimes seemed a bit condescending about what they considered Hwae's lack of culture and polish, along with the Assemblies' mere one planet and a few stations. But the family of Omkem tourists, none of whom could speak to each other, was a venerable and still-reliable way to get laughs out of a Hwaean audience.

"But think how fortunate you are, my dear," continued the woman, apparently ignoring her companion entirely, "you don't have to travel far to see such wonders! People come from all over space to see what's dull everyday to you."

"Yes, excellency," Ingray agreed, though in her experience it was mostly the Omkem who were so fascinated by the glass. "Though I wouldn't say dull. Have you come to see our ruin glass then?"

"More than see," said Netano. "They're applying for permission to dig up the glass in the Eswae Parkland."

"All of it?" For a moment Ingray was at a loss. She knew that visitors from the Omkem Federacy would often pay good money for large pieces of ruin glass, and would spend as much or more shipping it back home. But there were other places to find glass that weren't in a district nature preserve. There was little difference between the chunks of glass there and the ones anywhere else. "All at once?"

"Not all at once, of course," said the Omkem woman with a condescending smile. "We're really looking for information, not just glass. It's a very specific thing we hope to find, and we think we know where to find it, but we will have to do quite a lot of digging."

"I'm so very interested to hear about it," said Ingray, suppressing a shiver. "And so very glad to have met you. Mama, if you'll excuse me, I'm going to make the staff very unhappy, dripping on the floor like this." She heard Danach laugh again, briefly, but didn't turn her head to look at him. Decided, all things considered, that she might play up her sorry state, just a bit. "It was a long, wet walk from the transport hub."

"Are you just come down the elevator from the station, then?" asked the Omkem man. "Did you see the Geck?"

"I was halfway down before I heard the news they were in the system," Ingray lied. "But I don't imagine there'll be much to see. I don't think they like leaving their ship any more than they like leaving their homeworld."

"What times we live in!" exclaimed the man. "Who would have thought we would ever see any of this, eh? The Radch in chaos, yet another treaty conclave—and such a conclave! I remember the uproar when the Rrrrr were first discovered, what was it, thirty, thirty-five years ago now. Or is it closer to forty? But this, well, this is something else, isn't it." As he spoke the Omkem woman stared off in the other direction, as though he were not there and she did not hear him. Her lips slightly pursed, as though if she did hear, she disapproved and wished he had kept silent.

"The Geck went through Tyr Siilas back then, too," said Netano. "But they didn't come here. I can't even imagine why they would come here, but they must have some reason." She turned to Ingray. "Ingray, dear, go get dried off." Her gaze flicked over Ingray's shoulder, and then back. "Our guests are staying with us for the next few days, and there are no empty rooms. Your...friend will have to stay with you."

No hint of disapproval in her mother's voice, but Ingray had navigated Netano's moods before and knew it was there. Even not slouched and staring down, Garal wasn't terribly prepossessing. But that suited Ingray just now; it meant, she was fairly sure, that Netano had not noted eir similarity to Pahlad, or thought much more about em than that e was bedraggled and badly dressed. Ingray said, soberly, "Yes, Mama." She gave a brief nod toward Netano and her guests—none at all for Danach—and turned and left the room, Garal (she trusted) trailing behind her.

Ingray's room was hardly the largest in the house, but it had its own small bath (enormous luxury after the even smaller facility on Captain Uisine's ship) and a window that looked out onto the rainy garden. Garal sat on a bench by a gold-and-mother-of-pearl-inlaid dressing table, drinking serbat, wearing a lungi Ingray had found, though it wrapped nearly twice around em and ended several more inches above eir ankles than was strictly fashionable. As e drank, e looked at the vestiges hung on the wall behind the dressing table, and Ingray found herself just a bit embarrassed. Invitations to parties that mattered to no one but her, including one to her own majority dinner. A few mass-produced vestiges, from places Ingray had visited, garish pink or orange blobs of glass or plastic or wood with place names and dates printed on them; a few leaves and flowers cased in resin; a strip made up of a dozen or so small folded and interlocked pieces of paper, from a friend she barely remembered and hadn't seen since she'd come to live with Netano Aughskold. Garal, the expert, surely knew a valuable vestige when e saw one. What must e be thinking, looking at these?

It shouldn't matter. She had never cared about the kind of vestige collection that had so absorbed Danach. She sat on her rolled-up mattress, toweling the ends of her hair dry, reminding herself that there were other, more important things to worry about. "Are you," she asked, setting her towel into her lap for a moment, "thinking what I'm thinking?"

E turned away from eir examination of her vestiges. "Are you wondering just exactly how big a bribe those two would have brought to get Netano Aughskold to help them get permits to dig up Eswac Parkland?"

Ingray blinked in surprise. "Not exactly." She already knew how much that might cost. Or at least, she knew how much it would take for Netano to entertain these people and maybe lead them to believe she might get them the permits they wanted. It would be a very large number. And probably a cut of the future sale of any usable pieces of ruin glass they (or anyone else) wanted to remove, just as a sweetener on top. Picking up her towel again, she said, "You're right, though, it must be huge. But the Omkem Federacy has been trying for the past five or six years to get the Assemblies of Hwae to agree to let a military fleet through our gate to Byeit."

"Because the Omkem/Byeit gate is down, and that was Omkem's most convenient access to Tyr."

"Yes," Ingray agreed. "They want to restore that gate but they can't do it unless they control both ends of it, the Omkem end and the Byeit end. And the Omkem Federacy has ships that can make their own gates, but I suppose they don't have enough of them to recover Byeit." She set her towel in her lap. "They really don't like having to make that extra gate trip through Hwae to get to Tyr."

"No, of course they don't," Garal replied. "And if I were a Tyr executive, I'd have been very happy to see the Omkem/Byeit gate go down. The Omkem Federacy may not be as large as it used to be, but it's never been content with just being able to go somewhere. They'd much rather own it outright."

Or at least run it. And Omkem, unlike Byeit (or Hwae for that matter), didn't share a gate with Tyr. If the Omkem Federacy wanted to resume their unfettered access to Tyr and its dozens of gates, they'd have to rebuild that Byeit gate somehow. "I wonder what Mama is thinking, taking such a large contribution from them." Certainly such a large amount of money coming to Netano from the Federacy would look as though it was meant to secure political favors, no matter these visitors' stated purpose. And Ingray had spent far too long in Netano's household to believe any contribution was innocent.

"I thought that was odd, too," agreed Garal. "But isn't it coming up on campaign season? She could use that money to have another go at prolocutor, and win or lose, if the Omkem try to call in too many favors she couldn't go wrong publicly denouncing their expansionist ambitions and their transparent attempt to manipulate Hwaean affairs. My..." E closed eir mouth suddenly on the rest of what e had been about to say. "I doubt there's a politician in this system who hasn't taken Federacy money in one form or another. Netano may be thinking that, or thinking another run at prolocutor is worth it. I'm not sure this is a good decision on her part, though."

Ingray paused for a moment before replying. "Surely it's obvious to the Federacy that if she were one of the four prolocutors she wouldn't be able to do the things they probably want and keep her office? She'll have to repudiate them if they try to get anything substantial out of her. So maybe that's not what these people are after." Except if Ingray's guess was right, the amount of money would doubtless raise suspicions that Netano's political opponents could use to their advantage.

Before Garal could reply, the door to the hallway opened, and Danach came in, a tray in one hand. "A servant was bringing you some bread and cheese to tide you over till supper, but I told em I'd do it." He smiled insincerely.

"How nice of you," said Ingray with just as much sincerity as he set the tray down on a small table.

Danach sat on the floor, next to the table. Leaned against it in a way meant to show off his height and breadth to advantage—he knew he was Netano's favorite, and he knew he was far better-looking than Ingray.

Still smiling, he said, "So I'd ask you how much you were willing to pay me to not tell Netano what you're doing, but as far as I can tell you're completely broke."

This—this was an old, familiar game. Ingray widened her smile. "I wasn't aware there was anything I was doing that Mama might want to know," she said, sweetly. "And I'm sure if there were, you'd eventually tell her anyway, no matter how much I paid you."

"Well, for one thing, you lied when you said you hadn't gotten the news about the Geck until you were halfway down the elevator," said Danach. "I talked to Oro and he told me he met you on the station—you looked a mess, he said—and told you himself. You were just off a ship from Tyr Siilas. So I knew you were on your way home. With someone else, whose fare you were paying. It made me curious, so I took a look at who it was and, Ingray, if you'd wanted a false identity for someone you should have come to me. Whoever did this one was more or less competent, but what documentation they provided you didn't stand up to a really determined search. Before you even stepped off the elevator I knew that Garal Ket didn't really exist. I've been wondering all this morning who it was you'd gone to such trouble to bring home. I considered offering you a ride from the transport hub, but I thought it would be awkward if it seemed like I was involved with whatever you were doing. Turns out, I was right." He looked over at Garal, staring down into eir cup of serbat. "What are you doing here, Pahlad Budrakim? I thought we were well rid of you."

Garal straightened in eir seat on the dressing table

bench, eir slouch disappearing. E smiled faintly and Ingray was struck again by how much e could look like Pahlad Budrakim. "Hello, Danach. I'd say it was nice to see you again, but you're still a malicious little shit." E turned to Ingray. "When we talked at Tyr Siilas, you said you and I had never met. But we have, it was just a long time ago. Do you remember your first formal reception? It was during campaign season and all the news services were there and you must have been just out of the public crèche. You were very small. And your somewhat older sibling Danach kept pinching you, probably trying to make you cry and disgrace yourself in front of not only Netano but the entire public."

Ingray, astonished, could not speak. How could Garal know this? No one knew it. No one, so far as she knew, had noticed Danach; all the grown-ups had been intent on exchanging polite greetings.

But obviously someone had noticed. And Garal—or whatever eir real name was—had learned all sorts of small details about the system's wealthy and prominent families. Such details were, after all, part of eir stock-in-trade as a forger of vestiges.

"How's your foot, Danach?" Garal continued. "I do hope you limped for a few days afterward."

"I didn't remember you were there," said Ingray.

"I'm willing to forget the past," said Danach, picking a piece of bread up off the tray, "if you'll tell me where the Budrakim vestiges are."

Could it be that easy? Ingray had imagined carefully working to convince him that Garal was, in fact,

Pahlad, and that e knew where those vestiges were. And that Danach would have some reason to be interested in that information. "No, Danach," she said, renewing her efforts to towel her hair dry, as though she was completely untroubled by any of this, "I don't think so."

"Have you been at Tyr Siilas all this time, Pahlad?" asked Danach, ignoring Ingray. "I can't imagine you ever actually went to Compassionate Removal, because if you'd gone in you'd never have come out. So you must have found some way to escape being sent there. I imagine it involved lots of money, which you probably got from the sale of at least some of the vestiges you stole. And no doubt you've made some of that back from my sister, unless, of course, she spent all of her money and quite a bit more that wasn't actually hers just to find you."

Garal kept silent, just smiled that small smile, and took a drink of serbat.

"Whatever the plan," Danach continued, "it has to involve those vestiges. Because you have nothing else to offer, do you?" He did not wait for a reply. "No, you don't. So, where are they? I'd assumed you'd sold them outsystem—no one in Hwae would be stupid enough to buy them, no matter how much money they had, no matter how much they wanted them. But here you are, and there must be some reason for that."

"You're right," said Garal. "Those vestiges would be impossible to sell. So why would I have stolen them?"

"Spite," replied Danach, pleasantly. He took a bite of the bread he held, chewed and swallowed. "Resentment.

Watching over the Budrakim Lareum was your entire future, likely from the day you were adopted. If I were in your place I'd have wanted to burn that lareum down. Though, you know, I'd have tried to implicate my father's heir in that, and tried to take that place myself. I can think of several ways you could have done it."

"Then why didn't I?" asked Garal.

"Because you're not as smart as you think you are," said Danach. Evenly, dispassionately, as though he were talking about the weather, or the latest ki-ball scores. "Neither is Ingray. You'd think she'd have learned better after all these years, but no." He smiled at Ingray. "You're in serious trouble. If anyone finds out that you've brought Pahlad Budrakim back from Compassionate Removal—in theory back from Compassionate Removal, anyway—I don't think even Mama could help you. And that's assuming she'd want to."

Ingray considered pointing out that if Danach got what he wanted here—payment from Ingray to keep quiet, preferably in the form of the location of the stolen vestiges—he would be in just as much trouble if they were discovered. Instead, she bit her lip in the hope that she could keep her face as expressionless as possible, and continued drying her hair.

"That would be it for you, too, Pahlad," Danach continued, scooping up some cheese to add to his bread. "Whoever kept you out of Compassionate Removal certainly won't want that exposed, and you'll be on your own."

"I don't know about that," said Garal. "If nothing

else, how can *I* be blamed for the crimes of someone who is legally dead?"

Danach made a snorting noise. "You really aren't bright, are you. All it would take would be a request for Pahlad Budrakim's identification in the archives and a bit of DNA from you. And the Garal Ket identity, well, it won't stand up to serious scrutiny."

Garal considered Danach for a few moments. "Fine," e said then, and set eir cup of serbat down. "I see you've thought this all the way through. I suppose we don't have any choice but to bring you in."

"No!" cried Ingray. The note of alarm in her voice was quite real. This was going too fast; she wanted to talk to Garal first. "No, don't!"

"Sorry, Ingray," said Garal. "You're a nice kid, and I'm grateful for your help so far, but I'm not going back to Compassionate Removal. And this has turned out to be way more complicated than we thought." E turned back to Danach. "The real vestiges are in Eswae Parkland."

Ingray nearly laughed. *Are you thinking what I'm thinking?* she'd asked em, and e had been. She bit her lip again and made herself frown, so that she wouldn't laugh.

Danach wasn't watching her. He stared at Garal, unblinking for a few moments. "You can't be serious. Why would you put them there?"

"It's under protection," said Garal. "No one can do much of anything there without a permit. And it's in Arsamol. Netano's district."

"So if someone found them, it would look like she'd done it?" guessed Danach. "Or whoever found it might bring it to Netano's attention and she wouldn't fail to use it against your father?"

"Take your pick," said Garal.

"Gods of the afterlife!" Danach swore. He threw the fragment of bread and cheese he was holding onto the table. "Are you fucking kidding me?" He pointed toward the floor. "Those travelers downstairs, they've just promised a donation to Netano's reelection fund large enough to finance another run at prolocutor. And *just coincidentally* Netano is supporting their application to dig up the ruin glass in Eswae Parkland. It's a huge project, and they're obviously stinking rich, which means they'll hire help, and they don't like using automated mechs for that kind of digging—something about soil layers, I'm told. It made no sense to me. But the upshot is, there'll be mech-pilots all over the parkland. And it'll be months before any work actually starts, assuming Mama can get this through the right committees, but there'll be all kinds of surveys before then. Those two are supposed to go out to the parkland tomorrow, in fact. Supposedly they can see recent disturbances of the ground, and where it's been dug out and filled in again, and they've been talking about looking for exactly that sort of thing. And on top of that Netano's close to getting things tied up in the District Council—this has been under serious consideration since shortly after Ingray left for Tyr Siilas, and the amount of money involved gave Mama a very strong motivation to push things through. Fucking ascended saints! We'll have to get there before they do. Where are the vestiges, exactly?"

"I'm not entirely sure," said Garal. "I never intended to retrieve them, so I didn't pay much attention."

Danach stared at em, and then said, "I should just turn you in."

Ingray, having used the last minute or so to muster up more of a frown, dropped her towel and crossed her arms. "I should turn you *both* in. Do you think that permit will be approved once everyone knows where those vestiges are?" Danach and Garal both turned to stare at her. "We had a *deal*," she said to Garal.

"When we made that deal," Garal said, very patiently, "we didn't know about people digging up the ruin glass, did we."

"You won't turn us in," said Danach dismissively. And to Garal, "She'll get over it. And you'd better remember where you put those vestiges." He blinked and looked off into the distance. Brought his focus back to Ingray and Garal. "In the meantime, I have to get ready for a party. Taucris Ithesta's naming is tonight."

"What?" Ingray was startled out of her posed anger. "Did Ocris finally make a choice?" Ocris was Ingray's age, had been a quiet child, ill at ease in large groups. Ingray had liked them, but once she'd claimed her own adult name she'd seen very little of Ocris. Had almost forgotten them.

Danach gave a short laugh. "I thought they—sorry,

she—never would. She never did like making up her mind, and if she was going to be content to stay a child playing at cops and robbers for the rest of her life, well, she can do as she likes, her nother is rich enough to support her. But I hear her nother threatened to cut off her allowance if she didn't declare. Honestly, I think most of her friends had written her off. I certainly had. I wouldn't be going tonight, except her nother *is* very rich, and Mama *is* considering another run at prolocutor. So there's no avoiding it." He rose. "We'll talk more in the morning." And he left.

Ingray looked at Garal, who said nothing. "Well," Ingray said after a bit, wary of servants, or of Danach having some other way to hear what went on in her room. "I suppose it can't be helped. But there are still... financial issues." Danach had taken the bait, swallowed a good deal more of the hook and line than she had ever expected, much sooner than she had expected. But there seemed to be no chance to get any money out of him, not as things stood.

"Don't worry," said Garal. "We'll work something out." E seemed remarkably untroubled. "Maybe since your mother is going out tonight, we can have our supper up here. It might be a good idea to look at some maps and pictures. I'll see if I can't... remember something."

"No," said Ingray, summoning the household schedule into her vision, and blinking through it. "Netano's guests aren't going to the party. They need to be up early tomorrow morning for their trip to Eswae Parkland.

They might decide to eat in their rooms tonight, but they might not. I'll tell staff we'll be at supper at the regular time—that's in about an hour and a half—and we'll go to the sitting room afterward. We can play counters."

"That sounds fun," said Garal, perfectly seriously.

6

Eswae Parkland was a bit more than an hour by ground-car from Netano's house. The land had been owned by one of Netano's predecessors in the Assembly, who had donated it to the people of the district quite a long time ago. Kilometers of grass and tree-covered hills, of little streams edged with outcrops of ruin glass running down to the Iogh River. The whole parkland was strewn with great boulders and piles of colored glass, and it was a common belief that the hills were made of the stuff. Certainly quite a lot of the parkland was just a layer of soil over glass rubble. Not terribly convenient for buildings or farms, which was why it was a park instead.

Ingray mostly knew it as a place to pose for photos—just a few years ago, Netano had negotiated the passage of a resolution in the Assembly that among other things had funded the renovation of several walking trails in the parkland, and so of course she and her family had been there at the reopening, clean, neat, and smiling in front of Eswae's most famous landmark, a broad tumble of huge glass blocks, red and blue and yellow and green, some of them ten meters or more wide, in all sorts of eccentric shapes. Blocks and slabs and twisting arcs, an entire hillside of them sloping down into the river. The rest of the hill was grass, a copse of rovingtrees at the top. The public vestige from that event was a smooth slab of basalt, lying flat in the grass at the foot of the hill, beside the path, with the date of the resolution's passage cut into it. Yesterday's rain had washed the sky a cloudless blue, and the day was bright and warm. It was late enough in spring that the rovingtrees weren't shedding anymore, though here and there a tuft of gray fibers was caught in the grass.

Ingray had never been as strangely obsessed with ruin glass as Omkem visitors all seemed to be. But this glass, this hillside in the parkland, was a landmark. One of the most famous landmarks in Arsamol. It was part of her home, and the thought of digging mechs pulling it all apart... "Surely you don't mean to dig this up," said Ingray to the foreign woman. Her name was Zat, and she had been unfailingly cheerful on the groundcar ride and the subsequent long walk into the parkland. "Not the hillside."

"Oh, goodness, no," Zat replied. The man walked beside and just behind her—Hevom, he'd named himself when Ingray asked, though of course Zat never said his name, or spoke directly to him. "I wish I could dig up that hill! I would love to have confirmation of some of my hypotheses—or denial, yes, that's always a possibility, you know. Perhaps what I find elsewhere on the site will help convince others to support me in exploring the hill. But for the moment, it's out of reach. Still, I can learn quite a lot from being able to take various sorts of images. Perhaps that will tell me a great deal, yes?"

"You haven't taken them already?" asked Garal, standing beside Ingray. Today e wore a green-and-white tunic and a pair of trousers that were several centimeters too short for em even though they hung baggy all around eir thin frame, but there was no help for that. No shoes—Ingray hadn't had any that would fit em, but e had said it wouldn't matter, and had not complained or seemed uncomfortable, even after the morning's walk. E still carried that black bag on eir shoulder, though Ingray could not imagine what might be in it that e thought e might need. "You'll forgive me, excellency," Garal continued, speaking Yiir, as they all had been all morning. "I know just a bit about this sort of research, and I understand it's customary to start with a survey—or at least images that might give some indication of what's under the ground and its extent."

"Ah!" Zat brightened further, clearly pleased at Garal's interest. "Yes, so very right. That is where we should begin, with a survey. Images, and also a...what is the word, a walk? Ordinarily I would have many mechs walk the ground and then look at the recordings for small details. But, you understand, the Assemblies are not happy to have foreign mechs flying around taking pictures of the planet, nor large numbers of them combing the parkland. We asked, of course, and of course were refused. Nor are they happy to have a number of foreign students descend on the parkland with any intention beyond enjoying the scenery. I have only been able to survey what I and my little Uto here"—she gestured at the small, boxy bright pink mech walking alongside her on four thin, flexing legs—"can reach on our own. We hope to be allowed access to the government's own images eventually, though we cannot expect that, and will have to plan as though it will not happen. We will hire people here on Hwae to survey and dig when we have the permissions to do so. In the meantime, it's just us." A glance, not at Hevom, but at little pink Uto, stepping along beside her on the path.

"You really think it was a city?" asked Ingray. At dinner the night before, Zat had explained what it was they were looking for, why they hoped to dig here. "You think there are *buildings*?"

"There is surely quite a lot here." She gestured to the slope of huge glass blocks. "I think—I cannot prove it yet—that these hills were intentional structures. Temples, palaces, treasuries. What might be inside them, hidden all these centuries?"

"But," objected Garal, "isn't it odd that there was a city here once, but there isn't one now? Isn't that usually the way it is with cities, they're built on top of an old one, or very nearby?"

"It can't have been a human city, though," Ingray put in. "It was here before the first humans found this planet."

"Was it, now?" asked Zat. "I am not so sure. Humans may have reached this planet earlier than many think. I am certain that they did."

"But not much earlier, surely." As soon as she said it, Ingray realized she probably shouldn't have. Zat was, after all, a guest of Netano's, and one Netano was hoping to gain from, financially. "I mean, we know how far humans would have had to come, and we know how long it would have taken them." A very, very long time before the first intersystem gates were built. "And the atmosphere, when the first humans arrived, wasn't breathable." She seemed to recall a tutor saying it had been very thin, and mostly carbon dioxide and sulfur before the terraforming started.

"So the official histories say," said Zat. "But what if they're wrong? What if the place the histories claim to be the birthplace of humanity isn't? Or what if humans left their homeworld much sooner than claimed?"

Ingray hadn't paid overly close attention to ancient history lessons. "I suppose that would change things, yes," she agreed. "But...I mean no disrespect, excellency, but why go to all this trouble? I mean, I do understand wanting to know things, and I understand being interested enough to go to some trouble to find things out. But why make so much effort, for so long, over this particular question?"

Zat still smiled. "Most Iwacans I've met feel this way. Your esteemed mother does, I believe, and cares only for the contribution to her reelection fund. I must say, no disrespect intended, excellency, but I have never understood this. You live surrounded by this"—she gestured around, meaning, Ingray supposed, to indicate the parkland and its profusion of ruin glass—"and have so little curiosity about it! Perhaps you use the pieces of it to build a wall. And yet, a floor tile from a building that, it is claimed, one of your Founders might have stood near, badly made to begin with, ugly and cracked and in reality not three centuries old, you will call that a priceless treasure and argue over it bitterly—yes, I see the look on your face when I mention it, I know that the Kaheru family still holds the grudge against Netano for that, though she is not the same Netano and it was a hundred years ago. When this, so much more ancient and precious, you care nothing for. But surely you cannot be unaffected by real beauty, and surely you see that to know your past is to know who you are."

"In that case, excellency," said Garal, "who are *you*, if ruin glass was left by humans who left the ancient homeworld thousands of years earlier than supposed? And why is it worth so much to you to be able to claim that?"

Hevom laughed, startling Ingray. He had been entirely silent for hours. "Quick, very quick," he said.

Zat frowned, ignoring Hevom as usual. Not offended, it seemed, so much as searching for a way to answer the question. "I believe," she said, finally, "that the earliest inhabitants of Omkem came from Hwae. By the time your own ancestors arrived they were gone, and had left only these ruins."

"So you are closer to the original source of humanity

than we are," Garal suggested. "No disrespect meant, of course, just a fact." Eir voice was entirely, impressively, without rancor or sarcasm. "And as descendants of Hwae's actual first inhabitants, you might want the right to have some say in Hwae's affairs, yes? In particular, several members of the Omkem Federacy would like some control over traffic in the gates here. Or maybe they'd just like the Federacy military to be able to travel freely through the Hwae/Byeit gate, so they can reestablish control there, and rebuild the gate that was taken down. It was so much easier for them to get to Tyr before the Byeits revolted and took that gate down."

"That wasn't a revolution," said Hevom, his voice just barely noticeably angry and impatient. "That was a few terrorists."

Zat, as always, completely ignored what Hevom had said. "I am not a politician. I care only for knowledge. I want only the truth. These other concerns"—she gestured them away, minor irritants—"they are irrelevant. But I do not expect you to understand this."

Garal said nothing. Ingray, who had grown up in a politician's very political household, smiled and said brightly, "That's quite fascinating! And of *course* the truth is important. Thank you, excellency, for being so patient with our questions."

"Of course, excellency!" replied Zat. "Now, I know the parkland Safety officer warned us not to climb on the blocks there, for very good reasons, but I am going to see if my little Uto here can take some detailed visuals for me. The officer did say that would be all right." She started off into the grass toward the slope of the hill, the little pink mech trailing behind her.

Hevom did not follow her. He stood silent for a moment, watching her walk away. And then, with surprising venom, "It's a waste of time. So many other important issues to worry about, and this is what we expend so much on?"

"Then why did you come?" asked Ingray.

"I had no choice. When one is a poor junior cousin of a sister's daughter's affines, one does not refuse." Ingray wondered what possible reason Zat could have for bringing along a resentful junior cousin who she could not speak to or, Ingray suspected, speak about directly. But before she could ask, Hevom continued. "A person with a hereditary seat on the Directorate and a great deal of money can have a disproportionate effect on the Directorate's priorities." Ingray suspected he wasn't speaking generally but was mentioning Zat as specifically as he could. "The Directorate devotes whole sessions to discussing ancient history and finding the means to make expeditions like this one. But do they give any attention at all to..." He seemed to stop himself, and think better of what he meant to say. "Or do they think of sending representatives to the Conclave?" He made a disgusted noise. "I would rather be home pressing that far more important issue. We can't leave the human vote up to the Radchaai! They're sure to oppose the AIs joining the treaty, but it's absolutely vital that they be accepted!"

"I don't know," said Ingray, watching the little pink

mech clamber onto a huge glass block as Zat reached the crown of the hill and sat down in the shade of a slender rovingtree. "What if it's a Radchaai ploy to begin with? The AIs are their own ships and stations, they built them and programmed them. They're impossible to separate from Radchaai space." It was one of many reasons the Radchaai were so frightening. "If they're accepted into the treaty, then it's possible the Radchaai will have two voices in treaty affairs, not just one."

"I would agree with you," said Hevom. "Except for the fact that it's become increasingly obvious that the Radchaai are fighting each other. The news from Athoek alone should be enough to make that clear. Anaander Mianaai is tearing herself apart, and has lost control of at least some of her artificial intelligences. I don't think it's a deception; there would be other, far less damaging ways of achieving the same ends."

"A sudden attack of conscience, for instance," suggested Garal. "Demanding the conclave herself, instead of being apparently forced into it in such a humiliating way. And if that's the case, treaty recognition of their AIs will tear Radch space apart."

"Or make the whole idea of Radch space meaningless," agreed Hevom.

"But independent AIs," Ingray protested. "Independent *warship* AIs!"

"By the treaty, they can't interfere with us," Hevom pointed out. "If the Conclave refuses to admit them, and the Radchaai lose control of them—"

"Which it seems they have already, at least partially,"

Ingray concluded. "Yes, I see. Put that way, it does seem best if the machines are admitted to the treaty." Just saying it made a shiver start at the back of her neck.

"Every human government that can should be sending forces to the Conclave, to be sure Translator Seimet Mianaai speaks for humans, not Radchaai." Hevom spoke emphatically, angrily. "Instead we're spending money and time on *this*. Your pardon, excellencies, but I find it very frustrating. And of course I can't speak of it as I'd like to."

"No, of course," replied Ingray. "We understand entirely." Though she didn't, not really.

"Well," Hevom said, clearly still angry. "Well. Excuse me, excellencies. I'm supposed to examine the area where the glass meets the water."

"How does he know he's supposed to do that," asked Garal, as Hevom stalked away toward the riverbank, "if Zat never speaks to him? She never even looks at him."

"I don't think anyone understands the Omkem except the Omkem," said Ingray. Most Omkem Ingray had met seemed entirely normal, except for things like this.

"Indeed," said Garal. "Why don't we walk around ourselves, and look for some likely spots? And maybe keep an eye on what areas your Omkem guests are most interested in."

"I don't think you can claim to have buried the vestiges in the hill," Ingray said, gesturing toward the mass of bright-colored glass boulders that made up the hillside. "I don't think it's possible to dig very far down there, and it's not like you'd forget putting them there."

"Not likely, no," Garal agreed. "But somewhere near here, I'd say. This is where the Omkem seem most interested. Let's walk a bit, and keep an eye on where else they might be poking around."

Ingray and Garal spent an hour or two strolling along the trail that ran by the river and curved around the glass-bouldered hill, or wandering into the grass beside the trail. Hevom walked up and down the riverbank, occasionally stopping and stooping to splash a hand in the water or peer more closely at something by his feet. Despite the looming hillside, he was nearly always in view. Zat sat on the top of the hill, her back against a slender rovingtree. Her small bright pink mech bobbed into sight every now and then among the hillside glass, once or twice climbing out of the rocks and toddling over to Zat, and then away, back into the boulders again, its luminous pink bright against the blue, purple, yellow, red, and green of the glass.

At length, Ingray and Garal's walk returned them to the basalt slab. Hevom looked up from whatever it was he was doing by the water and walked toward them. "Well," said Ingray, quietly, "even if we don't find any suitable site, it's a lovely day." Under the sunlight she had begun to relax, in a way she hadn't for weeks, all that time on stations and ships. She hadn't realized how much she missed the light and the breeze, and open spaces.

"I've been thinking," said Garal, also quietly, though it would take Hevom a minute or two to come within earshot, "we might be able to get away with the hill. I could claim it was dark and I was in a hurry. Or"—with a glance at Hevom—"I could say I threw them in the river."

"Oh!" That was an excellent idea. Except that it didn't quite match what they'd already said to Danach. "I suppose you might not have mentioned that particular detail, and don't remember quite exactly where you threw it in." She thought a moment more. "We should find out what their interest in the river is. If they're going to be spending time dragging things up from the bottom, we could make sure it was wherever they were going to be doing that."

"Has there been any movement on the hilltop?" Hevom asked as he came up to where they stood talking.

It took Ingray a moment to understand that he was asking if there had been any word or sign from Zat. "No, there hasn't been." She glanced up at the hilltop. Zat was still seated, leaning against the rovingtree, for all the world as though she hadn't moved all morning.

Ingray composed a brief message with a request for immediate response and sent it off to Zat, but there was no reply, and the figure on the hilltop didn't move. "I wonder if she's fallen asleep."

"Not likely," said Hevom. "Uto's automated routines are very limited. It's certainly been under control all the times I've seen it."

"Have you seen it recently?" asked Garal.

"Not for a half hour or so," Hevom replied. "It's really rather vexing. I know the servants packed us some lunch, but I can't possibly eat it just yet."

Before or without Zat, Ingray supposed that meant. And he couldn't just tell Zat what he wanted. "Garal and I can take the lunch out," suggested Ingray. "You could say it would have been rude not to join us."

"I'm afraid I still wouldn't be able to eat," said Hevom, with an aggrieved sigh.

"Well, we won't put you in that position, then," said Ingray, though she really did want some lunch, now Hevom had mentioned it. She reminded herself that it wasn't Hevom's fault that he was Omkem, and a younger cousin of Zat's affines, whatever that might mean.

Of course, she wasn't under the restrictions Hevom apparently was. She could go say something to Zat, maybe even suggest lunch. Ingray looked up at the top of the hill, where Zat was sitting in the same place she'd been for the last couple of hours. Ingray really should go up the hill and say something to her.

"Oh, look," said Garal. "Your brother has decided to favor us with his presence."

Ingray, Garal, and Hevom all turned to look as Danach came toward them on the trail, walking slowly. "You look tired," said Ingray sweetly as he reached them. "Did you not get enough sleep?"

"Fuck you," Danach replied, with an almost sincere-looking smile. In Bantia, presumably so Hevom could not understand.

"You were sleeping so peacefully when we left," said Garal, in Yiir, "and we knew you'd had a late night. We didn't want to wake you."

Danach looked at Ingray and then at Garal. "Entirely

127

out of kindness, I'm sure." In Yiir, now. "Did you find what you were looking for?" The barest hint of menace in his voice.

Ingray was quite sure Garal heard it, too, but Hevom seemed oblivious. "My goodness, no, excellency! It will take much longer than an afternoon to find what we're looking for." His tone was just slightly exasperated.

"We've narrowed it down," Ingray said, in Bantia. And then, in Yiir, "I was about to go up the hill and ask Excellency Zat if she'd like some lunch."

Danach scoffed. "You left the lunches in the ground-car. I'm not walking all the way back there." He dropped down to sit in the grass and crossed his legs. Ingray knew he worked out regularly—this would be a result of Danach's late night, and his anger at Ingray and Garal. Danach continued. "Did it not occur to you to message Excellency Zat instead of walking up the hill? Or to just have lunch without her?"

"She's not replying to messages." Ingray did her best to keep her irritation with her brother out of her voice. "And it would be rude to start lunch without her." Which Danach knew, of course. She looked at Garal, who was as expressionless as usual, and at Hevom, who frowned. "I'll go up the hill and wake her," Ingray said.

Hevom's frown cleared. "Thank you, excellency."

From the top of the hill, even with the small copse of rovingtrees, Ingray could see the whole area of the parkland they'd been walking in over the past couple of hours, the grass, the walking trail, Danach sitting beside it, Garal apparently talking to him. Hevom gazed toward the bright silver ribbon of the river curving and foaming around the swath of colored glass blocks and slabs. Zat hadn't stirred as Ingray approached, so she was certainly asleep, still leaning against the tree. From where Ingray stood, she could see the Omkem woman's right shoulder and arm, her hand resting flat down on the ground beside her, her legs stretched out in front of her. "Excellency," Ingray called. "Excellency Zat." No response. She walked around the tree to face Zat.

For a moment, she could not make sense of what she saw: Zat, eyes closed, her head pushed hard up against the slim trunk of the rovingtree. Something dark crusted one corner of her mouth, and it took Ingray another moment to admit to herself that it was probably blood. Like the wide, dark stain on the front of Zat's tunic was probably blood.

Zat's chest didn't seem to be moving under that stain, no rise and fall of breath, and Ingray couldn't think what it was she ought to do next, even if it was true, but it couldn't be true, she must be mistaken. "Excellency Zat," Ingray said again. Made herself step closer. A flat, empty seedpod dropped from the rovingtree, brushed Zat's cheek, landed on that dark stain on her tunic.

Suddenly terrified and sick to her stomach, Ingray made herself take a deep breath and swallow. Carefully, hoping the nausea wouldn't overcome her. She turned to look down the hill again, where Garal and Danach waited, where Hevom still stared at the river.

She needed to tell them what had happened. And then what? Then she needed to send a message to Planetary

Safety. They would take care of it after that, they would know what to do. But she found she couldn't bring herself to think out any sort of message, so instead she walked back down the hill. Maybe she would be able to say it by the time she reached the bottom, maybe she would be able to tell everyone that Zat, her mother's guest, hadn't moved for hours, or replied to messages, because she was dead.

7

The parkland's Safety office was mostly a visitor center—restrooms, some snacks for sale—bean crackers, three flavors of roasted cicadas, milk sweets—and a fabricator that would make various sorts of customizable vestiges. A counter where a Safety officer sat, with a few rooms behind that. Offices, Ingray had always assumed, though it turned out that there was also a small holding area, in case someone had to be detained.

Ingray, Garal, Danach, and Hevom sat in one of the larger rooms, one that looked as though it might be used for meetings, or perhaps it was one the officers used for breaks or meals, because there was a wide table and a few benches, no windows, the walls set to a pattern of blue, brown, and yellow zigzags. Emergency procedures notices hung on the wall opposite the door, actually physically printed on sheets of plastic, so that they could be read even without overlays, and under those a scratched wooden shelf holding a few mismatched cups and a half-empty bottle of pepper sauce. "Can't we just go home?" Danach had asked, when they'd first been escorted to the room, and only received a long, apologetic response that had added up to *definitely not.* "I'm messaging my mother," Danach had said then, a threatening undercurrent to the pleasant tone of his voice, and the Safety officer had said that he was quite welcome to do so, but had still refused to let them leave.

That had been several hours ago, and Netano hadn't answered. A curt message had come to both Danach and Ingray from Netano's chief of staff—their nuncle, Ingray's boss if she hadn't yet lost her job—telling them to be patient and cooperate with Planetary Safety. On receiving that message, Danach had descended into silent, gloomy anger. But honestly, Ingray couldn't imagine that Netano being here, let alone any of her staff, would make much difference. If this had been something minor, no doubt she would have pried her children free of Planetary Safety by now, but a murder was something else entirely. Especially given that she was considering another run for prolocutor. Ingray suspected that Danach himself might have been much more noisily belligerent had he not known that the behavior of any of Netano's household right now could be an issue in an upcoming election.

So they sat in the office, waiting for some Planetary Safety official to send them home. Danach sulked. Hevom seemed stunned, staring blankly into space, not touching the lunch he'd been so eager for, which an officer had brought in from the groundcar. Garal seemed completely untroubled, and once e had eaten eir lunch e sat quietly, seemingly unworried, to all appearances content to read the emergency notices. Ingray remembered that e was accustomed to the company of murderers or worse.

Both Ingray and Danach turned immediately toward the door as soon as it opened. Neither Garal nor Hevom moved. A tall and broad-shouldered neman in the green-and-gold jacket and lungi of a deputy chief of Planetary Safety entered. "Good evening," e said, in heavily accented Yiir. Not Bantia, presumably so that Hevom would understand em. It was a language most well-educated Hwaeans knew at least a bit of, though the deputy chief's accent didn't sound well educated. Sounded, in fact, as though e wasn't from this area but from Lim District. "I apologize for keeping you all waiting so long. I'm Cheban Veret, Deputy Chief of Serious Crimes. And this"—e gestured to the shorter, slimmer person behind him, in a similar uniform, though with an odd, wide, darker green stripe from jacket collar to shoulder to wrist that Ingray had never seen before—"is my assistant, Taucris Ithesta."

Danach gave a short, bitter laugh. "Taucris! I thought you left the party last night because you were bored."

"I told you," said Taucris, "I had to go to work this morning. Hello, Ingray."

"Hello, Taucris." Ingray nearly slipped and used her child-name instead. "I'm sorry I didn't get home in time to congratulate you properly." Oblique, not saying directly what those congratulations would be for. Ingray had claimed her adult name in her late teens, like nearly everyone she knew. Taucris was nearly twenty-five, so much older than expected that it might be embarrassing to them...to her, to have it pointed out.

Taucris gave a tiny lift of the corners of her mouth, barely a smile. "Thank you."

"Excellencies," said Deputy Chief Veret after a moment of silence. "You've already given the parkland officers an account of your visit here this morning and afternoon, for which, thank you. I do have some additional questions, and once those are addressed you can be on your way. To begin: Excellency Garal Ket. Or, should I say, Pahlad Budrakim."

Garal smiled. An actual smile, not just eir normal quirk of the mouth. "I'm sorry, Ingray," e said. "You're a nice kid, for an Aughskold. I didn't want to lie to you but I didn't see any other way." And then, looking at the deputy chief, "She didn't know. She found me on Tyr Siilas. I gave her a sob story, and she helped me get back to Hwae. Nice kid, like I said."

"How could she know?" asked Deputy Chief Veret. "I barely believe it myself, and I've seen the data. How did you get out of Compassionate Removal?"

"I obviously never made it there to begin with," said Garal—no, Pahlad. Calmly. Lying with such familiar smooth conviction. "I never intended to come back. Not at first. But I've decided I want to tell all of Hwae what I did with the Garseddai vestiges."

And e knew. If e was really, actually Pahlad, e had

to know what e had done with them. E had known the whole time e'd been talking about places they could pretend e'd left them. Ingray was trying to get her thoughts around that.

"Well," said the deputy chief. "That's as may be. At the moment I'm most interested in the murder of Excellency Zat. It's been difficult to piece together what must have happened, not least because I haven't been able to find any reason anyone within kilometers of the parkland today would have wished her dead. Until your name came up."

"But," said Ingray, still feeling as though nothing around her was quite solid, not even the bench she sat on, "e was with me the whole time! We both watched Zat go up the hill, and Garal was never out of my sight after that until I went up the hill and found..."

"Yes," agreed the deputy chief. "That is a problem. In fact, no one was near the deceased from the moment she went up the hill until you found her body, excellency. But she was certainly murdered. Stabbed through the heart with what was probably some sort of knife. And she'd been..." The deputy chief hesitated. "She'd been spiked to the rovingtree." Ingray thought of Zat's head pressed so firmly against the tree trunk, the blood at the corner of her mouth. "Presumably so that she'd stay sitting up. The spike was a marker stake. It's used in construction, and also in various kinds of"—e hesitated, looking for a word or phrase—"historical excavation work. Zat's mech was carrying six of them, she declared them on entering the system. But we don't know where her mech went. We're looking for it now. In the meantime we still need to understand why it was done. As I said, no one anywhere near seemed to have any reason to kill Excellency Zat. That is, until the name Pahlad Budrakim came up."

"Ethiat," Pahlad suggested, "doesn't like the plan to dig up Eswae Parkland. Is it because he doesn't like the idea of Excellency Zat trying to legitimize Omkem claims to a history in the system? Or does he object to the disruption to one of our planet's beautiful natural areas?"

"Tearing up nature," said Danach. Still sullen, but unable to resist a jibe at Prolocutor Budrakim. "He hasn't said anything about the Omkem."

"Ah," said Pahlad, with only the slightest hint of bitterness. "He'll have been getting Omkem money himself, then. At any rate, whatever his objection, he'll have discovered it when he saw it might be a way to limit the influence of Representative Aughskold. But surely you don't think I'm acting for Ethiat Budrakim. Besides, I rather suspect he's got his hands full dealing with more important issues. Like finding some political advantage in the Geck being here."

Deputy Chief Veret said, "I had a long talk with Representative Aughskold before I came in here." Ingray looked quickly at Danach, who showed no sign of reacting to that news. The deputy chief continued. "She tells me she and Prolocutor Budrakim had a very acrimonious conversation on the topic just last week. The prolocutor was adamant that he would prevent the disturbance of Eswae Parkland if it was in his power."

Pahlad smiled again. "Is that a fact."

"If you please, Pahlad," said Taucris then, "put your bag on the table."

"Of course," said Pahlad, still smiling, and did so.

Taucris held out her hand, and the dark green stripe on her sleeve raised itself up on dozens of legs and swarmed down and across onto the table. It ran onto Pahlad's black bag, pushed at it here and there until it opened, and then dived inside. Nutrient blocks tumbled out onto the table, and then, "Ah," said Taucris, frowning, focusing somewhere in the air in front of her, and the mech slid out of the bag, several of its many legs clutching the handle of a knife.

It was the sort of knife the cook in Netano's house might use to slice meat. In fact, Ingray was quite sure it *was* one of the cook's knives.

"I stole it from the kitchen," Pahlad said in answer to her look. "I went to the kitchen late last night looking for food, and I saw the knives. It just made me feel safer to have it."

One end of the mech opened, like a mouth. It brought the knife closer to the opening and spat out a plastic blob that it pulled and patted until it enclosed the knife. "It matches," said Taucris.

"What?" asked Ingray, startled.

"It matches the wound," said Deputy Chief Veret. "It could have been the knife that stabbed Excellency Zat."

"But there are three or four more just like it in my mother's kitchen," Ingray protested. "And probably lots of other kitchens."

"Maybe," said the deputy chief. "We'll look into that. In the meantime, Pahlad Budrakim, I'm afraid we're detaining you on suspicion of murder."

"Really?" Pahlad seemed entirely untroubled by this. "Not for escaping an unescapable prison and coming back alive when I wasn't supposed to?"

"I don't think anyone's ever done that before," admitted the deputy chief. "Not that I know of. And I don't think there's any legal provision for it happening."

"Well, that's something, isn't it. I presume Officer Taucris Ithesta will give me a receipt for my bag, with an inventory of its contents?" Taucris gestured confirmation of this. "Not my first time being detained, you know." E stood. "Goodbye, Ingray. You really should take the captain's advice."

When Taucris had led Pahlad out of the room, and the deputy chief had told the rest of them they could go, so long as they remained available to Planetary Safety for further questions, Danach said, "Who is the captain and what was his advice?"

"No one you know, and none of your business," said Ingray. "Let's go home."

By the time they arrived back at Netano's house, it was quite late, but lights still shone through the blue and green and red glass blocks. A servant opened the door, and Ingray, Danach, and Hevom entered to find Netano herself, in businesslike formal skirts and jacket and sandals, her unruly black hair braided into neat submission. "Ah, you're back," she said, on seeing them enter. "Excellency Hevom, I am so very, very sorry for your loss."

Hevom managed to pull himself out of his stunned reverie. "Thank you, Representative. I...thank you."

"Please make yourself at home here, for as long as you need. Ingray, a word in the sitting room."

Danach smirked. "Good night, Mama," he said, and headed up the stairs. Hevom followed.

In the sitting room, Netano gestured Ingray to a seat, the armchair where Danach had lounged the day before. "Planetary Safety has asked the news services to hold off on reporting Excellency Zat's death," Netano said, having taken her own seat on a bench opposite. "So, I'm sure, has Prolocutor Budrakim. Pahlad's return isn't something the news services know about, but of course once they start poking around it probably won't be long before they discover it. I predict they will restrain themselves for two or three days, at the most. There's no possible way this can be kept quiet indefinitely. So explain to me."

Clearly Danach had told Netano something in his messages to her. Just what, though, Ingray couldn't be certain. "I met em...I met Garal, or I suppose e's really Pahlad. I met em on Tyr Siilas. E looked so much like Pahlad I said something to em about it, but e said e wasn't. And I got to talking to em and e said e was stranded and out of money and had no one to help em get home, so I thought I would help." Netano didn't visibly react to any of it; her round face held just a pleas-ant, listening expression. "And we got here, and Danach immediately thought the same thing I'd thought, that this person looked a lot like Pahlad Budrakim, only he decided that e must really *be* Pahlad, and came to my room to tell us he knew who e really was. And we just kind of played along."

"Only it turned out the person you were dealing with really was Pahlad Budrakim." Ingray gestured agree-ment. "Deputy Chief Veret assumes that Pahlad obtained eir own false identification at Tyr Siilas. Danach, on the other hand, is quite sure that it was *you* who purchased it. But you didn't just buy a false identity for a random stranger you met on Tyr Siilas, no matter how forlorn they seemed. You'd already bought it for something else, hadn't you. Who did you intend it for?"

Ingray took a deep breath. "I'd had a plan. I went to Tyr Siilas to . . . well, when I got there I discovered the thing I wanted to do wouldn't work. It wasn't any good to me anymore, but Garal—I mean, Pahlad—really needed it."

"The fact that you had a false identity on you to begin with, and that it was so easily transferred to this person you happened to run across, and who you brought here, and the alacrity with which you confirmed Danach's identification of em—an identification you tell me you believed to be incorrect—suggests to me that your plan wasn't entirely legal or aboveboard to begin with," said Netano. "And no doubt your plan was aimed at your brother." Ingray's face heated, but she said nothing. "It's probably better if I don't know the details. I don't intend to say any of this to Planetary Safety. But if the deputy chief discovers it for emself, well, this would be a bad time for those details to come out."

"Yes, Mama." Ingray didn't have anything else to say to that.

"You're certain that Pahlad was with you the whole time, in Eswae? And e couldn't have been piloting a mech part of the time?"

Ingray was relieved that Netano wasn't pursuing the issue of her having brought Pahlad Budrakim home any further, but wary, too—it didn't mean her mother wouldn't bring it up again sometime in the future. "The only mech anyone saw was Excellency Zat's Uto." Ingray thought of the marker spike and suppressed a shudder. Whoever had killed Zat had to have used her own mech to do it. "I can't imagine Pahlad would have had access to that. And e never seemed distracted, or like e was thinking about something else." Then again, Captain Uisine never had, either, even when he'd been drinking, and Ingray knew he was almost always piloting one— or, unheard of, two or three—at any given time.

"Well." Netano sighed. "Your timing isn't very good, Ingray. You know it's coming up on campaign season. I would hate to have a family scandal cost me an election." Her tone was mild, but Ingray knew it for a warning. "But it may be we can get some advantage out of it. My sources tell me that the prolocutor left for Hwae Station the moment he heard about the Geck arriving. But he's turned right around and is on his way back home, because of Pahlad."

"The prolocutor himself?" asked Ingray, frowning. "Not his daughter?" Ethiat had already given his name to his heir, and she often made appearances or visits for her father now. It was technically the same as being there himself, though of course everyone knew the difference, and interpreted which of them went where as a judgment on what or who the prolocutor felt was most important.

"The prolocutor himself," confirmed Netano. "Even though he could—and should—have sent his daughter." When Netano said *should*, she certainly meant politically, the way it would look to Prolocutor Budrakim's constituency. The news services hadn't yet learned of Pahlad Budrakim's presence on Hwae, or eir involvement in the death of Excellency Zat, and so most people would find the prolocutor's sudden return inexplicable. "I am no longer confident that the prolocutor values the interests of Assembly electors the way he ought, and I am on my way to the station now to be certain that *someone* will. But I also have good reason to stay home and deal with this situation. If I had named my heir, the way that the prolocutor has, my course would be very simple—I would leave that Netano here to handle this situation." Of course. Politics before family, unless family *was* politics. Which it often was.

But trust Netano to find some political advantage in any situation.

"I've let the ambassador from the Omkem Federacy know that Excellency Hevom is welcome to stay here as long as he likes," Netano continued, "and that my own children are looking after him. I am extremely unhappy that my guest has been murdered, and I want very much for Planetary Safety to find the person who did it. I expect every member of my household to cooperate fully and openly with Planetary Safety's investigation of this matter. It would be very unfortunate if anything unsavory came to light in the process."

"Yes, Mama." Ingray knew that for a warning as well.

"The groundcar is here," said Netano, rising, "and I can't miss the elevator. I won't be available for anything but the most urgent of emergencies, so you'll have to call Nuncle Lak if anything comes up that you can't handle on your own. Be good." And she kissed Ingray on the cheek, as though Ingray had still been a small child.

Ingray wasn't sure whether to be pleased at that, or to be very, very afraid.

In the morning she had a quick breakfast in her room and told the head house servant to message her if Excellency Hevom needed anything staff or Danach couldn't handle—though she trusted Danach to be self-interested enough to be very solicitous with Hevom—and ordered the household groundcar for a trip to the district Planetary Safety offices. While she ate, she considered the advisability of letting her nuncle know what she was planning, but she was quite sure that e would forbid her to speak to anyone at Planetary Safety without eir advice or possibly even eir presence, neither of which Ingray wanted. As it was, she could take disingenuous refuge in Netano's *anything you can't handle on your own* from the night before. It wouldn't be the first time she, or any other Aughskold, had done such a thing.

It took ten minutes for the groundcar to bring her to Planetary Safety. As she got out, it slid off to find somewhere to wait until she needed it again. Arsamol District Planetary Safety Headquarters stood on one side of a broad court, sunlit today, and paved with scuffed and time-rounded black stones, each of which was a vestige from the founding of the district. The flat black basalt vestige in Eswae had been an imitation of them, though these were smaller and much, much older. Older even than the existence of the Aughskold household, let alone the first Netano. Ingray had never thought about that before, but now, since hearing Garal—no, Pahlad—talk about how easy it was to forge at least some vestiges, it seemed she couldn't stop thinking about them in odd ways. Why had Netano chosen a design for that vestige that would remind people of the court here in the district center? Had she known that she was doing that?

But Ingray had more important business. Before she'd left the house, she'd checked to see that Taucris was available for a meeting and had made a request to speak to her in person, and now as she entered the building a half-meter-high, four-legged, green-and-gold mech broke off from a line of identical mechs along a far wall. "Ingray Aughskold," it chirped, reaching her. "Ingray Aughskold."

"I'm Ingray Aughskold," she said.

"Ingray Aughskold," chirped the mech in reply, "I am unpiloted and can only lead you to your appointment.

Stay within two meters of me until you reach your destination. Do you understand?"

"I understand," said Ingray, who had expected something like this—the various Assembly office facilities had
escort mechs nearly identical to these—and the mech
toddled off, Ingray following.

Taucris actually smiled when Ingray entered her office,
and she was struck by the strangeness of it. Taucris had
not smiled much when Ingray had known her better. Or
not the last few years before Ingray had taken her adult
name, and then lost touch with her old friend. "Ingray,
good morning. It's good to see you. I would have invited
you, the other evening, if I'd known you were back
home."

"Was it a nice party?" asked Ingray.

Taucris gestured Ingray to the other seat in the small
office. "Not really. I didn't want to have *any* sort of
party, or maybe just a very small one, but Nana insisted.
I didn't think e would, I was sure e would be too embarrassed that I took so long. And embarrassed at this." She
gestured around herself, the narrow plastic desk, the two
chairs, the walls, one set to show notices and announcements, one a view of the black-paved court outside,
people strolling across it, or standing to talk, the occasional groundcar sliding along the court's perimeter. "I
couldn't help but feel like everyone was snickering at me
behind their hands. I actually caught Danach at it, but I
pretended I didn't notice."

"I'm really impressed," said Ingray, sitting, though she
had to admit to herself she'd been taken aback. "Assistant

to the Deputy Chief of Serious Crimes on your first day! And you already seem like you're so good at it."

"It's not really my first day," said Taucris. "You know I did all those tours with the Young Citizen Volunteers." Taucris had always been fascinated by policing and crime. Her nother had indulged it, and everyone had assumed she'd grow out of it, or that it would stay a hobby. "And I've been doing internships for a couple of years. In fact..." She hesitated. "I wouldn't have chosen yet, except I'd been doing a lot of this job for a while and the deputy chief really wanted me to actually officially have it. But as long as I wasn't legally an adult I couldn't. And of course Nana really wanted me to finally choose. E tried to be patient, but e really didn't understand." Ingray didn't know quite what to say to that. "And I'm mostly glad I did. I wanted this job so much, and I'm glad to finally have it for certain, officially. But...you won't laugh at me, will you?"

"No, of course not." Ingray couldn't imagine what there was to laugh at. Though she could think of quite a few acquaintances who would sneer at Taucris's actually going to work for Planetary Safety like this.

"Danach would laugh at me." Taucris hesitated a moment more, on the verge of saying something, and then finally said, "Ingray, how did you know? How did you know you were ready?"

"I don't know," replied Ingray, baffled at the question. "I guess it just seemed like everyone expected me to choose."

"But I never felt like...like a grown-up," Taucris said. "I still don't, not really. Nana said I should just listen to myself and I would know what was right. But it never seemed right." She sighed. "Thank you for not laughing." And then, "I've always been kind of jealous of you. You just always seem to have everything so together. Danach keeps trying to knock you over, but you always just brush it off. I just wish I could...I don't know; I wish I could be that sure of myself."

"I wouldn't laugh at you," said Ingray. And meant it, but also found herself astonished at the rest of Taucris's confidence. "And I don't...I'm not sure I really have everything together." Did she? She didn't really think so. "And I don't think I've ever been able to just brush Danach off." She thought of Pahlad's story about having met her when she was small and intervened in Danach's trying to hurt her. Thought about how she'd gone to such lengths just to get back at Danach. "But I'm glad it seems like it. That makes me feel a little better about it."

"You've always been so kind to me," said Taucris, very seriously. "But I'm taking up your time—I assume you're here to talk about the case."

"Sort of," admitted Ingray. "I have some information from our cook. E said e'd searched the kitchen and found two knives missing, not just one."

"And there was nothing on the knife in Pahlad's bag except eir own fingerprints," said Taucris. "I don't think that's much better, though. And we're still looking for the mech."

Ingray thought of little Uto, bobbing up and down among the glass blocks that spilled into the river, bright pink against the blue and green. "Did you look in the river?"

"They're looking there right now," said Taucris. "I suppose the other knife won't be far off, if it was the one the murderer used. And I can't see how Pahlad could have piloted the mech—e wouldn't have had the access and from all I can find e was never much of a mech-pilot to begin with."

"Excellency Hevom might have access," Ingray suggested, "and I think he and Zat had some disagreements. Though there was some kind of Omkem family thing keeping them from talking to each other directly. And he seems completely devastated by her death."

"Omkem." Taucris waved away the eccentricity of foreigners. "It's the Omkem consul the deputy chief is meeting with right now. Hevom apparently contacted the ambassador sometime last night, and he sent the consul here. The consul wants us to let Hevom go home immediately. The deputy chief, of course, considers Hevom a suspect and wants him to stay until this is resolved."

"So the deputy chief hasn't settled on Pahlad, then?" asked Ingray.

"Oh, no, e hasn't settled on anyone. Everyone's still a suspect. Well, you aren't, not really. Danach might be, if it turns out that the murderer used a Hwaean mech. But that marker spike was Zat's, and had to have come from Uto. I doubt Danach even knew what a marker spike was, to be honest, let alone how to use it. Besides,

Danach has no motive. Everyone knows he's going to be the next Netano, so he'd only be hurting himself if he did this. So I don't think he's really a suspect."

"If Excellency Zat's Uto was involved," Ingray pointed out, "there's no way Pahlad could have done it, either. You know how different outsystem mechs can be—I don't think mechs from Omkem work quite like ours. I can't imagine many Hwaeans have the right implants."

"No, you're right," Taucris admitted. "It matters whether the murderer used Uto or a Hwaean mech. If it was Uto then you and Danach and nearly every other Hwaean are cleared. But, you know, Pahlad's situation is...complicated. E was supposed to be in Compassionate Removal, but e's not, and we don't know how long e hasn't been there, or where e went in the meantime. E could have gotten any sort of modifications or implants. We'll check for that, of course, but even if e's cleared of Zat's murder..."

Ingray sighed. "Yes. And that actually brings me to the thing I wanted to ask you. Do you think I could talk to em?" She wasn't sure how that worked, visiting or talking to people Planetary Safety had detained. Well, she knew how it worked in entertainments, but real life was often different. And Pahlad's situation was, as Taucris had said, complicated.

Taucris frowned. "Probably not—I'm supposed to turn aside any requests to talk to em, actually, but I'm fairly sure the deputy chief meant to keep any news service workers from poking around and happening onto something they shouldn't just yet. But let me check something." Her gaze turned inward for a few moments. "All right, the deputy chief says you can, if Pahlad will agree to talk to you, but e wants to make sure you understand that anything you say to Pahlad, or Pahlad says to you, is going to be recorded and examined."

"All right. Thank you. Thank you so much."

8

It turned out that talking to detainees of Planetary Safety was a lot like in entertainments. Taucris ushered Ingray to a small gray-walled room with a two-meter-long backless bench of scratched and dingy white plastic. "Have a seat," said Taucris. "It'll just be a few moments."

Not long after Taucris left, the wall in front of Ingray dissolved from gray to an image of another, identical small room, except there was no bench and Pahlad stood there. E wore gray tunic and trousers, and was barefoot. "Ingray," e said, with eir tiny barely-a-smile twitching on the corners of eir mouth. "I don't think you should be here."

She stood—it felt wrong to sit there while e had no way to sit emself. "I probably shouldn't." She had thought about it all night, and all during breakfast. She knew that she should distance herself from Pahlad as quickly as she could. For just a moment she felt that dismaying feeling that she was about to fall. "But I couldn't just leave you here. Especially when I realized I owed you for stepping on Danach's foot that one time."

E smiled—a real smile this time, though still a small one. "I'm fine. I have a room all to myself and they feed me regularly. Nothing like the food at your mother's house, but still. There's no need to worry about me."

"The prolocutor is coming," said Ingray.

Pahlad seemed entirely unsurprised at that. Though, Ingray realized, e never had been very easy to read. "Yes, of course he is."

He. There was no reason to assume that Ingray had meant Pahlad's father, and not eir sister. Unless e already knew. "Did they tell you?"

"No. But I knew he would come, as soon as he heard I was here. I knew he wouldn't send my sister. He's going to come here as soon as he arrives and demand to speak to me."

Ingray wanted to ask why, and then reconsidered. The Budrakim family hadn't been like the Aughskolds. So far as Ingray knew, there had never been any doubt that Ethiat Budrakim was going to give his name to his eldest biological child, had brought her up himself, rather than fostering her out, and trained her accordingly. Any other of the Budrakim children had known from the start that their futures would be different, and presumably their places in the house didn't depend on how well they did in some competition for his approval. Maybe he had come straight here despite how it would look to the public because after all, no matter what e might have done, Pahlad was his child.

But then, the prolocutor had done nothing to prevent Pahlad's being sent to Compassionate Removal, when he almost certainly might have. And she remembered Pahlad telling her she should take Captain Uisine's advice to get as far away from her own family as she could. Maybe that was based only on knowing something about Danach, and having spent an evening in Netano's house. But maybe not.

"Will you agree to meet him when he comes?" she asked. Wondered a moment if Pahlad would be allowed to refuse. "Will you be all right?"

"I'll be fine until they send me back to Compassionate Removal," Pahlad said. "Ingray, you've already done so much to help me. More than you really should have. I still don't think you should be here. But since you are, will you do some things for me?" And just as Ingray was opening her mouth to answer, e added, "Don't say *yes* until you've heard what they are."

"All right, then, I won't."

The corners of eir mouth twitched into that barely perceptible smile, and then it was gone again. "Would you get my things? I know you probably can't get the knife back. Please tell your cook I'm sorry about that. But the bag, and the other things in it. There are probably fewer nutrient bars in it than you remember. If you could put a few more in I'd appreciate it."

"I'll try," said Ingray. "Do you just want me to keep it?" She almost said *keep it until you get out* but of

153

course it wasn't very likely Pahlad would get out, except to go back to Compassionate Removal. Pahlad's situation, abstract to Ingray except where it might cause herself problems, suddenly seemed all too real. What was going to happen to em? Ingray's troubles with her brother, her potential trouble with her mother, maybe even the difficulties she would have if anyone discovered her role in bringing Pahlad here, it was all nothing compared to the situation Pahlad was in.

"Yes," e said. "Just keep it." Serious and straightforward. "That's the easy one, actually. Would you also be here when my...when Ethiat Budrakim talks to me? I don't want to talk to him alone. Ever. I know I technically never am alone, here. But I don't just want Planetary Safety here. I won't blame you for saying no. You probably *should* say no. It would probably be much safer for you."

But not safer for Pahlad, for some reason Ingray didn't understand. She wasn't sure how her presence could make any difference at all. She thought of Pahlad lying to her so smoothly about who e was—and wasn't—back at Tyr Siilas. "Was it so bad, in Compassionate Removal?" she asked. "I thought the whole point was people could live there and just be away from everyone else."

E hesitated before e answered, and took a breath. As though thinking very carefully about what e wanted to say. "It might be all right if there were enough food for everyone. There's supposed to be. We're supposed to be able to grow our own food, but there are only certain places in Compassionate Removal where you can do that, and people have already laid claim to most of it. If you can get in with some of them, if they're people you can trust at all, you might be all right, but that's not easy to do. And growing all your food, without mechs, that's an awful lot of work. If your timing is right and you've got control of one of the places where the occasional supply drops arrive, you can keep everything for yourself and your allies."

Ingray didn't know what to say to that.

"There was a small war, after the last supply drop," Pahlad continued, into her silence. "Even people who'd scratched out their own living and weren't bothering anyone else wanted those medical supplies. I know no one out here really cares. After all, it's Compassionate Removal. It's only what the people there deserve." Ingray suspected eir words were bitter and sarcastic, but there was no trace of it in cir voice. "I really don't want to talk about it. If I thought you had any chance of being Netano, I would say more. But I don't think you do. No offense. It's better for you if you don't. If my sister were coming instead of...she might have some chance of doing something about it. If you see her, will you tell her?"

"Yes. Yes, I'll tell her. And I'll be here if you want me to, when the prolocutor comes."

"Thank you." Eir face was blankly serious.

At home, Ingray did not stop to do anything, not even put down Pahlad's bag that now hung from her shoulder, but went straight into the reception room. Today the blocks of ruin glass glowed a bright green and blue, and the mossy gray stones, the trees and flowers through the broad wall of windows were lit by the sun. The consul for the Omkem Federacy sat with her back to the courtyard, and Danach next to her, speaking, midsentence. "Consul," Ingray said before Danach could finish, let alone protest her interruption. "I'm Ingray Aughskold. It appears we missed each other at Planetary Safety. I went there myself first thing this morning to try to speak to the deputy chief, but you were already with em. I went to take care of some other business, and when I came back, you had gone. I must have just missed you."

"Excellency Aughskold," said the consul, rising to a startling height even for an Omkem. She wore trousers and a tunic, though it was an outfit that struck most Hwaeans as far too casual for serious business matters. Ingray guessed she wanted to be very conspicuously Omkem just now. "How kind of you. This whole situation is quite unfortunate. I cannot make the deputy chief understand that Excellency Hevom could not possibly have been involved in the death of Excellency Zat. On the contrary, the very reason Hevom was here to begin with was that he was the one person Excellency Zat knew would never harm her."

Danach frowned, distracted, it seemed, from the matter of Ingray's entrance not going the way he'd probably hoped.

"Of course he couldn't harm her," agreed Ingray. "He couldn't even speak to her."

"Nor even touch her." The consul did not sit. "I will

admit, Zat could occasionally be quite abrasive, and she had her enemies. But Hevom could not possibly have been one of them."

Ingray thought of Hevom's words at Eswae the day before. *It's a waste of time. So many other important issues to worry about, and this is what we should expend so much on?* "You surprise me, Consul. How could Zat possibly have made such enemies?"

"It would be difficult to explain, without first summarizing decades of Omkem politics," said the consul, with a smile. "I suppose we should be grateful that Hevom hasn't been detained. But he cannot possibly stay here alone. He ought to at least be able to come up to the Omkem Chancery on the station. Frankly I'm disappointed your excellent mother isn't here to bring some pressure to bear on the deputy chief. The timing of all of this has been very inconvenient."

"It has," Ingray agreed. "Have you had a chance to see Excellency Hevom? He was sleeping when I left, and of course I didn't want to disturb him, but I knew that Danach would take good care of him." She didn't look to see if Danach reacted to that condescension and assumption of authority. Was quite sure, in fact, that he wouldn't, not visibly.

"I understand he's only just now ready to receive visitors," said the consul. That explained why she hadn't sat back down. "I'll be going up to see him in a moment."

"Of course, Consul," said Ingray. "Please don't hesitate to call on anyone in the household if you or Excellency Hevom need anything."

When the consul had left the room, Danach, still sitting, said pleasantly, "Of course, that's not why you went to Planetary Safety this morning. Has Pahlad turned on you yet?"

"I'm sure I don't know what you mean," said Ingray. She considered sitting down but decided she didn't want to get trapped in a long conversation with Danach. She turned to leave, but then reconsidered. Danach would never miss an opportunity to snipe at her in private, but he would always cooperate when the family's interest was at stake. "Did it seem strange to you when the consul said that Hevom might be the only person Zat would be safe from?"

"That wasn't exactly what she said." Danach's voice was scornful. "And if you'd been here instead of off doing who knows what for the last month or two, you might have had a chance to actually talk to our guests. Zat considered herself to be above politics. She was only interested in the truth, or so she said. But her project here wasn't as apolitical as she liked to think."

"Yes," agreed Ingray, before he could lecture her on the topic. "There would be political implications to evidence that the Omkem were here before we were."

"There would be," Danach agreed. "Zat believed that the Omkem—at least, the Ewet Omkem—stopped here on their way to their eventual home system. But quite a lot of Ewet believe that, in fact, Omkem is the original home of humanity, that they—the Ewet—were born there and have always been there." Ingray frowned. Danach continued. "They can't both be right. Actually, I'm fairly sure neither of them is right, but I'd never have said it in front of Zat and I won't say it in front of Hevom or the consul. But if Zat was right, if we can be convinced she was right, the Omkem might have some extra leverage in getting us to let their fleet through our Byeit gate. Which the Omkem Federacy has badly wanted for several years now."

"I don't think that would give them leverage, though. Not with us." Ingray thought a moment, and saw Danach smirk. "It's not just us they care about, is it. It would also be about the Federacy justifying their actions to their own people."

"Probably," agreed Danach. "If nothing else, it lends legitimacy to a certain faction of Omkem."

"And if Zat was proved wrong—or if she was prevented from ever being able to prove she was right—then that faction loses political and moral leverage."

"And any other faction that might gain leverage from it," Danach agreed, "won't be able to use that leverage against Hwae so easily. Zat wasn't just spending her own money on this—she was rich, but not *that* rich. She'd been granted Federacy funds."

Surely the Federacy knew those funds would ultimately go to Netano. "They thought if they could help Mama become a prolocutor she'd owe them favors," Ingray suggested. Did the Omkem Federacy—or a wealthy faction in the Omkem Federacy—really think that Netano as one of Hwae's four prolocutors would help them bring their fleet through Hwae's gate to Byeit? "Among other things."

"Among other things. Mama was certain Zat wouldn't

find what she thought she'd find. She wouldn't have agreed to any of this otherwise. But maybe someone from the Federacy wasn't so sure, and didn't like the idea of Zat finding any proof the Ewet Omkem were the first people here."

"So aside from Hwaeans who seriously objected to the parkland being dug up..."

"There are some number of those," Danach put in.

"Of course. But if any of them had been near the parkland yesterday the deputy chief would have brought them in. So, besides them, the only people who would have wanted Zat dead were from the Omkem Federacy." And likely only people from the Omkem Federacy could have operated Zat's Uto. But there wasn't yet proof that Uto had been involved, and Ingray didn't bother saying it to Danach. "Hevom was the only other Omkem anywhere near." And the Federacy consul seemed strangely anxious to get Hevom off the planet. "So why hasn't the deputy chief brought him in?"

"If you ask me," said Danach carelessly, "it's because Deputy Chief Veret is Hatli, from Lim District. They still claim that some of the Arsamol vestiges in the System Lareum were stolen from them. It wasn't Netano who put them there, and they don't have the Aughskold name on them, but they're still associated with us, and you know how the Hatli love to pretend they're disadvantaged."

Every year a delegation from Lim District arrived to ask for the return of those vestiges, and every year Netano refused to bring the matter to the System Lareum. "So you think the deputy chief is just being difficult, delaying arresting the one real suspect, just to give the Aughskolds trouble? But it's trouble for us no matter what e does about it, or when."

Danach gestured unconcern. "In the end e'll let Hevom leave."

"But if it was Hevom who killed Zat? And if we protect Hevom and the consul takes him out of the system . . ."

"The deputy chief will just pin it all on Pahlad. Which will hardly make any difference to Pahlad emself, considering. So it's let a murderer get away with it in the hope that Zat's money will still be coming . . ."

"It won't, if what you say is true," interrupted Ingray.

"Or arrest and convict Hevom and send him to Compassionate Removal. And make enemies with the faction that's apparently protecting him—and which might be on its way to pushing the faction that supported Zat out of power, now she's gone."

"We should talk to Nuncle Lak," Ingray said.

"We?" asked Danach. "If I were you, I wouldn't want to meddle in this. After all, I don't imagine you warned either Nuncle or Mama that you were going to Planetary Safety. That conversation can only go badly for you. And besides, I'm the one of us who actually knows something about this situation. And you're going to have your hands full once Prolocutor Budrakim realizes that you were the one who brought Pahlad back to Hwae. I don't think Mama's going to like the results of that, not just before campaign season." He smiled maliciously.

Before Ingray could reply to that, an orange emergency alert flashed in her vision, and something thudded against the door to the sitting room. The door opened, and in stepped a spider mech, a terrified-looking servant right behind it. "Ingray Aughskold," whistled the spider mech. "Where is Tic Uisine?"

Ingray blinked, and stared. "Ambassador?"

A pause; the Geck ambassador motionless for nearly a second. Then she knocked one claw against the floor, a gesture Ingray had seen on the docks at Tyr Siilas. "Where is Tic?"

"I...I don't know where the captain is, Ambassador. I haven't seen him or heard from him since we...since I left his ship, days ago."

Another second passed. The ambassador struck her claw against the floor again, three times, hard. "Where is the other one? Where is Garal Ket? I cannot find em."

"Ambassador, how did you get here?" Ingray asked. There didn't seem to be anyone with the Geck ambassador except that one frightened and worried Aughskold servant standing anxious in the doorway. No Planetary Safety officers, or diplomats, or politicians, or anyone who might be the ambassador's own security, though Ingray supposed security wasn't so urgent when it was only a bio mech and not the ambassador herself.

Another motionless second. Of course—the ambassador herself was in orbit, far enough away that there was a delay between her and her mech. "Do not concern yourself with how I came here," whistled the ambassador. "Where is Tic Uisine?" She raised one weirdly jointed, hairy limb and pointed it at Danach, who sat speechless and staring. "Who is that?"

"That," said Ingray, "is my brother Danach. Danach, may I introduce the Geck ambassador." She blinked, silently summoning the groundcar again. It had just dropped her off at the front entrance; it couldn't have gone far.

"What," said Danach. After a pause, the ambassador turned all but one of her stalked eyes to look at him. "Ambassador," he said, recovering himself and rising, "an honor to meet you."

Pause. The ambassador's eyes swiveled back to Ingray. "Take me to Tic Uisine. He stole those ships. You know. You were there, on Tyr Siilas. I have been in the company of humans many times and I see you now, I see you. You will try to tell me a thing that is not so and maybe you will succeed and maybe you will not. *I see you.*"

"Danach, give me your jacket," said Ingray.

"What have you gotten this family involved in, sis?" Danach demanded.

"I do not care about a jacket," whistled the ambassador. "I want Tic Uisine."

"Toss me your jacket, Danach," Ingray insisted. Hoped frantically that this would be one of those occasional moments when Danach behaved like a brother and not a competitor.

Every one of the ambassador's eyestalks strained toward Ingray. "Captain Uisine." She knocked her claw against the floor again. "Where is Garal Ket? Garal Ket will know."

"Truly, Ambassador," said Ingray, "I don't know where Captain Uisine is. And I think your being here

163

without any escort"—or likely any permission—"may be a breach of the treaty. *Danach, the jacket.*"

"I hope you know what you're doing," said Danach. And pulled off his jacket.

After a second, the ambassador's eyestalks relaxed, but she still kept all her eyes focused on Ingray. "Not a breach of the treaty, but near it," she whistled. "I know the treaty well."

And a message blinked into Ingray's view to tell her the car was again waiting out front. "I recall you saying that. Maybe you should go back to your ship?" How she was supposed to do that without anyone finding out that she'd been here, Ingray had no idea. But the ambassador had managed to come all the way here, apparently without being discovered. Ingray thought of the gelatinous way Captain Uisine's mechs changed their shape, or sprouted extra limbs, and shivered.

"I will go back to my ship after you show me Tic Uisine," insisted the ambassador.

"Ambassador," replied Ingray, trying to keep her voice calm and reasonable, "Captain Uisine is a citizen of Tyr. You don't have any authority over him, and if he wanted to talk to you he'd have done it back at Tyr Siilas."

At that moment Danach stepped quickly up behind the mech and dropped his jacket over its eyestalks. "Oops," he said. "I was trying to throw it to you, Ingray, just like you asked."

She couldn't thank him, or stop to think, but dashed out of the reception room, the servant in the doorway jumping, startled, out of her path, and Ingray ran through the entrance hall and out the door to the waiting groundcar. "Take me to Mama's office!" she cried as she got in, as though she were a child again and didn't have the implants that would let her control the car without speaking. "And tell Nuncle Lak I need to talk to em right away."

Lak Aughskold was actually with Netano's staff in the capital—several hours away by flier. But e kept an office here in the Arsamol District seat. It was a small room, the only vestige an entry card for the first Netano Aughskold's first session as an Assembly representative in a plain, narrow-bordered case that hung on otherwise undecorated dark brown walls. But there was no mistaking the plainness for austerity—the two low chairs that faced the display wall were cushioned in gold brocade, and the table between them had been cut from a single block of green-and-white-veined stone.

"Wait," said Lak Aughskold's image on the display wall, though Ingray had asked em not to interrupt until she had given em the whole catalog of the day's events. Nuncle Lak was short and stocky, and eir size and quiet calm often led new acquaintances to underestimate em, though not for long. To all appearances e was just a few meters from Ingray, sitting in one of two low gold chairs facing her, with another polished green stone table between them. But she knew e was thousands of kilometers away, and the wall behind em, and the colors and to some extent the shapes of those chairs and table, were custom generated to match the room

165

where Ingray sat. Nuncle Lak continued. "You went to Planetary Safety and *asked to speak to Pahlad Budrakim*? It's bad enough you brought em into the system to begin with. With a false identity that…" E sighed. "What was that for, Ingray? I expect this sort of thing from Danach, but you…" Partway through eir last few words the door to the office where Ingray sat opened and her nuncle fell silent, the expression on eir round, dark face suddenly blandly cheerful. A servant came in with a cup of serbat and set it on the glassy green-and-white surface of the table beside Ingray. When the servant had gone again, Lak said, "I don't think this is one of the rare occasions when you and your brother are working together."

"No, Nuncle," Ingray admitted.

"I never expected trouble from you, Ingray." Withering disapproval in eir voice.

"I'm not done!" Ingray protested, though she really wanted to flee, out the door of the office, out of the building, into the street…but then, where after that? There was nowhere to go. "Pahlad asked me to be there when eir father came to talk to em. E was very sure Ethiat Budrakim would come, eir father, not eir sister. And I agreed. And then…"

"Oh, that might be helpful." Finally, cautious approval in Lak's voice. E took off eir peach silk jacket, laid it on the back of the chair e sat on. Pushed a stray braid out of eir face, and picked up eir own cup of serbat from the table beside em. "Maybe this isn't all bad, then. Go on."

"And then I went home," Ingray continued, the

sensation that she was in freefall suddenly overtaking her, "and the Omkem consul was there..."

"Yes. Your mother has already heard from the consul. At length."

"The consul was very concerned about getting Hevom off the planet. I know he's family to Excellency Zat, and she's—she was—very influential, but it seems odd, doesn't it? I mean, it's not like Hevom is under arrest, he's staying at the house, and the staff has orders to make him as comfortable as possible."

"Mmm," said Lak, and took a drink of serbat. "Indeed. Go on."

"So anyway, I told the consul I'd gone to Planetary Safety to talk about Hevom. Which was a lie, I went there to talk to Pahlad." No change of expression on Lak's face when she said that. "And the consul said she was unhappy that Netano wasn't here, and then she went up to see Hevom. And then." Just the plain fact of what came next was enough to stop her speech for a moment. "And then the Geck ambassador came into the house."

"So it really isn't as bad as I thought it was at first," observed Nuncle Lak, after the briefest silence. "It's worse."

"Yes," agreed Ingray. "The ship Pahlad and I came home on was a little cargo carrier owned and captained by a Tyr citizen called Tic Uisine. And while we were at Tyr Siilas, the Geck arrived and saw his ship and thought it was one that had been stolen from them. Captain Uisine had all the documents to prove he's the legal owner of the ship, but the ambassador didn't want to believe that. And I guess they followed us here. The ambassador kept asking me where Captain Uisine was. But I don't know! And I don't know how she got as far as the house without anyone knowing she was here, either. I mean, she's just a mech. Or, the ambassador herself is somewhere in orbit, because there's a delay, talking to the mech. Anyway, she kept asking me where the captain was, and I don't know! And then she asked me where Pahlad was, or Garal, that's the name e was using at the time. And then..." She thought for a moment what would be the best way to explain what happened next. "I asked Danach for his jacket, he was in the room..."

"Ah, I knew Danach would be in it somewhere."

"I asked Danach for his jacket, and he tossed it to me but it landed on the ambassador's eyes—she's got nearly a dozen of them. And I ran out of the room before she could take it off and see where I'd gone, and I went right to the groundcar and came here."

After a moment Nuncle Lak set down eir cup of serbat and sighed. "I remember when you first came to Netano's house. You were such a quiet little child. *At last*, I thought, *my sister has brought someone sensible into the family.*"

Ingray blinked, astonished. "Really?" Lak wasn't given to drama or overstatement. E was unfailingly calm and, when e needed to be, brutally straightforward.

"I know, it's kind of ridiculous in light of the last few days, isn't it." E sighed again. "I'm glad at least to see you and your brother working together."

"I don't...we aren't really..." Ingray was at a loss.

But it was true—Danach had understood what she'd meant when she'd asked for his jacket, and helped her when he didn't have to.

"When the family is threatened, or the stakes high enough, he'll do the right thing. If your mother would have…but no, that's a conversation for another time." E shook eir head. "So I'm guessing you aren't here to ask for advice, or, ascended saints help me, instruction."

"No, Nuncle, I do need advice!" Ingray protested. "I promised Pahlad I'd be there when the prolocutor talked to em, and I know that maybe wasn't a good idea, but it was my own choice, and I can handle whatever happens after that." Maybe. She wasn't actually sure she could. "But the Geck ambassador is a whole other thing."

"So you haven't completely taken leave of your senses," observed Lak. "That's something, anyway." E closed eir eyes, then opened them again, gazing unfocused somewhere in front of em. Probably reading or listening to something. At length, e said, "The Geck demanded to see Captain Tic Uisine as soon as they came into the system, but the captain had left dock by then and had filed a route that would take him to one of the non-Hwaean outstations. He'll have left Hwae-controlled space by now."

He probably hadn't, not legally speaking. The non-Hwaean outstations were most of them quite distant. But no doubt it was convenient to be able to tell the Geck that Captain Uisine was out of reach. "It shouldn't matter," Ingray said. "He's a citizen of Tyr, and the chief executive of Tyr Siilas herself refused to hand him over to the Geck. We wouldn't want to make trouble with Tyr

Siilas. And besides, he's human and the Geck have no authority over him."

"Which makes me wonder why the Geck want him so badly," said Lak. "But you're right, we can't hand him over. If nothing else it would set a bad precedent for our dealings with the Geck. Which, to be entirely honest, really shouldn't exist to be an issue at all. We've never had to talk to the Geck about anything before. The damned Radchaai ambassador to the Geck ought to be handling this, but I'm told just now that the ambassador, who is in fact aboard the Geck ship, claims she can't do anything about it. What good is she then?"

"I don't know, Nuncle."

"Captain Uisine has probably done us at least a small favor by fleeing. It's odd, though, that he got advance word of the Geck arriving, when only a few people knew at that point." E waited a moment, as if expecting Ingray to say something. When she didn't, e asked, "Is the ship stolen?"

Wary of lying directly to Lak, Ingray replied, "He had all the documents, like I said. Clear back to the shipyard."

"That wasn't what I asked. Which I suppose answers my question. So why did you go to Tyr Siilas to begin with? And what did you buy there? You've come back with no money at all."

She needed a moment to find a plausible answer to that question, so she picked up the cup of serbat.

"Ingray," said Lak as she took a sip, as though e had been struck by a terrible thought, "you didn't go to a broker and ask them to bring Pahlad Budrakim out of Compassionate Removal, did you? Please tell me you didn't."

Ingray's mouth was full of serbat, and she couldn't find a way to swallow it, or spit it back into the cup. Then she managed to move again, managed to make her throat work, to set the cup down instead of dropping it. To say, maybe even calmly, "That would be ridiculous." But she knew she had taken too long to answer.

Lak sighed. "I told Netano it wasn't right to make you children compete. I told her from the start. And I warned her to be careful about rewarding her children for taking big risks. But she was going to do things her way, no matter what I said. I think she realized her mistake when Vaor left. I know you and Danach both think e was sent away, but e wasn't. E left to get away from Netano—to get away from the whole household, but it's Netano who made that household. And I know you probably don't believe this, but it upset Netano very much. Our own mother was...well. There's a reason my sister didn't have children until after our mother died, and a reason none of those children are biological ones. Netano very much did not want to be the same kind of parent as ours had been. So Vaor leaving, that was..." Nuncle Lak shook eir head. "I think Netano has tried to change how she deals with you two, but my sister is who she is. And besides, the damage is done. Although, even so, I always thought it would be Danach who would do the outrageously ambitious and destructive thing."

Ingray found she had nothing to say, not even a protest.

"Who did you go to—Gold Orchid, I assume? And they took your payment, then, and brought you Pahlad?"

It hadn't been anywhere near that straightforward, but... "Yes," Ingray acknowledged.

"I have some thinking to do about this," said Lak, into her silence. "There are some complicating factors you aren't aware of, and that at the moment I can't tell you about. And no matter what, if this business about Pahlad comes out there will probably be nothing either your mother or I can do to protect you. It probably won't come out—I suspect there isn't a representative in the Assembly who hasn't done one or more deals with a Tyr broker that would get them in serious trouble. Them or a family member. And I can think of several reasons the government would prefer word of such a thing never got out. But I can't make you any promises."

"Of course not," she agreed. Not even sure anything around her was real except the overwhelming sense of shame and doom. Why had she done it?

"Well, it is what it is. Take the groundcar to Planetary Safety. If the ambassador follows you there, tell her very politely—and in front of witnesses—that you really can't talk to her and that her being onworld without authorization is likely a breach of the treaty."

"I did that, at home."

"Good. Tell her again. And then don't say anything else to her. I'll have your mother send a message to the Radchaai ambassador to the Geck, complaining of harassment."

"Thank you."

172

"Thank me," said Lak, "by telling me everything the prolocutor says to Pahlad. I'm very interested in how quickly Ethiat Budrakim turned around, when he heard Pahlad was back, and even more interested in the fact that he's come himself and not sent his daughter, even given the Geck being here. There's something else going on that I can't see. You don't happen to know what it is, do you?"

"No, I don't. I swear I don't." But e was right. Ingray was sure e was right, now that e'd said it. Realized, though she should have seen it before now, that Pahlad had had eir own agenda from the start, from, at least, the moment e had agreed to stay on the ship and come back to Hwae. Ingray's plans had been incidental to that. Pahlad's arrest was apparently also incidental to that agenda. "I'm sorry."

"Sorry won't unbreak the cup," said Lak. "Now, go. I'm keeping people waiting right now who really shouldn't be kept waiting. And, Ingray, just…you haven't taken any advice in this so far, and I despair of you beginning now, but whatever you do, I beg you, *keep me informed.*"

"Yes, Nuncle," Ingray said.

9

In the groundcar, Ingray dropped Pahlad's black bag onto the floor, settled back into the seat, and closed her eyes. The ride from Netano's offices to the district's Planetary Safety headquarters was a short one—she could have walked it, would have on another day, but she didn't want to run into someone she knew, or worse, someone from a news service. Or worst of all, the Geck ambassador.

The moment she had the thought, a whispery, whistling voice said, in Yiir, "Excellency Ingray, please don't scream." She opened her eyes. The voice continued. "It's me, Tic Uisine. You don't strike me as the screaming type, but just in case." The bag at Ingray's feet had sprouted a single stalked eye and three weirdly jointed, hairy legs.

She sprang to her feet—or tried to, and hit her head on the ceiling of the groundcar.

"Is there an emergency?" asked the car's control

panel as Ingray collapsed back into her seat with a cry of surprise and dismay. "Authorized voice confirmation required within fifteen se..."

"No emergency," said Ingray, pressing herself into the seat back, as far away from the suddenly appeared spider mech as possible. "What..." She wasn't sure she had any more words than that.

Another stalked eye popped out of the surface of the bag. It had never been a bag. Or the spider mech was able to be a bag—that went some way to explaining how the ambassador might have gotten as far as Netano's house with no one realizing she was even on the planet. "Did Pahlad...I mean Garal..." She tried to think which name Captain Uisine would recognize. Pahlad had been carrying the bag when Deputy Chief Veret had named em. "Did Pahlad know that..."

"I just wanted to keep an eye on Pahlad," the spider mech said, interrupting her, continuing on as though she hadn't said anything. "Not that e needs it, necessarily, but it turns out e needs it." Of course. The captain was far away, far enough to delay any communications with him. The ambassador had been delayed about a second. Captain Uisine was presumably even farther away. The spider mech continued. "Pahlad in the custody of Planetary Safety only has one outcome for Pahlad, and it's not a good one. And that's not even counting the Federacy's involvement. I know you've realized that, because your shit of a brother mentioned it back at your mother's house. You'll have figured it out yourself, though. So the question is, what can we do about it?"

Ingray waited a moment, to see if he was still talking, but he seemed to have stopped. "Why do you care?" she asked.

"What kind of a question is that?" asked the spider mech, about a second after Ingray had finished speaking. "We don't have time to waste. It seems likely to me that the Federacy consul is going to insist that Pahlad be handed over to them for Zat's murder, even though Hevom obviously did it. Why he did it, I'm not sure. Maybe it's something to do with Federacy politics, maybe it's just feuding families, he is an affine after all. But the Federacy doesn't mess around with things like Compassionate Removal. They'll publicly execute Pahlad if they think that's what they need to do. You know some influential people. So does Pahlad, of course, but they're not going to be any help to em. Your mother is most of the way to the station by now, but that nuncle of yours seems like e might be willing to help you. Up to a point, at least. So if I know anything about you, you're going to be confused for at least the next five or ten minutes, and then you'll come up with something. But we don't really have five or ten minutes, because we're pulling up to Planetary Safety now, if I've counted right." The spider mech pulled itself back into a bag shape. No, it really was a bag, even if it was also a mech, because Pahlad had kept things in it.

"Wait, what?" Ingray asked as the groundcar stopped in front of Planetary Safety. "But, no, why are you doing this?" No immediate answer. Of course. And she couldn't just sit here arguing with a bag. She picked it up and got out of the groundcar.

"All right, five or ten minutes then," whispered the bag, one second after she'd spoken. "That's all we can afford. Now pick me up and let's go."

Ingray didn't answer. One second. That was all the delay was. The same as the Geck ambassador. She shouldered the bag, suppressing a shudder, and headed into the main entrance of Planetary Safety.

She wasn't sure who she should talk to, to complain about an alien ambassador bursting into her home, but she thought she might begin by asking to see Taucris. Taucris had confided in Ingray earlier, and she had always been friendly. And besides, she was well acquainted with Planetary Safety and would have a better idea of where to go than Ingray.

But as soon as Ingray came through the main door into the vestibule, a spindly, three-legged mech came to life and lurched out of its corner. "Miss Ingray Aughskold, please follow me," it said. "The assistant to the Deputy Chief of Serious Crimes will see you immediately."

"What?" asked Ingray, astonished. There hadn't been even the merest chance for her to ask to see Taucris. "Has something happened?"

"Miss Ingray Aughskold," the mech said again, "please follow me. The assistant to the Deputy Chief of Serious Crimes will see you immediately."

"All right," said Ingray, still puzzled. But something must have happened. "I'll follow."

Taucris met Ingray in the corridor, outside her office. "I was just about to message you," Taucris said as the spindly mech spun and lurched away. "Then I heard you'd come into the building. Prolocutor Budrakim is..."

The next door along the corridor opened. Prolocutor Budrakim strode out, tall and broad, his square face chiseled and even-featured, his hair meticulously braided and gathered to the back—doubtless he knew his good looks were a not inconsiderable part of his power, and he never appeared outside his home in anything less than perfectly groomed and ordered fashion. He was saying, "I'll speak to the Planctary Head of Serious Crimes. I will litigate if I have to. This is..." He stopped suddenly, catching sight of Ingray standing there.

Ingray, trained since small to handle any interaction with Netano's political opponents with aplomb, smiled quite automatically and said, with a small bow, "Prolocutor Budrakim. How good to see you."

"Miss Aughskold," said Deputy Chief Veret, coming out of eir office behind the prolocutor. "I'm glad to see you. It appears that Pahlad Budrakim has refused to speak to anyone without you being present. The prolocutor is here wanting to speak to em, and has been unable to."

"Netano's behind this," said the prolocutor, to Ingray, ignoring the deputy chief. "You were the one who brought Pahlad here to begin with."

"I'm sure I don't know what you mean, Prolocutor," Ingray responded, smile still fixed on her face. "I'm happy to assist right now."

"Your assistance is not required. I demand to talk to Pahlad without anyone listening in or recording," said Prolocutor Budrakim. "E is my child, after all."

"Prolocutor," said Deputy Chief Veret, "as I have already explained, no one in the custody of Planetary Safety is ever allowed to speak to visitors without observation." Eir Lim District accent was at odds with the punctilious formality of eir words, to Ingray's ear. Doubtless to the prolocutor's as well. "Any exceptions that may have been made in the past"—a slight, very slight hesitation—"were not under my authority, and are not relevant to me. My job is to uphold the law."

"I suspect you'll be looking for a new job soon," said the prolocutor, and Ingray realized that at least one of those exceptions the deputy chief had spoken of must have involved the prolocutor, and Pahlad emself. Which possibly explained Pahlad's insistence on a witness now.

"With all due respect, Prolocutor," said Ingray, "I don't think it's fair to blame the deputy chief if it's Pahlad who's refusing to speak to you." Felt panic as she spoke—Netano had taught all her children to be exactly polite to Ethiat Budrakim, to say whatever courtesy dictated but absolutely no more. "But I'm happy to help."

"Of course you are," said Prolocutor Budrakim, only the barest trace of sarcasm in his voice. He turned to the deputy chief. "I told you not to call her."

"E didn't," said Ingray. "I happened to arrive just now on my own business." The prolocutor scoffed. Ingray turned to Taucris, who had been standing in her own doorway all this time, watching silently. "Taucris, I need to consult you about something. Can I see you when we're done with Pahlad?"

"Of course," said Taucris. "Come to my office when you're ready." And she stepped back and closed the door.

Ingray turned back to Ethiat Budrakim. "I'm at your service, Prolocutor."

The same bare, dingy room, the same scuffed white bench. Pahlad apparently standing there, but of course e was only an image on the wall. Eir mouth quirked, just slightly, when e saw Ingray, but e otherwise stood silent, waiting.

"I'm hurt," Ethiat said, at length. "My own child won't speak to me."

"I never said I wouldn't speak to you," said Pahlad. "I said I wouldn't speak to you unless Ingray was here. Hello, Ingray, thank you for coming."

"You're welcome," said Ingray.

"How did you get out of Compassionate Removal?" asked the prolocutor. "I'm sorry to say I found it beyond my means to keep you out, or get you out after."

"Let's dispense with the lies," said Pahlad. Calmly and seriously. "You said you would keep me out, or get me out if I went, but you never intended to do any such thing. I believed you when you said it, or things would have gone very differently, but I don't believe it now. I've made every sacrifice for the good of the family that it was possible to make, and I'm done." No vehemence, no anger in eir voice. Just a calm, matter-of-fact statement. "I'm sure that at the first opportunity I'll be asked—again—what I did with those vestiges. Some of the guards here have already mentioned it, as it happens. It's what I'm famous for."

"No," said the prolocutor.

"You were willing to send your own child to Compassionate Removal for their theft. What wouldn't you do to have them back again?" E turned to Ingray. "The truth is, I didn't steal the vestiges. No one stole them. They're right where they've always been."

"But last night," protested Ingray, "you said you were ready to talk about what you'd done with them." And then as soon as she spoke, realized how ridiculous that was.

"I did say that," Pahlad acknowledged. "And I would appreciate it if you would tell the news services that I buried the vestiges in Eswae. I recall hearing that Prolocutor Budrakim opposed the excavation of the parkland. Knowing the vestiges are buried there, though, well of course he'll have to change his tune. He made such a show of wanting them found. Wanting them back. If the only way to get them back is to dig up the parkland, well, that's what he'll have to do."

"The news services don't know you're here," said the prolocutor. "And if any discover it, they won't find it in their interest to report the fact."

"I suppose we'll discover who has more pull with the local news services," Pahlad observed, still calmly. "You, or Representative Aughskold. I'm sure she'd jump at the chance to publicly embarrass you. It is coming up on elections, after all."

"What is it you want?" asked Prolocutor Budrakim, harsh and blunt.

"I want your political career ended," replied Pahlad. Calmly, evenly. "I want everyone to know what you did to me. The problem is, I don't have any evidence. Or not any evidence I didn't have at the time of my trial, and"—e waved a hand—"we know how that went. I'm well aware that I could tell the story of what you did to me to every news service reporter from here to Hwae Station and it likely wouldn't change a thing. Or if it did, it wouldn't be until after years of litigation, and you'd spend those years making life miserable for anyone who dared to help me. But you taught me to be pragmatic. I'll settle for embarrassing you any way I can." E turned to Ingray. "Away from this system, people laugh at us and our vestiges. Partly because they find the idea ridiculous, but partly because some of the most famous of them can't possibly be what they're supposed to be. You know the panel in the System Lareum? The one that's supposedly part of the airlock of the first crewed explorer to arrive in the system? It's from a ship type that didn't exist until six or seven hundred years after the actual event."

"It's a fake?" asked Ingray, astonished.

"It is," Pahlad agreed. "And the *Rejection of Further Obligations to Tyr* is also a fake. Not the text itself, of course, that's genuine, those were the words that were presented to Tyr, when the debt was fully paid off. But the actual document in the System Lareum is a fraud. The lettering is a style that didn't come into use until

183

well after independence, and the fabric is only about four hundred years old. Really, anything in the System Lareum that was suddenly 'found' in someone's attic or a dusty storeroom was probably ginned up a few months before. As soon as you try to do any kind of research or authentication outside Hwae, it becomes pretty obvious."

Ingray wasn't sure what to say. The *Rejection of Further Obligations to Tyr*, a fake? She remembered looking at it, and even though she had often been in the buildings where the Founders had stood, and met people whose names had come down in an unbroken line since before then, seeing that document, the original copy of the very basis of Hwaean independence and government, had impressed her to thoughtful silence. But if it was fake, then there was no difference between seeing that sheet of linen in the lareum and reading it in an information file. It was only the words themselves that were real.

"My actual crime," Pahlad continued, as the prolocutor looked on in stony silence, "was trying to learn more about the family vestiges that it was my duty to care for. I went looking for information in places where they know more about the Garseddai. And I discovered that away from here, nearly every expert in the topic knows about the Budrakim vestiges, and knows they're fake. I didn't believe it at first, but the more I learned the more obvious it became. So I told my father what I'd discovered. Because it was a very serious matter. If the vestiges that proved Ethiat Budrakim's origin and ancestry were fake, well, where did that leave us? And besides, the family vestiges had been placed in my care, and I took that responsibility seriously."

"You tried this lie when you were first confronted with your crime," said the prolocutor, with a sudden grave sadness. "It failed to convince me then."

"Oh, no, I convinced you! Which is why a few weeks later you suddenly discovered they were actually inferior copies of the originals, and accused me of stealing them. It was easy enough to use the information I myself had given you to make a case for them being forgeries. And now if I told anyone the truth, it would sound like a desperate lie. But it would be all right, you assured me when I was arrested. It was the only way to preserve the reputation of the Ethiat who had set them up as family vestiges to begin with, and you would take care of me so long as I kept my mouth shut. And oh, you took care of me." E turned to Ingray again. "Like I said, what I want is to tell the news services about the way I was unjustly convicted of a crime I didn't commit, and hopefully end the prolocutor's political career—or maybe even see him end up in Compassionate Removal, but I'm not sure I could manage to do it. But forcing him to play along with digging up the parkland when there's nothing there, well, that I might be able to do... and if I'm lucky it will ultimately lead to the same result. So do me a favor and be sure to tell the news services that I buried the vestiges near the hill where Excellency Zat died."

"Oh, they'll like that," said Ingray in admiration, unable to stop herself.

"Won't they just," agreed Pahlad with a tiny quirk of

a smile. "Be sure to tell your mother, too. I'm certainly planning to tell every guard I meet from here on out."

Prolocutor Budrakim appeared to have reached a conclusion. "But our conversation here is being recorded," he said. "You've just claimed that you never stole the vestiges, so how could they be in Eswae?"

"Good point," said Pahlad. "Do let's have the entire conversation sent to the news services. The public can make up their own minds about it."

That seemed risky to Ingray—if nothing else, she doubted any Hwaean would react favorably to Pahlad saying the *Rejection of Obligations* was a fake, and Pahlad had contradicted emself several times during the conversation. But it seemed Pahlad had decided e had nothing left to lose. And Ingray knew when to play along. "It *is* coming up on elections, after all," she said, her voice pious.

"And you've just said the System Lareum is full of fakes," pointed out Prolocutor Budrakim. "That won't exactly make you popular, or convince people to listen to you."

"It'll get me a lot of attention, though," Pahlad pointed out. "And now I'm done talking. To you, anyway, Prolocutor. I have plenty to say to the news services, I find." E smiled, a slight upturn of the corners of eir mouth that did not reach eir eyes at all. Ingray shivered.

Prolocutor Budrakim was stonily silent as he walked through the door into the corridor. A spindly mech came up beside him and chirped an offer to see him out, but he only turned and walked away, the mech tottering after him.

Another mech took Ingray back to Taucris's office. "Ingray," said Taucris, rising from her seat as Ingray entered. "There's a problem." She glanced over Ingray's shoulder as the mech that had accompanied her backed out and shut the door. "The Omkem consul has said the Federacy is going to litigate to get Excellency Hevom released to them."

"I expected that," said Ingray.

"Yes, and that's bad enough. Just an hour ago, searchers found Excellency Zat's mech. And the knife. The other knife, I mean, the one that Zat was stabbed with, not the one Pahlad had in eir bag." Her eyes went to the black bag, still on Ingray's shoulder, and back to Ingray's face. "It was in the storage compartment inside the mech itself."

"Where was the mech?"

"In the middle of the river. One of its legs was caught in a crevice between pieces of glass on the bottom."

"And one of its marker spikes was gone."

"Yes," Taucris acknowledged. "So it's obvious the mech was used to murder Zat. And it couldn't have been anyone but Hevom. We already knew no one else could have controlled it—it was manufactured in the Federacy. It's like we said earlier, even if anyone else had known the accesses, it likely wouldn't have been compatible with their implants. We'll check that to be sure, of course, and we're in the process of checking Pahlad, but I doubt anyone else within kilometers of the parkland that day had compatible wiring. And if that's the case, no one but Zat or Hevom could have put the knife into the storage compartment. So there's really no question that Hevom did it, we just don't know why. But that's not the problem. Or, it is a problem, because the Federacy is essentially asking us to declare a murderer innocent and send him home. But the problem I meant is, the Omkem Chancery is also demanding that Pahlad be turned over to them, to be tried for the murder of Excellency Zat."

Ingray thought she felt the bag twitch, and pressed her arm against it, squeezing it more tightly to her side, as a warning. "But Pahlad couldn't have done it!" And then, realizing, "And how do they know e's even here? Wait. Hevom." Hevom had been in the room when the deputy chief had named Pahlad. And when the knife had been found.

"Something's *wrong*, Ingray. It just doesn't make sense. Zat was rich and influential. She had lots of friends and supporters."

"And Hevom was the poor relation," Ingray agreed. "So why are they protecting him? And why"—she found herself suddenly nauseated—"are they trying to pin the murder on Pahlad?"

"Maybe they feel like they have to punish someone, and it's easier to think one of us did it than one of their own," Taucris suggested. "Even so, it just feels wrong. I feel like there's something else going on and I can't figure out what it is. Pahlad definitely didn't murder Zat, and we can prove it. And the deputy chief has said that to the consul, but they're still going ahead with the litigation. And calling in representatives to support their claim, and I'm afraid Prolocutor Budrakim would be only too happy to get rid of em. It won't matter if e can get the news services to believe the thing about the Budrakim vestiges if e's hauled off to the Omkem Federacy and executed for a murder Excellency Hevom committed."

Realization struck Ingray. "You were listening in."

"I was," Taucris admitted. More abashed than necessary, Ingray thought, given that doing so was no doubt part of her job. "Pahlad is your friend, isn't e? E trusted you to be there when e had to talk to eir father, and if that's what happened, if the prolocutor sold em out to protect the reputation of fake family vestiges, then I don't blame em for not wanting to talk to him alone."

"Yes," said Ingray. "Yes, e's my friend."

Taucris nodded, as though Ingray had said something more that had needed her agreement. "And I don't think there's anything I can do. I don't know if there's anything anyone can do. Pahlad is still legally dead, but e's here and not dead, and I don't think that's ever happened before."

"I'm beginning to wonder if it has, and we just don't know about it." Ingray frowned. Suddenly the reason she'd come to see Taucris seemed out of place, even trivial. Though it wasn't. The presence of an alien ambassador on the planet—even if she was just a piloted mech—was possibly even worse news than the danger Pahlad was in. But there was quite possibly nothing

Planetary Safety could do about it. The Geck ambassador would do whatever she wanted to do, but she couldn't stay indefinitely, and at least Tic and his ship were safely out of her way. "Taucris," she said, and saw a fleeting expression on Taucris's face. Embarrassment? Pleasure? Just at Ingray saying her name? Taucris had always been shy, but...and suddenly it became clear to Ingray why Taucris might have confided in her earlier, why she was so concerned about someone who might be Ingray's friend. "Taucris," she said again, and yes, there was that expression again, and she found she didn't mind the implications of that at all, but this was not the moment to stop and explore that. "The Geck ambassador is on the planet." She explained about the ambassador holding up the ship at Tyr Siilas, and the accusation that Captain Uisine had stolen his ship, and the ambassador confronting Ingray at home that morning.

"But," Taucris protested, when Ingray had finished, "how did the ambassador get off the station? And I thought the Geck needed to be near water all the time? I remember hearing that."

"It's not really the ambassador. She's piloting a mech. And it's...it's a weird mech. It's kind of like a spider, but kind of not, and it can change its shape quite a lot." She was suddenly acutely aware of the bag hanging from her shoulder.

Which was a mech almost exactly like the one the ambassador was piloting.

"I don't think there's anything Planetary Safety can

do," Taucris was saying. "I mean, if she injures you, that's probably a treaty violation. And they have to leave eventually. But I think that even if you report it, you'll be told there's nothing we can do. We'd probably do whatever she asked, actually, so long as it didn't hurt anybody. I bet if Captain Uisine hadn't left so quickly the Assembly would be arguing over whether to give him up to them, even if it would make problems with Tyr. He's not Hwaean, after all, and nobody wants trouble with the treaty."

"Right," agreed Ingray. She had that free-fall feeling again, and it was terrifying, but almost familiar by now. "But I *can* report it, right? I can make sure there's an official record of the fact that she's here, and bothering me, and trying to find Pahlad? Who do I report that to?"

In the groundcar, Ingray set the bag on the floor— she didn't want it to become a spidery thing again while she was touching it—and waited.

After a few minutes a stalked eye poked out of the bag's side and turned toward Ingray. "So it took more than five or ten minutes," the mech whispered. "But I was right otherwise. You have a plan. So tell me, how are we getting Pahlad out of there?"

"Have you known who e is the whole time?" asked Ingray.

Two seconds. Then, "I have difficulty believing *you* haven't known who e was the whole time. Gold Orchid doesn't make that sort of mistake. E's an impressively good liar, I'll grant you that, and that's only to be expected, given eir upbringing. You do fairly well yourself on that score, and I doubt you have anything like a natural ability for it. But Gold Orchid would never have delivered em to you if they weren't absolutely certain e was Pahlad. It was pretty obvious that e didn't know what you were up to and didn't want to be pulled into whatever it was. Once e had some idea of the situation, well, then e changed eir mind. And before you ask, e's right about how people away from Hwae think of vestiges. And e's right about the Budrakim Garseddai vestiges—from everything I've been able to find, they were obvious fakes from the start. Are you going to tell me you thought all those bits of trash displayed on the station were real, or *important*?"

"They're important to us!" Ingray insisted, stung.

"It doesn't matter," said the mech. "This is a distraction. What's your plan?"

"It's..." Suddenly the idea that had seemed so brilliant and obvious back in Taucris's office looked incomplete and ridiculous. "So, the mech you're using. It looks exactly like the ambassador's." Stopped. Afraid to go on and say more, because the entire idea was utterly foolish.

"Ingray," whispered the mech, "what is it you do for that nuncle of yours? Please tell me e consults you whenever e needs an outrageous and brilliant strategy. So you want me to impersonate the ambassador and demand Pahlad's release into her custody. My custody. Our custody."

"Can you do that?"

192

"Of course I can. I've known her since I was born. Well, she was *he* some of the time, and a few other pronouns this language doesn't have other times, but I've known that entity all my life. I can play her well enough for this. It wouldn't fool any of the Geck delegation. Well, I would probably fool the Radchaai ambassador, she's useless."

"That's the problem," said Ingray. "The Radchaai ambassador is in contact with Hwaean authorities. She'll know it's not the Geck ambassador doing this."

"No, she won't," Tic whispered, contempt somehow managing to come through in the mech's odd, whistley voice. "The Geck ambassador won't speak to her. Never has. She's spent her entire posting—most of her life, I suspect—watching imported Radchaai entertainments and playing dice one hand against the other. And complaining she can't find a decent cup of tea. So she's not a problem."

"The ambassador herself is a problem," Ingray pointed out.

"Maybe," Tic conceded. "But if you recall, she was looking for Pahlad because she knew e was on my ship with me, not because she wanted to hurt em. I'd much rather hand em over to the Geck delegation than the Federacy. Which might happen, if we get em to the station but can't get em onto my ship before we're caught."

"You're not actually very far from the station," Ingray said. "Your delay is too short."

"Good catch. No, I didn't take my filed route. I changed the ship's appearance a bit, and I'm sending out

193

a false ID. I'm not docked, though, and I doubt my ID would stand up to scrutiny well enough for me to get permission to dock without tipping off station authorities. Or the ambassador."

"So, why are you doing this?" It still bothered her. They had known each other for a few weeks, certainly, and he had seemed to be good company. She thought of Tic drinking, just the slightest bit drunk, saying to Pahlad, *I like you.* The spider mech in the ship's tiny galley running its claws through Pahlad's newly short hair. The fact that Pahlad, hearing that the Geck had come into the system, had immediately messaged the captain, even before Ingray had thought of it. "Are you and Pahlad..."

"We are not," whistled the mech decisively. "E's certainly not ready for anything like that right now. If it's something e's even interested in."

"Hah!" Ingray exclaimed. "You've got a thing for em!"

"Maybe instead we should talk about that young police officer who very obviously has a thing for *you.* She's quite fetching in that uniform, I'm sure you've already noticed."

Ingray refused to be embarrassed. "So what if I have? And it isn't any of your business."

"My point exactly," returned the mech. "So where are we headed right now?"

"Home," said Ingray. "I've checked with the staff, the ambassador is gone. And I want to talk to Hevom. Something's wrong. I mean, there's something more going on here: Nuncle has said it, Taucris has said it, and they're right. I want to know what it is. Hevom probably won't tell me anything, but I want to see what I can find out. And I want some lunch."

"And after lunch, we go back to Planetary Safety and get Pahlad," agreed Captain Uisine.

10

Ingray left the bag—the mech—in her room, and went looking for Hevom. She found him in the house's little garden, sitting on a bench in the shade of the willow tree, staring blankly ahead. The very picture of emotional devastation.

She opened the windowed door, but instead of stepping out onto the mossy stone path she closed the door again and stood there. She told herself that she ought to just walk away. She could go to the kitchen; there would be people there, at least one or two servants who'd known her since she was a child, and she could say that she didn't want to be alone right now, which she realized, staring out at the garden, was the truth. She could sit out of the way and have a cup of serbat and listen to the staff chat as they worked.

She had been moving more or less constantly, thinking

constantly, calculating constantly, from the moment she'd awakened that morning. It was like working a meeting or a campaign event for Nuncle Lak—so many details to worry about and direct, not to mention possible bad outcomes to prevent, and all of it happening *right now*, no time to actually be worried or afraid about any of it, not till later, and then it was all done.

This wasn't all done. But looking out at Hevom, sitting beside the tree—maybe it was seeing the tree, when all the morning's talk of knives and spikes and who might or might not have killed Zat had not brought the image so vividly to her mind as it was now, of Zat motionless against the rovingtree, blood at the corner of her mouth. The seedpod fluttering down and brushing her unmoving face.

Ingray put her hand over her mouth. She didn't want to think about that. Couldn't.

Couldn't stand the thought of Hevom in the garden, in her own house. Well, it was Netano's house, and if it was politically advantageous to keep Hevom there, Netano would, no matter how many murders he might have committed. Ingray knew that. It had been a fact of her life for years. She had never questioned it.

She didn't have to go out into the garden. She didn't want to talk to Hevom. But she wanted to know, needed to know, why he'd done what he'd done. Needed more than guesses and theories. Because she couldn't push it away anymore, the memory of Excellency Zat, leaning against the rovingtree. Dead.

What if Hevom hadn't done it? But it had to have been him, no one else could have.

She lowered her hand from her mouth and took a deep breath. Opened the door again, and picked her way along the mossy stone path, and sat beside Hevom on the bench. He looked at her, briefly, and then away again.

"How are you doing, excellency?" she asked. Amazed at how steady her voice was, how pleasant her tone.

He was silent a moment, no change of expression. "As well as can be expected, I suppose." Silence again. Then, "I couldn't stand to stay in my room one more minute, but there's nowhere else I'd want to go. Except home, of course." He turned, then, to look at Ingray. "I don't mean to sound ungrateful. Everyone here has been very attentive."

Yes, thought Ingray, *of course they have. Because no matter what you may have done, for the moment it's politically useful to pretend you haven't done any of it.* Sitting here, beside someone she was sure was an actual murderer, she remembered wondering if Garal—who she'd told herself at the time wasn't Pahlad—had maybe murdered someone, to get emself sent to Compassionate Removal. It had seemed so abstract at the time. And, it turned out, e'd been sent to Compassionate Removal not for anything e had actually done, but because eir father had wanted to conceal what Pahlad had found.

She was horrified at what Hevom had done, and, yes, frightened to find herself sitting beside a murderer. And, she realized, she was angry. "I know this is a very difficult time for you," she said, her voice smooth and concerned. "It can't be easy to have actually killed someone, even if you hated them." No reaction from Hevom, but her heart sped up, hearing herself make the accusation. Long practice at pretending to be calm and cheerful for the news services kept her voice steady, and her tone sympathetic. "There are a few things I don't understand, though. Why did you do it to begin with? I know you hated her, but that's not enough of a reason." Hevom turned his face away again, stared ahead. Ingray continued. "And why did you use the knife? You could have killed her just with those spikes. So why stab her with the knife, and then hide it in the mech and put the mech in the river?" Still no answer. A breeze set the willow branches waving, and speckles of sunlight and shadow danced across the stones. "And why is the Federacy so insistent on getting you back to Omkem so quickly?"

"Is this what passes for a murder investigation here?" Hevom asked, still staring away. "No wonder the consul is so insistent on getting me away. I knew Hwaeans were credulous and uncultured, and of course what you call law enforcement here is a joke anywhere civilized, but I hadn't realized you were quite that bad."

Ingray couldn't find an answer to that, not right away. Though she could smile and look as though nothing troubled her for hours on end, she had never been good at the instant, witty reply. "And why are you trying to pin the murder on Pahlad? E never did anything to you. E's in enough trouble as it is, why are you trying to get em killed for what you did?" Hevom didn't answer.

"There's so much about this that doesn't make sense. I'd just like to know what's going on."

"No doubt you would," he observed drily. As though he actually found it amusing. "I don't much care what happens to Pahlad Budrakim. And neither does anyone else here."

Ah. And that was why pin it on Pahlad. All the individual steps made sense—the plan to murder; the murder itself, except for the knife, and maybe that made sense when you added Pahlad in. Maybe seeing Pahlad—had Hevom recognized em? Or just seen someone who was apparently without wealth or family who Planetary Safety might happily assume was guilty? Or had the knife been meant to throw suspicion on anyone at all in Netano's house, but when Pahlad's identity was revealed, e became the obvious target? It all hung together. The only part that was missing was that very first step: why do it at all?

"You must really have hated Excellency Zat," observed Ingray. "It can't have been the only reason you killed her, as I said, but you'd never have done it unless you hated her. Why? I know you had political differences, but that's not enough to want her dead, is it? I know she was, what, an affine?" The word didn't quite translate into Bantia, or Yiir for that matter, where it would have meant the relatives of parents your siblings didn't share with you. "Surely you can talk about her now she's dead."

On the bench beside her, Hevom stiffened. Turned to look at her, indignant anger on his face. "You have absolutely *no* understanding of common decency, do you."

It hadn't been the accusation of murder that caused that reaction. It was something else—could he be offended at the idea of talking directly about Excellency Zat, even now when she was dead, and moreover he had certainly killed her?

"Well, I am credulous and uncultured, after all," Ingray said, not quite believing the words had left her mouth.

Hevom made a disgusted noise and turned away again.

A thudding crack startled Ingray, set her heart racing. She turned. A large, quivering, many-eyed black spider mech came lurching through the suddenly open door out onto the mossy stones. "Ingray Aughskold!" it whistled. "I see you, Ingray Aughskold! You have tried to hide from me the person called Garal Ket, but you have failed. I know where this person is. You will take me to Garal Ket!"

"Am...Ambassador?" She had been so absorbed in her distress at talking to Hevom that she had forgotten that she and Tic had planned exactly this. Her startlement was real, and for a moment she wasn't certain this wasn't the ambassador herself.

"Garal Ket!" the mech insisted, and knocked one claw on the stone in front of it.

It had to be Tic. And really, if it was actually the ambassador, how bad could that be? "Of course, Ambassador." Ingray stood, and turned to Hevom, who was staring at the spider mech. "If you'll excuse me, Excellency Hevom, I find I have urgent business elsewhere."

Hevom looked at her, and back at the spider mech, but still said nothing. "Follow me, Ambassador."

"Where is the brother, Danach?" asked the spider mech. "I will not be deceived again, with the jacket."

Ingray frowned. Sent a quick, silent message to the household staff. "I don't know where Danach is." The reply to Ingray's question appeared in her vision— Danach had gone out, and would be gone several days. He had not said where he was going. Did Ingray need help? Should the staff call Planetary Safety?

Whatever Danach might be doing wasn't her concern. She blinked a reassurance to the staff and requested the groundcar again. "As far as I can tell, Ambassador, Danach is quite far away. Let's go out front and wait for the groundcar, and I'll take you right to Garal Ket."

Deputy Chief Veret took one look at the Geck ambassador— or at the mech that apparently was the Geck ambassador— and called Nuncle Lak.

Less than ten minutes later, Ingray, the mech, and the deputy chief were in a meeting room nearly identical to the one in Netano's local office, except the walls were light blue, and the chairs and table an easily cleaned and less luxurious flat black. The deputy chief sat in one chair, Ingray in another, the spider mech on the floor between them, its eyestalks pointing some at Ingray, some at the deputy chief, and some at Nuncle Lak on the display wall, eir own chairs and table now the same black, the wall behind em blue.

"I've left a message for the Extra-Hwae Relations Office," Deputy Chief Veret said to em, "but they haven't replied."

"They will," said Nuncle Lak. E looked at the spider mech. "Ambassador, I'm sorry but the deputy chief can't just release a prisoner to you. There are procedures for this sort of thing. And besides, Garal Ket is human, and a citizen of Hwae. This is a human matter, and a matter of Hwaean law, and with the greatest respect, Ambassador, you have no grounds to demand that e be turned over to you."

The mech did not move. "I listen," it whispered. "Garal Ket is not a citizen of Hwae. Garal Ket is not Garal Ket. Garal Ket is a person who is dead, and if that person is dead e does not exist anymore. Humans exist. A person who does not exist is not human."

Deputy Chief Veret frowned. "But e very obviously does exist. And it's not always the case here, Ambassador, that someone who is dead doesn't exist anymore."

"But it's the case for Garal," said Ingray. "Or for Pahlad, I mean. Isn't it? E didn't get anyone's name but eirs, and didn't give eir name to anyone." And even if e had, eir going to Compassionate Removal would have made that irrelevant.

Nuncle Lak gave Ingray a calculating look. "But e's not actually dead, Ingray. And even so, whoever e is now e came into Hwaean space on false pretenses and is breaking the law just by being here."

"The Geck will apologize for this," whispered the

spider mech. "And pay a fine. At Tyr Siilas we were told that payment resolves all such difficulties."

"That was Tyr, Ambassador," said Deputy Chief Veret. "Our legal system doesn't work that way."

"And there is still the matter of the Omkem Federacy," Nuncle Lak put in, "who are also demanding custody of Garal Ket, so that they can try em for the murder of Excellency Zat. We've given them the same answer. The Deputy Chief of Serious Crimes can't just let prisoners go to anyone who asks for them. You'll have to pursue litigation, Ambassador."

The spider mech knocked a claw on the pale yellow tiled floor. "You hold a person who belongs to the Geck. This is a violation of the treaty. Do not argue with me about the treaty. This Garal Ket is a person who belongs nowhere human. I now declare that e belongs to the Geck. If you give Garal Ket to these Omkem you will violate the treaty. Do not argue with me about the treaty. You do not know its contents better than I."

"I'm not sure it works that way," said Nuncle Lak.

The spider mech raised its body up several centimeters and pointed one claw at the image of Nuncle Lak on the wall. "Do. Not. Argue. With me. About. The treaty."

A soft tone sounded, and another person appeared on the display wall, standing beside Nuncle Lak, a person wearing all white: white coat, somewhat rumpled, as though it had been folded for a very long time and only recently taken out; white trousers, white shoes. White gloves. Their dark hair was short enough to stick up, haphazard, all over their head. *Her* head—those gloves meant Radchaai, and at least in Bantia, Radchaai were conventionally called *she*. This person seemed disconcertingly uncategorizable, not a man or a woman or a neman. "Hello?" she said, in heavily accented Yiir. "Oh, there you are, I couldn't see you at first. Hello. I am Tibanvori Nevol." She sighed, weirdly incongruous with the Radchaai accent that made her sound like a villain in a melodramatic entertainment. "I am the human ambassador to the Geck." She sounded unconvinced of that. No, she sounded as though she were reading out something she didn't entirely understand. She probably didn't speak Yiir very well and was using some sort of translation device.

"Thank you for joining us, Ambassador Nevol," said Deputy Chief Veret.

The ambassador sighed again. "Tibanvori. And I'm not an ambassador, I'm an ambassa...oh, this thing is hopeless. And I can't help you. I've tried to explain but no one is listening to me. I don't have any control over this situation. I don't know why the Geck ambassador is so...so fixated on this runaway mech-pilot." She sighed again. "I can't blame her for running away; if it were me I'd put as much distance between me and the Geck homeworld as I could."

"Her?" asked Ingray.

"Her. Him. Em." The emissary made an exasperated noise. "Whatever. And when we were at Tyr Siilas, we learned that Pilot Uisine had claimed Tyr citizenship. Which was entirely within..." She winced. "His? Rights, under the treaty. The Geck no longer have any authority over... him. The pilot. The captain now, I suppose. Though actually she... he *did* steal that ship. More than one. It caused quite a lot of inconvenience, actually." Ambassador Tibanvori smiled, just a bit, as though the memory of it was amusing to her. "But the Geck ambassador knows this. She knows the treaty as well as anyone does, and she must know she has no legal grounds for pursuing this pilot. She might be able to file a petition for compensation for the stolen ships with the Tyr Executory, which has *been suggested* to the ambassador, by people she *ordinarily* will listen to." Ambassador Tibanvori made an odd, shoving-away gesture with one gloved hand, as though she were pushing the entire matter away from her. "I myself am not one of those people. So there's really no point to my being here."

"It's kind of you to take the time, in any case," said Nuncle Lak. "Perhaps since you're here, you could answer some questions for us. You must know the treaty fairly well, yourself, I think." Ambassador Tibanvori made a gesture that Nuncle Lak took for assent. "Her Excellency the Geck ambassador to the Presger is making the claim that a particular Hwaean citizen actually falls under Geck authority."

Ambassador Tibanvori rolled her eyes and made an exasperated noise. "I don't know what the ambassador is playing at. No Hwaean could possibly be a Geck citizen."

"This is an unusual case, Ambassador," Ingray said.

"The person *was* a Hwaean citizen, but e's been declared legally dead. E wasn't supposed to ever be able to come back to Hwae, but e has, with an illegally obtained false identity."

The emissary frowned. "So e holds no citizenship anywhere? E has no legal existence as a human?"

"Basically," agreed Ingray, ignoring Nuncle Lak's sharp look in her direction.

Ambassador Tibanvori's frown deepened. She was silent for a moment. Then she said, "Huh. Well. In that case, it seems to me that if this person declares emself Geck, and the Geck will have em, e can probably be Geck. Why e would ever *want* to is beyond me, though."

"But there's more to it," said Deputy Chief Veret. "This person is currently under arrest on suspicion of murder. Of the murder of a citizen of the Omkem Federacy, in fact, and the Omkem are demanding e be turned over to *them*."

"E didn't do it!" protested Ingray. She looked at the deputy chief. "You *know* e didn't do it."

"Well that's a relief," said Ambassador Tibanvori. "Because if e had, and e's Geck, that would have been a violation of the treaty. I honestly don't see what your problem is here. Give the actual murderer to the, who are they, the Omkem? And give this other person to the Geck. Simple enough."

"Thank you, Ambassador," said Nuncle Lak. "You've been very helpful."

When the ambassador had disappeared from the display, the spider mech, which had sat still and silent at Ingray's feet this whole while, said, "Give us Garal Ket."

Not acknowledging the recent presence of the human ambassador at all.

Nuncle Lak said, "Ambassador, please understand, we still can't just release em to you. There are procedures to follow. And the Omkem demand is still an issue here. You'll have to make a formal request, and the authorities will have to make an official ruling. The deputy chief will assist you in filing that request, and I'll be more than happy to make sure myself that the committee knows they need to consider it alongside the Omkem request for custody. It seems likely to me that the committee will rule just as Ambassador Tibanvori has suggested, but these things take time."

"Delay delay delay," whispered the spider mech.

"I'm sorry, Ambassador," said Nuncle Lak. "But there's really no other way to make this happen."

"Very well, then," whispered the spider mech. "But now I will speak with Garal Ket."

In the prisoner visiting room, Pahlad appeared to be utterly unsurprised at the presence of the Geck ambassador. Though e had no doubt had the walk from wherever he was being held to the meeting room to compose emself. "Ingray," e said, with a small nod. "Deputy Chief. And Ambassador, I'm honored. What can I do for you?" And before anyone could reply, e added, "I'm afraid, Ambassador, that I have no idea where Captain Uisine is. So I won't be able to help you with that."

The spider mech waved a claw, then pointed it at Pahlad. "You are Geck," it said.

Pahlad blinked, visibly surprised for just a moment, and then the expression was gone. "Am I?"

"You are," insisted the mech.

"It's complicated," said Deputy Chief Veret.

"I remember Captain Uisine saying that," Pahlad said. "If I remember his remarks correctly, I'm guessing that the fact that my legal status with a human polity is... ambiguous suggests that under the treaty I might be able to claim citizenship with the Geck? Is that what's happening here?"

"It is," Ingray said.

Pahlad's mouth twitched, and e bit eir lip and turned eir head away, as though e was about to smile broadly, or even laugh, and didn't want anyone to see it. After a few moments e looked at the ambassador again. "I take it you plan to file a petition to have me released into your custody, since because I am a Geck citizen who's broken no laws Planetary Safety has no authority over me."

"There's the false identity," Deputy Chief Veret said.

"That's minor, really," Ingray said. "And the ambassador has already offered to apologize for that and pay a fine."

"It's up to the committee," the deputy chief said, firmly.

"This person called Garal Ket is Geck," said the spider mech. "Say it, Garal Ket."

"I am Geck," said Pahlad. "And it's true I came into the system with a false identity. I apologize for that. It was wrong, and I shouldn't have done it. I haven't broken any other laws."

"You came back from Compassionate Removal," pointed out the deputy chief.

"No one comes back from Compassionate Removal." Pahlad's voice was bland and even, but Ingray thought she heard just the slightest edge to it. "To enter Compassionate Removal is to die, to lose even the possibility of your name continuing. I can't possibly be the person you seem to think I am."

Silence for a moment. Then the deputy chief said, "If you got out, if you came back, who else has?"

"That does appear to be a potential problem for you, Deputy Chief. But since I'm Geck, it doesn't matter very much to me personally."

"Delay delay delay," whispered the spider mech. "Garal Ket is Geck. E has said so emsclf. I have said so. Now tell this committee, and give me Garal Ket."

Deputy Chief Veret sighed. "If you'll come back to my office, Ambassador, I can put you in contact with the committee and get your petition filed with them. As I said I would." E frowned then. "But I don't like this. The laws are there for people's safety. They aren't meant to be played with, or bent for your convenience."

"You're right, Deputy Chief." Pahlad's expression didn't change, but eir voice was almost regretful. "They aren't meant to be bent for people's convenience, but they are. It happens all the time, it probably always has and probably always will. And in this case, I imagine it will solve one or two problems facing you right now. It does clear up the question of just what to do with me, doesn't it."

"It does," Deputy Chief Veret admitted. "But I don't have to like it."

"No." Pahlad's voice was still regretful. "You're an honest neman. Honest enough, I hope, to keep asking those questions about Compassionate Removal."

The deputy chief looked at Pahlad for several seconds, silent. Then e said, "Ambassador, if you'll come with me." And turned and left the room.

Halfway through the process of composing the petition, Taucris came to Ingray where she sat in a chair in the corner of the deputy chief's office, handed her a cup of serbat, and whispered, "Ingray, have you eaten?" And Ingray suddenly realized how late in the day it was, nearly suppertime, and she'd barely had even a moment to herself. To just sit still. And yes, to eat.

Deputy Chief Veret, who had been explaining a detail of the petition process to the spider mech, looked up. "We're going to be a while, Miss Aughskold. And you don't need to stay for this."

"Yes, yes," whispered the spider mech, waving a hairy leg. "I will stay here with Garal Ket. You go."

Ingray should stay. She should make sure everything happened the way it ought to; she couldn't just leave Tic here by himself, pretending to be the Geck ambassador.

She really wanted to be by herself somewhere, for just

a few minutes. To close her eyes and not do anything in particular. "Call me if you need me."

The deputy chief gestured assent. The spider mech waved its leg again. Taucris said, half hesitant, "Let's go get something to eat."

11

Taucris brought Ingray to a small courtyard, a few plastic benches and tables here and there, black walls relieved by a thick fall of leaves and tiny white flowers cascading down a trellis. "Thank you," said Ingray as she sat down on the nearest bench.

"You're welcome," said Taucris, sitting beside her with a small smile. "You looked like you needed a break. This is all very strange. Why do the Geck want Pahlad so badly?"

"I suppose the ambassador has decided I'm not going to help her find Captain Uisine, so she's going to see if Pahlad will."

A spindly mech came tottering into the courtyard with two boxes. Taucris took them, handed one to Ingray, and shooed the mech away. "It doesn't make much sense," she said. "Then again, she is an alien." She opened her own box and the smell of fried spiced beans wafted out. "But if she's an alien, why is she *she*? I mean, aliens won't work like humans, right?"

"I don't know," said Ingray, opening her own box and picking up a round of breaded and fried mashed beans. "Maybe it's because she has to speak Yiir. We don't have Geck words for things because we're not Geck, so that's the best she can do. Although." She took a bite. "Oh, this is delicious."

"It's from a place around the corner," Taucris said. "Try the sauce, it's really good."

"Although," Ingray continued, dipping the round in the well of sauce, "Captain Uisine said the ambassador had had lots of different pronouns in the time he'd known her, she was just *she* right now."

"They *change*?" asked Taucris, leaning slightly forward, food forgotten. Her straight dark hair, curling just a bit at the ends, still growing out of child-short, slid forward to rest on her cheek.

Ingray suppressed an urge to brush it back. Took another bite of food. "This is so good."

"Isn't it?" Suddenly Taucris seemed to realize how close her face was to Ingray's. She straightened and looked down at her food. Looked up again. "Nana's always been one of Netano's supporters, so of course I grew up thinking of Ethiat Budrakim as a liar. Untrustworthy. But I never..." She picked up a fried round, then put it back down again. "I never imagined he'd throw his own child into Compassionate Removal to keep a political advantage. And such a small one!"

"The last prolocutorial election was awfully close," said Ingray. Wondering, as she said it, how it was that Taucris suddenly seemed so...attractive. But then, Ingray hadn't seen Taucris as an adult until yesterday. And not just adult but confident, sure in a way Ingray had never noticed before. "If word about the Garseddai vestiges had cost him just a small percentage of the votes, Netano would be prolocutor now. That's not a small advantage."

"It's not enough to throw your child away for," insisted Taucris. "As much as I know I've disappointed my nother, I don't think e would ever do anything like that to me."

They ate in silence for a few minutes, until the boxes were empty even of crumbs. "You know, sometimes I feel sorry for Danach."

"Sorry for him!" Ingray was astonished.

"I've known since I was little that I was a foster-child," Taucris explained. "That my biological family gave me up. They probably only had me so they could foster me with Nana, because that was a connection that might get them something. Well, they already have quite a lot to begin with, right? Because you can't just show up at Nana's door with a baby like that. But, you know. They could have kept me but they didn't. It doesn't really matter, because Nana is my nother. Not because I showed I was worthy or anything, just because I'm eir child. I never worried I wouldn't be good enough to stay in the family. Danach, he has another family, too, and he hardly knows them. And they never really wanted him, they just wanted Netano to foster one of their children. But I think he's always afraid that if he messes up, he'll be out, and he has nowhere to go but back to the family that never wanted him to begin with, except as an investment that didn't pay off. Or, he could go out entirely on his own, but either way he doesn't like not being important. He's expected all his life that he would be important."

"At least he'd have somewhere to go," Ingray said, unable to keep some bitterness out of her voice. She herself had no one but the Aughskolds. She had lost even the small promise of friendly crèchemates long ago. She took a breath and focused on steadying her voice. "Besides, it's not like there's any question. He's going to be the next Netano."

"Maybe," said Taucris. "Probably. It seems like it. But what if Netano doesn't choose the way everyone expects her to? Or, you know, what if she does but Danach still worries about it?" Ingray didn't answer, and after a few moments Taucris took Ingray's empty box and said, "I think I should tell you that Danach has gone to Eswae."

"What?" She wasn't sure if she was more surprised by Danach going to Eswae or by Taucris knowing that.

"We're keeping an eye on everyone in your household right now." With her free hand she made an indefinite gesture. "We want to be sure we're not missing anything."

"Right." They'd been watching Ingray's movements, too, then. But she'd only been home, and to Mama's office, and here. All of them perfectly reasonable places for her to go. "Right, that makes sense. But...Eswae? Do you mean the parkland, or the town?"

"The town," said Taucris. She walked over to a recycle slot in the wall and shoved the boxes in. "But of course that's very near the parkland, and I can't imagine why he would have gone there to begin with." Eswae Town was mostly shops and services for farmers who lived in the area, and a stop-off for hikers. Not Danach's kind of place at all. "He's used a false ID to take a room and hire an excavation mech." She came back and sat down on the bench beside Ingray again. "It looks a lot like he's planning to dig in the parkland, but we set guards as soon as we heard what Pahlad said, about telling people the vestiges were buried there. Even though it hasn't gotten to the news services yet. We could have Danach arrested right now. It would be better for him if we did; your mother would almost certainly get him clear of it one way or another. But the deputy chief is inclined to wait until Danach actually tries digging in the parkland. After all, he might sober up and change his mind, and just bringing him in on the false identification wouldn't really be worth the effort for us, considering." Taucris sighed. "I really shouldn't be telling you this. But Nana has always supported Netano, and you're...I mean... if Danach tries to dig in the parkland he'll almost certainly be arrested. And if the news services get hold of something like that, Prolocutor Budrakim will get whatever he can out of it, you know that. Or, I mean. Netano could distance herself from Danach, and probably be all right. But it would be very bad for Danach. And he's an ass and totally deserves it, but he *is* your brother. Or if you know he's about to get himself in trouble, you could make sure you didn't get caught in it." She hesitated just a moment, looked away, and then said, still not looking at Ingray, "Or you could take advantage of it. Nana may not be a politician, but I know how these things work."

But what was Danach doing? "The news services haven't reported Pahlad's presence here, have they? You said they didn't know yet. So it's not like anyone but us and maybe a few guards know what e said about putting the vestiges in the parkland." No. Wait. Just the night before last Pahlad had told Danach that the Budrakim vestiges were hidden in Eswae Parkland. And he hadn't heard Pahlad say that it had been a lie.

Stop and think. Nuncle Lak's constant advice. Which she didn't take as often as she should. What would happen if the news services found this? If Ingray right now sent Danach a message wondering (fretfully, anxiously?) where he was because they needed him at home, so it was obvious she didn't know what he was doing, and had nothing to do with whatever his project was?

It would depend. It would depend on what the news services knew. And whether Ethiat Budrakim wanted to keep any of it quiet. Danach digging in the parkland for stolen vestiges would look bad for Netano and therefore good for the prolocutor—but those vestiges were Budrakim vestiges, and Netano wouldn't hesitate to point that out, or bring Pahlad's story to the news services if she could.

But Pahlad might well be easy to discredit. E was a

convict, here illegally, and had said straight out that the *Rejection of Further Obligations* in the System Lareum was a fake. Whether it was true or not, no Hwaean would like hearing that. Ingray didn't herself. She suspected it was probably true, and she was having trouble believing it.

None of that would matter much to Netano, if she was willing to throw Danach out the airlock.

Netano would have to start over with another potential heir. Ingray herself was already too involved in this, and besides she'd never stood a chance at being Netano in the first place. Had already been planning to walk away from the household, so that was all right.

If Ingray did nothing, she wouldn't be any better off. But she wouldn't be any worse off, and at least she'd have seen Danach humiliated. And Taucris was right; he did deserve it.

Taucris was still sitting beside her. Silent. Patient. Ingray remembered Taucris confiding in her. Taucris worrying about whether Ingray had had a break, and something to eat. Taucris leaning close, her hair brushing her cheek, *fetching* Tic had said, and, yes. *I never imagined he'd throw his own child into Compassionate Removal to keep a political advantage,* Taucris had just said, disapprovingly. And of Danach, *He's an ass and totally deserves it, but he is your brother.* Taucris had quite possibly risked her job—a job that was important to her, that she'd wanted badly for much of her life—giving Ingray this information. Which Ingray could use to try to mitigate whatever trouble Danach was getting himself into, or to hurt him. Taucris had said as much. *Nana may not be a politician, but I know how these things work.*

She was still looking away from Ingray, her head turned toward the tumble of leaves and white flowers across the small courtyard. Giving Ingray room to think. And suddenly it mattered very much to Ingray how Taucris would look at her, when she turned to face her again.

"Fucking ascended saints," Ingray said, vehemently. But there wasn't any other choice she could make, not really. She wanted to kick something, but her feet were bare and there was nothing nearby but the bench, and the stone walls of the court. "I'm going to have to go try to get him out of this somehow, aren't I."

By the time Ingray reached Eswae it was dark, a few flutterglows flickering red and yellow in the even darker shadows of the hostelry where Danach had taken a room. It wasn't the sort of place that had an actual human being working there—just a panel at the end of the long building, with an interface you could use to pay for a bed. Though it wasn't that late, the street was empty. A hundred meters or so off, light spilled into the street from a food shop, a place that sold ready-made meals to tourists. She'd looked in there before she'd come to the hostelry—she could imagine Danach there much more easily than she could believe he would spend any time at all in the tiny little compartments the hostelry likely offered.

She'd knocked on the door of his compartment and gotten no response. She could go back to the eatery and ask if anyone there had seen Danach. But if they had, what good would that do? She might learn what he'd eaten for supper that day but likely not much more. And besides, she knew where he'd gone. Asking would just waste time.

She got back in the groundcar and told it to take her to the parkland.

"Eswae Parkland is closed from one hour after sunset to one hour before sunrise," said the car as Ingray settled into the seat.

"I know," she said. "I'm looking for someone. I just want to go slowly along the road and see if I can find them."

"Do you require the assistance of Planetary Safety?" asked the car.

"No," said Ingray. "It's not that kind of thing." Yet.

The groundcar lurched into motion. Within a few minutes the only light was the groundcar's headlights. More flutterglows floated and flickered under the trees on either side of the road. The empty road—all the hikers and travelers were back at the town by now, probably having a nice warm supper in the bright and cheerful eatery Ingray had left behind her. If Ingray had stopped in there, to ask after Danach and maybe have some serbat, she would be there now. Surrounded by light and people. Distracted from her own thoughts. Tic had said—or his mech that he was using to pretend he was the Geck ambassador had said—that he would rather stay at Arsamol Planetary Safety with Pahlad. So she had taken the trip alone, and her thoughts had increasingly, disturbingly, centered on the memory of Excellency Zat on the hilltop. Which she needed to not think about right now, because she had to find Danach, and it was so dark. If he'd taken a different way she'd never be able to find him.

He hadn't taken a different way. Just before the bridge over the Iogh River the groundcar's lights brushed the back of some kind of large construction mech that had slid off the road and into the edge of the trees. "Stop," said Ingray, and got out.

There were no lights but the groundcar's, and the ribbon of stars above the road, thick and bright this far from an actual city. She should have thought to bring a hand light, but it hadn't occurred to her until now. "Danach?" she called. "Danach, are you there?" No answer. She girded up her skirts and stepped carefully off the road, into mud—a good thing she'd worn shoes for this. She reached out and put one hand on the two-meter-high mech and took one slow step toward its front end. If this mech was like others Ingray had seen, it would be about three meters long, not including the massive shovel on the front, which could swing in nearly any direction and dig from whatever angle the pilot liked. Somewhere toward the front there would be handholds that would let a pilot climb up on top, and while there wasn't an actual seat, there would be room to sit. Danach would probably have been sitting there when the mech went off the road—she couldn't imagine him walking this far in the dark, when he could ride an excavation mech, just like in children's entertainments.

She stepped very slowly, wary of tripping or putting a foot wrong in the dark. The mech was silent, and cold against her hand. The shapes of trees began to resolve themselves out of the black, Ingray's eyes adjusting now that she'd come a little away from the groundcar's lights. "Danach, are you all right?" No answer. Suddenly she was truly afraid—what if he'd been injured when the mech slid off the road? What if he was unconscious, or dead? She reached the front end of the mech, put a hand on the folded-down shovel. "Danach?"

Danach's voice, out of the dark, just above and behind her. "What the fuck are you doing here?" Angry.

She looked up and back. Saw Danach sitting on top of the mech, only a shadow in the starlight and what light reached here from the groundcar. "I'd ask you the same thing but I already know the answer." Relieved, but she said nothing about that.

"I suppose it's a good thing you're here," said Danach, from atop the mech. "Now you can tell me where the vestiges are, once I get this fucking mech back on the road, and I won't have to dig randomly and hope I guess right."

"They aren't here," she said. "They aren't in the parkland. They never were."

"Nice try." Danach's voice was contemptuous. "If you don't help me find those vestiges, I'll spill the whole story to Mama."

"Go right ahead," said Ingray. "If you don't come

down from there and come back home with me, I'm calling Planetary Safety." It was a threat she knew she had to be willing to make good. She knew that Planetary Safety getting involved in this would likely be a disaster for her, but she'd had time on her way here to think about what choices she had, and what Danach was likely to do, and what she might do in response.

"No," Danach said. "You're not calling Planetary Safety." With a groan the mech's shovel unfolded and rose high and swung, just missing Ingray's head. She stepped back in alarm, tripped, and fell sprawling. Danach swore, and the shovel swung back the other way and slammed into something—it must have been a tree. The tree cracked and groaned as the shovel pushed against it, and the mech seemed to tip toward Ingray and then steady, and the shovel swept back toward Ingray again, lower this time, she could feel the breeze as it passed.

She rolled over and crawled toward the road. "You think this is going to keep Planetary Safety away?" she gasped, and got a mouthful of muddy strands of hair.

"It doesn't matter." There was a crack as the shovel slammed into the tree again. "By the time anyone gets here I'll be kilometers away, and there are at least a dozen people who'll swear I was home all…" Danach's words turned into a strangled cry.

And then a whispery, whistling voice said, "The brother Danach is not a good brother."

Ingray stopped crawling. "Tic?" And then realized that what Tic had said had sounded much more like the ambassador—he was still in character. Of course he was. "Ambassador?" Realized, too, as she got to her feet and walked cautiously toward the now-still mech, that the Geck ambassador assaulting humans had to be some sort of treaty violation. Good thing that wasn't actually what was happening. "I thought you stayed with Pahlad."

"Bad brother Danach," repeated the spider mech. "Will you kill the brother Danach, Ingray Human? It tried to kill you."

"I wasn't going to kill her!" Danach's voice, hoarse and terrified. "Fucking ascended saints! Ingray! What kind of person do you think I am?" In the starlight Ingray could see a looming, hunched shadow atop the mech.

"You are the kind of person who tries to kill their clutchmate," said the spider mech. "Your mother may eat you if she finds you too young, but your clutchmates you rely on from the moment you hatch until age takes you. I am sorry I cannot kill this bad brother, Ingray Human. It would be a violation of the treaty. But if the brother Danach fell in front of this machine it might roll over him."

Ingray found the set of rungs and climbed up the side of the excavation mech. "No! Ambassador, don't!" She didn't think Tic would really kill Danach, but even through the mech, even with its strange whistling voice, he managed to sound menacing. "And you almost did kill me, Danach." Or at least almost injured her very badly.

"You were going to call Planetary Safety! That wouldn't have just been bad for me, it would have been bad for the whole family!"

The spider mech had wrapped several legs around him and held him down flat against the top of the excavation mech. One claw gripped Danach's hair, pulling his head back. Another claw hovered over his throat. Still clinging to the side of the mech, Ingray said, "I had to stop you somehow. I'm telling you the truth, the Budrakim vestiges aren't in the parkland."

Still tight in the spider mech's grip, Danach closed his eyes. "Then where are they?"

"Where they've always been," said Ingray. "Pahlad never stole them. The prolocutor made that up because Pahlad discovered they were forgeries to begin with. Prolocutor Budrakim didn't want that to come out, so instead he made up a story about the real ones being stolen and replaced with fakes."

Danach's eyes opened. "What? That's fantastic!" He tried to sit up, but the spider mech still held him down. He made an exasperated noise. "Have you told Mama?"

"No, because I just found out today. And Pahlad has every intention of going public with the story emself, if e can get around the objections of the prolocutor, who's going to do everything in his power to prevent the news services from saying anything at all about it."

"We can take it to one of the local independent services," Danach suggested. "Talk it up, get it passed around. It might take a while for it to build up to where the planetary services can't ignore it anymore, but that's just a matter of some work. Nuncle Lak could do it easy. Hell, even *you* could do it, Ingray."

Ingray said nothing, only waited.

"No," Danach said after a moment. As though she had said something. "Nobody knows I'm the person who rented this excavation mech, I used a fake ID. So we'll just leave it here and go home."

Still, Ingray waited. The silence stretched out.

"Okay, so I wouldn't have found anything. But nobody would ever have known it was me, so I don't see what difference it makes."

"How do you think I found you, Danach?" asked Ingray. "Next time you want a false identity you really should come to me. Whoever did this one was more or less competent, but it didn't stand up to a really determined search."

A silence. Then, "Oh, fuck."

"Bad brother Danach," said the spider mech. "Ingray sister has been very generous to you although you do not deserve it."

"Let him go, Ambassador," said Ingray. "You know you can't hurt him without causing some kind of diplomatic incident. You really shouldn't be holding on to him like this."

"He tried to kill you," insisted the spider mech, but it loosened its hold on him.

"It was an accident!" Danach protested. He sat up, rubbing his throat. "I was only trying to scare you so you wouldn't call Planetary Safety. I wouldn't kill you!"

"You wouldn't be sorry if I was gone, though," suggested Ingray.

A pause. "Infernal powers, Ingray! I'm not a *murderer.*"

"Ingray Human has been *very* generous to you," repeated the spider mech.

"Here's what we need to do," said Ingray. "We get in the car. We go home. If anyone asks, yes, you rented this excavation mech. You were drunk, you were thinking about the murder, you got upset. You'd gotten to know Excellency Zat and liked her; she was a gentle soul who only cared about knowledge. You were angry and sad that she'd been murdered. You're not really sure what you were going to do with the construction mech but whatever it was, it made sense on a bottle of arrack. It probably had something to do with Dapi the Dirt Mover." That was the central character of a children's entertainment that had run for decades. There weren't many Hwaeans who hadn't at some point in their childhoods harbored an ambition to be a heroic construction mech-pilot on account of it. "You couldn't control it, it crashed..."

"I couldn't," Danach put in. "I've hardly drunk anything at all and this thing is a huge pain to drive. I didn't think it would be that difficult, I've piloted mechs before."

"Is not easy," whispered the spider mech. "Important to practice."

"*It crashed,*" said Ingray again. "You're very sorry. You're going to pay for the damage to the excavation mech. Out of your allowance. Without being asked. You're going to think hard about whether you're going to be doing any more drinking in the future. Pahlad

230

being Pahlad, and the business with the vestiges, all of that will take you completely by surprise."

"I can't get down if you don't move," said Danach. And then, when Ingray didn't move, and didn't say anything, "All right. All right, *thank you*." Graceless and resentful. "I would have been completely fucked if you hadn't turned up. Even if I'd managed to get into the parkland with this heap of junk. Is that what you wanted?"

Ingray took a breath. Considered answering, but instead she climbed back down to the ground and walked carefully back to the road, and the groundcar. Behind her there was a *plop*, and a scrambling sound, and the spider mech came alongside her. "You'll probably have to be a bag again," said Ingray. "It won't help if the news services get the idea the Geck were involved in this."

"A bag, a bag," whispered the spider mech. "Hah! The bag. I see now. But no, I will make my own way." It trudged onto the road and shoved itself underneath the groundcar.

"Whatever you like," said Ingray. Suddenly she shivered. She hadn't been paying close attention, had been thinking two and three steps ahead. What had the spider mech just said? *Hah! The bag. I see now.* A nauseatingly horrible thought occurred to her. "Tic?" she called. "Tic, that is you, isn't it?" But it had to be. Why would the Geck ambassador threaten to kill Danach like that? That was certainly an unambiguous violation of the treaty.

"Let it alone," said Danach, coming up behind her. "*You* might have made friends with it, but I don't want to ride with that thing anywhere near me. It's so...so squishy." He shuddered. "And it almost strangled me."

Ingray opened the groundcar door. "Right, let's go."

12

By the time the groundcar pulled up to Netano's house, it was well after midnight. The house was dark, except for a faint glow of light through the blue and red glass around the doorway. And bright against it, casting a yellow glow on the pavement at an exactly legally allowed distance from the house, the tall, four-legged bright orange column of a news service mech.

Danach swore. *"District Voice?"*

"District Voice," Ingray confirmed, peering out the window at the black lettering across the mech's front panel. "But it's the only one. The news about Pahlad must have gotten out, but only *District Voice* is doing anything about it."

Danach gave a short, tired laugh. "The prolocutor must be leaning on the big services. If it is about Pahlad, then I imagine they're here for you, sis." That last a trifle smugly.

"What a time for you to be so very drunk," said Ingray. "I'm going to have to call a servant to help me get you into the house."

"I think I'd have sobered up some by now," Danach pointed out.

"You drank an awful lot, and you've had an exhausting night. You've passed out and I don't want to try to wake you up, or risk you saying something awkward to the *District Voice*. Besides, I've already called for help."

"Ingray," said Danach, sounding suddenly, unaccountably pleading. "I really wasn't trying to hurt you. I just... I thought you were there to get me in trouble, or take credit for finding the vestiges, or..." He trailed off.

"Why do you do any of it, Danach?" asked Ingray. Her anger and frustration had receded during the ride, as they always seemed to, but at Danach's halting attempt at an apparent apology it broke out afresh. "You know Mama's going to choose you. You know I'm no danger to your future prospects, I never was."

"I don't know that. I never did, not either one. Mama doesn't always do what anyone expects her to. And Nuncle Lak likes you better than me. You know e does. And Mama listens to Nuncle Lak." Danach sighed. "Look, I didn't mean to start another fight. I've been sitting here thinking what would have happened if you'd been hurt or even killed back there. And I just...I don't want that, Ingray. I never wanted that. I just, it seemed like I had this thing, that I was going to have a chance of coming home and laying the Budrakim vestiges in front of

Mama, right before elections, and Mama probably won't wait much longer to name her heir, and you turn up to take that away."

"That's not why I was there." She wanted to say more, but he sounded actually sincere. And she knew what that felt like, that anxiety to please Netano, the feeling that her life, her future, depended on it.

Then the front door of the house opened, and the news service mech spun to see who it was but lost interest when two servants came out. "That was quick," observed Ingray, and opened the groundcar door. "I'm so sorry to trouble you at this hour," she called as the servants came to the car. "It's just Danach. He's"—she lowered her voice, though not enough to conceal her words from the news mech—"drunk rather a lot. He's either asleep or passed out, but I don't think the street is the best place to find out which one."

"Of course, miss," said one servant, without even blinking, and between the two of them they slid the limp, resistless Danach out of the back of the groundcar and carried him into the house.

"Miss Aughskold!" said the news mech, as Ingray followed them. "Can you explain your involvement in the return of Pahlad Budrakim from Compassionate Removal? What is eir involvement in the murder of the Omkem Excellency Zat? Why are the Geck involving themselves in this? And what about the Budrakim vestiges? And how in the world did you come to be covered with so much mud?"

Ingray smiled as she walked past. "I'm so sorry. It's been an eventful night and I'm a bit worried about my brother just now. Perhaps we can talk later."

"What do you take me for?" asked the news mech. "This isn't the first time Danach Aughskold has been carried home drunk. He'll be fine once he gets past the hangover. And it's you I want to talk to, not him. Did you know who Pahlad Budrakim was when you brought em to Hwae? Do you think it's true that the prolocutor lied to the Magistracy Committee about his family vestiges being stolen? Do you think Pahlad is right when e says the *Rejection of Further Obligations* in the System Lareum is a forgery? Could Pahlad have stolen the real one emself?"

"I'll be happy to talk to you in the morning," Ingray promised as she reached the door of the house.

"Oh, right, after the big services get here," complained the mech. Not moving from its spot—it couldn't legally come any closer to the door, or Ingray, without an explicit invitation. "Come on, Ingray, a little help for the local news service."

"In the morning!" She stepped inside and the door closed behind her.

Inside, in the dim, nighttime entrance hall light, she found Danach, uncharacteristically submissive-looking, standing in front of Nuncle Lak, who sat on the bench beside the stairs. "Ingray," Nuncle Lak said. "I got in less than five minutes ago, and I've been wondering where you were. Didn't I ask you to keep me informed? And how *did* you come to be covered with so much mud?"

"That's my fault, Nuncle," said Danach.

"Ascended saints," replied Nuncle Lak with mock surprise. "Danach admitting responsibility. It really is true what they say, anything can happen and there's no end to surprises in this life." E turned to Ingray again. "Not that I'm letting you off the hook. I did ask you to keep me informed."

"I'm sorry, Nuncle."

"Well, don't be too sorry," said Nuncle Lak with a sigh. "While you were gone, I threw you to the *District Voice*. I didn't warn you, I knew you'd be expecting it."

"Yes, I noticed," said Ingray, and Nuncle Lak laughed. "I wasn't surprised." There was no rancor in her saying it. "In fact, that's why I went after Danach. When I guessed where he'd gone, I knew someone had to bring him back. I didn't bother you, I knew you were probably busy with everything else."

"And where," Nuncle Lak asked, "had Danach gone?" E turned to Danach expectantly.

Ingray couldn't see Danach's face, but she could tell by the sullen hunch of his shoulders that he didn't want to answer. But he did. "I went to Eswae." And stopped there.

"And why, dear nephew, did you go to Eswae? I am having difficulty imagining any particularly good reasons for such a thing."

Danach made a resentful, disgusted noise. "I recognized Pahlad when Ingray brought em home. When I confronted em, e told me that the Budrakim vestiges were in Eswae Parkland. I thought I could at least try to find them before it got out. I figured it might never get out; the prolocutor would do everything in his power to prevent it." He gave a sort of abbreviated shrug. "There was a chance I might find them, anyway. And then we'd have had that over the Budrakims."

Nuncle Lak just looked at him in silence. After a few moments Danach said, "If I'd stopped to talk to you or Ingray I'd have known it was a bad idea." Still Nuncle Lak was silent. Danach continued, voice disgusted. "I've already thanked Ingray for getting me out of it, what else do you want?"

"Are you out of it?" asked Nuncle Lak.

"He was upset about Excellency Zat," said Ingray. "He got drunk. He doesn't remember exactly what he was thinking when he rented the excavation mech. I guessed where he'd gone, from something he'd said earlier in the day, and I went out to stop him from making an absolute fool of himself. He's going to pay for the damage."

"The damage to . . . ?" prompted Nuncle Lak.

"I crashed the mech before I ever got to the parkland," admitted Danach. "The thing was a beast to pilot."

"You know there are people who work piloting construction mechs their whole lives," Nuncle Lak pointed out. "They aren't toys. It takes training and practice, it's not just something you can pick up and do on the spur of the moment if you've never done it before." Silence. "You know what I'm about to say."

Danach replied, still sullen, "Things would go better for me, now and in the future, if I treated my sister as an ally instead of an adversary."

"Netano's favorite thing," said Nuncle Lak, "is for one of you children to present her with a surprise. Some plot even she didn't know you were working on. She's actively encouraged it, and it's always been the most reliable way for you to impress her. I'll give you credit for that, Danach, you've always been eager to impress your mother. And being able to turn the Budrakim vestiges over to her would no doubt have impressed her quite a lot. Probably even enough to justify this rather uncharacteristically harebrained scheme of yours. We won't mention the attraction of a chance to do your sister one better in a scheme of her own that you'd discovered. But..." E looked expectantly at Danach.

Danach sighed. "I should have made sure I had accurate intelligence before I moved. And I'd have had more accurate intelligence if I'd talked to Ingray. And if I hadn't tried to blackmail her and Pahlad when they arrived. And..." He looked up, as though he'd noticed something interesting painted on the ceiling. "It won't help me to be so worried that Ingray might outdo me that I end up hurting myself, not only now but in the future."

Astonished, Ingray suppressed a frown and brought her teeth firmly together so that she would not make any noise of surprise. That had sounded like Danach reciting words he'd heard over and over again.

"You can manage to be polite and even charming with people you don't like," said Nuncle Lak. "You're very good at it. And you're entirely capable of being diplomatic when it's called for, when it's not your sister we're talking about. I know family gets under your skin—ascended saints, do I know. And I know that by encouraging you children to compete for her approval, your mother has to some extent set you up for this. But you need to be smarter than this, Danach. I know you *are* smarter than this."

Danach said nothing.

"Well," said Nuncle Lak. "I'll be honest, nephew of mine, if Ingray had decided to leave you to your fate tonight, I wouldn't have blamed her. And no, don't tell me what your mother would or wouldn't have done in that case, this is not the time to be playing games like that. Though I'm well aware you're not the only child of my sister's to be playing games right now. I've been trying to understand what's been happening, and I've come to some conclusions. Ingray, we've already talked about exactly why you went to Tyr Siilas. I think you need to share that information with your brother."

Ingray took a breath. Couldn't bring herself to speak. But if Nuncle Lak wanted Danach to know, Danach would know, whatever Ingray said or didn't say now. "I went to Gold Orchid to ask them to bring Pahlad back from Compassionate Removal so I could ask em where e'd hidden the Budrakim vestiges." Danach didn't say anything, didn't visibly react.

"And Gold Orchid obliged you." Nuncle Lak's voice was unbelievably calm, as though e were talking about a catering order, or the wording of an announcement to the news services. "How much did you pay them?"

Ingray, acutely aware of Danach standing beside her

hearing her confess, wished she could be anywhere but here. Out in the woods in the mud, or walking miserable through town in the rain. Better yet, somewhere nicer, where she was safe and the people around her didn't demand so much of her. Still aboard Captain Uisine's ship, maybe. She named the sum.

"That's what I thought," said Nuncle Lak, then. "If you'd had a little more information you'd have realized that was far, far too small a price for what you were asking. And all of this, including what I'm about to say next, does not ever go beyond the three of us." E looked at Danach, who made an indignant noise. "Ever. Ingray is not the first Aughskold to ask Gold Orchid to bring someone out of Compassionate Removal. They—and every other broker approached—refused. They explained their refusal—and they never explain their refusals—by saying that they would never, under any circumstances, undertake such a commission, which would not only involve kidnapping but also would very directly undermine law enforcement in another polity."

"But who..." began Danach. "Why would..."

Nuncle Lak cut him off. "Your grandmother was a piece of work. More than that I will only say to Netano." By that e meant, e wouldn't answer Danach's questions until Danach himself was Netano. "The price Ingray offered is only a small fraction of what Gold Orchid refused on that occasion. What changed?" Silence. "And I can't help but wonder if Pahlad is acting on Tyr instructions."

"E was in a suspension pod when I picked em up,"

said Ingray. But then she remembered Pahlad saying *I think I'd like to visit the Incomers Office.* "But the captain wouldn't let me take em on the ship without em saying e wanted to go, so we thawed em out. And e acted like e didn't know who I was, and said e wasn't Pahlad, and went to the Tyr Siilas Incomers Office. E didn't want to come to Hwae, I had to find em and convince em to come with me."

"Maybe it wasn't you who convinced em," suggested Danach. "It suited someone for Pahlad to come back."

"It suited *Tyr* for Pahlad to come back," corrected Nuncle Lak. "And Tyr may have been able to compel Pahlad to come back to Hwae, but now that e's here e has nothing to lose and might as well do as e likes. Of course, the Tyr Executory isn't stupid and likely knew what e would do, once e got here, whatever instructions they may have given em."

"It suited Tyr to embarrass Prolocutor Budrakim, then," said Ingray. "But I don't see how what Pahlad is doing helps Tyr at all."

"I can't help but notice," said Nuncle Lak, "that the prolocutor has recently spoken in favor of seriously considering the Omkem Federacy's request that we allow their military through our gates, so they can reestablish contact with Byeit."

"Why would Tyr care about Omkem's access to Byeit?" asked Danach.

"We're not just one gate away from Byeit," Ingray said. "We're also only one gate away from Tyr."

"A lot of traffic goes through Tyr," agreed Nuncle Lak.

"A lot of information, and a lot of money. I don't think I'd like to try their defenses, but perhaps the Federacy would disagree. Perhaps they're not interested in Byeit. Or, not *only* interested in Byeit. Perhaps they would like to have a foothold here, too, especially now they're cut off from the system that used to be their easiest access to Tyr. And that thought has occurred to plenty of people right here. I'm sure the possibility has also occurred to the Tyr Executory."

"But surely," protested Ingray, "if that's their plan, Prolocutor Budrakim wouldn't take part in such a thing." And then, at a thought, "If he knew."

"He'd be stupid not to know," asserted Danach.

"You yourself didn't know, a moment ago," reproved Nuncle Lak. "But I imagine he does know, or at least suspects what the Omkem Federacy's aim is in this. Ethiat Budrakim is many things, but he is not stupid and he is not a traitor. He probably thinks it doesn't matter much to Hwae who's controlling the Tyr Executory, but it might be useful if whoever it was owed Ethiat Budrakim favors for helping put them in charge. And besides, I'm sure he thinks he can take Omkem money and wiggle out of any obligations they think they've put on him. Your mother thought the same, despite my advice otherwise. Though it's true Excellency Zat didn't care at all about whether Federacy military had access to Hwae. If anything, she was against it, or so Netano told me."

"Hevom cared," said Ingray. "Hevom killed Zat."

"And the ambassador is so eager to get him back," agreed Nuncle Lak. "And, coincidentally, so eager to have Pahlad stand trial in the Federacy, for a murder committed on Hwae. Perhaps as a favor to Ethiat Budrakim. Or perhaps they just see an extra opportunity to take offense when their demands are refused."

"They want an excuse for military action against Hwae," guessed Ingray. It seemed ridiculous. Unreal.

Nuncle Lak gestured agreement. "The Geck have interfered, at least as far as Pahlad is concerned. I imagine the committee will rule that Pahlad is Geck and send em up to the ship. From what I can tell, they don't have much choice about it. What that will mean for Pahlad, I have no idea. E seems entirely unworried at the prospect. But then, as I said, e has nothing left to lose."

"And Excellency Hevom?" asked Ingray.

"I doubt we're the only people to think this is meant to be a pretext for Omkem aggression. It's possible the committee will release Hevom to the Chancery, on the condition that Hevom boards the first ship leaving for the Federacy and never enters Hwae space again. Or it's possible the committee will be angered by the rather insulting and arrogant demeanor of the Omkem ambassador and insist Hevom face the magistracy here. Either way, we're likely to have some sort of decision in the morning. Or, I should say, in just a few hours."

"Infernal powers!" swore Danach. "I didn't think any committee could come to a decision in less than a few weeks."

Nuncle Lak ignored him. "This is why I gave what I did to the *District Voice* tonight. We'll stay with the story that Ingray found Pahlad on Tyr Siilas and didn't know who e was. She felt sorry for em and brought em home. It's the sort of thing she'd do, we all know that, and moreover it's the sort of generosity to fellow Hwaeans that her mother has instilled in her. Everything else has been a complete surprise." E looked at Ingray. "So you know how to play this, in the morning. Because you're going to be there when Pahlad leaves Planetary Safety. It will draw attention away from this house, and Hevom's own departure—either for the Omkem Chancery on the station, or a cell in Planetary Safety. And besides, the Geck ambassador has repeatedly insisted on it."

In a whole night of bizarre events, this was, for Ingray, the most puzzlingly unreal. "Repeatedly?"

"The ambassador," said Nuncle Lak, very calmly and straightforwardly, as though what e was saying made any sense, "somehow got past the guards and into Pahlad's cell. She refuses to leave em. She's been there all night."

"All night?" asked Ingray, surprised that she was actually able to speak aloud, with such a steady voice. "How strange." Danach, beside her, said nothing. And really, what was there for him to say? *That's impossible, the ambassador just tried to strangle me outside Eswae Parkland a few hours ago to stop me from murdering Ingray?*

Tic had been with Pahlad all night.

It really had been the ambassador who had assaulted Danach. And who had doubtless followed them back home, and doubtless realized that Tic was here, or his mech was, and what he was up to. What would happen in the morning when the ambassador appeared at Planetary Safety and revealed their fraud?

"The whole thing is strange," Nuncle Lak was saying. "And you can see why this is not the time for petty squabbles between the two of you."

"Yes, Nuncle," said Danach. To all appearances submissive, his voice obedient, but Ingray knew that no matter how repentant he seemed right now, he'd be searching for some way to turn what he'd just learned to his advantage. He didn't know about Tic's spider mechs, but he had heard Ingray call out *Tic?* when the mech had first spoken. It wouldn't take him long to put the two things together. Maybe he already had.

And Ingray had no choice but to say, herself, "Yes, Nuncle."

At Planetary Safety, Deputy Chief Veret offered Ingray serbat and a seat in eir office—very much like Taucris's, only larger, with more, and more comfortable, chairs for visitors. "When Taucris gets here," the deputy chief said, handing Ingray her cup of serbat, and then sitting emself, "I'll have her bring in some breakfast for you." For some reason, e said it just a bit stiffly, as though e was trying to conceal anger or discomfort.

"Have you been here all night?" Ingray asked. She herself had at least been able to doze in the groundcar to and from Eswae.

"Yes," said the deputy chief. E did not pour any serbat

for emself. "But I wouldn't have gotten much sleep last night anyway."

For a moment Ingray was puzzled. But of course, judging by eir accent Deputy Chief Veret was from Lim. And now she noticed, on the deputy chief's desk, the small square plain black lacquer tray that held, in a tumbled pile, a string of dark blue, gold-veined beads. Everyone knew the Hatli had some odd religious practices, and regular days throughout the year when they were obliged to fast, or sit up all night praying, or some other odd thing. And there were perfectly good foods the Hatli wouldn't eat.

She'd known the deputy chief was from Lim, and known that had probably meant e was Hatli, even before Danach had said it the morning before. But she hadn't thought that someone well-educated enough to take a job like this, let alone to speak Yiir as well as e had the other day, would still believe eir ancestors required such observances.

"Don't get the wrong idea about last night," said Deputy Chief Veret into her exhausted silence. "I have never been a supporter of your mother's. Not that it does me any good to say so in this district. Anyone else who could realistically challenge Netano Aughskold would almost certainly hold positions just as repugnant to me, and anyway I am so much among the minority here I might as well not vote, for all the good it does."

Ingray didn't know what to say to that, so she said nothing.

"I'm used to it by now," e continued. "Mostly. Every now and then something comes up that I can't ignore. Every now and then someone says it out loud—*You speak so well, Deputy Chief! But surely you're too educated to be like all those other Hatli, Deputy Chief!*—instead of just thinking it. Yes, I know you thought it just now."

Ingray started to protest. But realized that no matter what she said, she would only make things worse.

The deputy chief gave a sardonic smile. "It's usually pretty obvious. And every now and then politics dictates how I handle a case. Not just the planetary chiefs telling me who to arrest or what to say to the news services, not just a litigation committee ordering me to release people I believe should never be released, no, that's part of the job. They're my bosses. Maybe my judgment is wrong, and that's why we have litigation to begin with. But things like this." E shook eir head. "A cold-blooded, carefully planned murder, and I can't arrest the murderer, and he'll almost certainly be allowed to leave. And I won't be able to say anything about it. And then there's Ethiat Budrakim and his fake Garseddai vestiges." E reached over, toward the blue and gold beads in their tray, as though e wanted to pick them up, but pushed the tray a few centimeters away instead. "My own family has names that have been here on Hwae since long before the Budrakims ever came to this system. That's truth, but what vestiges we Hatli have of our ancestors are either sneered at as trivial or kept in a side hall of the System Lareum, as though we aren't really Hwaean. Or they're stolen outright and proudly displayed with some other family's name on them. But the Budrakims! Late-comers to Hwae, like all the Garseddai here—or the people here who claim to be Garseddai. And the vestiges?" E made a disgusted noise. "Fakes from the start. And him willing to throw his own child into Compassionate Removal to conceal it. And I can say nothing about it, except as it serves the interests of Netano Aughskold." E looked, it seemed reflexively, at eir desk. Closed one hand and opened it again, as though there were something e wanted to pick up. A cup of serbat e couldn't have because e was fasting, maybe.

"I know Hevom killed Excellency Zat," said Ingray. "I don't think he's even trying to hide it."

"He won't speak to us. It's probably better that way. The Omkem consul was so aggressively condescending I'm not certain I could take any more of it, from her or from Hevom."

"I keep thinking about finding Excellency Zat," said Ingray. "Most of the time I think I'm all right and it won't bother me anymore and then I'll be doing something else and just remember it. Remember her there." Her back against the slender tree trunk, the blood at the corner of her mouth.

"It's like that," said Deputy Chief Verct, gruffly but, she thought, with real sympathy.

"I don't want him to go free, either. But it's not up to us."

"I'm aware of that, Miss Aughskold," e said. "I just wanted to say it. I just needed someone to hear it, and it seems I'm not going to be able to say it outside this office." E was silent a moment. Looked over at the wall where the slowly brightening plaza in front of Planetary Safety was displayed, the sky above still a deep, dark, early-dawn blue, the glow behind a row of buildings across from where they sat the first traces of sunrise. "I wanted," e said, turning back to Ingray, "to be sure that it was said. When Pahlad Budrakim went to Compassionate Removal, do you imagine that no one was aware of what e said, yesterday? That outside Hwae the Budrakim vestiges are well known to be fakes? I've been thinking about that. I wasn't there for Mx Budrakim's conviction, but I cannot believe that not one of the prolocutor's many opponents didn't think of using that as a weapon against him. And in the capital there's an entire Planetary Safety office that investigates forgeries and frauds. And I requested access to the records of Mx Budrakim's arrest and trial and there is not a trace of anyone having looked into the claim that the Garseddai vestiges were fakes from the start. Even though, by the prolocutor's own statement, Mx Budrakim initially made that claim in eir own defense." Deputy Chief Veret gave a sharp, disbelieving *hah*. "Their jobs are as subject to politics as mine, I don't doubt. And I can't blame anyone for staying silent, when their own reputation and livelihood are threatened. But no one protested, no one said anything. Looking back all I can see is the dozens of people who were apparently content to send an innocent neman to Compassionate Removal because of Ethiat Budrakim's political ambitions. I want someone to know. I want someone to know that I think it was wrong. That it's wrong to set a murderer free, wrong to shuffle Pahlad Budrakim off to the Geck instead of dealing with the fact that e's here and not in Compassionate Removal, and dealing with the fact that e was apparently wrongfully convicted from the start. Dealing with it legally, I mean, and not just a few days' breathless news items that'll be forgotten the next time one of your lot throws a large enough party or wears a new hairstyle." E sighed. "And look at me, protesting to you and no one else. Certainly not anyone who'll actually do anything about it."

"I've been wondering, actually," said Ingray, "why my mother didn't do something with it." She probably could have asked Nuncle Lak. It was possible e wouldn't have told her. "But really, the next step would be asking what else was fake." As Pahlad emself had already pointed out. "It's easy to dismiss things people say outside Hwae. They don't understand, or they've got some reason to insult us or think less of us. But it wouldn't be like that, would it, if it were our own Magistracy Committee. It wouldn't be so easy to dismiss." She raised her cup of serbat to take a sip and then, self-conscious, lowered it again. "In the parkland, just before... just before Excellency Zat went up the hill, Pahlad asked her who she was, if her theories about where the ruin glass came from turned out to be true." And also asked why it had been worth so much time, money, and effort to find that proof. "And I had never really thought about it that way before. Who are we if our vestiges aren't real?"

"You never thought of it before," said the deputy chief, "because nobody has ever really questioned your being who you say you are. No one has ever told you your own vestiges are false, or that they mean you're not really entirely Hwaean."

"People have told me I wasn't really an Aughskold," Ingray pointed out. Defensive. Feeling insulted for some reason she couldn't name. "I came from a public crèche."

The deputy chief said nothing. And Ingray thought of what e'd said before, about people saying e was surprisingly well-educated, or calling eir religious beliefs superstition. Which she'd done herself, just hadn't said it aloud. She wanted to take back her words, say she was sorry, but she didn't know what she could say that would make it any better, and besides, she was still stung, and wasn't sure why.

The office door opened, and Taucris came in. "Excuse me, Deputy Chief. Can I borrow Ingray a moment?"

"Of course," said Deputy Chief Veret. "We were done here anyway."

"I put in an order for breakfast around the corner," Taucris said. "It'll be here in about twenty minutes."

Ingray rose. "Thanks for our talk." Still searching for the right thing to say. "I'll think about what you've said."

E said nothing, only gave a small nod and a brief wave of eir hand. Ingray followed Taucris out into the hallway.

"I didn't really need you for anything," Taucris said, when the office door had closed. "It's the end of a fast day for em and e's probably got some prayers or something e needs to do at sunrise. Same with breakfast. I could have brought it with me, but the deputy chief can't eat for another fifteen or twenty minutes. There are allowances for if someone has to work, and the deputy chief doesn't like to make a fuss, but most times it's easy enough for me to manage things so e doesn't have to worry about it. Oh, and breakfast is from the same place that did supper last night. They're the only place nearby that will make things for the deputy chief without butter or milk, without making a face at you." She hesitated. "It does mean some extra time sitting with me in my office. I hope you don't mind."

"Oh," said Ingray, with a smile, "I don't mind that at all."

13

It was past noon before the committee reached its decision, and another hour before Pahlad was brought out of the cells, once again wearing the green-and-white tunic and trousers e had borrowed from Ingray, the spider mech beside em. Tic—really Tic, Ingray was sure, but Ingray couldn't ask, not in the hallway outside the deputy chief's office, or on the walk down to the lobby. "It's all yours from here, Miss Aughskold, Mx Budrakim," Deputy Chief Veret said. "I've already referred all questions directed at me to the litigation committee." Through the doors Ingray could barely see the black stones of the plaza through the waiting crowd of news service mechs, and even actual people from the news services, all standing the prescribed fifteen meters from the entrance.

"Goodbye, Deputy Chief," said Pahlad. "Thank you

for having me, the last few days. Everyone was very polite, and your food here is better than what I had in my home district's Planetary Safety headquarters. And at least Excellency Hevom won't be getting away with murder." The committee's decision not to hand Hevom over to the Omkem ambassador hadn't been publicly announced yet, though Hevom himself had already been escorted into the Planetary Safety building through a side entrance and would be in a cell within the next few minutes if he wasn't already. It was only a matter of time before the Omkem ambassador managed to make his objection public.

"I don't see the groundcar," said Ingray.

"It's there," Taucris replied. She was standing just behind Pahlad. "They'll have to move out of our way. Even the people will." Though they could legally come closer than the mechs could.

"It'll be all right," said Pahlad. "I've done this before. And I suspect that if Ingray hasn't done this particular version of it, she's certainly had to face a crowd of news mechs at some point."

"Not quite like this," admitted Ingray. "But yes." Taucris, who was going along with them, wouldn't have to say anything at all. "Are you ready? Are you sure you want to stop for them?" They could all four of them—Pahlad, the spider mech, Ingray, and Taucris—just walk straight ahead to the groundcar.

"Oh, I definitely want to talk to them," replied Pahlad, with a smile.

The moment they stepped out the door, the clamor

surrounded them, echoing off the nearby buildings so that the crowd sounded larger than it was. Above, bright green and red and yellow against the blue sky, hovered several airborne news mechs, rising and falling on the mild breeze, always just outside the legally allowable distance. After Ingray had been out in the dark all night, and indoors until now, the sunshine felt strangely incongruous, even unreal. The sound of the shouting mechs resolved into comprehensible words. "Mx Budrakim! Mx Budrakim!" And Ingray was suddenly disappointed not to hear her name, even though she had been dreading it the moment before.

"I don't answer to that name," announced Pahlad, in a clear, loud voice. E stopped, four steps outside the door, and Ingray, the spider mech, and Taucris stopped with em. "I'm Garal Ket."

Despite how loudly e'd spoken, none of the news mechs had seemed to hear it through their own noise. But as Pahlad stood there, Ingray and Taucris and the mech beside em, the crowd gradually quieted, shushing each other to near silence. "I don't answer to that name," Pahlad said again, eir voice carrying to the news mechs this time. "My name is Garal Ket."

For just the briefest instant all noise ceased, the mechs motionless but for the bobbing of the airborne ones, the few actual humans frowning, puzzled, and then the *Out and About in Urade* mech said, "Mx Budrakim!" and the clamor started up again, echoing across the stones of the plaza.

Pahlad—no, Garal, Ingray supposed—looked at Ingray,

then back at the crowd of mechs, and began to walk forward, the spider mech close beside em. "Mx Budrakim!" called the mech nearest em. "Did you kill the Omkem Excellency Zat?" Garal ignored it. Taucris stepped ahead to wave the mechs in front of them aside.

"Mx Ket!" called a voice from the back of the crowd, pitched higher to carry over the general noise, expertly aimed to echo off the solid façade of the Planetary Safety building, Ingray thought, and probably turned up just a hair over the legal volume. "Mx Ket, did you kill Excellency Zat?"

Garal stopped abruptly and looked a question at Ingray.

"*Arsamol District Voice*," she said, quietly, as all the other news mechs fell hopefully silent.

"I did not kill Excellency Zat, *District Voice*," e said, loudly and clearly, for everyone to hear.

"Mx Ket!" cried the *District Voice* mech again. "We saw a recording of you telling Prolocutor Budrakim that you had never stolen the Budrakim vestiges, that they were frauds from the start. Is this true?"

"It is true, *District Voice*," said Garal. "I did say that; the recording that was released is accurate and unedited, at my request. Why don't you come up front here and walk us to the car?" The few humans in the crowd gave involuntary cries of protest. "Aenda Crav," said Garal, eir tone mild but eir voice still loud enough to carry halfway across the plaza, "and Thers Rathem, and you, Chorem Caellas, you all flew here from the capital this morning so you could shout questions at me in person, but you can't bring yourself to use the name I want to go by. None of you can, apparently, except for *District Voice* here."

District Voice's bright orange mech pushed its way to the front of the now-quiet crowd and came stepping right up to Garal. "Thanks for the invitation, Mx Ket. Miss Aughskold. Officer Ithesta. And I take it this is the Geck ambassador to the Presger? Honored to make your acquaintance."

The spider mech, which had already fixed a half dozen of its eyes on the mech, said, "What is? What is this thing?"

"It's a mech from the *District Voice* news service," said Ingray. "Piloted by a human reporter. And if you don't want to answer her questions, just say that and she'll leave you alone." With a significant look at the orange news mech.

"But you can't just decide what we call you," protested Chorem Caellas, a short, stocky woman from the most popular of the planetary-wide services.

"I'm not talking to anyone but the *District Voice*," said Garal, as Taucris shooed the mechs away from the groundcar.

"Miss Aughskold!" cried a news service mech, starting a desperate chorus of *Miss Aughskold* from the others. And suddenly, just as she'd felt slighted when they'd called for Garal and not her, now she wished they would just ignore her. But she knew how to handle this; she knew what it was like, the babble of questions, the mechs pressed close to each other all around, and all she had to do was keep her expression pleasant and not say a single word, or even look directly at any of the brightly colored news mechs.

"If the prolocutor were here," said the *District Voice* mech as Taucris opened the groundcar's passenger door, "none of them would need to pay any attention to you, they'd just talk to him."

"If they could get what they wanted from the prolocutor," replied Garal, "none of them would have come all the way here to talk to me in person. If it's all right with Ingray and Taucris, you can ride with us to the transport that's taking us to the elevator."

"And the Geck ambassador?" asked *District Voice*, collapsing its body down to half its height and clambering into the groundcar after Garal and the spider mech.

Ingray got in herself. "I notice you got into the groundcar before you asked about the ambassador's opinion," she observed before Garal, beside her, or the spider mech on the floor, could answer. The news mech had taken a seat opposite Garal. "And look, you were worried about what would happen when the big services got here."

The *District Voice* mech gave an amused little chirp. "Thanks for helping a girl out, Ingray. Hey, Officer Ithesta, am I going to get anything besides the official statement from the Deputy Chief of Serious Crimes?"

"You aren't," said Taucris, sliding in to sit next to the news mech and pulling the door closed. "So you just pretend I'm not here, all right?"

"Right, right," agreed the *District Voice* mech. "So, Ambassador. We're all having trouble understanding why you're saying Garal Ket is Geck. I mean, we all understand why e's agreeing with you, but that's another thing entirely, isn't it."

The spider mech turned all its eyes on the news service mech. "I do not want to answer questions." It sat all the way down on the floor of the groundcar, its legs curled beneath it. "Garal Ket is Geck."

"All right then," said the *District Voice* mech, quite cheerfully. "So, Garal. How did you manage to get out of Compassionate Removal? The place is built so that no one can get out, right? All one-way entrances? And it's guarded, isn't it?"

"I won't talk about getting out of Compassionate Removal," replied Garal pleasantly. "I'll talk about being in, if you like. And of course I'm more than happy to tell you about the Garseddai vestiges."

"That's a pretty shocking allegation you made in that recording," *District Voice* said, still cheerily. "How can you..." The orange mech paused. "Wait! The committee has just ordered Excellency Hevom to be arrested for the murder of Excellency Zat! And here I thought you were doing me a favor letting me go with you!"

"We are," said Ingray. "Tell the other *District Voice* reporters not to rush over to the house. Hevom has been gone for an hour or more; there's nothing to see and you won't get to talk to him."

"And the deputy chief isn't going to say anything more about it than e already has," put in Taucris.

"Oh, Ingray," said the news mech. "You are a jewel of the district." It turned its attention to Garal. "So, Mx

261

Ket, what I'd really like best is to sit down with you and talk about the situation with the Budrakim Garseddai vestiges. I'd love to do an in-depth piece on that. But we don't have time for it, so instead I'll ask you why you felt like you had to claim that the *Rejection of Further Obligations* is a fraud."

"Because it is," said Garal. "Not the words, no, we have the drafts of the resolution, we have recordings of the Assembly sessions where it was hammered out. But in all those recordings there's no sign of anyone making a physical document. Not like the one in the System Lareum. There were vestiges made, of course; all the representatives who were at those sessions got a specially made copy that they did all physically sign, but there never was one actual original."

"Are you claiming we're still obligated to the Tyr Executory?" asked the *District Voice* mech.

"Not at all. Just look at the history of the document in the System Lareum. About four hundred years ago Tauret Valmor was nearly broke and about to lose her seat in the Second Assembly. Her name was an old one, and one that was indeed there during the drafting of the *Rejection*, but there were questions about whether she held it legitimately—the Tauret Valmor just before her had died on the way to one of the non-Hwaean outstations, without giving eir name to an heir. The new Representative Valmor returned to Hwae claiming the elder had given her eir name just before e died, but there were no witnesses to that. But of course, her predecessor had told her about the secret storage compartment where the family's most precious vestiges were kept, including the actual original of the *Rejection of Further Obligations*, which of course e never would have told anyone but eir actual successor, and of course there was a nice detailed account of how it had gotten into Representative Valmor's possession to begin with. The donation practically founded the System Lareum; no one had wanted to give up anything really significant before that. It was a magnanimous gesture, and it went a long way to securing Valmor's Assembly seat, not to mention the fortunes of the next few Taurets. The most obvious giveaway is the lettering, which is nearly a century too late for the supposed date of the document. Whoever Valmor commissioned to do the work should have been more careful, but I suppose it doesn't matter, because it worked. But there are other problems with it, including the way such an important vestige suddenly appeared, when no one had even suspected it existed before that, and appeared right in time to be useful to the person who produced it."

"But if you were able to figure this out," protested the news mech, "why hasn't anyone else? The keepers at the System Lareum, for example?"

"Oh, I guarantee you that some of them know. There's no way they don't. But either they refuse to believe it, or they're keeping quiet. If they say anything they'll surely lose their jobs, and likely many of their friends and associates. And after all, it's the words that matter, the fact that the *Rejection* was sent and accepted and the Assemblies established, and just by being on display in the System Lareum that copy has become important. It's a real vestige now, even if it's not the one everyone thinks it is. So why should it matter if it's really a forgery?"

"Why should it matter?" The news mech's voice was outraged. "Of course it matters! How can you even say that?"

"Look into it, *District Voice*," said Garal. "Treat it like your most serious investigative story. Publish it, and then come ask me why the curators at the System Lareum might keep quiet and tell themselves it doesn't really matter."

"I won't be able to ask you," observed the *District Voice*. "You'll be well away from all of it, off gallivanting with aliens. You don't have anything to lose here."

"Nothing that matters more than everyone knowing what Ethiat Budrakim did to me, no." All this time Garal's voice had been calm and even, but Ingray thought she heard, for the first time, an undercurrent of anger. "I don't really care about anything else. But once you start looking at the evidence, once you really look at those Garseddai vestiges, there will be questions about other vestiges, and if you're afraid to ask those, *District Voice*, you might as well just stop now."

"And I'm back to wondering if you really did me a favor asking me along like this," said the news mech ruefully.

The spider mech spoke up from the floor of the groundcar. "Mech from the *District Voice* news service, you are very stupid."

"Be nice, Ambassador," said Ingray. "Aren't you a diplomat?"

"And the *District Voice* has a point," said Garal. "I've put her in a difficult position, while I myself, as she's just said, have nothing to lose. But I'm telling the truth."

"*Diplomat* does not mean nice," muttered the spider mech. "*Diplomat* means tell the aliens to leave us alone."

"Let me give you some names," said Garal to the news mech, as though the spider mech hadn't spoken, "and some places to start looking, and you can do whatever you want with them."

The car that ringed the massive, multistranded elevator cable was huge, with several decks, luxury cabins for those who could afford them, and shops and restaurants. And, of course, kiosks where one could buy a vestige of the trip.

Extra-Hwae Relations had lost the debate over what sort of quarters Garal—and not incidentally the Geck ambassador, traveling with em—was due. Surely an alien diplomat, who was getting her way largely because everyone was afraid to break the treaty she represented, ought to have as comfortable a trip as could be provided. Planetary Safety had pointed out that the ambassador was a mech, the comfort of which wasn't much of an issue; Garal Ket, Geck citizen or not, was a convicted criminal; and besides, Extra-Hwae Relations wasn't intending to actually pay for any of it. So they had a tiny private compartment with a single bunk the three humans sat on, with the spider mech crouching on the floor.

They were more than halfway up the elevator before Ingray could muster the courage to confess to Taucris that they had all lied to her, even Ingray, and the Geck did not in fact want custody of Garal Ket. The elevator had passed its midpoint several hours before, and gravity had begun to return—or, Ingray knew it wasn't exactly gravity, just felt like it, but it was close enough. Enough for them all to sit on what had previously been the underside of the bunk, the spider mech sitting now on what had hours before been the ceiling but was now the floor.

Was there any point in delaying it? They could tell Taucris what was really happening at the last possible moment, when they got off the shuttle from Zenith Platform to Hwae Station. That would be wisest. That would be safest.

Ingray didn't want to do that to Taucris, didn't want to see Taucris's face at that moment. But if she confessed now, what would Taucris do?

Ingray took a breath. Opened her mouth. "Taucris," she began.

"Oh, shit," said Taucris, sitting straighter. She stood quickly, or tried to, shoved too hard off the bunk in the slowly increasing gravity and hit the opposite wall. "Oh, shit," she said again. "We've got a problem. I mean, not just us. But we do. Ingray, turn your messages back on. And look at a station news service."

Ingray did, and her vision was flooded with urgent messages, and even more urgently worded news items. And once she saw what those were about, she couldn't even bring herself to swear.

*   *   *

A week before Ingray, Garal, and Tic Uisine had come out of the Tyr gate, two freighters had come out of the Enthen gate and docked at Hwae Station. They had declared the sort of cargo large freighters carried—a miscellaneous assortment of things that for whatever reason couldn't be produced at their destination: arrack, medical supplies, replacement parts for interstellar gates, even tea, not all of it from Radchaai space. They unloaded some but not nearly all of their cargo at Hwae, and while they waited for cargo they were scheduled to take on, their crews did the sort of things that freighter crews did on stations. None of it unusual, none of it alarming. None of it illegal, which in retrospect might have been suspicious in itself.

Enthen was one gate away from Hwae. It was also one gate away from Omkem. The freighters were not, in fact, carrying arrack or gate parts or Radchaai tea. Or not much of those things. They had actually been packed full with Omkem military mechs. And an hour ago those mechs had marched out of their freighters and blasted their way out of the docks.

"What is it?" asked Garal, who had not been reconnected to Hwae's communications network when e had left Arsamol Planetary Safety.

"Very bad, is what," whispered the spider mech. "I should have been watching the news from the station, but I wasn't."

Taucris was too involved in her own various sources

of information to notice how differently the spider mech had just spoken, far more like Tic than like the Geck ambassador. "Shuttle service between Zenith Platform and the station is suspended," she said. "Everyone on the station has been ordered to seek shelter."

"*What's happened?*" insisted Garal.

"It looks like the Omkem Federacy has happened," said Ingray. "They've managed to get armed mechs onto the station and there's fighting. I don't think anyone knows what their goal is, or why they're doing this."

Garal frowned. "It can't be about Excellency Zat. They couldn't possibly have gotten here so quickly."

"No," said the spider mech, "it looks like the ships they came on have been here for a week or more. It can't be about Zat. Or if it is, they knew about it before it happened. And now we have a problem."

"Did they know?" asked Taucris, no doubt, like Ingray, having reached the point where all the chaotic, fragmented reports from the station had ceased to give her any useful or accurate information. "Was Excellency Zat's murder all about giving the Federacy a pretext for invading?"

"It's possible," observed the spider mech, very obviously Tic Uisine now. "They probably told Hevom they'd get him out, but he's a poor cousin; I imagine no one will try too terribly hard to rescue him just now."

"Ambassador?" Taucris had finally noticed the change in the spider mech's personality.

"No," whispered the spider mech, curtly. "We don't really have time for long introductions or explanations, so I'll keep it short. I'm Captain Tic Uisine. I really did steal my ship, and a number of bio mechs along with it. Not coincidentally, they look very much like any Geck ship mechs. The ambassador really has been harassing Ingray in an attempt to find me. She has not, however, demanded custody of Garal Ket. That was me. The Geck ambassador almost certainly knows I've done it, and has done nothing to stop me. She's very possibly on this elevator somewhere and I imagine she's waiting for more specific information on where I actually am."

"I..." Taucris looked at Ingray.

"I'm sorry," Ingray said. "But the Omkem were talking about trying Garal for murder, when it's obvious e didn't do it, and besides, the murder happened here on Hwae and we know Hevom did it! They obviously just wanted someone to pin it on, and they'd decided that was Garal. And even if e wasn't turned over to them, e was probably going to end up back in Compassionate Removal. For something e didn't even do!"

Taucris stared at her, and then looked at the spider mech, and then at Garal.

"The plan," said Tic, "was to get to the station, and then for Garal—and Ingray if she wanted—to get into vacuum suits and go out on the station hull. I was going to have mechs pick em up and bring em to my ship. It's a long trip in a vacuum suit, but worth it if I could get em away. Worst case, the Geck would intercept em. I don't think they would hurt em."

Still speechless, Taucris looked at Ingray.

"I'm sorry," said Ingray again. "I couldn't just leave Garal there."

"This conversation was probably going to happen at some point anyway," said the spider mech. "The problem right now is that my mechs are already on their way to the station. It'll take a while for them to change course for the platform. I'm calculating that right now. It'll be a near thing, but I'm fairly sure I can do it. The question is, who's coming with me? Garal, of course, and I don't think Ingray was planning to but for various reasons—the most urgent being the fact that her family is in the middle of what would seem to be the Omkem's supposed motivation for sending armed mechs onto Hwae Station—for that and for other reasons, I suspect and hope she will change her mind. But you, Officer, we will be leaving in a difficult position. You were supposed to deliver Garal to the station, and ultimately to the Geck, under the assumption the Geck had demanded custody of em."

Taucris stared at the spider mech for a long, tense moment. Then she said, "That situation still applies, doesn't it? The treaty still says Garal is Geck if e declares emself Geck."

"Well," admitted the spider mech in its whistling whisper, "the Geck also have to accept em. Which they haven't actually had a chance to do."

"But they might," Taucris said. "And you, Captain Uisine, is it? We can't get Garal to the station or to the Geck, as things stand. But you could. You'll take Mx Ket to the Geck, right?"

The spider mech hesitated. "No."

Taucris frowned and folded her arms. "That wasn't how you were supposed to answer."

"I'm trying to be honest with you," said the spider mech testily. "As I said, we're potentially putting you in a very difficult position." Taucris made a disgusted sound. "Look," the spider mech insisted, "Ingray is going to be really unhappy if I get you in trouble, and you're going to be really unhappy with Ingray if you find out we lied to you any more than we have already. What else am I supposed to do?"

"You'd take me to the Geck if I wanted to go, though, right?" asked Garal, cir voice mild.

"Of course," replied the spider mech. "I just don't see why you'd want to."

"Last I heard," suggested Ingray, "the Geck ambassador was still insisting Tic was Geck. And Taucris is supposed to deliver Garal to the Geck."

"Well," admitted Taucris, arms still folded, "I'm supposed to deliver em to Extra-Hwae Relations, so *they* can deliver em to the Geck. But I can't do either one now."

"Right," agreed Ingray. And then her nausea flooded back. Not from microgravity this time. She swallowed, and breathed very carefully through her mouth.

Taucris unfolded her arms and sat down again in the space between Ingray and Garal. She sighed. "You'd probably better go with them, Ingray. The...Captain Uisine is right, it might be safer for you to be away for a while."

The spider mech patted Taucris's knee with one claw.

271

"Don't worry, Officer. We'll get her back to you as soon as we can. Or, you know, you could come with us."

"Not without losing my job," Taucris said. "And I might anyway, as it is. Besides, people are going to be panicking up on the platform, and Safety might need my help. Have you finished calculating?"

"I have," whispered the spider mech. "And I have a plan."

14

By the time the elevator had nearly reached Zenith Platform, the news of events on the station had been out for
hours and elevator staff had informed passengers that
while the elevator would finish its trip—it had to—no
passengers would be allowed onto the platform, let alone
onto a shuttle bound for the station.

"That ought to work to our advantage," Taucris said.
"We have Extra-Hwae Relations and Planetary Safety
behind us, we should be able to convince them to let us
through, and we won't have lots of people around us so
you three will have an easier time getting right out on
the platform hull without anyone noticing what you're
up to."

But by the time they left their small cabin, a good hour
before docking at Zenith, announcements had changed
from *No passengers will be allowed to exit the elevator*

at this time to *Please keep the corridors clear and do not approach the exits,* not just over communications but by loudspeaker. Repeated, over and over every few minutes. Usually at this point in the trip people were packing things up, looking for lost items, rounding up traveling companions, or forming an almost last-minute line at the vestige kiosks and the sanitary facilities. But despite announced orders, all of the many people they saw in the wide, shop-lined main corridor were headed single-mindedly for the lifts and even the stairs to the exit level, bags in hand.

And having reached the bare, brown-tiled exit level, they couldn't reach the first exit they headed for. Frustrated, complaining passengers and their luggage filled the corridor. "Why are they here so early?" asked Taucris, her voice exasperated. "Why do they want to go onto the platform?"

"Why do we?" asked Garal.

"It's hardly the same," said Ingray, but there they were, and as she watched, one woman turned to a neman beside her and complained that it was ridiculous, she had important business to attend to on the station.

"I have family there," agreed the neman. "And I'm supposed to just turn around and leave them?" E turned and caught sight of Taucris's green Planetary Safety uniform. Opened eir mouth to complain but some disturbance in the crowd pushed the person ahead of em back. E stepped hastily out of the way and tripped over the bulky bag at eir feet.

Taucris and Ingray caught eir arms before e could fall

headlong, but Taucris had to shout at the people ahead who had backed into the neman, to get them to clear room to put the neman safely on eir feet again. "This isn't good," said Taucris, with a perfunctory gesture at the neman's flustered thanks. More people had come up behind and were pushing to find a path through the crowd.

"Change of plan," said Tic, and the people nearest the spider mech flinched and stepped back, having apparently just realized that it wasn't just a strangely shaped package, starting a new wave of collisions and potentially dangerous falls behind them. And more people were arriving, filling the corridor behind, groaning in dismay to see the crowd already there.

"I have to stay here," said Taucris, and then, pointing at the newest arrivals and raising her voice, "You! Clear the exit corridor! This is an official warning!" Though she was, technically speaking, out of her jurisdiction.

"What about them?" cried a man, gesturing to the crowd ahead.

"They can't go anywhere with you in the way!" Taucris replied, loud and authoritative. "You have been officially warned! Ten more seconds and I start giving out fines!" A few people turned to go. Taucris said, more quietly, "I have to stay here. This could get bad, a crowd like this, even if everyone means well. I need to stay here until Elevator Safety can get here, and I need to help them."

"Yes," agreed Garal.

Ingray, seeing the few who had turned to go, and so

many still there and clearly dubious of Taucris's authority, said, "You can't stay all by yourself."

"Go," said Taucris. "I'll be fine. I've already called Elevator Safety, and they're sending someone but it will be a few minutes." She leaned forward and kissed Ingray on the mouth, firmly. "I'll see you when you get back."

Garal took Ingray's arm. "The officer said to clear the corridor," e said in a carrying voice, pulling Ingray along as e followed the spider mech scurrying away. "Let's do as she says." And then, more quietly, "Don't look back, you'll trip. And anyway she's fine."

"You're right," Ingray agreed, sounding more confident than she felt. But she did look back, for just an instant, and saw Taucris frowning, speaking sternly to the people who were standing there. "She'll be fine."

It was easy to get a lift to the top level—everyone else was going down, and only a few people had taken Taucris's orders seriously enough to move to another level. "This might actually be better," Tic said when the doors closed and they were alone for a few moments. "I'll pick you up from the elevator; it'll be docked with the platform soon enough and I'm already headed there. And in all this, no one will be paying attention to us. There'll be airlocks up top that will let us get out on the hull, it's just a matter of walking the circuit until we find one. I don't imagine there'll be anyone there to see us; everyone's trying to get to the exits."

The top level was the upside-down mirror image of the bottom. It had been the entrance down on Hwae, and there were no shops or restaurants or cabins along the brown-tiled curving corridor, just bare brown walls punctuated by doors marked EMERGENCY EXIT or ALARM WILL SOUND or AUTHORIZED PERSONNEL ONLY. Ingray had always assumed that it was empty once an ascent began.

But it wasn't empty. To judge by the occasional scattering of luggage and jumbled blankets, a few passengers who were unable or unwilling to pay for a cabin slept here. And quite a few of those had unpacked again, if they'd ever packed at all, and were apparently resigned to going directly back down.

Some passengers also appeared to use the mostly empty corridor as a place to stretch their legs, so that even once Ingray and Garal had strolled all the way around the circuit as casually as they could with the spider mech skittering along beside them, and Tic had settled on a likely door in an empty stretch of corridor, people would still walk by far too frequently.

Finally, after nearly five minutes of too-casual loitering by the chosen door in the hope of a break longer than ten seconds, Tic said quietly to Ingray and Garal, "All right. I'm going to do something drastic. It may mean I'll have to stay behind to cover for you."

"But..." began Ingray. But it seemed as though there would never be an opportunity otherwise, and this wasn't really Tic, just a mech. Tic was safely away on his ship somewhere.

"Don't worry about me," said Tic. "Here, just in case." The spider mech spat out a shiny black blob and handed it to Garal. "If I'm not with you, put that on the airlock controls. It should do the trick."

"What are you going to do?" asked Garal.

In reply the spider mech spun around and reared up to walk on its four hindmost legs, waving the front ones menacingly. It stretched a half dozen of its eyes at the nearest strolling passenger and whistled, "Do you look? At what do you look? I look, too! Am I food? *Are you food?*" Only to turn its attention on the next passenger as the first one fled. *"And you, do you also look?"*

Minutes later, their stretch of corridor was clear. "Quick now," Tic whispered then, scuttling back to them, "before someone sends elevator staff to deal with us." He reared up again and leaned against a door, flattening and spreading to cover it entirely, until Ingray could read the words AUTHORIZED PERSONNEL ONLY through its gelatinous body. Its legs seemed to have disappeared, though eyestalks protruded at seemingly random places. Ingray suppressed a tiny shudder as it pulled itself back into its not-quite-a-spider shape.

"Time to go," said Tic, as the door snicked open. "My other mechs aren't quite here yet so we may have to wait for a..." Footsteps sounded, and voices, someone saying, *It was right up here, Officer...* "Go! I'll see you soon!"

Garal grabbed Ingray's elbow and pulled her through the door as the spider mech scuttled up to the Safety officer who rounded the corridor's curve. "You!" whistled the spider mech, waving three or four clawed legs, eyestalks writhing. "I will make such complaints to you!" The door closed again with a click, and Ingray and Garal stood in the grimy quiet of a service passage. "We can't wait around, even here," said Garal.

"I know." Ingray took a steadying breath. She was still dizzy, though whether that was from knowing she was about to climb outside the elevator, or the close call moments ago, or from Taucris's kiss back on the lower level, she wasn't sure. "Let's go."

They found an airlock easily enough, and a rack of vacuum suits and helmets. For a few terrifying and frustrating minutes it seemed as though there wouldn't be one to fit Garal, but e said, "Start checks on yours, I'll look at the next airlock." Five minutes later e was back, dragging a suit. "Yours good?" e asked. Quietly.

"Yes." Ingray finished her last check. And then froze. It was time to put the suit on, check once more, and then go outside. Where there would be nothing between her and hard vacuum but the thin shell of the suit. She'd done it before. Had thrown up in her suit, but she'd passed the test. In theory she was fully qualified to do this, to go out into the suffocating nothing of space. Where she would die if she'd made any mistake.

"We'll be all right," said Garal, checking over eir own suit.

Ingray wasn't sure if e was saying it for her benefit, or for eir own. She feared any reply would come out breathy and shaking. Feared she was hyperventilating, and yes, her tingling fingers said she was. *Calm. Just stay calm.* She'd done this before.

Garal made eir last check. Looked at Ingray. "Are you all right?"

"I'm scared," admitted Ingray, and yes her voice was breathy, but it didn't shake quite as much as she'd feared it would.

"I'm not," said Garal, with the smallest suggestion of a smile. "I'm fucking terrified." Ingray couldn't manage to laugh at that. "Suit up," Garal continued. "We go through the airlock and step out on the ledge and wait for Tic. That's all we have to do."

"Right," agreed Ingray. She girded up her skirts. Shoved and pulled herself into the suit—it was more or less her size but hadn't been made to fit someone quite as round as she was, and getting it on properly strained the limits of the suit's adjustability. She closed all the seals and tried to pull on her helmet, but it wouldn't sit right until she pulled out her hairpins. And then stared helplessly at the pile of pins in her hand. Keeping them wouldn't do her much good—her hair had only stayed up as long as it had because a servant had done it, back at Netano's house.

Garal snapped on eir own helmet and closed eir last seal. Looked a question at Ingray.

She stowed the pins in a pouch on her suit, snapped her own helmet into place, stopped herself from testing the communications—they didn't want anyone hearing them, noticing them—and before she could think too hard about what she was doing she touched the outer airlock control and stepped through the hatch when it opened. Garal came into the lock beside her, triggered the door closure, and pressed the shiny black blob Tic had given em over the inside airlock controls. They stood, waiting for the lock to depressurize. Hopefully without sounding any alarms that might bring elevator staff. Ingray counted, trying to time her breaths, trying to keep them deep and even and not let them go jagged and gasping the way they clearly wanted.

After forever, the outside door swung open. One more breath. Another. And Ingray stepped out into sunlight.

The ledge here was two meters wide. With a rail, thank all the gods of the afterlife. Above towered the elevator cable—or really, cables, a massive bundle of them, shining white, here and there refracting the sunlight into thin rainbows. And looming above that, Hwae. Night darkened half the deep blue Iths Ocean, and east of that the Ados peninsula was laid out clear as a map, striped and whorled with a dozen shades of green. Fine, wispy clouds made a gauzy white veil over the green and brown of Southern Ustia, and though her feet were firmly on the elevator ledge Ingray clutched the rail, terrified. She'd seen this before, from inside the elevator, from inside Zenith Platform, but there it had been merely deliciously disorienting. Out here, she felt that she would slide off the ledge and tumble away into the ocean overhead.

Garal touched eir faceplate to hers. "Look at your feet, Ingray."

"I can't!" she gasped.

"Look at *me*, Ingray!"

She dragged her gaze down. Garal's own eyes were wide, the first visible sign of fear or anxiety she had seen in em.

"There," e said. "That's better. Don't look up again." Which was nearly impossible; the broad, bright, rainbow-shot cable led so inexorably up to Hwae, so near and so huge. "If you panic and anything happens to you, you'll never get to kiss Officer Ithesta back."

Ingray made a breathy sound that began as a laugh and ended as a sob. "How long until Tic gets here?"

"Not long," Garal said. "Maybe fifteen minutes?" E seemed so calm, but eir own voice trembled, just a bit.

I can't do it, she wanted to say, but movement caught the corner of her vision. She turned her head, slowly. Carefully. A black, many-eyed spider mech scuttled along the ledge. "No, he's here. He's here already." She lifted her faceplate away from Garal's and raised her hand.

The spider mech raised one claw, ran right up to her, and wrapped six legs around her. Another mech came scuttling around the bend of the ledge, and then another. And another. Ingray hadn't realized that Tic had so many of them.

It wasn't over. It would still be hours and hours. But she didn't have to do anything now, and she could close her eyes and Tic would take care of the rest, and eventually they would be aboard his ship, where she knew they would be safe. "See you aboard," she said, though of course Garal couldn't hear her now their helmets weren't touching. But e'd seen her mouth move, said something in reply that Ingray couldn't interpret, as two spider mechs put their hairy legs around em.

The mech already holding Ingray reached out one claw

and tugged on her hand that still held the rail. "Oh," she said, and made herself let go, and then the surface of the ledge lifted away from her feet and she lost any sense of up or down. She closed her eyes and tried very, very hard not to scream. Tried to think of nothing but counting her breaths.

She lost count, lost all confidence that she hadn't repeated the same few hundred numbers over and over, thought maybe she'd dozed at some point but there was no way for her to be sure. The view outside her faceplate was uninformative, claustrophobic black. She could look at the time just by blinking; she wouldn't need to query the system communications to do it. But she was afraid of what she'd see—that it had only been a few minutes and there was still all the rest to get through. Or that it had been days and she'd somehow missed the destination, was drifting aimlessly away from anyone and anything that might get her out of the prisoning suit. She shouldn't have done this. She should have stayed on the elevator and risked facing Planetary or Elevator Safety, or Omkem military mechs.

An alarm buzzed in her ears. She opened her eyes and saw the flashing orange of an alert. "Tic?" she gasped. "My air is getting low." He'd said he'd bring extra; the distance to his ship was too long for a single vacuum suit's supply. But, she realized, trying very very hard not to panic, she hadn't seen any of the spider mechs carrying tanks.

"Not long now," came the thready reply, barely audible

through her faceplate. She had no idea where it was coming from, had never seen any of the spider mechs use a mouth to speak. "Stay calm."

"I'm trying," she said. But of course talking, and breathing hard the way she was now she wasn't concentrating on taking each breath perfectly calmly, would just use up more air. She closed her eyes again and struggled to slow her breathing. Which worked for a while, but eventually her fingers were tingling again, and she must have been clenching her teeth, because she had the beginning of a headache. But Tic had said to stay calm. Had said it wouldn't be long. She had no idea how much time had passed since he'd said that. It would be all right. She was not going to throw up here in the suit, because even though the suit would almost certainly clean up most of the mess it was still not a good idea to vomit in microgravity, and besides, she just wasn't going to. There was a *thunk*; she'd run into something, or something had run into her. *Down* returned suddenly to the universe, beneath her feet. The ship, it must be. The gravity was a relief, and all she had to do now was wait for the airlock to cycle, and she could do that. She could wait, now she knew she was safe, and she was still *not* going to throw up. But it was going to be a near thing, and her head was hurting worse, and she couldn't keep from gasping, and her helmet separated from her suit with a click and it felt so, so good to actually feel like she was getting air when she breathed again. She fumbled at the seals of her vacuum suit, and one of the spider mechs that had brought her here pulled at the others and helped her out of the suit.

She stood a moment, unsteadily, in a dimly lit compartment. Beside her a spider mech was helping Garal out of eir own suit, and e seemed to be all right. And a voice that Ingray couldn't put a name to, but that seemed oddly familiar, said, "Oh, it's you!"

Ingray turned toward the voice. Slouching in the doorway, in rumpled white coat and trousers and gloves, was the Radchaai ambassador to the Geck, Tibanvori Nevol. "I didn't know you were coming along. But no one here tells me anything. You're not claiming to be Geck, too, are you?"

"There isn't anything like tea here," said Ambassador Tibanvori, twenty minutes later, "or I'd offer you some." She'd taken off her rumpled white coat but still wore a white shirt, trousers, and gloves. "The Geck humans drink warm water with salt in it in situations like this." She grimaced. "I'll have some brought if you like."

"Thank you, no," said Ingray. She sat beside Garal on a ledge—or, it wasn't a ledge, exactly. More of a growth that rose out of the inner surface of the shadowed room. Which was narrower at the entrance than where Ingray and Garal sat, with no corners at all that Ingray could see, and half a dozen large and sinuous protrusions in various places, including the walls and ceiling. "I'm sorry about your coat."

Ambassador Tibanvori waved that away and sat on a

nearby protrusion. "Thankfully, you don't seem to have eaten much before you set out. Still, I must say, the next time you plan to make a long journey in a vacuum suit— though it's not the best idea to begin with—you might want to be sure you have enough air. Is your head feeling better?"

"Yes, thank you, Ambassador."

"Is this ship still docked with Hwae Station?" asked Garal.

"It is," Tibanvori acknowledged. "Treaty or no treaty, we'd have been better off leaving days ago. But no, the ambassador had to find this Tic Uisine person. And her ship. His ship." She sighed.

"What's happening on the station?" Ingray asked. The last she'd heard, military mechs had shot their way out of the docks, and that was still all she knew. "Is there still fighting? Do you know…" She knew people who lived and worked on the station. Netano was there. She risked a quick query to the station's various news services, but all she found were warnings to seek shelter and remain there. That was a bad sign, she thought. But she would not allow herself to think too hard about that until she knew what was going on. Nuncle Lak certainly either knew where Netano was right now or was looking for information about her, and e would share what e knew when e knew it. There was no need for Ingray to add to the chaos by sending out queries of her own.

"I have no idea what's happening on the station," replied Tibanvori. "And you shouldn't, either, if you're claiming to be Geck."

"I'm not," said Ingray. "Garal is."

"Well, all I know is, there was some shooting on the docks a day or so ago, and we've been left alone."

A person came through the door, the first person they'd seen besides Tibanvori. Dripping wet. Tall, broad in an odd way that Ingray couldn't quite make sense of, their head rising straight out of their shoulders as though they had no neck whatever. They seemed to be wearing a very tight-fitting greenish-brown suit of some sort, with a series of dark almost-horizontal lines on either side. Something about their face was just barely familiar, but Ingray couldn't think why. "Ingray Aughskold," the person said in a quiet, strangely breathy voice. "Garal Ket. Come with me. The ambassador would like to speak with you."

"Of course," said Garal, as though this were merely a courteous social invitation. E rose, and Ingray did as well, and, with a polite nod to Ambassador Tibanvori, followed the person out. Not into a corridor exactly—there seemed to be no corridors on this ship, just a number of strangely shaped compartments. Ingray remembered Tic saying he'd had his own ship refitted— had it been like this on the inside, when he'd stolen it?

But she would have to remember not to say that here. Had to remember that as far as she knew, Tic had bought his ship quite legally.

At length, the person brought them to a room like any of the others, except for a pool of dark water, about three meters wide, with four curved and snaking seats around it. "Sit," said the person. "Do not get in the water. Some of what's in it is not good for you. The ambassador will be here in a moment." And the person dived into the pool. In the brief instant they were visible below the surface of the water, Ingray saw those horizontal lines flare open, and she realized with a dizzying shock that the person had not been wearing any sort of suit at all, and those lines had been gill slits.

"We might as well sit down," said Garal. Ingray turned to look at em. "Sit down, Ingray," e repeated.

"That person had gills," said Ingray.

"Yes," agreed Garal, as they both sat on one weirdly curving bench. Ingray thought about saying *So that was what Tic wanted to be*. What he'd thought he was going to be when he grew up. What he still resented not being, it seemed. She opened her mouth to say it but stopped and closed her mouth again.

She flinched as something green and glistening surged up out of the still-sloshing water. It rose, dripping, a smooth and shining blob that leaned over and...oozed onto the margin of the pool. A hole appeared in it, one that stretched wide and then pursed. "Garal Ket," it whisper/whistled. "Ingray Human." There was more of it below the water, a massive, dark shadow. This must be the ambassador herself, then. One of the aliens that no one Ingray knew of had ever actually seen. Well, besides Tic, of course.

This was important. She had to think straight. And tired and confused as she was, Ingray knew how to handle this. "Ambassador. Thank you for..." She wanted to say *for inviting us* but of course there had been nothing like an invitation. "Thank you for having us here."

"You are Tic's friend, I think," said the green blob, as though that were a reply that made sense. "Garal Ket, you have no legal status as a human, yet you are a human, and you have claimed to be Geck. It only remains for the Geck to accept your claim. You have done this in fear of your life; I have heard many things and seen many things and so I understand this. Tic Uisine intended that this should remove you from danger. I know you are not clutchmates, you cannot be even by the standards of humans. I have known many humans. I understand humans. Not everyone understands humans so well; humans are difficult to understand, even when they are Geck. And Tic Uisine..." The ambassador hesitated, then made an odd, sighing sound. The green blob had shifted somehow to a bluish color. "Tic Uisine is not Geck anymore. I do not wish to say it, but it is clearly so. Still, I understand him well. You are Tic's friend, I think. We are considering what to do with you, Garal Ket." The blob flared a brighter blue for just a moment, and then turned pale green.

"I thank you for your patience, Ambassador," said Garal. "And Captain Uisine will be pleased to hear you've recognized his status as human."

"Yes," whistled the ambassador. "Yes. I had not believed he would be, but I think now he will. Ingray Human, I have caused you some trouble. I have broken the treaty by assaulting your clutchmate, the brother Danach."

Beside Ingray on the bench, Garal turned to stare at Ingray. "What?"

"I'll tell you later," said Ingray. "It doesn't matter right now. Ambassador, you didn't hurt him, and everything came out fine. I took him home, and all of that is straightened out now."

"Still," replied the ambassador. "I should not have done these things. And I admit to you that I am not glad that the brother Danach was not hurt, but I should still not have done it. I have thought since then, and I have not done well. I have not. I have done things I should not have done. I must say to you, *I apologize, Ingray Aughskold*. Those are the words. I say them."

Silence. The water in the pool still sloshed, little waves breaking at Ingray and Garal's feet and against the once-again-darker-green blob, as the rest of the ambassador moved under the water. Or Ingray assumed so, she couldn't quite see what the rest of the ambassador looked like, or how much of her there might be. "It's all right, Ambassador," Ingray said after a moment.

"It is not all right," insisted the green blob. "It is not. I will tell you a thing. I will tell you. When humans first appeared, many things died. So much died, and the humans were bad to eat. Many wished to remove them, but some said, no, they are very strange and things die all around them, but they are like people in some way. And they have come here to live, how could they live outside the world? Nothing could. Imagine being outside the world, it is a terrible thing. Do we kill these strange, so very strange maybe-people for that? When we might instead help them live? And so we changed them, and now things do not die all around them, and they can live in the world."

"Most of them," Garal said.

"Be more patient, Garal Ket," said the ambassador. "This is the next thing I am going to say. The change is not perfect, and some cannot live in the world. But this is the way of eggs, and hatchlings, is it not? One spawns thousands upon thousands, but only a few survive. I myself, my clutchmates numbered in the thousands on the day I hatched. Hundreds, days later, and only twelve of us lived to maturity, and of those two failed to swim down."

"That's...not how it works for humans, Ambassador," said Ingray.

"No," the ambassador agreed. "It cannot work this way for humans. It could not. For years human hatchlings must be cared for, carefully attended, fed, taught, before they can swim with a clutch. And long before then the hatchlings you have cared for might as well be your own clutchmates. Perverse, yes. But so it is with humans. You cannot abandon your own clutchmates to death, or leave them to be eaten. A hatchling that thinks only of its own survival makes an untrustworthy adult, and if every hatchling behaved so, far too few would survive.

"The change was not perfect, and because of this some human hatchlings cannot stay. But they are clutchmates. They cannot stay, but they cannot be sent out of the world. Who does this to a clutchmate? But the humans had built a place on the edge of the world, and in this place those hatchlings can live, and even be useful."

"Tic's gills didn't come in," observed Garal. "He told us that."

"I have done a wrong thing," said the ambassador. "I must say to Tic Uisine, *I apologize, Tic Uisine.*" The ambassador fell silent then, only the sound of the water echoing off the room's smooth walls.

"What did you do?" asked Ingray finally.

"One of my clutchmates who survived to swim down with me," said the ambassador, "was Geck human. His daughter is Tic Uisine's mother. She is not a clutchmate of mine, but she is like a clutchmate to my clutchmate. Do you understand? Even though she is not my clutchmate, even though she has her own clutch, a different one, still I feel that. My clutchmate is a human and I cannot help but love his daughter, because he does. And humans cannot help but grieve for their hatchlings, when they do not survive, and so when her hatchlings failed to survive swimming down, every one, I could not help but grieve with her. Do you understand? We changed the humans so they could live in the world, and now the humans have changed us. I do not know if we should have let them stay in the world. I do not. But oh, she grieved, once, twice, three times. Do you understand? If her hatchlings had not been able to swim down they would have been sent to the edge of the world. If her hatchlings had gone to the edge of the world, at least they would be alive and she might not grieve so much. I saw from the day she showed Tic to me that he would never survive swimming down. He would be like the rest. Do you understand?"

"No," admitted Ingray, horrified by what she was hearing, though she hadn't really understood any of it. Frightened, though she wasn't sure why. "I don't understand."

"*You* did it," said Garal. "Somehow you made it so that Tic's gills didn't come in."

"I did it," agreed the ambassador. "I did a wrong thing, but if I had not done it, Tic Uisine would not have survived swimming down. If I had allowed him to swim down, he would be dead. I did the thing I did so that at least he could be alive and in the world. But then he stole ships and left the world. It was like him to do such a thing. It was not like Geck to do such a thing. He would not have survived swimming down. No. He would not." Silence. Then, "His mother grieved. My clutchmate grieved. What can live outside the world? There are creatures that live outside the world, but they must be creatures of endless sorrow and pain and death. The conclave before, I went, and did what was needed, and returned to the world. I did not want to be outside the world at all, but to keep the aliens away I must do so. I returned to the world as quickly as could be. I thought to do so again, this time. But we saw our ship, and I thought to myself that Tic Uisine might be there, and it might be that I could bring him back, and he would not be any longer in endless pain and suffering because he would be in the world again, and his mother would cease to grieve. But Tic Uisine was always headstrong. Always! From a larva he was headstrong." The blob paled again, pulled itself under the water, and then oozed back up onto the margin of the pool, water streaming off it. "Perhaps I am headstrong as well. A bit."

"A bit," agreed Ingray, when the ambassador seemed to pause for some response. Garal said nothing, and Ingray thought it might be better if she didn't look to see eir expression.

"Yes," agreed the ambassador. "I followed him here. It may be that in pain and suffering, surrounded with sorrow and death, he does not act as he should. And it is the wrong thing that *I* have done that has caused this. So I follow. I am afraid, I do not want to be out of the world, it is terrible to be out of the world. But I look, I see. I hear, I listen. You are very strange, Ingray Human, but you do not seem to live in endless pain and sorrow. No, you swim here as though this were the world, and live your very strange life as though all was right and well. And I think to myself, is this not where the humans came from? They hatched outside the world; this is their home water. The hatchlings at the edge of the world, do we do a wrong thing, to keep them?"

"I imagine," said Garal, then, "that many of them are quite happy there. It is their home, after all."

"But not all are happy, Garal Ket," said the ambassador. "Not all. And until now I could not think that thought, that anyone could wish to be outside the world. But now I think it. And so I talk to you. I have a thing to say to Tic Uisine, but I think he will not agree to speak to me. And you, Garal Ket, and Ingray Aughskold, you are friends of Tic Uisine. Will you say to him that if he truly wishes to leave the Geck, then I acknowledge his human citizenship, and no longer claim he is subject to the Geck? Will you say to him that I apologize? Will you say to him that he can come back to the edge of the world if he wishes, even if he is not Geck, and that I do not care about the ships, only that he is well? That if he is happy and well outside the world, I will be happy for that, and I will tell his mother that even though he is outside the world, he is well, and he swims in waters better suited to him, and has friends, and she will try to cease to grieve? Will you say this to Tic Uisine?"

"I..." Ingray stopped, not sure what to answer. "I think it would be best if you said this yourself, Ambassador. But maybe he won't want to talk to you at all, and..." She faltered. *And I couldn't blame him for that.* There was no diplomatic way to say it.

"I would not want to talk to me at all," said the ambassador.

"So you say you'll leave him alone," Ingray said, emboldened by the ambassador's frankness, "but you won't leave him alone. You'll just ask us to chase him for you. I think you should send what you just said in a message to him, and he can listen to it or not. And then just leave him alone, unless he says he wants to talk to you."

Silence. Ingray realized that she was clutching at a handful of her already creased and grubby skirts, still tucked up from being in the suit. And, she realized, she was exhausted. And hungry. And she needed a bath. She'd left her hairpins with the vacuum suit; she'd been so miserable and so relieved to be free of it. Garal, quiet beside her, was very likely in similar shape, though she knew em well enough by now to know e'd never give any sign of it if e could help it.

The ambassador said, "I do not like to hear this, Ingray Human. But I will think about it. I will think. Garal Ket, you are Geck. If you wish to stay outside the world, you may. I will have to explain it somehow, back in the world, and there is no way to think about doing that, but we will have to think about doing that, for the sake of the hatchlings at the edge of the world."

"Thank you, Ambassador," e said.

"But do not break the treaty!" insisted the ambassador. "You must study the treaty, and never break it. The treaty keeps aliens out of the world. Ingray Aughskold, I do not understand what is happening on this station, but I think it would not be safe for you to leave the ship at this moment. There is food and water here that is safe for you to eat and drink. There are places for you to sleep. I will think. Later we will talk again." And the green blob pulled itself back into the water, and was gone.

15

A spider mech showed them to a room where one or two of the ridges rising out of the floor seemed somewhat tablelike, and then scurried off—not quite as gracefully as Tic would have, but far more so than the ambassador. A few moments later it returned with three of its arms full of packets and dumped them on a table. "Here is food," the spider mech whistled.

"Thank you." Garal seemed far more self-possessed than Ingray thought possible. "Is there hot water somewhere?"

"You're going to *eat*?" asked Ingray, exhausted and incredulous. The spider mech gestured vaguely toward one end of the room, and left. "With everything that's going on?"

"There's food here now," said Garal. "Everything will be going on whether we eat or not. And it's easier to think things through when you're not hungry and thirsty."

Ingray frowned, and opened her mouth to argue, but then she remembered Garal on the trip to Hwae, saving food. Talking about how difficult it could be to get something to eat in Compassionate Removal.

"You haven't eaten in way too long," Garal said.

She didn't trust herself to answer but went to the back of the room, in the direction the spider mech had indicated. She found a niche in the wall with a basin of body-warm water in it. Gingerly, she scooped up a small handful and tasted it.

"It's plain warm water." Ambassador Tibanvori's voice. Ingray turned to see her come into the room. "They won't make anything hotter, even if you ask."

"What do they eat, then?" asked Garal, sitting down on an extrusion beside the table.

"Raw things," Tibanvori said, with utter disgust. "Or rotted ones." She gestured at the packets on the table. "This is your kind of food, though. We took it on board at Tyr Siilas. I have no idea what any of it is."

"Nutrient blocks," said Ingray. "Those are mostly yeast with flavors." Ambassador Tibanvori wrinkled her nose.

"Noodles," Garal added. "You add hot water to them. I guess warm water will do."

"It won't," said Tibanvori with disdain, sitting down next to Garal.

"And there's serbat." Garal looked over at Ingray. "Instant serbat."

"I could do with some serbat," Ingray said. "Are there

any cups or bowls or…" She trailed off, unable to quite complete the thought.

"Touch the wall above the basin," said Tibanvori. Ingray did, and the surface of the wall contracted away from her fingers, exposing a cavity underneath that held a stack of shallow bowls, some small cups, and a few large, deep spoons.

"It's disgusting, isn't it," said Tibanvori, behind her, and she had to agree at the very least that there was something disturbing about the way the wall had reacted, how it felt. Like a muscle, or at least something biological, not a nice, solid, dependable wall. Tibanvori continued. "Those spoons are only for scooping up water. They eat with their *fingers*." She shuddered. "What's serbat?"

"It's a hot drink," Garal said. "It's serbat."

Ambassador Tibanvori gave em a sideways, disapproving look and then sighed, rose, and came over to where Ingray stood. "Here." She took a stack of bowls and cups out of the cavity and handed them to Ingray, then scooped a few cupfuls of warm water out of the basin. "Whatever serbat is, it can't be worse than poick. The salt water I was telling you about before," she added, to Ingray and Garal's exhausted incomprehension. "The noodles you just have to let sit longer. I don't know about the sort you're used to, the ones I've had are generally not very good cold, but it's better than live sea worms or algae paste."

"I like algae paste," said Ingray, following Tibanvori back to the table. "And I like fish, cooked or not. I don't know about worms, though."

"Trust me, they're horrible." Tibanvori took the dishes out of Ingray's hands. "Sit down." Brusquely, but, Ingray realized, she had been standing there clutching the stack of bowls, unable to form any idea of what to do with them.

"I'm sorry," Ingray said. "I'm very tired."

"Apparently," Tibanvori agreed, tearing open a serbat packet and peering at the contents. "You mix this with water, I take it?"

"Yes," Garal agreed, as Ingray sat. And stared as Tibanvori poured lukewarm water onto noodles, and into cups of serbat powder.

"And I need to know what's happening on the station," said Ingray.

"Not bad," the Radchaai ambassador said, after a sip of warmish serbat. She sat at the table. "Not tea, but not bad. I wonder if I can get some of this shipped back to the Geck homeworld. Tea is hopeless when you can't get hot water. Real tea, the way it should be drunk, I mean."

"I need to know what's happening on the station," said Ingray again. She blinked open her messages, but she was too tired to make much sense out of what she saw. Nothing from Netano at any rate, and nothing from Nuncle Lak. She sent them both a brief, barely coherent message asking for whatever information either of them had.

"Whatever's happening on the station doesn't concern us," Tibanvori said. "Your friend is right, you should eat something. And then see if you can find some news, I suppose. And get some sleep. Though I'm sorry to say there's nothing like civilized sleeping quarters here. These people, the ones who live in orbit, they generally just lie down on the ground wherever they are. This room"—she gestured around with the cup of serbat still in her hand—"is a concession to foreign habits. Even the Geck humans on the station generally eat squatting or standing. Though I guess you don't need anything like comfort or manners when you're just shoveling slimy animals into your mouth with your bare hands."

"I can't imagine why the Geck ambassador doesn't like you," Garal said.

Tibanvori made a sharp, sardonic *hah*. "Well, I don't much like her, if it comes to that."

Ingray sat, and took her own cup of lukewarm serbat. She would know when Nuncle Lak's reply came. There wasn't much else she could do right now anyway. "Then why are you still the human ambassador?"

"The people who appointed me were not friends of mine. Or my family's. We have a figure of speech, I don't know if you have it." She took another swallow of serbat and used the spoon handle to poke experimentally at a bowl of slowly rehydrating noodles. "Ah, this may be it—kicked upstairs. Being the representative of all humans to an entire alien race may sound important, but not when that alien race is the Geck. They care nothing about what goes on away from their own planet, and only pay any attention when it's a matter of keeping the rest of the universe out. They don't want any communication or really any sort of relationship at all with humans, so there's nothing to do unless

301

a conclave should happen along, and even then there's really no point to my office. I don't need to be at this AI conclave, not really. I had nothing to do at the last one, when the Rrrrr were admitted to the treaty. I might as well have stayed away this time. I only insisted on coming along because there might be civilized food there. So being ambassador for humans to the Geck may sound like a wonderful opportunity, an important job for the most distinguished and accomplished of diplomats, but in reality it's just a way of disposing me and my career in the most insulting way possible."

"So why don't you quit?" asked Ingray, still baffled.

"I do. Every year. And every year I'm told that since my service has been so invaluable and I myself am irreplaceable, the Translators Office refuses to accept my resignation." She poked at the noodles again and frowned. "The other thing that might be at the Conclave is someone who'll help me get away from this hole of a post." She looked up, then, at Garal. "I don't think you realize what you've gotten yourself into. You may find yourself wishing you were back in prison."

"No," said Garal. "I won't."

"Are you sure you want to go back to the Radch?" asked Ingray. "The news right now..."

"It's my home," Tibanvori said. "It's civilization. Where else would I go? Certainly not here. As you already know, there was shooting on the docks just the other day. Not our part of it, as I said we've been left alone, thank the gods. But this is hardly a safe or civilized place."

"Do you have any idea at all what's happening now?" asked Garal. "I know you said it doesn't concern us, but surely you've heard something."

Ambassador Tibanvori sighed. "The last I heard, Station Security had managed to confine, who are they, the Omkem? The Omkem are confined to their end of the docks and part of one level of the station itself. I don't think your Station Security was very heavily armed, so unless there was already a heavy military presence here, either the Omkem commander must be extremely stupid, or taking over this station isn't what she's after, and what she's done so far is just one step of another project entirely."

"Like what?" asked Ingray.

Tibanvori shoved a nutrient block across the table toward Garal, and another toward Ingray. "How should I know? I don't live here. What would the Omkem want from you?"

"Access to our gate to Byeit," said Garal.

"Or Tyr," Ingray added.

"Well, there you go," said Tibanvori. "I imagine they either want to threaten the station—or someone on it—to guarantee your acceptance of whatever terms they're looking for, or this is a distraction from the real threat that's already on its way here. Not a good time to move, with the Geck here, but they can't have known the ambassador would have some incomprehensible alien fit over a stolen ship, and the distances involved make it impossible to do things like this on the spur of the moment. Probably the forces here have to act based on when more ships will arrive, and those will be, as I've said, already on their way."

"We have to tell someone!" Ingray cried. Almost alarmed enough to stand up, exhausted as she was.

Tibanvori waved dismissively. "If military authorities here haven't already figured all of that out, no amount of warning will help them. Eat." She nudged the nutrient block nearest Ingray. "Get some sleep. Then decide what you're going to do. You"—she turned to Garal—"have already made your decision."

"Yes," agreed Garal. "The ambassador is right, Ingray. There's nothing you can do right now, and you'll make better decisions when you've had some sleep."

She managed a few bites of nutrient block and a mouthful or two of cold, soggy noodles, and then found a dark chamber nearby to lie down in. The floor wasn't soft, not exactly, but it was surprisingly comfortable. She was asleep in less than a minute.

And dreamed endlessly of being in the vacuum suit, of seeing only black through the helmet visor, the sound of her breath loud in her ears. She knew she was dreaming, could feel that she was somehow not all the way asleep. Could sense the darkened chamber around her, thought every now and then she could hear voices somewhere else on the ship, and yet the dream was still there, she was still prisoned in the ill-fitting suit.

She woke. Blinked for the time. She had slept for far longer than she'd thought; at some point the vacuum suit dream must have trailed off and she'd finally slept deeply. The floor had shifted underneath her, had flexed to support her the way her bed at home would have. She lay there a moment, and then blinked open her messages and news again.

Ambassador Nevol had said the Federacy mechs were confined to part of one level of the station. In fact they had taken control of the System Lareum, and the nearly adjoining First Assembly offices and chambers, and they also held the path from there to where their ships were docked. It was an inconveniently long route that went away from the closest exit out of the docks and doubled back on itself, and for a moment Ingray wondered why they hadn't taken the straightest way. She knew there was one—when she and Garal had arrived, just days ago, they'd taken it.

She looked closer at the information the news services were giving out. There was doubtless a lot they weren't saying, but they had carefully mapped out the stretch of bays where the Omkem freighters were docked, and marked the location of the two freighters with bright orange dots. And down the way toward the more convenient exit a green dot marked another ship.

The Geck. It was the bay where the Geck ship was docked. This ship, which Ingray was on. The back of her neck prickled. If she went out onto the docks she could probably see them. Unless System Defense had that way blocked off by now, which she imagined they did. But so close.

She didn't need to read the accompanying report to realize that the Omkem had been wary of interfering with the Geck in any way. Just the ship sitting there— and possibly several spider mechs or Geck humans going back and forth on business—had been enough to make them go the long way around to their goal.

There wasn't much other information available. Station residents should remain calm. Hwae System Defense was in control of the situation. Station Administration and Hwae System Defense would provide fuller information soon; in the meantime residents were asked to keep local communications clear for official use, and to refrain from spreading false information. All the news services were sending out the same exact statement.

Everything else Ingray found was gossip and rumor. The station's hull had been breached, killing dozens of people. The hull hadn't actually been breached, but emergency doors had been triggered. Several hundred children had been evacuated from the lareum in the nick of time. No, dozens of children were dead or captive or otherwise missing. The Omkem troops had shot at least sixteen Hwaeans on their way out of the docks—there was an image of a man lying on the ground in what looked like a docks corridor, blood smeared across the floor beside his head. Ingray blinked that away, quickly.

Netano wouldn't have been on the docks. Netano had come here to be seen involving herself with the Geck's unexpected presence. She might well have been in one of the First Assembly offices. Nuncle Lak hadn't replied to Ingray's earlier message—which might mean e hadn't had time to look at eir messages, or might mean e had nothing yet to report. Or it might mean communications with Hwae Station had been crushed under everyone in Hwaean space urgently trying to contact anyone and everyone they knew might be on the station, all at the same time, and a message from Nuncle Lak might take a while getting through.

None of that was reassuring. And no doubt Netano's messages were flooded with people asking if she was all right, but surely she would understand if Ingray was one of those people.

She sent the message, a quick query that she knew would go straight to Netano's personal attention. All Mama had to do to reply was blink an automated acknowledgment, that was all Ingray had asked for.

Nothing. Maybe Netano was asleep? Maybe she was perfectly fine but too busy to spare a thought for Ingray.

And then the message from Nuncle Lak arrived.

She had to get off the ship and onto the station. They had to let her off, she was human. She had to find someone—a spider mech, or the Geck ambassador herself—and tell them that she had to leave. She scrambled to her feet and headed back toward the room they'd eaten in.

"Garal!" she called, coming in the door. "Garal, I need to get off the ship."

Garal sat at the table extrusion eating a bowl of soggy noodles, a bit rumpled-looking but otherwise awake and alert. "Why?" e asked. "Has something happened?"

"The Federacy seized the System Lareum and the First Assembly Chambers," Ingray said. "And Mama was in the lareum. She's still there."

"How do you know this?" Garal asked, quite reasonably. "There's nothing on the official news the Geck are receiving but warnings to take shelter and stay there."

"I finally got a message from Nuncle Lak," she replied. "E says they probably wanted to take the First Assembly captive while it was in session, but the Geck being here forced them to take a longer route than they'd planned on. By the time they got there the Assembly Chambers were evacuated. But the lareum hadn't been, not all the way. And Mama was there to meet a crèche trip from Arsamol District."

A moment of silence. Then Garal asked, "And the children? Are they still in the lareum, too?"

"Yes! Most of the children are there, and Mama and a couple other people. They have the Prolocutor of the First Assembly, Prolocutor Dicat. And some of the lareum staff."

"If they couldn't get hold of the First Assembly," Garal pointed out, "Prolocutor Dicat is a good second best. Though I imagine it's the senior Dicat they have."

"Yes," Ingray acknowledged. "E was meeting another crèche trip. Eir heir was in the Chambers, but he got clear." The First Prolocutor's heir, named decades ago, had been attending to prolocutorial business for years. In terms of Assembly affairs the prolocutor might as well not be captive at all.

"Sit down," said Garal. "Eat something. Have some poick. It's..." E wrinkled eir nose. "I suspect it's an acquired taste. But sit down and eat something and make a plan before you go charging off. Netano probably isn't in immediate danger, and if she is, well, you won't be able to help."

Ingray had no intention of eating anything. But she needed to talk to Garal. She sat down. "I already have a plan. I don't think they came here to take a crècheful of children hostage. They were after the First Assembly. Nuncle Lak says there hasn't been any communication from the Omkem—or there hadn't been when e sent the message, but System Defense is expecting them to make demands."

Garal reached across the table to set a cup down in front of her, and then a bowl of still-stiff noodles in a pool of tepid water. "I'm sure I'll be on any list of demands. Not anywhere near the top, of course. Still."

"Probably," Ingray admitted. "Nuncle Lak didn't say. But you're Geck now, so they can't have you. But I'm the one who brought you here, and I was actually there when Zat was murdered."

E stared at her for a moment, then said, "You want to exchange yourself for Netano."

"And the children."

Garal was silent a moment, regarding her. "Do you think they would agree to that? I don't doubt Hwae would be willing to make some pretty big concessions for the sake of those children. Why would the Omkem let them go just to have you?"

Ingray had already thought about that. "There are at least two crèches there—the one my mother met, and the one that Prolocutor Dicat was there with. So anywhere from forty to a hundred children or more. Even if the crèche caretakers are with them, that's a lot of frightened children to deal with. I don't know if there's any kind of negotiating going on, but the longer it takes..."

"The more the Omkem have to deal with a lot of tired, terrified children."

"And the longer System Defense has to come up with some way to free those children that doesn't involve any kind of negotiations." Ingray took a careful breath. "The longer it takes, the more danger they'll be in. The Omkem are going to want something important in exchange for them, but I don't think System Defense will trade anything *really* important. They might not even be talking to the Omkem about it at all."

"They probably aren't," agreed Garal. "It's not a good idea to let your enemies know that they can just take some hostages and get whatever they want from you."

"Right," agreed Ingray, with a shiver. "But I could offer it myself. Last I knew the Omkem ambassador was still complaining about Hevom." And about Garal being sent to the Geck, but e already knew that. "I was there when Zat died. I can tell them what I know. I'll tell them they can have me, if they let the children go, and Mama. She hasn't named her heir yet; if anything happens to her..."

"This isn't actually about Hevom," Garal said. "Zat's death is just a convenient excuse, a justification. It's the

First Assembly they were aiming at. The First Assembly represents Hwae Station. And the six Hwaean out-stations. And what residents there are on Zenith Platform. So whoever controls the First Assembly controls access to the gates." And access to the planet's resources from space. "It's probably not a coincidence that they've done this during one of the times the Assembly is meeting in person. Excellency Zat's only been dead a few days. The freighters the Omkem troops came in docked a week ago, and freighters aren't exactly fast. They'll have left Enthen weeks before that. Having you won't make any difference. And once they have you..."

"I have to try." Ingray didn't know how else to explain. "All those children."

"You're not responsible for their safety," Garal pointed out. "If they're even still alive."

They very possibly weren't. "And Netano is my mother."

"She is," agreed Garal. "I know. You and I are both out of a public crèche. Any little bit our parents gave us, it's everything we have. Our families expect us to be grateful for it, and so does everyone else. And we do feel it. I felt it for so much longer than I probably should have, and Netano never did anything to you even remotely like what Ethiat Budrakim did to me. From the moment you joined her household you knew what you owed Netano. And she hasn't given her name to Danach yet, so if something happens to her now, that's the end of Netano. But if something happens to you, that's the end of *you*. Ethiat Budrakim aside, I'm under the impression that quite a lot of parents would actually prefer to risk themselves to protect their children, rather than the other way around."

"Yes," agreed Ingray, her stomach heaving with an anxiety she'd been trying to ignore since she'd waked. "But that's exactly why…"

"And you were thinking about leaving," Garal cut in. "You've been thinking about leaving the Aughskolds. I know you have. You didn't do all this"—e gestured toward emself—"thinking it would get you into Danach's place. Or, I imagine you sort of hoped it would but you'd never have seriously thought it would happen."

"No." Ingray's face heated with embarrassment. She had barely even admitted that to herself; it was humiliating to hear Garal say it straight out. But also a relief, in a strange way she couldn't quite explain.

"No one expects you to do anything like this," continued Garal. "Least of all Netano. And if she does, well…" E waved away any concern for Netano's opinion in that case.

"I couldn't really afford it," Ingray said. "It turns out no amount of money is enough to get any Tyr broker to break someone out of Compassionate Removal. I didn't know that at the time but I should have realized it."

Garal went suddenly still for the briefest moment, then finished lowering eir cup of poick to the table. Ingray might not have even noticed, if she hadn't gotten to know em as well as she had.

"Are you working for Tyr? Or, were you? I guess you can't be now, if you're Geck." No reply. "I've been thinking about it. I imagine they thought I'd thaw you out when we got to Hwae and then you'd do... something that would benefit them? But Tic wouldn't let you on board that way, and you didn't want anything to do with whatever it was I was planning. You didn't even want to talk to me when I found you at the Incomers Office. And there was nowhere there to sleep and nothing for you to eat, but you could have at least cadged a meal out of me or Tic, or tried to." And if there was one thing Garal had been obsessive about—still was— it was access to food. "So why did you wait until next morning?"

"I'm not working for Tyr," e said. "I told them I wouldn't work for them. I told them I wasn't going back to Hwae no matter what they did. And they told me that since I didn't technically exist and there was no one who knew or cared that I was on Tyr Siilas except you—and I'd cut that avenue off myself—they would be happy to toss me out an airlock if I didn't agree to whatever it was they wanted. And I thought maybe once I got that identity in my hands I might have at least something to work with." E gave the tiniest of smiles. "Well, you know how that worked out. I couldn't leave when the Executory put Tic's ship under interdict. And by the time I might have been able to, I decided it would be better to stay with you."

"What did they want?" asked Ingray. "No, I know what it was. They wanted you to embarrass Prolocutor Budrakim."

"Among other things," agreed Garal. "That much

at least I didn't mind doing. But I told them I wouldn't work for them, and I haven't been. And even if I were—and if I weren't Geck now—it wouldn't do any good. They won't come charging in to help me, or offer any kind of assistance at all. Even when they were trying to convince me to work for them they wouldn't make any promises to help me out if I landed in trouble here. Not even as a lie to get me to do what they wanted, right?" No, of course not. Among the few serious crimes the Tyr recognized, breaking a contract—even an implied one—was among the worst. "They knew they didn't have to offer me anything. The Tyr will act if they think it's in the best interest of the Executory, and not before, or for any other reason. If it helps, I'm sure they've tried other things than just sending me. I'm sure there are Tyr agents on this station right now. The question is who they are, and what good they'll do you."

"And the answer to that last," agreed Ingray, "is not much unless it suits their own goals."

"And the Geck won't interfere," said Garal. "It would be a potentially serious breach of the treaty. And that means that I can't do anything. It also means you're safe here. And if your mother is even a half-decent parent, she'll want you to stay safe."

"But see, listen," insisted Ingray. "The Omkem wanted to be able to hold the First Assembly hostage, so they could control the system gates. I'm sure that's what they were after. But they couldn't do that, and now what they've got is the empty Assembly Chambers, the lareum, and some hostages. But why are they in the System Lareum to begin with?"

"It's right next to the Assembly Chambers," Garal pointed out.

"Right," agreed Ingray. "But what I'm saying is, they've had to change their plans." Garal frowned. "Don't you see?" continued Ingray into eir incomprehension. "What's in the lareum? All the things that tell us we're Hwaean. The *Rejection of Further Obligations to Tyr*, which tells us that Hwae exists, and what it is. And what's in the First Assembly Chambers, even after the representatives are evacuated?"

"Oh." Understanding, finally, in Garal's expression. "The Assembly Bell." The bell was, in fact, a large ceramic bowl from the days when the First Assembly had been the only Assembly, and had only just begun meeting, only just begun to contemplate ending their indebtedness to Tyr. Every Hwaean knew that it had been used to pickle cabbage, before the sound of the spoon against its side had become the signal of the official start of Assembly business. "But, Ingray, it's just a vestige. The Omkem don't care about vestiges."

"They do," insisted Ingray. "What else was Zat looking for, in the parkland? And I know you said people outside Hwae laugh at our vestiges, but it wouldn't need to be something important to them. Just important to us. And the First Assembly can't legally meet without the Assembly Bell. It's not the same as having control of the Assembly itself, but it's something. And now they're in this and can't go back, the Omkem probably at least want to have *something*."

"The *Rejection* is certainly a forgery," said Garal. "You know that by now. The Assembly Bell..." E hesitated. "The Assembly Bell is from the right time period, and yes, the first Assembly meetings were small and somewhat makeshift, and it wouldn't surprise me if someone banged a spoon against a cabbage-pickling crock to bring those meetings to order. But, Ingray, besides the Assembly Bell, have you ever seen an actual crock for pickling cabbage?"

"No," admitted Ingray. "But I don't see what..."

"They're not shaped like that," said Garal. "They mostly have straight sides. Or mouths smaller than the container itself. The idea is to seal off the cabbage, right? It won't ferment right in the air. So either the story about pickling cabbage isn't true, or the Assembly Bell isn't the actual original Assembly Bell."

"But it's the Assembly Bell *now*," insisted Ingray. "And I guess if something happened to it the First Assembly would find some replacement. Just like if anything happened to the *Rejection of Obligations* that's in the lareum, that wouldn't mean Hwae would suddenly not exist. But the Omkem aren't here to make us not exist, they're not interested in invading. They just want to make the First Assembly do what they want. And if they've taken all the things that make the First Assembly the First Assembly..."

"To most Hwaeans, at least," agreed Garal. "I see

your point. But what difference will it make if you're in there?"

Ingray took a breath. "So," she said, and took another breath. "Maybe we could steal it back."

"We." Garal's voice was even as ever, but Ingray heard a trace of bitterness. "You've forgotten that I'm Geck."

"No, I haven't. I just thought you could maybe give me some advice. Some suggestions."

"You've also forgotten that I'm not actually a thief." E pushed eir bowl of noodles aside.

"No, I know you're not. But you know thieves, don't you. When we met, you said you were a forger. You're not, but the best kind of lie has some truth in it. You were talking about a real person. Someone you'd met in Compassionate Removal. You knew enough about em to know eir work when you saw it in Mama's house. You've never been a forger but you learned things about forgery from the people you've known. You've never been a thief. But you know things. You can give me advice. It won't break the treaty, we're just talking over breakfast." She picked up the cup Garal had set in front of her when she had first sat down. Took a sip. Tasted lukewarm salt water and made a face. "Ugh. Is this poick?"

"Like I said, I'm pretty sure it's an acquired taste. And you're right, I learned things in Compassionate Removal, but not anything that will help you. The people who pull off the kind of theft I was accused of—the kind of theft you're proposing now—by and large they do it with overwhelming physical force. Which our own forces would have used by now if they thought it would work, and you don't need me for advice about that sort of thing. Where a theft isn't carried out by force, it's an inside job, or else the people responsible for guarding the vestiges were manipulated in some way. It's not like entertainments, where there are ancient alien artifacts with alarm-canceling powers, or elaborate plans." E took a sip of eir own poick and grimaced. "Well, sometimes there are elaborate plans, but those almost always go wrong somewhere and everyone involved ends up under arrest."

"I don't want an elaborate plan then," countered Ingray, in what she hoped was a calm and reasonable voice. She had wanted an elaborate plan. She had wanted assistance from Tyr. Or anyone who might give it. "Just one that works. And if I can't do that, at least Mama and those children will be out of danger."

"What does your nuncle Lak think about this potential plan of yours?"

"Are you kidding?" Ingray used her fingers to fish some noodles out of the bowl in front of her. "I haven't said anything to em about it. E'd probably tell me not to do it."

"The more I know your nuncle, the better I like em," observed Garal.

"If I always consulted with Nuncle Lak, you'd still be in Compassionate Removal," Ingray pointed out. Put the noodles in her mouth and immediately wished she hadn't. She wasn't sure she could eat at all, and the cold, soggy noodles weren't remotely appetizing, but she made herself chew and swallow. "I'm glad you're not."

Garal sighed and closed eir eyes. "You're going to do this anyway, aren't you."

"Yes," Ingray said, managing to sound halfway certain of herself. "I am."

16

Ingray's name was enough to get her the attention of Over Captain Utury, of Hwae System Defense. The over captain met her in a small room somewhere on the station. Utury was short and broad, imposing despite her lack of height, her blue-and-gold System Defense uniform vivid against the plain beige of the walls and the stiff plastic bench and table.

"Absolutely not," she said, when Ingray had explained what she proposed to do. "We're trying to get civilians away from danger, not send more in. And to be entirely frank, I only agreed to meet with you now because my superiors would prefer not to have your mother upset with them. Just personally, I understand how you feel right now, but the best way to get any hostages to safety is to stop wasting my time and let me do my job." And then added, belatedly, "Respectfully. Miss."

"But, Over Captain..." Ingray began.

"No." Over Captain Utury didn't raise her voice, but her tone cut right through Ingray's words. "I have met with you, I have heard your request, and I have denied it. You will go immediately to the nearest civilian shelter and stay there. If I see you again I will have you arrested, I don't care who your mother is. *Do I make myself clear?*"

Ingray felt tears well. But she would not cry. She wouldn't. "Yes, ma'am."

"Good," said Over Captain Utury, and turned and left the room.

A few seconds later a soldier came in. "I'm here to escort you to a shelter, miss."

"Oh," said Ingray, and she couldn't stop the tears anymore. She'd failed. All she could do now was sit in some shelter somewhere, with people she didn't even know, and wait. "Is there..." She sniffled, and wiped her eyes with the back of her hand. "Is there a restroom I could use first?"

"I have to take you straight to a shelter, miss," said the soldier. "Over Captain's orders."

"I know," Ingray said. "I just need to wash my face. And... you know."

"There's a restroom right behind you, miss," said the soldier. "I'll be waiting right here for you."

The restroom was tiny and cramped. Ingray shut the door. Blew her nose, washed her hands. Splashed some water on her face. She could do this, she could go to the shelter and wait. She had no other choice. She'd done her best.

A hairpin clattered into the wash basin. She grabbed it before it could slide down the drain.

Movement caught the corner of her vision. She looked around. Looked up. A black spider mech clung to the ceiling, its many stalked eyes staring directly at her. "So," it whistled, quietly, "I hear you want to break into the System Lareum."

Ingray could only stare.

"It's me, Tic," the spider mech said. "I can get you close to the lareum, where if System Defense doesn't stop you in time, you can propose a trade. If you really want to do that. I don't think it's a good idea."

"I do want to do that!" said Ingray. Very quietly, mindful of the soldier outside.

"As far as getting hold of the *Rejection of Obligations* and the Assembly Bell, I can't make any promises. I can't even suggest any plans until I know where everything is, how it's laid out, and what's happening. It'll take a while to figure all that out. And in the meantime you'll be in danger."

"Tic!" whispered Ingray urgently, "I don't have time to talk about this! I just need to do it!"

"All right," said Tic. "Then let's do this."

The façade of the System Lareum was two levels high, though the wide doors were only half as tall. They were mottled gray, scorched and scored, panels of what was allegedly part of the hull of the original Hwae Station. At the moment they were shut, the open space in front of them—black-and-green-tiled, high-ceilinged and echoing, and nearly always thronged with visitors and passersby—was empty. Or it looked empty—Tic had told her that Hwaean System Defense was all around, and there were certainly Omkem military mechs behind the half dozen broad closed doors of the lareum.

Well, here she was, and the longer she delayed the more danger she was in. Of course, she was already in a good deal of danger just standing here.

She took a deep breath. "My name is Ingray Aughskold," she called. In Yiir because she didn't know if any of the Omkem would understand Bantia. "I'm Representative Netano Aughskold's daughter. I was there when Excellency Zat was murdered, I can tell you what really happened. Send the children out unharmed, and my mother, too, and you can have me instead."

Silence. Well, even if the Federacy ultimately accepted the trade, they'd want to think about it first.

"Miss Aughskold!" That hadn't come from the lareum entrance—the voice was behind her. She turned her head. A small boxy cleaning mech trundled a meter or so closer to her, and stopped. "Miss Aughskold, what are you doing?" Ingray stared. "The over captain didn't think it was a good idea to send an obviously armed mech here at this particular time. We're pretty sure there are Omkem mechs right inside that entrance. This isn't a safe place to be, miss."

"I didn't think it was," Ingray said. Despite her best intentions, her voice shook a little.

"Then what are you doing here, miss?"

"I thought it was obvious. I'm exchanging myself for

those children the Omkem are holding, and my mother. Or trying to."

"How did you get out of the civilian shelter?" asked the cleaning mech. "For that matter, how did you get *here*?"

"I walked." Which was mostly true.

"We can't let you do this, miss. I'm going to ask you to walk with me back behind our line. If we're very lucky there won't be any trouble."

"Sorry." She managed to make her tone careless, but her voice still shook. "I'm staying here." But she was becoming less and less convinced that this was a good idea.

"Then I'm afraid we'll have to pick you up and carry you out of here, miss."

"Oh, won't that look good on the news services," Ingray remarked. "System Defense manhandling me out of the way, when all I want is to rescue children. And my mama!" Her voice broke at that last, and she swallowed hard. If she lost her balance now, if she wept or shouted, she would collapse entirely, she was sure of it.

They'll try to remove you, Tic had said. *Be stubborn. If you haven't changed your mind, that is. I'll do what I can to stop them.* But Tic had left her when she'd walked out into the middle of the empty tiled floor. And she didn't know what there was that he could do against System Defense.

"You're assuming you'll be allowed to tell the news services any of this," the cleaning mech pointed out.

"You just try and stop me," said Ingray.

The cleaning mech was silent. Ingray made herself turn again and look at the doors to the lareum, still closed. Still silent. Wanted to close her eyes, but she was feeling dizzy and she was afraid she'd fall over if she did that. Instead she counted her breaths—it had worked in the vacuum suit, so maybe it would keep her from panicking here.

After what had to be five minutes—Ingray had cut her connection with Hwae's system communications, and refused to summon up the time in her vision—the cleaning mech said, "The over captain wants you to know that she's not responsible for anything that happens to you, miss."

"Of course not," replied Ingray, still staring at the lareum doors.

"And if you survive this, miss, she'll see you up for trial."

Trial. Well, of course. She was interfering with a System Defense operation. And it didn't matter. What mattered was getting into the lareum. Getting Netano and the children out. And the vestiges, if she was that lucky. "I look forward to it," she managed to say, though not very convincingly. She waited for the cleaning mech to do something more—try to persuade her to change her mind, approach and attempt to physically remove her—but it did nothing. After a few minutes, she heard it trundle away. Then silence.

She was alone. *I can't come in with you,* Tic had told her. *If there's even the smallest chance they'll detect my presence, your life will be in danger. I'll have to find my own way in*. Presumably that was what he was doing now.

After a while her still-trembling legs grew tired, and she sat carefully down on the floor. What if the Omkem didn't take her offer? What if she'd done all this for nothing?

It didn't matter. It didn't matter that she felt stupid and scared sitting out here all alone. And at least her hairpins were staying in—that was something, anyway. Of course, it was probably because the spider mech had put them in, while they'd discussed what passed as a plan.

She gave in to her impulse to blink on the time—nearly two hours had passed since she'd come here. Blinked it off again. There was no point staring at the seconds as they flashed by.

With a click, one of the wide lareum doors opened, just a crack, and a voice said, in heavily accented Yiir, "We will make the exchange. You will bring nothing. You will be searched. Stand up."

Slowly, carefully, Ingray got to her feet.

The door opened wider, and a line of children slowly filed out, two dozen of them, in rumpled beige tunics and trousers. A public crèche then, and probably a station crèche, since some of the children were quite small (and sniffling and tearstained), and a visit to the System Lareum didn't involve travel if you were already on the station.

One small child turned their head to look at Ingray. Sniffled. Opened their mouth. An older child behind them hissed, "Shhhh! Keep walking!" Quiet and urgent. Tears welling.

At the end of the line of beige-uniformed children came Netano. Despite having been a prisoner in the lareum for the past few days, she seemed only slightly disheveled—her skirts and jacket just a bit creased and rumpled, no hair at all escaping her braids. Ingray bit down on the cry of *Mama* that wanted to come out of her mouth. As if she had heard anyway, Netano looked directly at her but did not change her bland, neutral expression. If Ingray had been younger, with a guiltier conscience, she'd have shivered to see that. Now, older, she knew that expression concealed any strong emotion Netano needed to hide, not just anger and disappointment.

"Exchange now," the voice from behind the door said, in Yiir, loud and toneless. "Walk forward. If there is any difficulty you will be shot." Without looking back, Netano kept walking.

For a moment Ingray wondered why they'd let so many children go before they were sure she was in their hands. But there was no time to wonder. She walked toward her mother.

Behind Netano was another, shorter line of children. They all looked to be about eight or nine years old, and Ingray recognized their blue-and-yellow uniforms. And of course. Netano had been in the lareum meeting a crèche from Arsamol District. The same crèche Ingray herself had come from.

They walked toward each other, slow and measured. A few steps from meeting Netano in the middle, Ingray, unable to help herself, said, "Mama." She wasn't going to cry. She *wasn't.*

"Ingray, dear," said Netano, drawing closer. "I won't forget this."

I won't forget this. A chill went down Ingray's back. Whether from the ambiguity of Netano's words, or from the realization of what it was Ingray was doing, she didn't know.

And then Netano was past, and Ingray was walking past the children, each one of whom turned their eyes in Ingray's direction but did not turn their head or hesitate in their steady walk forward.

Inside the lareum doors stood a hulking, dark gray mech with a wide, boxy body, four jointed legs, and a large gun in one of its three upper appendages. But Ingray could keep her face bland and neutral, just like Netano. Well, almost like Netano; Ingray had never managed to seem quite as confidently in control as her mother could. But it didn't matter, she didn't have to be her mother, never would, never could be Netano. She was only Ingray Aughskold, but she had something these Omkem wanted, and she had gotten the children clear of this. And Netano, so that she could appoint her heir and be sure her name would go on. Ingray hadn't done that for Danach, but she hoped he would be conscious, every moment of his life from here on forward, just how much he owed Ingray after this.

Two more mechs waited farther in, past the vestiges of the lareum's former chief caretakers, past the wide strip of linen on which the lareum's charter had been written in the hand of the Prolocutor of the First Assembly at the time. Past the kiosk that, for a fee, would print out a numbered and dated entry card. For a moment Ingray wondered if the hulking, armed mechs would let her stop at the kiosk. Surely a vestige of this occasion would be worth something—Danach would no doubt pay her good money for it. It would be worth more with some kind of personal impression, though. She should sign the card, and get the Omkem to do so as well. She imagined one of these big gray military mechs, holding the thin cardboard with one appendage and a brush with another, and a giant gun in the third, and bit her lip to keep from giggling. Or from crying, she wasn't sure which. Tic should sign it, too. Was he nearby, even if she couldn't see any sign of a spider mech? But no, he'd said he would find a different way in.

Off to the side of the kiosk, a jumbled heap of blue-and-purple sticks and boxes. No, it was a half dozen or more lareum guide mechs, smashed to pieces. She didn't think they were the sort of mech that was ever controlled remotely, but the Omkem weren't taking any chances, it appeared.

"Ingray Aughskold," said one of the waiting mechs, "come this way." In almost impenetrably accented Bantia, which Ingray thought was odd. The mech behind her had spoken in Yiir, and all the Omkem she'd ever met had spoken Yiir and almost never Bantia.

But none of that mattered. She followed, not looking to see if the mech from the entrance came behind her.

The mech brought her directly to the center of the lareum, a long, wide hall lined with vestiges of Hwae's founding, paper or linen or groupings of clay tiles on the dark green walls, and between them, or dotted along the length of the hall, the sort of vestiges that did not hang well: cups, serbat decanters, a necklace or two, even a pair of sandals, all cased in glass and standing on plinths.

At the far end of the hall the *Rejection of Further Obligations* hung, suspended vertically in a clear case that rested on its own long, low diorite plinth. From this angle, walking down the length of the hall, Ingray could only see it edge-on but she could recite the words painted on it without even half a thought. *Let this document certify that the Assembled Representatives of the People of Hwae*... It was those words that mattered, wasn't it? Even if Garal was right and this particular document was a fake.

Full of vestiges as it was, and signs and notices so that even children could understand what they were visiting, the long room seemed oddly empty without the overlays of text and images that Ingray would have seen if she were connected to Hwae's communications network. She found herself blinking to summon them, but of course nothing happened. She'd cut off her own access before coming here, but she knew from the news service reports that there were no communications coming from the prisoners in the lareum. No doubt the Omkem had managed to prevent it somehow.

There were five mechs here, two like the ones Ingray had already seen, one at each entrance to the room, and a third in the center of the hall, standing over two people who sat on the buff-tiled floor, watching her approach.

331

One of those people, a stout, gray-haired neman, Ingray recognized immediately as the Prolocutor of the First Assembly, Prolocutor Dicat. The other, much younger, not much older than Ingray in fact, thinner but obviously taller even sitting, was...it took Ingray a moment to place her. Yes, she was the appointed heir of the senior keeper of post-Tyr vestiges.

Near the end of the *Rejection*'s case stood two smaller mechs that looked more like humans than machines. They both turned toward Ingray as she approached. "Miss Aughskold," said one. "Please stay where you are." In Bantia.

She stopped. The smaller of the two more humanlike mechs walked toward her. It didn't move like a mech at all, and she realized that it wasn't, that neither of them was a mech. They were both humans in dark gray armor. Like a lot of Omkem they were much taller than Ingray was used to, and the armor gave them an intimidating bulk besides.

The second armored human said something Ingray couldn't understand.

"Miss Aughskold," said the first, still in Bantia, "would you please remove your hairpins?"

"Certainly," Ingray replied. Her voice didn't even shake the tiniest bit, she was glad to hear. She pulled out her hairpins and held them out to the armored person who'd spoken to her. "What should I do with them?"

The first armored person spoke again. She wasn't sure what language it might be.

"Please set them on the floor, Miss Aughskold," said the other, "and step away from them."

She bent to lay the pins on the floor, then straightened. She had a little travel translation utility that supposedly functioned away from Hwae's network. She'd used it a few times during her stay on Tyr Siilas. It wasn't very good, and she hadn't had a chance to load it with a dictionary, but maybe she could still use it. Maybe it would recognize this language. It would be better than nothing.

The first armored person stared at the small pile of hairpins, then spoke. "Floor them apart," said a flat voice in Ingray's ear.

The second bent and tried to scoop up the pins, but three of them tumbled out of their armored hand. "Fiddlesticks," they said. According to the translation utility, anyway. The armor on their hands retracted, disappearing somewhere into the figure's arms. Then they reached up and pulled off their head—no, pulled off a helmet. Revealing a pale-skinned man with thick dark hair and a genial expression. "I don't know how these soldiers do this." And, to a disapproving exclamation from the first armored figure, "Fie, Commander. Absence was your own mouth. I absent soldier." He scooped up the hairpins in his bare hand, stood, and smiled at Ingray. "Excuse me a moment, Miss Aughskold. Please stay right there." He went, then, over to one of the mechs at the nearer entrance, which popped open a wide panel in the side of its body, and the man dropped the hairpins inside and pushed the panel closed again. Came back over to Ingray. "Please don't be afraid. There's no reason this has to be unpleasant."

"I wasn't afraid, until you said that," replied Ingray.

He made a small *huh*. Not a laugh, not quite. "The commander and I have a few things to discuss. But can I ask you a question? Do you think this"—he gestured to the *Rejection of Obligations*—"is genuine?"

"I...I've always thought it was." Ingray supposed she should be glad to have such immediate confirmation of her guess that the Federacy troops, denied control of the First Assembly, had turned their attention to Hwae's most important vestiges. Even after the things Garal had said, the *Rejection of Obligations* was still very nearly the most important vestige in the system.

He turned to the commander. "Perceive. As my own mouth."

"In the ordinary remain," said the commander. "The ordinary is not. The attention is, the argument is prolocutor. Doubt required and the level lowered. I theorize look elsewhere."

"Remain," said the man who had spoken to Ingray in Bantia. "Insufficiency the days before, insufficiency this moment."

"Who are you?" she asked the man. "And why are you doing this?"

"My name is Chenns. I'm a...you would say I was an ethnographer. I specialize in Hwaean cultures. And that"—he gestured toward the other armored figure—"is Commander Hatqueban. And as for what we're doing here, I'm surprised to hear you of all people ask that question, Miss Aughskold. I knew Excellency Zat. I can't say I liked her much. She was quite arrogant, and contemptuous of those she considered her inferiors. She was absolutely convinced of the most ridiculous historical theories. Though to be frank, I wince at dignifying them with the word *theory*. She promoted these ridiculous ideas, and convinced others—or forced them—to invest time and valuable resources attempting to prove them. But she didn't deserve to die."

"No, she didn't," Ingray agreed. "But this isn't really about Zat. For one thing, Excellency Zat has only been dead a few days, and the ship you probably came on had to have started out weeks ago. And for another, it was Zat's affine Hevom who killed her. None of us here has anything to do with that, except for them both having stayed at my mother's house."

"Excellency Hevom doesn't deserve to be condemned for a murder he surely didn't commit," continued Excellency Chenns, as though Ingray hadn't spoken. "Your own Planetary Safety arrested Pahlad Budrakim for Zat's murder. What's more likely, that an escaped convicted criminal killed her, or that her own affine, who couldn't touch her, couldn't even *speak* to her, did it? And I know the ruin glass is mostly just a nuisance or a curiosity or a building material to you, but Zat's crackpot theories about the origins of that glass had political implications. Implications that would offend most Hwaeans."

"Yes," Ingray agreed, "she wanted to prove that Hwae was the original home of the Omkem. Or at least the original home of the Omkem who were related to her. I know. She told me. But it's a crackpot theory, as you've said yourself. She could have dug up every piece of ruin glass on the planet and not proved it."

"She'd have made whatever she did find fit whatever suited her," Chenns replied. "And there would have been repercussions in the Federacy. Believe me, Miss Aughskold, it was always about convincing possible allies in the Federacy. Convincing Hwaeans wasn't ever the point. Zat couldn't have cared less what Hwaeans thought, except where it might get her what she wanted. I can't imagine your mother didn't realize that when she invited Zat to stay with her."

No, Ingray couldn't imagine it, either. What had her mother been doing? But then, refusing to let Zat dig up the parkland might only have allowed Zat to cry conspiracy, where the actual results of the digging might well speak for themselves. "Listen to me," Ingray said. "I was there that day. I was there when Zat died. She went up the hill—you know the one with all the glass down to the river, it's in all the pictures of the parkland. She went up there to have a view, I suppose, while she sent her little Uto mech searching for whatever it might find on the surface." Which would have been precious little. "She went up the hill, and sat down, and nobody went near her until lunchtime and I went up to get her because she wasn't answering messages, and she was..." Ingray stopped. *And she was dead.* Chenns watched her, saying nothing. "Garal...Pahlad Budrakim, but I didn't know that's who e was then, was with me the entire time. And don't tell me e was piloting a mech. E wasn't, I was talking to em the whole time, and the only mech that went up the hill was Uto. Garal doesn't have the right implants to pilot a Federacy-made mech. The only person nearby who did was Hevom. And Hevom was the only person nearby who hated Zat enough to kill her. I was there."

Excellency Chenns just looked at her, frowning slightly, and said nothing.

"Why did she even bring Hevom along? They couldn't speak to each other; it would have been better to bring an assistant she could actually talk to, who didn't resent her so much."

Chenns grimaced. "It was cruel of Zat to make him come along. More cruel than I think you can understand. Some of Hevom's senior relatives had defied Zat's family over a, I guess you would say a political matter. The…the affinage I guess you would say"—the word he used was an awkward coinage, a Yiir word with an unaccustomed element pasted on—"was meant to settle the consequent dispute, but Zat herself did what she could to make its terms as humiliating as possible to Hevom's family. Hevom made the mistake of protesting. Zat compelled him to come as a sort of lesson, for him and for his relatives."

"That sounds like a motive to me," said Ingray. "And once he'd resolved to kill her, it was easy enough to pin the murder on an innocent Hwaean. After all, we're…" How had Hevom said it? "Ignorant and uncultured, and our legal system is a joke. So are our lives, it seems."

337

Excellency Chenns sighed. "I wouldn't exactly call Pahlad Budrakim innocent."

"Eir name is Garal Ket now. And e *didn't kill Zat.* I was there." And it was beside the point anyway. The Federacy couldn't have Garal, because Garal was Geck now. And none of this was happening because of Zat, or Hevom. These people, these mechs and soldiers, had shipped through the Enthen/Hwae gate long before any of it had happened.

Unless of course someone knew ahead of time that Zat would die and Hevom would be accused of the murder.

"You still don't understand," said Chenns. "You can't. Murdering Zat would have been literally unthinkable for someone in Hevom's position. Even if I try to explain it to you, you wouldn't understand, because your families don't work that way. Imagine...imagine someone killing their parent."

"Someone might call that unthinkable," replied Ingray. "I can't even imagine what sort of person would kill a parent. But it's happened."

Excellency Chenns looked over his shoulder at the still-armored commander, then back at Ingray. "You're here, Miss Aughskold, because of your involvement with Zat's death. Commander Hatqueban would never have agreed to the exchange otherwise. She'll want to speak to you directly about it. Not now, at the moment there are more pressing issues, but sometime soon. She doesn't speak Bantia at all"—Ingray had already guessed as much— "and her Yiir isn't very good. She has a translation utility, it's not bad really, but she doesn't quite trust it, so I'll be there to translate for her if she feels she needs it."

"Is she related to Zat, too?" asked Ingray, as innocently as she could manage.

"No," said Chenns. Did Ingray detect some chagrin? "She's related to Hevom. She won't appreciate you dragging her...cousin, I suppose is best. She won't appreciate you dragging her cousin's name through the mud."

"Chosen especially for this mission, was she?" asked Ingray. "What an incredible coincidence."

Some reaction Ingray couldn't quite read crossed Chenns's face. But he only said, "Go sit down with the others, Miss Aughskold."

"Whoever planned this didn't care much about what happened to Hevom," said Ingray. "I suppose they promised him they'd get him out of it, but you'd think they'd have given him better resources to do it with." If this were an entertainment, Hevom would have come with forged evidence, with a way to put fake fingerprints or DNA on the knife, and to place falsely incriminating messages in the system for Planetary Safety to find and eventually unravel. The Federacy could probably do some of that, if not all, with enough planning. If they thought it would be worth it. Hevom apparently wasn't.

"Sit down, Miss Aughskold," Chenns said again. "I don't want to have to resort to threats."

"That's all right, excellency," said Ingray, with as false a smile as she'd ever managed in her life. "The commander and her soldiers will be happy to do it for you."

And still smiling she turned away from him, from the *Rejection*, and walked unhurriedly over to where the two other Hwaeans sat, not to give the impression that she was unafraid and unintimidated, but because if she moved too quickly she'd be unable to stop herself from running in panic. And because the more deliberately she moved, the more she might be able to conceal the fact that she was trembling with fear.

17

Ingray sat down between the Prolocutor of the First Assembly and the senior keeper of post-Tyr vestiges, pretending to ignore the armed four-legged mech standing over them. The young vestige keeper gave her a glance, and then stared straight ahead.

"Well," said Prolocutor Dicat. "Netano's well out of it. And she gets to personally deliver the children safely back to their crèches. Though it's not as if the Omkem weren't going to let them go at the first opportunity. They cried and sniffled and had to go to the bathroom every few minutes and of course the Omkem couldn't just let them run around loose. We're lucky the commander over there wasn't ruthless enough to just shoot them all, because not one of them had influential families to make up for the trouble of keeping them. But Netano will get to play the hero for the news services, and no doubt if anything happens to you she'll get some extra sympathy come election time. You can't possibly be her own offspring, let alone a foster from one of her cousins or prominent supporters. Only a child from a public crèche could be so easily sacrificed. Or so willing to go along with it. They're the only ones who don't have anywhere else to go."

So easily sacrificed. Well, it was true, and Ingray had known as much for most of her life. *I won't forget this,* her mother had said. Ingray knew she had meant it. Knew, also, that Netano would wrest whatever political advantage she could out of Ingray being here, whether she survived or not.

She wanted to protest at the no-doubt-intended insult. And the disdainful assessment of the crèche children. But if she opened her mouth to say something indignant, she would probably scream, or start to cry. Instead she said, as sweetly as she could, "It's so good to meet you, Prolocutor." And closed her mouth on anything else that might want to come out.

On Ingray's other side the keeper of post-Tyr vestiges began to weep silently. After a few minutes, Prolocutor Dicat snapped, "Oh, do stop sniveling. You're as bad as the children and it won't do anything except get things wet and annoy the rest of us."

Ingray leaned toward the keeper of post-Tyr vestiges. "I'm Ingray Aughskold. I think we've met once or twice before."

"Nicale Tai," said the young woman. "And I'm not crying on purpose."

"I feel like crying, too. Maybe if we all cry hard enough, the room will flood and it will short out the mechs." Ingray didn't know where that had come from, the words had just appeared in her mind and come right out of her mouth. Maybe it was knowing she was so close to death. Or maybe it was knowing that Tic was trying to get here, that he might be here even now.

Nicale gave a weak, shaking *hah*. Wiped her eyes with the back of her hand, though the tears kept falling. "The atmosphere control would probably suck all the moisture out of the air before very much could build up. Humidity is bad for the vestiges."

"We'll need another plan, then," said Ingray. Light-headed with fear, still not sure how or why she could say any of this. "Maybe we need to cry right onto them." The mech, gun clutched in one appendage, loomed over them. "Are you waterproof?" Ingray asked it. It said nothing. "I bet it is."

"It would be kind of foolish to go to war with mechs that weren't," agreed Nicale. "You could just fight them off with buckets and hoses."

"Oh, *will* you be silent," snapped Prolocutor Dicat.

Nicale teared up again. Had Prolocutor Dicat been needling her all this time?

Prolocutor Dicat had a reputation—widely admired by eir constituents—for saying things plainly and directly, not dancing around issues, or spending much effort being diplomatic. But Ingray knew that anyone who couldn't exercise diplomacy effectively would never have made prolocutor. "Are you very uncomfortable, Prolocutor?"

Ingray asked. She looked up at the looming military mech. "What are you even thinking," she demanded, in Yiir, "making this poor, enfeebled, elderly neman..."

"Enfeebled!" interjected Prolocutor Dicat, indignant.

"...making em sit on the floor like this, with no cushion and no back support. You could at least bring em a bench!" The mech did not respond. "Would you treat your own grandparent like this?" Still no answer.

"Young lady," began Prolocutor Dicat, "I'll have you know..."

"Oh, be quiet!" cried Nicale. "We're all three of us going to die, and if you won't be polite to us, why should we be polite to you?"

"Silence!" The Omkem commander strode toward them. Her voice must have been amplified by something in her armor, because her face was still hidden behind the dark, smooth helmet. Chenns the ethnographer followed close behind her. "You're as bad as the children."

"Commander Hatqueban," Ingray said, "don't you know the prolocutor has a bad hip?" It was true, e did. Ingray remembered it being an issue at a meeting the prolocutor had attended at the foot of the elevator a few years ago. "And a bad back, too, and e probably has pain medication e hasn't been able to take, and you're making em sit on the floor like this with no..."

"Silence!" The commander again, in Yiir, voice deafening. "Or you will be shot."

Beside Ingray, Nicale hunched down, shoulders suddenly drawn inward. "Not before we open the *Rejection*'s case

344

for them," she muttered. "If they set off the alarms the doors will all close and they'll have to cut their way out."

Ingray looked up at the flat dark gray of the Omkem commander's armor. Felt the dizzy freefall of terror—she herself was not a member of the First Assembly, or necessary to open anything here. The business about Zat was, as she herself had pointed out, incidental, even if for some reason it was important enough that they'd kept Netano, and agreed to trade her and the children for Ingray. And if the prolocutor was right, Commander Hatqueban had been looking for a reason to send the children away. If Ingray caused too much trouble the commander might easily decide to be rid of her by the simplest possible method. So why was Ingray taking a breath to say something? She ought to keep silent. And after all, she was just Ingray, nobody special, not beautiful or brilliant or particularly important to anyone.

No. She was Ingray Aughskold, who had freed a wrongly convicted person from inescapable Compassionate Removal. Who had, completely unarmed, faced down Danach threatening her with a huge dirt mover. She'd had some help there, but she was also a person who sometimes had help from mysterious and unnerving aliens. She might have help here now.

"This is unacceptable," she said to the Omkem commander's blank helmet, voice flat and disapproving. "You will bring a chair for the prolocutor. One with a back and a cushion." Commander Hatqueban said nothing. Beside her, Excellency Chenns frowned and opened his mouth to speak. "Do not argue with me about this!" Ingray ordered, astonished with herself. Apparently all she had to do was think of the Geck ambassador and she herself would produce a passable imitation of the alien diplomat. "Bring the chair."

"Stupid child," said Prolocutor Dicat. Quiet and vehement. "I have been doing my best not to get us killed."

"They're not going to kill you," Ingray retorted. "Not until they get whatever it is they want you for, anyway. And they might as well let you be comfortable until then." Though she wasn't entirely sure she believed it. And she herself had no protective usefulness. Not really.

Excellency Chenns said something too quiet for Ingray's translation utility to catch.

"Hah!" said the commander. "Chair process you several silent."

"The commander will have a chair brought," said Excellency Chenns, "if you will all promise to be quiet."

"What, even if you ask us something?" Nicale asked. Very quietly.

"I advise you not to push your luck too far," Chenns said. "The commander is not in a mood for games."

"You're not going to do anything to Nicale until after you get her to open that case for you," Ingray pointed out. "I think we all know that. Or, excuse me, excellency," she added sweetly. "The commander won't. *You're* not a soldier and you don't threaten people."

Chenns only said, calmly, "The chair is on its way." And he and the commander walked away, toward the *Rejection*.

After what seemed like an interminable wait, a mech came into the hall with a chair and a cushion and set them beside Prolocutor Dicat. It also dropped three bottled water rations and three paper-wrapped packages onto the ground.

"That's our supper," whispered Nicale. "Nutrition blocks. I can't read the writing but I'm pretty sure they're dust-flavored." And then, even more quietly, "I don't think the prolocutor can get up from the floor by eirself."

But e could get up with Ingray and Nicale on either side, to support em. E said nothing, no word of criticism or thanks as e settled into the chair, and Ingray and Nicale sat back down on the ground and opened their nutrition blocks.

They had all three eaten, Ingray was trying very hard not to look around and try to see if Tic was anywhere nearby, and Nicale was dozing, leaning against the side of Prolocutor Dicat's chair, when footsteps echoed in the long room—Commander Hatqueban and Chenns walking toward where they sat. Nicale startled awake. Prolocutor Dicat didn't even look up at them as they approached, just stared ahead of emself.

"Miss Aughskold," Chenns said, "the commander has some questions for you."

"Commander Hatqueban," acknowledged Ingray, feeling a somehow surprising sting of anger.

"Miss Aughskold," said the still-armored commander, in Yiir. "Tell me the truth about the death of Excellency Zat."

347

"I've already told Excellency Chenns," Ingray said. She wanted to stand up, so that she didn't feel so small and helpless, so that Commander Hatqueban and the ethnographer Chenns and the large armed mech were not looking down at her from such a height. But neither did she want to give the impression that she cared much what any of them thought. She leaned back against one leg of Prolocutor Dicat's chair. "I was there. Garal Ket was with me the entire time."

"Who is Garal Ket?" asked Commander Hatqueban.

"Designation Pahlad Budrakim existing," murmured Chenns to the commander.

"Excellency Zat was in view the entire time," Ingray continued. "There was no one on the hilltop with her, and the only mech I saw was her own Uto. You can't miss it, it's bright pink."

"Utos are," agreed Chenns. "It's so you can see them easily."

Ingray gave him the briefest of glances but no other acknowledgment. "I found her. Zat had been stabbed with a marker spike, one that came from Zat's own store of them, which the Uto held. And then, after she died, she was stabbed with a knife that came from my mother's kitchen. Planetary Safety found that knife in the Uto's storage compartment. The Uto itself was at the bottom of the Iogh River, caught between pieces of ruin glass."

"Pahlad Budrakim might have had that knife from your mother's kitchen," Commander Hatqueban pointed out. "Or you."

"Eir name is Garal Ket now," Ingray said, coldly.

"Have you ever tried to pilot an unfamiliar mech from an entirely different system?"

A pause. "Actually, excellency, I have. But I will grant that it was not a simple proposition, nor a spur-of-the-moment thing. Still, your own military likely has methods for doing exactly that."

"Garal was never military," Ingray pointed out. "E's a vestige keeper. I'm quite sure e's never done more than the kind of mech-piloting anyone does for fun. And even if none of that were true, why use the knife? The marker spike did the job." She felt a tiny shiver at the back of her neck that wanted to spread further but somehow didn't. "If the goal was to falsely accuse Excellency Hevom, then the knife only muddied things. When the Uto is the murder weapon, Excellency Hevom is the first, obvious suspect. And Garal had no reason to kill Excellency Zat." She thought of pointing out that Garal would certainly not be working for eir father. But, she realized, there was no true statement she could make that Commander Hatqueban couldn't dismiss as deception by some means or another. And, she remembered, Chenns had said that the commander was Hevom's cousin. She wasn't sure how close a relationship that might imply, but Chenns had seemed to think it would mean that Hatqueban wouldn't want to think Hevom was a murderer. That probably also meant the commander wasn't pleased with how Zat had treated Hevom. "*You* probably had more reason to wish Zat dead than Garal did. In any event, this business with Excellency Zat can't have been part of your orders when you started out. If they were you wouldn't be asking me any of this, because you'd know it was set up." But that wasn't a useful direction to go. Commander Hatqueban was no naïve child, she was an experienced soldier with orders to follow, and she would surely follow them, no matter what she might privately think of those orders. "You were already on your way here, with orders to do this," or something a lot like it anyway, "long before Zat died. So all this concern about who killed Zat and all these questions, none of it makes any sense."

"And so you know what it is to be a soldier," replied Commander Hatqueban. "Orders often make no sense, or not good sense. One follows them regardless, the best one can."

The best one can. This operation had clearly not gone according to plan and Commander Hatqueban was likely trying to salvage as much of her original orders as she could.

Commander Hatqueban said into Ingray's silence, "Tell me why the Geck are here."

"They're here looking for a former citizen of theirs." *Citizen* couldn't possibly be the right word. But Ingray wasn't sure what other word would do. "Someone the Geck ambassador knows personally. She was concerned about this person's welfare." Maybe Tic was here, even now, watching. Waiting for some reason to act.

"You're not speaking of Pahlad Budrakim," said the commander. Not a question. "Or, excuse me, Garal Ket."

Ingray frowned. And then realized that the specifics of what the ambassador had wanted had never been discussed on any of the news services. "No, not Garal. Someone else."

"The Geck don't leave their homeworld," argued Commander Hatqueban. "Not unless they absolutely must. And they aren't human, so a Geck could hardly pass unnoticed anywhere else."

"There are humans who are associated with the Geck," Ingray said. "They count as Geck under the treaty. The person the ambassador was looking for is one of these. Or was at one time."

"And the Geck have claimed that Pahlad...excuse me, Garal Ket, is also one of these? Why?"

Ingray gave a small careless wave of one hand. "You'd have to ask the Geck. But it doesn't really matter. Garal didn't kill Excellency Zat. Believe what you want about Hevom, but it wasn't Garal."

"It might have been you," suggested Commander Hatqueban. "After all, the knife came from your mother's house, and you could easily have put it into the body when you came up the hill."

Ingray blinked in surprise. "Now, why would I have done that?"

"No reason that makes sense," replied Commander Hatqueban. "It would muddy the water, as you have already pointed out, but not in any way helpful to you or your mother. Or Garal Ket."

"Who is beyond our reach now," added Chenns.

Commander Hatqueban said nothing, only turned and strode away, back toward the case that held the *Rejection of Obligations*.

Chenns looked at Ingray and gave an apologetic smile. "The commander has a lot on her mind right now."

"Does she." Ingray was not disposed to be sympathetic.

Chenns crouched down, so that his face was more on a level with Ingray's. "She doesn't understand Hwaeans. Or Hwae. She's disgusted that the parents of the children we were holding didn't demand their release."

"But they..." Ingray stopped.

"I know." Chenns looked over his shoulder at the commander, and then back. "I wasn't...sure about the wisdom of explaining who those children were. It probably wouldn't have made a difference. The commander isn't the sort to shoot children." Ingray considered asking why, if that was the case, Chenns had neglected to mention just how few people would care very personally if anything happened to these particular children. "And actually, between you and me, she's relieved to be rid of them. It's just that she wonders why you troubled yourself over them, when no one else did and they're no relations of yours. And it's difficult for her to think that your mother allowing you to take her place makes any kind of sense, but Netano went with the children immediately, with no hesitation or even any sign that it might trouble her. Even though the commander agreed to the switch, she's very suspicious of your presence here, for that reason."

"But Mama hadn't named her heir yet," Ingray protested. "And it wasn't ever going to be me anyway." Behind her, Prolocutor Dicat snorted.

"I know," said Chenns. How he stayed squatting the way he was, not quite all the way down, in that armor,

Ingray didn't know. Unless it was supporting him some-how. "I've explained, and she trusts that explanation, or you wouldn't be here, but she doesn't really understand it. She might understand better if I told her you were a foster-child, but she would understand better in the wrong way. I don't know if that makes sense."

"Not really."

He gave that apologetic smile again. "I didn't think so. At any rate, there were good reasons for agreeing to the exchange, but the commander is still not sure it's not some kind of trick. I'm here because I speak fluent Bantia. Translation utilities can only do so much. And when you don't understand a language or a culture very well, it's easy to make simple mistakes that undermine what you're trying to do. That much the commander does understand. She also understands just how unlikely it is that the Geck have come into this system at all, let alone at this particular moment. Add their interest in... in Garal Ket, and it becomes perhaps a bit too much to accept as mere coincidence."

"It *is* a coincidence," Ingray insisted. "Coincidences happen."

"But as a result of this one," Chenns said, "our plans have been disrupted. It's not just the presence of the Geck that's done this. Garal Ket's presence here has also changed conditions we were depending on."

Ingray frowned, puzzled. Then remembered that Pro-locutor Budrakim had been on his way to the station when he'd learned that Pahlad Budrakim had returned from Compassionate Removal.

But he'd been on his way because of the Geck. If the Geck hadn't come, would he have been on the station now for some other reason?

The First Assembly had been in session. In theory all eight members could hold meetings long-distance easily enough. In practice they did need to meet in person every now and then, and besides, anyone interested in running for Prolocutor of the First Assembly needed to be familiar to the voters of Hwae Station, who just from sheer numbers tended to dominate prolocutorial elections.

The Omkem had been delayed taking the Chambers because the presence of the Geck had compelled them to take a longer way there. If not for the Geck, Commander Hatqueban might have been able to hold the entire First Assembly hostage, and with it, legal authority over Hwae Station. And authority over Hwae Station ultimately meant control of the system's most valuable resources—the station itself, the gates to other systems. Access to the planet.

It suited Tyr *for Pahlad to come back*, Nuncle Lak had said. And Ingray had replied, *It suited Tyr to embarrass Prolocutor Budrakim*. And Garal had confirmed both statements.

Would Prolocutor Budrakim have gone up to the station at this time even if the Geck hadn't come? Ethiat Budrakim was Prolocutor of the Third Assembly, not the First. He wouldn't have had any reason to be with the First Assembly when the Omkem captured it. But maybe he had known this was coming, and had some role to play. The heroic negotiator who ended a tense and dangerous standoff, maybe?

Tyr couldn't have known, could they? Certainly they couldn't have known about the Geck, but could they have known the Omkem were planning this? Maybe not this thing specifically, why would anyone try to counter an invasion with an escaped convict? But something. Something they thought Ethiat Budrakim might be involved in. *Ethiat Budrakim is many things, but he is not stupid and he is not a traitor,* Nuncle Lak had said.

"The Federacy has been paying off Prolocutor Budrakim to speak in favor of allowing your fleets to get to Byeit through our system," said Ingray. "I imagine you've been sending gifts to any Assembly representatives who might sway the argument in your favor, but you'll have focused on the prolocutors. You expected Prolocutor Budrakim—and maybe other specific representatives—to be on the station when you arrived. Either in the First Assembly Chambers to be captured, or outside to advise System Defense to stand down so that he could negotiate a settlement. Right?" No change of expression on Excellency Chenns's face. "But he got turned around when he learned that Garal was back, and the others were evacuated when it took you too long to get to the Assembly Chambers because the presence of the Geck made you go the long way around." Chenns said nothing, just looked at her, serious. Still expressionless. Ingray supposed that it was possible the younger Prolocutor Budrakim wasn't in on it, or the elder Ethiat Budrakim didn't want her taking part for whatever reason. Garal had suggested that e might still speak to eir sister, if e had the chance. Or maybe she had known, but refused to do it. "That was the plan, right? Prolocutor Budrakim was supposed to broker some kind of agreement to get your hostages released in return for letting the Federacy use our Byeit gate. You would get your access, which he didn't care much about one way or another, and he would come out of it looking like he'd done something heroic, something that might even get him a shot at archprolocutor. But Garal coming back, that concerned him far more than any plans he had with you, because if the story came out of how his own child had ended up in Compassion- ate Removal for something e hadn't done, and Prolocu- tor Budrakim knew it, his reputation would be badly damaged and as far as the prolocutor was concerned the whole exercise would be pointless." It couldn't have been this specific series of events Tyr had wanted to affect, Ingray realized. But someone must have seen Prolocutor Budrakim as a step for the Federacy's move closer to Tyr, and acted to remove that step. "Excellency Zat's death just gives you one more grievance to justify what you're doing, one more perfectly understandable demand to make, one that's bound to play well on the news ser- vices back home, on top of getting rid of Zat herself. I'm sure it's no coincidence that Commander Hatqueban is related to Excellency Hevom, or that Zat's death came as a surprise to her. I'm sure that it did—otherwise there wouldn't have been any reason to ask me about it. So I imagine the commander was chosen for this mission precisely because she would take personal offense at Hevom's arrest."

Still Chenns said nothing. Prolocutor Dicat, in eir chair, gave another snort.

"That's quite a story you've constructed," Chenns said, after a long pause. "Even with the news services pushing it, I imagine most Omkem would find the murder of Excellency Zat insufficient justification for military action. But I can think of quite a few people who would be glad to see her gone, and it's so much neater to take what you want and then place the responsibility for it well away from home. It would be easy enough for it to have been undertaken by people who had no idea that anything else was being planned."

"Or who did and thought a little extra grievance wouldn't hurt," suggested Prolocutor Dicat. "They wouldn't need to have told *you* about it ahead of time."

"No," said Ingray, "all they needed to do was assign this mission to Hevom's cousin."

Chenns sighed. "I'm going to go talk to the commander." He rose from his crouch. "Please, don't do anything rash. No one here wants to hurt any of you."

"Rash?" asked Nicale as he walked away. "What does that even mean? What are we likely to do that would be rash?"

"Don't be stupid," snapped Prolocutor Dicat. "They're running out of time. The commander is going to have to do something drastic soon if she's going to get what she needs before more Omkem Federacy ships arrive in the system. Whatever it is surely involves one or more of us, and if we resist we're liable to get killed."

They're running out of time. And Ingray hadn't heard anything at all from Tic, in all this time. Had he not been able to get in? But she didn't want to think about that. "Did you know? That Prolocutor Budrakim was involved with the Omkem like this?"

Prolocutor Dicat scoffed. "We've all been courted by the Federacy. You said it yourself, they've been trying to bribe anyone they thought would swing the prolocutors and Extra-Hwae Relations their way. Did I know Ethiat Budrakim was a greedy, power hungry traitor, is the question." E made a meditative *hmph*. "Well, he's always been greedy and power hungry. That's normal for an ambitious Assembly representative. The *traitor* is new."

"He might not think he was being a traitor," Nicale pointed out, timidly, looking to Ingray for reassurance. "If it was a question of just looking like he was saving Hwae from the Omkem."

"If he was stupid enough to invite the Omkem here and think they wouldn't take whatever they could, you mean," corrected Prolocutor Dicat.

"So Garal coming back actually did him a favor," Ingray suggested. "Sort of."

Prolocutor Dicat made a disgusted, incredulous noise. Opened eir mouth to say something more but a deafening bang sounded, startling Ingray into throwing her hands up in front of her face. Heart racing, she looked around to see what had happened. Commander Hatqueban strode past, headed for the mech at the entrance away from the *Rejection*. Its gun was pointed at the white-painted ceiling.

Chenns was suddenly beside her. "Don't move!" he cried. Gasping slightly. He must have run to them from Commander Hatqueban's side. He looked as startled as Ingray was. Nicale lay flat on the floor, her hands covering her head. Prolocutor Dicat was bent forward in eir seat.

As Commander Hatqueban neared the mech it fired and the sudden loud sound brought Ingray's hands up again. "What is it?" she asked, not even trying to sound calm.

"I don't know!" Chenns replied. "But you need to get down. The prolocutor needs to get down."

"E can't get down by eirself," said Ingray.

The mech swung its weapon toward another part of the ceiling and fired again. Dust and fragments of plastic dropped to the floor. Nicale, arms crossed over the back of her head, whimpered.

"We need to get the prolocutor down on the ground," insisted Chenns, and pulled his helmet on.

The mech fired again, seven shots in rapid succession. Something large and black appeared, clinging to the white ceiling for just a moment, and then it dropped and hit the floor with a splat, a few meters from where Nicale lay.

"Confound it!" said Chenns, according to Ingray's translation utility. "What is it?"

Ingray made a strangled sound. Three eyestalks tried

to lift but then flopped down again, and one of the thing's hairy, clawed appendages twitched. Blue fluid pooled around it, and more spatters of blue surrounded it.

"Fiddlesticks!" swore Commander Hatqueban, striding up to the bleeding, now-still spider mech. "Fiddlesticks! Fiddlesticks! Confounded *Geck ambassador*!" She turned to Ingray, said in Yiir, "She was following *you*."

Ingray felt tears start. She was in terrible danger and she was utterly alone. "No! She had everything she wanted, she had Garal, she had..." She couldn't allow Tic's name to come out of her mouth, or she would break down utterly. "She doesn't care about me at all!"

"Hatqueban," said Chenns. In Yiir. "Tell me we didn't just shoot the Geck ambassador to the Presger."

"But..." began Ingray, and stopped herself before the words *it's just a mech* could escape. How clear had the news services been about that? She wasn't sure. The mech had stopped moving, its eyestalks lying flaccid in a pool of... was that blue fluid blood? She couldn't keep from making a distressed moan.

"This isn't good," observed Prolocutor Dicat drily. E was again sitting up, leaning against the back of eir chair.

"Why was she here?" Commander Hatqueban demanded of Ingray.

"I don't know!" Ingray cried. "How am I supposed to know?"

"Hatqueban," said Chenns, and continued, not in Yiir, "for what reason is the event? No plausibility that the Geck might interfere for this one."

"The Pahlad the Garal Ket is this one's ally," replied Commander Hatqueban. "Or else curiosity. Erratic is the ambassador."

"If you've broken the treaty," observed Prolocutor Dicat, voice still dry, "I expect every human government will be more than happy to make the most abject apologies to the Geck, and as part of that they'll likely promise to do whatever will make the Geck forget about this, up to and including handing you and your soldiers over to them. The Omkem Federacy very possibly included."

"Be silent," snapped Commander Hatqueban. And stood then, motionless for a good minute. Considering, maybe, or communicating with her troops elsewhere. Or both. Ingray sniffled, and stifled a sob. She couldn't prevent the tears from rolling down her face.

Chenns pulled his helmet off again. "Miss Aughskold, are you all right?"

Ingray took a ragged breath. "I'm fine." But she wasn't. She was alone, and there was no help coming.

"Are you all right, Prolocutor?" asked Chenns.

"Do you actually care?" asked Prolocutor Dicat.

"Prolocutor, I assure you, I..." Chenns began.

"Excellency Tai," Commander Hatqueban said abruptly, in Yiir, seeming not to notice or care that she had interrupted Excellency Chenns. "You will open the case in which the *Rejection of Further Obligations to Tyr* is stored. Without triggering any alarms."

Silence. Then, "I won't," said Nicale.

"You will," said the commander, calmly. "Or I will shoot Excellency Aughskold." Some catch or compartment near Commander Hatqueban's hip came loose, and she pulled out a sidearm. A gun—Ingray didn't know much about guns, except the sort that turned up in the occasional adventure serial. This one was black, but somehow the circle of empty space at the end the commander now pointed directly at Ingray was even blacker. The bore. That was what that was called, the channel a bullet would travel down. Her entire attention was on that hole, on the gun. Everything else seemed distant and unreal. Fresh tears welled, rolled down her cheeks.

She was alone.

"Stand up, all of you," Commander Hatqueban continued. "We're all going to walk over to the case, and Excellency Tai will open it and remove the *Rejection of Obligations*."

"Why?" asked Ingray.

"Because the Omkem have to get out of here now before anyone realizes what just happened to the Geck ambassador," said Prolocutor Dicat.

"Because I've ordered it," said Commander Hatqueban. "Get up."

Ingray took another shaky breath, and climbed to her feet. She wasn't certain her legs would support her. All the fear she'd felt before—making the trade that had brought Garal out of Compassionate Removal, despairing of getting away from Tyr Siilas and back home, when Danach had tried to kill her with the dirt mover, the terrible, desperate trip in the vacuum suit—it was all nothing compared to this moment, to looking at the end of a gun pointed at her by someone who had declared their intent to kill her. She wanted to curl up and cry. She wanted to scream and run away. *Don't do anything rash*, Chenns had said.

She couldn't afford to curl up and cry. There was no point to screaming and running away. Or no point that wouldn't end with her dead. She made herself swallow and tried to slow her breathing. So that she could say, "Prolocutor, can I help you get up?" She wanted to wipe her eyes with the back of her hand, but the thought of startling the commander into shooting terrified her even more than she already was.

Still sitting on the floor, Nicale whimpered. "Get up, you stupid girl," snapped Prolocutor Dicat. "Get up and open the case."

"Prolocutor," Ingray reproved, her voice still unsteady with tears, feeling as though she was watching herself speak, and wasn't actually doing it herself. "There's no need to be unpleasant. This is difficult for all of us. Now, do you need help getting up?"

Prolocutor Dicat gave Ingray a baleful look but took Ingray's arm. Nicale got herself to her feet, sobbing now, too, but silently.

"Let's walk," said the commander, when they were all standing, and together they moved toward the case, Ingray and Nicale on either side of the prolocutor, the mech that had stood guard over them following.

Commander Hatqueban stopped them, several meters short of the *Rejection*. "Excellency Tai." Nicale wiped her eyes on her sleeve and stepped hesitantly forward.

The commander took Ingray's arm and brought the end of the gun right up against Ingray's head. As afraid as she had been before, now she found every muscle in her body frozen. Even breathing was difficult.

Nicale brushed her fingers on the diorite plinth the case sat on, then laid her hand flat on another part. Waited a moment. The front of the case split, though it had been clear and seamless the moment before, and at Nicale's touch the two halves swung aside as if hinged.

"Take the document out," said Commander Hatqueban, "and roll it up."

Nicale turned, face indignant. "It'll be damaged! It's hundreds of years old, it..."

"Take it out," Commander Hatqueban repeated. "And roll it up."

"What good is it to you," asked Prolocutor Dicat, on Ingray's other side, still holding her arm, "if it's destroyed when you take it out of the case?"

"I'll help," said Excellency Chenns, and bent to set his helmet on the floor and then stepped forward to help Nicale with the long, wide linen.

Between the two of them they unfastened it from the display, slowly and carefully rolling it up as they went. Stopping once near the end when the weight of the rolled fabric pulled too hard on what little was left and the edge ripped, a good six centimeters, and another two as they rolled past the tear. When they were done, Chenns left Nicale sobbing by the empty case and brought the *Rejection* over to the mech that had followed them from the middle of the room. The mech's wide side panel popped open—with distant surprise, Ingray saw that her hairpins weren't inside the compartment. They must be in a different mech—the ones Ingray had seen so far all looked alike, though she presumed the commander could tell one from another somehow. Chenns put the *Rejection* into the compartment, folding one end over to make it fit, to Nicale's audible distress, and the compartment closed with a snap.

"Now," said Commander Hatqueban, lowering her gun, "walk."

"I don't think the prolocutor can walk far," said Ingray. The fact that the commander's gun was no longer pointed at her was such a relief that it was nearly painful. She felt far more in danger of just giving up now, of just sitting down and crying. But she couldn't.

"The prolocutor will be carried, if that's the case," said Commander Hatqueban. "Move."

18

Ingray had always thought of the First Assembly Chambers as being practically next door to the System Lareum, but just walking to the lareum exit nearest the Assembly on one side of Prolocutor Dicat, still-weeping Nicale on the other, step by slow step, the distance seemed to stretch out to kilometers. And there was no distraction from each of those steps, no way Ingray could let her mind wander, knowing two hulking gray military mechs with guns were following behind, one pointing its weapon at the ceiling, the commander herself up front with her own sidearm ready in her hand, her head tilted to look up as well as forward.

They walked several minutes in silence through the lareum's vestige-hung rooms. Beyond the space where the *Rejection* had once hung, spindly-legged pale blue escort mechs lay here and there, smashed, legs askew.

"There's a tram," Nicale said, as they neared the exit to the corridor the lareum shared with the Assembly Chambers. She spoke at a volume that was quite plausibly conversational but obviously pitched to reach the ears of Commander Hatqueban, three meters ahead of them. She sniffled. "There's a little wheeled tram to get people through the lareum if they have trouble walking, and there's another one just outside the entrance to take people to the Assembly Chambers if they need it."

Without turning around Commander Hatqueban said, "We're not taking the tram."

"Why not?" asked Nicale.

"Don't go getting us killed," muttered Prolocutor Dicat irritably.

Commander Hatqueban said nothing. Beside her, Chenns glanced back for just a moment, expression apologetic, and then faced forward again.

"The tram between here and the Assembly probably isn't working," Ingray said, very quietly. "I bet it's shut down. I'm sure nobody wanted to make it easy for the Federacy to use it."

"Oh," said Nicale. "Where are they all, anyway? There were more mechs when they first took over the lareum. But we've only seen maybe three or four since then."

"Spread out, maybe," suggested Ingray, still quietly. "Keeping our own soldiers out." And then, struck by a thought, she whispered, "You may be right, Prolocutor, the commander probably wants to get away from here before anyone realizes what's happened." She wiped her eyes with the back of her free hand. She was not going to cry any more than she already had. She would not think about Tic's mech dead and bleeding back there. "So maybe we don't want to suggest faster ways to get to the Assembly Chambers."

Prolocutor Dicat sighed, whether from fatigue or impatience Ingray couldn't tell. "Finally. I was beginning to think neither of you had any brains to speak of."

Needled, Ingray opened her mouth to say something unflattering about the prolocutor. But then she closed her mouth. Prolocutor Dicat was likely in pain, on top of being held captive and now forced to walk a considerable distance without eir normal assistance—e usually used a cane, and the commander had probably taken it from em, or it had been lost somehow. So instead of saying anything, Ingray shot a glance at Nicale, who grimaced in response, but said nothing herself.

A few meters farther on they reached the entrance to yet another room in the lareum. Another tall gray mech waited there, and as they came even with it, it walked up to Prolocutor Dicat and lifted em up with two of its three arms.

"Are you comfortable, Prolocutor?" asked Excellency Chenns as the mech strode forward with the prolocutor in its grip.

"Excellency Aughskold, Excellency Tai," Commander Hatqueban said, not turning around, "please walk faster." The two armed mechs behind them sped up. So did Ingray and Nicale.

As they exited the lareum into the broad corridor that

led to the Assembly Chambers, Ingray was struck, as she always was coming this way, with a sudden sense of dislocation. The floor was the same brown-and-gold tile that could be found all over the station, but the walls showed images of the space outside, making it seem like they were walking on a bridge through the endless vacuum. It was a recording, not a live feed, and the sun was always underneath or behind something. Hwae wasn't visible just now, but it would swing in and out of view over time, she knew.

The memory of standing outside the elevator flashed into her mind, and she hesitated, but the thought of Commander Hatqueban ahead with a gun in her hand, and the armed mechs behind them, kept her moving. She couldn't stop herself from glancing up, though. And saw the broad, white ceiling. That was better. That was safe.

But *safe* didn't mean anything right now. Tic wasn't here. At least it hadn't actually been Tic they'd shot, just his mech. Though thinking of the dying mech, that blood—Ingray was sure somehow it was blood—made more tears well. She swallowed, and tried to blink them away.

Up ahead, Commander Hatqueban stopped abruptly. Turned to face Ingray and Nicale and the prolocutor. The back of Ingray's neck prickled. The commander's face was still hidden behind her helmet, blank dark gray like the rest of her armor. Her gun still raised, pointing off to the side now, at least. Chenns stopped when she did, turned to look at the commander with a puzzled expression.

"Stop," Commander Hatqueban commanded, in Yiir, "and be silent."

Ingray, Nicale, the mech carrying the prolocutor, all came to a halt. "We weren't..." Nicale began.

"Silent!" insisted Commander Hatqueban.

They waited in silence for what seemed like several minutes. Even though the commander was clearly in a hurry. Was she unnerved by the corridor, as Ingray had momentarily been? But no, the Omkem would have traveled it more than once by now, it would be familiar to them. What was she waiting for?

A click sounded, and Commander Hatqueban and her mechs turned suddenly to a doorway-shaped crack of light along the left wall. After a few seconds the door opened all the way, and Ambassador Tibanvori stepped through, hands at her shoulders, palm out.

Followed by Garal. Eir hands hanging at eir sides, like e was just coming into an ordinary room at an ordinary time.

Fear shot through Ingray—e was putting emself in danger! And then hope. Was e here to help her? But no, e couldn't be. Not in danger, and not here to help her. E was Geck, and Ingray wasn't.

"Commander Hatqueban, is it?" asked Tibanvori in Radchaai-accented Yiir. "You can put the guns down, or point them away at any rate. I'm here on your behalf, Amaat preserve us all. I have no idea why you would have done such a dreadful thing."

"We're not putting the guns down, Ambassador," said Commander Hatqueban. "We won't be in any trouble for shooting *you*. In fact, I gather some would thank me for it."

371

"But you can't shoot *me*," said Garal. Eir voice amazingly calm and steady, almost casual. "Not without getting yourself in even more trouble than you already are." Commander Hatqueban didn't answer, and Garal continued. "We're here for ..." E gestured. "You know."

Silence. Then Chenns asked, "Was it the ambassador?"

Tibanvori rolled her eyes and opened her mouth to answer, but Garal said, before she could speak, "Who else would it be?"

Tibanvori blinked, as though surprised, but said nothing.

"Why was she here?" asked Commander Hatqueban. "Why was she even *here*?"

"Apparently she'd taken an interest in Ingray," replied Garal. "But it hardly matters. We need to get the body and bring it back to our ship. We can't leave it here."

"It's still in the lareum," said Commander Hatqueban. "You can get it when we're gone."

"No," said Garal. "We'll get it now. You needn't fear I'll be any threat to you—the treaty protects you from me, just as it protects me from you. And Ambassador Tibanvori is here as an observer to ensure *your* safety, so you don't need to worry about her, either."

"*Our* safety," said the commander, flat and skeptical.

"It will be bad for all of us if the treaty is broken," said Tibanvori. "Though I'm beginning to wish I hadn't gotten myself into this particular situation."

"The Geck are very secretive," said Garal. "As you may already know, Commander. We can't wait till you're gone to do this." And suddenly Ingray understood what was happening. That mech had been Tic's—but it had been Geck to begin with. Clearly the Geck didn't want it falling into anyone else's hands. So they had sent Garal and Tibanvori to fetch it—Garal because the other Geck were so uncomfortable leaving the ship, but Ingray wasn't sure why Tibanvori would have come, or played along with the suggestion that it was actually the Geck ambassador herself who'd been involved. Unless Tibanvori hadn't realized that until now. Ingray thought Tibanvori likely would have refused to come if she'd known—there was no treaty violation if the Omkem shot Tic's mech, and she wasn't inclined to be helpful to the Geck generally.

Garal continued. "We don't trust the Hwaeans with what you've left back in the lareum any more than we trust you with it. It's essential that we do this as soon as possible."

"*And in a way that doesn't break the treaty*," said Ambassador Tibanvori emphatically, with a sidelong glance at Garal.

"We won't break the treaty," Garal replied, serious and even. "And you're here, Ambassador, to be *sure* that we don't."

Tibanvori rolled her eyes. "All of you," she said, her voice disgusted. "I've had it with all of you."

"I'll go with them," said Chenns into the silence that followed.

Commander Hatqueban asked, as though Chenns hadn't spoken, "Who killed Excellency Zat?"

"Not me," said Garal. "I was with Ingray the whole time, and besides I had no reason to kill her. She was arrogant and abrasive, it's true, but that's generally not something I consider grounds for murder." The commander didn't reply. "Ingray didn't do it, either. You really ought to let her go."

"No," said Commander Hatqueban.

Garal looked at Ingray. "Sorry. I tried."

"Is there another one with you?" asked Commander Hatqueban. "Another Geck? We can't see any, but I'm sure it's here."

"No," said Garal. "No, we didn't bring anyone else here. We didn't want to risk another…incident." Commander Hatqueban didn't answer or even move, and Garal continued. "You'd know if there was, you detected the ambassador, even though the Hwaeans never did. We're not here for anything but what we already said we were. Anything more…" E made a wry expression. "That would be interfering with an internal human dispute, and that would break the treaty. I wish I *could* interfere, though. Ingray is my friend, and if anything happens to her…" Ingray hardly dared breathe, sure that if she moved one muscle she would fall sobbing to the floor.

"If anything happens to her, you won't be able to do anything about it," said Tibanvori sharply. "So you can just stop implying that you will, before we end up with another interspecies incident."

"I'll go with them," Chenns said again. "If I don't come back you'll know something's wrong."

"It was an accident," said Commander Hatqueban, to Ambassador Tibanvori. "Will you tell them that?"

374

"I'll do my best," Tibanvori said drily. "I make no guarantees. You really shouldn't go around shooting at things."

Still in the clutch of a mech, Prolocutor Dicat gave a bark of laughter. "You should talk, Radchaai."

Tibanvori shot em an irritated glance. "I represent all humans in this matter. I don't want the treaty broken any more than you do. But I can't promise anything."

"I suppose we'll just have to live with that," said the commander. She gestured at Chenns. "Go with them."

As Chenns, Tibanvori, and Garal passed, Garal said, "I'm sorry, Ingray. I really can't do anything."

"I kn..." Ingray swallowed. "I know. The treaty..." Her voice failed her.

"At least there's *somebody* sensible here," said Tibanvori, and set off into the lareum, Chenns and Garal following.

Ingray couldn't bring herself to turn and watch them walk away. She wasn't sure she'd be able to move when Commander Hatqueban ordered them to start walking again. But she did, found herself walking alongside Nicale as though someone else were moving her legs and feet. The tears that had threatened just moments ago had receded, though she still felt the knife edge of panic. Once, when she had been small, and the Aughskolds were on their way to a public reception, Nuncle Lak had taken her hand and leaned down to tell her that if she was afraid, she should look around and take notice of all the people and things that were frightening, and then of all the ones that might help her. *What if there's no one and nothing?* she'd thought but not dared say, but e had been right, it had helped, even just to know where the bathrooms were in case of a humiliating accident, or to notice who in the crowd were Netano's supporters and disposed to think kindly of Netano's children as a consequence.

There wasn't much potential help here. Nicale, maybe, and the prolocutor. Chenns at least tried to seem kind, but of course he was going back to the lareum with… but Ingray wasn't going to think about that. She was going to be calm and sensible, and walk alongside Nicale, behind Commander Hatqueban, down the corridor to the First Assembly Chambers.

As important as the First Assembly was, the room where it met was relatively small, at least as Assembly Chambers went—a little over twelve meters wide and long. There were after all only eight representatives in the First Assembly, one for each of six Hwaean outstations, Hwaé Station itself, and the prolocutor, who presided and represented all of the First Assembly to the Overassembly. But the meeting room proper was circled by a wide gallery, set a meter higher than the center, with ramps down to where eight backed and cushioned benches and a few low tables surrounded a diorite plinth—just like the one that supported the *Rejection of Obligations*. Or had supported it. On this plinth, in its own glass case, sat the Assembly Bell—a deep, two-handled bowl of blue-and-purple glazed pottery. Next to it under the glass was a large plain wooden spoon.

The mech holding Prolocutor Dicat marched down the nearest ramp and settled em incongruously gently on a bench. Ingray and Nicale followed. "Sit," ordered Commander Hatqueban, standing by the Assembly Bell plinth, still holding her gun, still entirely armored, and gestured at the benches. Nicale sat on a bench near the one Prolocutor Dicat sat on, and Ingray nearly collapsed onto the one beside Nicale. It was cushioned and definitely more comfortable than sitting on the hard lareum floor. That was good. That counted as a help, even if it was a tiny, mostly useless one.

The mech that had been carrying Prolocutor Dicat had moved up another ramp to stand on the far side of the room. Another had taken up a position at the door they'd come in. It seemed as though a session had been in progress when the Federacy had attacked. Things were strewn across the low tables between the benches— a cup and decanter here, a handheld and stylus there, even a pair of shoes sticking out from beneath the bench Ingray sat on. If Prolocutor Dicat had been here instead of in the lareum, e would have escaped entirely. Or, no, Prolocutor Dicat *had* been here. The younger one, at any rate. This Prolocutor Dicat had chosen to meet a crèche trip instead. There was a gilded decanter on the table nearest Ingray, and a cup half full of serbat. It had obviously been sitting there undisturbed for a couple of days at least.

The commander stood silent by the plinth for several minutes. Nicale and the prolocutor sat silent on their own benches. Ingray clutched at her creased and grimy skirts and looked sidelong at the cup of serbat on the table beside her. Some of the liquid had evaporated and left a white line on the side of the cup, just above the surface of the serbat itself. There was probably dust in it, too. Entirely unappetizing, but Ingray realized she was thirsty. She clutched her skirts harder to keep herself from reaching for the decanter to see if there was anything drinkable in it.

After a while Chenns came into the Chambers, helmet in his hand. Blue blood smeared his armored forearm. "They're gone," he said, in Yiir. Whether because he'd been speaking that language the last while and was still thinking in it, or because he wanted them all to hear and understand what he was saying, Ingray wasn't sure. "Mx Ket insisted on getting…all of the ambassador, and it took a while to find…well, we got all of her. I had Mx Ket say it in Ambassador Tibanvori's hearing, that e agreed we'd gotten everything, and Ambassador Tibanvori agreed she'd heard em say it. Mx Ket refused to speak any further about the issue, e said e wasn't authorized to do that. But Tibanvori said it might work out mostly all right, she doesn't think the Geck want the treaty broken any more than we do."

Prolocutor Dicat had been silent all this time, but now e said, "Of course the easiest way to make it work out would be to hand the ambassador's killer over to the Geck."

For a moment no one replied. Ingray wondered why the prolocutor would say something so guaranteed to distress or even frighten their captors. Then she

378

remembered Ambassador Tibanvori saying that things like this couldn't be planned on the spur of the moment. The commander had failed to take control of the First Assembly, but she couldn't just leave, or she probably would have. No, she must have to achieve at least something before...before more Omkem ships arrived? At any rate, she was working with limited time. And that was before Commander Hatqueban had thought they'd shot the Geck ambassador. The business with Garal taking the mech away, with Tibanvori saying she'd try to straighten it out, doubtless came as quite a relief to Commander Hatqueban.

But Prolocutor Dicat was shrewd enough to realize that the more flustered or frightened their captors were, the more likely they would make a mistake. Of course, that mistake was as likely to be fatal to Ingray or Nicale or the prolocutor emself as it was to injure the Omkem. Ingray shivered as she realized the prolocutor was surely shrewd enough to realize that, too. No one was looking at her but she clutched her skirts tighter to keep her hands from trembling.

"I'll patch that leak when the pressure drops," said Commander Hatqueban, still in Yiir. "Prolocutor, can you open this case?"

"I imagine it's under the authority of the Assembly's vestige keeper," said Prolocutor Dicat. "He'll be the one who knows how to open it."

"He's not here," said Commander Hatqueban.

"What a pity," replied Prolocutor Dicat, drily.

Silence. Commander Hatqueban didn't reply. Then Chenns said, in Bantia, "Every child in every Hwaean crèche knows what the Assembly Bell is, and that the First Assembly can't do business without it. I know— I've tried to explain to the commander—that it's futile to think that holding you hostage affects First Assembly business at all." Prolocutor Dicat snorted, contemptuous. "The commander doesn't understand Hwae. But then, if she'd understood, she'd have let you go with the children, before I could convince her of the importance of some of the vestiges here. And then we wouldn't have anyone who could open this case for us."

"Open the case, excellency," said Commander Hatqueban, in Yiir.

Prolocutor Dicat looked at Commander Hatqueban a moment, then said, "Or else you'll shoot Miss Aughskold? Or will it be Miss Tai?"

"Either one," agreed Commander Hatqueban. "And if you still refuse, the other."

"If I say I'll open the case," asked Prolocutor Dicat, "will you let Excellency Tai and Excellency Aughskold go?"

"You don't ask to be released yourself?" asked Chenns.

"I'm dispensable," replied Prolocutor Dicat, eir voice cold.

"Not to us, Prolocutor," returned Chenns.

"Let them go, and then I'll open it for you," said the prolocutor. Voice still cold and even.

"No," said Commander Hatqueban.

380

"If we let them go," Excellency Chenns pointed out, "you have only to refuse to open it for us, and we have no way to compel you."

"But you don't actually need me to open the case, excellency," said Prolocutor Dicat. "One of your mechs could break it open for you. It probably wouldn't take more than a minute."

Ingray blinked, and then tried very hard not to otherwise visibly react to what the prolocutor had said. If the commander had one of her mechs smash the glass, alarms would go off. Nicale had said, back in the lareum, that the doors would close. The Omkem would be trapped here. Or at least it would take them time to get out.

Was that why all the mechs Nicale and the prolocutor had seen before were somewhere else? Because if the alarm was triggered by accident they'd all be trapped and it would be easier to contain them? Or maybe just make it more difficult for them to defend the path back to the freighters the mech had come on. Or the freighters themselves.

But in that case, why were the commander and the ethnographer still here in person? When it came time to open the case—this one, or the one back in the lareum— wouldn't it have been better to have only more or less disposable mechs present, so that if they were trapped when alarms went off, at least there would be no people lost?

They're cut off, Ingray realized. Or if not cut off, getting back to the freighter they'd come on must be riskier than staying here. Maybe Hwae System Defense was already pressing the Omkem. That, on top of the time limit Ingray guessed the commander was working under. Add in worry over the reaction of the Geck to the apparent murder of their ambassador. Commander Hatqueban was under a lot of stress right now, and maybe without many resources. There must be some way to push her into making some kind of mistake that would give System Defense a chance to finish this.

Commander Hatqueban raised her sidearm and pointed it at Nicale. "The time for discussion is past. Open the case, Prolocutor."

Nicale made a small, frightened noise but did not otherwise move. Ingray had a sharp, clear memory of the business end of the commander's gun in her vision. Her breathing tightened and once again everything else seemed to fall away. Having the *Rejection* would do the Omkem very little good—even if it was genuine, the questions Garal had raised would likely be seized on by Hwaeans eager for any advantage against the Federacy just now. And maybe having the bowl wouldn't do the Omkem much good, either, maybe—probably—Hwaean System Defense would fight on regardless, and the First Assembly would find a new place to meet, and vote into law some other vestige to open those meetings with.

This Prolocutor Dicat would gain very little by opening the case—some time, at most, before the next demand, or until the commander decided eir life wasn't worth preserving. But the Assembly Bell *was* important. It was part of the history of Hwae. It was what set official First Assembly sessions apart from other sorts of meetings. Without it, the First Assembly wasn't really the First Assembly. But then, would some other group of people using it be able to legally claim to be the real First Assembly? No, Ingray was sure it didn't work that way. But it was *part* of how it worked. If the Omkem couldn't put their hands on the Assembly itself, this was possibly a workable second choice. Or at least the best option facing Commander Hatqueban right now.

Delay might help Hwae System Defense. So the prolocutor—and Ingray and Nicale for that matter—would want to delay the opening of that case for as long as possible. And the most unarguable delay would be the prolocutor flatly refusing to open the case.

And if Prolocutor Dicat died refusing to open that case, e would leave a valuable political legacy for eir successor. Ingray had no doubt Netano would do her best to capitalize on Ingray's own death in very much the same way. Nicale—well, the senior Nicale Tai had time to choose a new heir, after all. They were all three of them disposable, at least in a certain sense. Replaceable.

Prolocutor Dicat hadn't moved. Hadn't even breathed. Everything seemed frozen, time slowed in the face of Ingray's racing, terrified thoughts, that gun pointed at Nicale. Prolocutor Dicat had been irritable and unpleasant. E was uncomfortable, likely in pain and no doubt frightened. But e was—e always had been—a shrewd politician. E had surely already seen what Ingray had just realized, that the best move now, for emself and for Hwae, was to let Commander Hatqueban shoot Nicale, and then Ingray, to steadfastly refuse to open that case. To make the commander break it. Which she certainly would, but not until she was forced to, not until Ingray, Nicale, and Prolocutor Dicat were all dead.

"I won't open the case," said Prolocutor Dicat.

And without even realizing she'd intended it, Ingray grabbed the gilded decanter beside her and flung it at the case on its plinth.

The lights went out. Something flashed, made a loud bang, and someone screamed. Ingray. Ingray had screamed, and thrown herself off the bench onto the floor, though she didn't remember actually doing it. More gunshots, deafening in the enclosed space. Ingray lay facedown on the cold tile and gasped, breathless, heart pounding. Her knee hurt, she must have wrenched it coming off the bench.

Silence. Then light that seemed to swing wildly. "Chenns!" Commander Hatqueban's voice. "Chenns, hear. Chenns!"

"I good condition," replied Excellency Chenns. "Say I told you so the helmet."

Still flat on the floor, Ingray dared to raise her head. Commander Hatqueban stood nearby, a light in her hand, and beside her knelt Excellency Chenns. Blood ran down the side of his face. "The armor absent the seem," replied Commander Hatqueban. "Communications the condition absent operate. The mechs absent motion."

The mechs absent motion. The mechs weren't moving, the commander must have meant. Communications had been cut off somehow. Ingray pushed herself up, just a bit.

"Don't move, Excellency Aughskold," ordered Commander Hatqueban sharply, in Yiir. "You almost got Excellency Chenns killed."

Not me, Ingray wanted to protest. All the guns had been on the commander's side, after all. Instead she said, "Where's Prolocutor Dicat? Where's Nicale?"

"Here." Prolocutor Dicat's voice. Commander Hatqueban swung her light in eir direction.

Prolocutor Dicat knelt on the floor beside Nicale's prone form. Eir hand on Nicale's shoulder, and in the dim, erratic light it took Ingray a moment to realize that there was blood between eir fingers. Nicale didn't move, and her breath came shallow and gasping.

She'd been shot. *My fault*, thought Ingray, in panicked horror. Nicale had been shot because of what Ingray had done. Now she might die.

No. No, if Ingray had done nothing, both Ingray and Nicale would likely have ended up dead. And Nicale wasn't dead yet. She was just... *Oh fucking ascended saints*, Ingray thought. *Don't let her die because of me.*

"There's an aid kit in the back of the gallery," Prolocutor Dicat said, icily calm.

Without a word, Chenns got to his feet and walked up the ramp to the gallery. A mech lay unmoving beside the ramp, as though it had tumbled off and not had a chance to right itself, its gun still clutched in one appendage. Commander Hatqueban pointed her gun at Ingray. "I will not hesitate to shoot, excellency."

"I'm sure," replied Ingray. There was no hiding the way her voice was shaking. She wasn't sure she could get to her feet if she needed to, she was shaking so much even lying on the ground like this.

Chenns brought the aid kit over to where Nicale lay, and knelt beside the prolocutor and began sorting through the kit's supplies. "Is there something the alarm did to block our communications?" asked Commander Hatqueban. "That wasn't in the information I was given."

Ingray presumed the commander was addressing her—Nicale was unconscious, and Prolocutor Dicat and Excellency Chenns were busy with the aid kit. "I haven't the faintest idea." Nicale Tai would have known. "I'm sure they don't announce the details of how security works to everyone."

"Don't move," said Commander Hatqueban. Ingray sighed and laid her head back down. Even if her knee didn't ache fiercely, even if she weren't still trembling, she posed no threat to anyone. And there was nothing she could do to help Nicale.

"I don't know if that's going to help," she heard Chenns say after a few minutes. "It's the best we can do."

"You've done enough, excellency," said Prolocutor Dicat, eir voice dry and sardonic, in Yiir though Chenns had spoken Bantia. Nicale's quick and shallow breathing seemed to slow. Was that a good sign? Ingray vaguely remembered learning about the signs of shock, something about breathing fast and being cold and confused. She wanted to ask Prolocutor Dicat and Excellency Chenns if Nicale's skin was cold and clammy, or at least look up to see if they'd raised up Nicale's feet, but that was foolish. Aid kits came with instructions, and besides, both Dicat and Chenns very probably knew what they were doing. She would only be in the way, and besides, she'd caused this, it was her fault that Nicale was hurt, even if it had been Commander Hatqueban or one of the mechs who had fired the gun. It had probably been Commander Hatqueban who had fired.

The light moved away, leaving them in the dark. Footsteps circled the gallery—Commander Hatqueban, it must be, checking the exits. "Condition trapped," said Commander Hatqueban's voice once she'd finished the circuit, coming down the ramp from the sound of her steps, and from the returning light. "Certainly ours present forcibly open upon awareness." The weird results coming from Ingray's limited translation utility were making at least some minimal sense to her. The commander thought her soldiers would begin working to break into the meeting room as soon as they realized they had lost contact with her. "Time is finite, but possession condition possession." Ingray frowned into the floor. There wasn't much time, or time was running out. But what in the world was *possession condition possession* supposed to mean?

"Hatqueban!" The alarm in Excellency Chenns's voice was enough to make Ingray push herself partway up.

Chenns still knelt at Prolocutor Dicat's side, next to Nicale. But he wasn't looking at Nicale. He was staring at the diorite plinth, with its glass case.

Its empty glass case. Commander Hatqueban aimed her light straight at it, but there had been no mistake, no trick of the shadows. The bowl and spoon were gone.

"What did you do?" she demanded, turning her light on Ingray.

Ingray blinked, suddenly unable to see anything except that light in her face. "Nothing! I threw the decanter, and then the lights went out and I fell off the bench."

"Stand up!" Hatqueban demanded.

Slowly, carefully, using the bench beside her as support, Ingray got to her feet. "I hurt my knee," she said. Commander Hatqueban still shone the light in Ingray's face, but she seemed to have reached some point beyond fear. Beyond guessing or even caring what might happen next.

Brusquely Commander Hatqueban patted down Ingray's legs and momentarily flicked up the hem of her skirts.

"She doesn't have it," said Chenns, in Yiir. "The bowl was too large to hide that way." And Nicale certainly didn't have it. Or Prolocutor Dicat.

After a moment the light turned away, and Commander Hatqueban strode over to the mech that lay beside the ramp. She leaned over and pressed something on the mech's side, and the compartment lid snicked open. The commander pulled the lid all the way up and shone her light inside. "*Rejection* absent!"

"The *Rejection* is gone?" asked Ingray.

"That's impossible," said Prolocutor Dicat. "When the alarm went off, the doors will have closed and locked."

"That's what the intelligence said would happen, yes," agreed Commander Hatqueban. "Perhaps they didn't close and lock right away."

"It wasn't even ten seconds before you turned your

light on," argued Chenns. Still speaking Yiir. "Someone came in here when the lights went out, and in less than ten seconds they opened the case and took the bell, and then forced open the mech's compartment and took the *Rejection*, and left without us knowing it? And they left behind the Prolocutor of the First Assembly, and the daughter of an Assembly representative? Not to mention a badly injured keeper of post-Tyr vestiges? No, Commander, it's impossible."

It couldn't be Tic. He wasn't here. Even if the Geck had been willing to risk breaking the treaty by sneaking him in when Garal and Ambassador Tibanvori had come, he would likely have been detected by now. Again.

"Undefined person condition present," said Commander Hatqueban, very calmly, and turned to Ingray, still standing in front of the bench, knee aching. "What did you do? *What was the plan?*"

"I don't know what you're talking about." Though she did. There had indeed been a plan—or at least a plan to make a plan.

"You set that alarm off on purpose." The commander's voice was steady, and icy.

"You were going to shoot me, or Nicale. You said so. And you were..." Her voice shook too hard to continue. She swallowed and tried again. "It was obvious you didn't want to set the alarm off because it would make things more difficult for you. So I set it off." Fresh tears welled, and she didn't try to stop them.

Silence. Commander Hatqueban didn't move.

"You can shoot me if you want," said Ingray. "The

children are safe, and my mama. That's all I came here for." Her voice still trembling so much she could barely speak. She tried to make herself lift her chin defiantly, wasn't sure if she managed it, or if she was only shaking so hard that it seemed like she might have.

The silence stretched out. *She let the children go*, Ingray reminded herself. Still weeping. *She gave Prolocutor Dicat the chair.* That didn't mean the commander wouldn't kill anyone—she was a soldier, after all—but maybe, just maybe, she would go to some lengths to avoid it, to avoid being cruel if she could.

After a few more seconds of silence, Commander Hatqueban said, brusquely, "If you move from that bench, or if you speak one more word, whatever it is, I will shoot you."

Ingray sat, and after a moment Commander Hatqueban began a circuit of the room, very slow and methodical, shining her light into every shadowed corner.

Tears still ran down Ingray's face. She sniffled, as quietly as she could, and shifted uncomfortably on the cushioned bench and then, careful of her injured knee, pulled her feet up and lay down, her arms crossed over her body. Commander Hatqueban made two more slow circuits of the room, ducking to shine her light under every table and bench, occasionally knocking on a wall or stomping one foot on a floor tile, as though searching for some secret hollow space.

Ingray didn't seem to be able to stop crying. Commander Hatqueban's light moved as she still slowly circled the room. Either Prolocutor Dicat or Excellency

Chenns had put some cushions under Nicale's feet, and there must have been a thin blanket in the aid kit, because it lay across Nicale's body and Ingray didn't want to think about the puzzle—the far too simple a puzzle—of whether it was her fault Nicale had been shot. She wanted to be home, in her room. With a plate of fruit and cheese and a decanter of nice hot serbat, and rain outside the window and nowhere to be, no one needing her for anything. And there was no way she could be, probably never would be again. There was nothing she could do about any of it but lie here and cry.

Halfway through the commander's sixth slow circuit of the room there was a loud *thunk* and then the hiss of a door opening, and suddenly light shone through a doorway and the mech by the ramp shuddered, and then righted itself. Ingray didn't move. She refused to move, to speak, to do anything. Across the room another mech rose that must have been concealed from her view by benches and tables until now. Of course—two mechs had followed them into the Assembly Chambers.

"Finally," said Commander Hatqueban, as another Federacy mech trundled into the room. "Good quick work. Specified several captive offer a turnip ship. Time is finite. Additional only these to exit. Search attribute exhaustive."

"Affirmed, Commander," replied the newest mech, as the commander strode out the door, followed by Excellency Chenns. The mech stepped down the ramp, lowered itself, and extruded a shelf with which it lifted Nicale and carried her out the door. The mech that had fallen off the ramp walked over to Prolocutor Dicat then, and scooped em carefully up and followed the first.

The third mech, the one that had been out of Ingray's sight until now, approached Ingray and said, quietly, "Are you all right besides the sprained knee, Miss Aughs-kold?" In Bantia.

Ingray blinked. "I... what?"

It was still the same large, squarish mech, four-legged and three-armed. Or she supposed it was the same one, she couldn't really tell one from another.

"Don't make any noises, miss," said the mech. "I'm Char Nakal, Hwae System Defense Specialist. Our troops have taken control of the Federacy freighters and disconnected the pilots there from their mechs. The commander and the excellency are in for a surprise, but we want you three well clear before they realize it. Commander Hatqueban is still armed, and we think Excellency Chenns might be, too. And none of us are quite used to these hulks yet, we'd prefer not to fight with them just now. I'm only telling you so that you'll know not to come up with some sort of idea for escaping on your own. I'm told you're liable to do that sort of thing."

"I'm..." Ingray began. And then, "What?" *I'm told you're liable to do that sort of thing.* Who would have...

Tic would have. Ingray opened her mouth to ask, *Is Tic with you?*

The mech lowered itself and scooped her up. "Quiet, now, miss. If we take too long here Commander Hatqueban will wonder why. Oh, here, don't forget your shoes." It hooked its huge gun onto its side and then picked up the shoes under the bench Ingray had been lying on and set them in her lap.

"They're not..." Ingray began.

"Hush now." The mech lumbered up the ramp holding Ingray in two of its arms.

Now wasn't the time for questions. Ingray kept still as they moved out into the corridor. The shoes were heavy in her lap, almost boots, with thick, hard soles, and definitely too large for her. Maybe it was something that had come into style in the months she'd been gone at Tyr Siilas. Or maybe the Assembly representative who owned them wanted to be thought of as someone who did hands-on, hard work, the sort that would require heavy foot protection. Well, it didn't matter. What mattered was that Specialist Nakal was going to get her away from here; the two hulking gray mechs ahead of her were being piloted by other Hwae System Defense Specialists and were going to get Nicale and Prolocutor Dicat safely away, too; and all she had to do to help was stay calm. Stay quiet. She could do that. It was easy. The corridors of the Assembly offices were dark, and the only sound was the clunking of the mechs walking. It was almost relaxing.

The corridor that led to the lareum was bright, lit by the recording of Hwae's sun. A sliver of Hwae itself was peeking up over the floor on the right-hand wall. The space here was broader than the corridor they'd come out of, and the other two mechs began to slow, just slightly, just enough to gradually come nearer to the one piloted by Specialist Nakal, holding Ingray. Up ahead she could see Commander Hatqueban's back, and Excellency Chenns's. He had his helmet off again.

The commander stopped abruptly. Turned. Chenns, a few steps beyond, turned, too, with a worried stare at Hatqueban. "Halt!" shouted Commander Hatqueban.

The three mechs came to an uneven, faltering stop. The commander's blank gray faceplate stared. A chill began at the back of Ingray's neck. She remembered the obvious difference between Tic piloting a spider mech and the Geck ambassador piloting one. Reminded herself that even though she knew that difference, she hadn't always noticed it, especially if she was assuming she knew which one it was, or if there were other things going on.

"Move not," ordered Commander Hatqueban, and slowly, deliberately, walked toward the mechs.

She knows, thought Ingray. But what could she do? Nothing but lie still in the mech's grip as the commander walked right up to the mech that held Ingray, pulled her sidearm, and fired.

The mech lurched. Commander Hatqueban grabbed Ingray's arm and pointed the gun at Ingray's head. "No one move," the commander said, in Yiir. "Or I will shoot Miss Aughskold."

Ingray wanted to shout in fear and frustration. But Specialist Nakal had said that Hwae System Defense had taken over the Omkem freighters, and the mechs. There must be System Defense troops nearby, ready to help. The question was, could they get here before Hatqueban fired? Was there anything *she* could do? She thought of Nicale, unconscious and bleeding, held by another mech. The commander had been pointing a gun at Nicale when Ingray had triggered the alarm, and Nicale had ended up shot. So maybe trying to surprise the commander right now wasn't a very good idea. Then again, things hadn't gone the way the commander had wanted them to, because of what Ingray had done.

"Get down, Miss Aughskold," said Commander Hatqueban, still holding Ingray's arm. "You and I and Excellency Chenns are going to walk undisturbed to the Omkem Chancery."

"You won't get that far," said Specialist Nakal.

"That's as may be," said Commander Hatqueban, as Ingray tightened her grip on the heavy shoe nearest her hand and swung it at Commander Hatqueban's gun.

There was a deafening bang, and a pain along her forearm, enough to make her vision go black for an instant, for her to drop the shoe. Was she shot? But she didn't have time to worry about it. She squirmed in the mech's grip despite the flare of pain from her arm, grabbed the second shoe with her other hand, and smacked it into Hatqueban's faceplate once, twice, as more gunfire sounded, and then the commander staggered back.

Or, no, the commander had been pulled back, by two blue-and-gold-armored Hwae System Defense troops. Behind her, on the ground, lay Chenns, helmet still in his hand. "Is Chenns..." Ingray tried to make some sense out of what she was seeing, what had just happened. "Is he...?"

"No need to worry about him anymore," said Specialist Nakal. "He should have kept his helmet on."

"Let us help you down, miss," said another blue-and-gold-armored figure who was suddenly in front of Ingray, cutting off her view of Chenns and Commander Hatqueban. "Char can't walk, the commander did something to his mech."

"Good to know that's a vulnerable spot, though," said Specialist Nakal, cheerily. "And were they ever right about you, miss."

"Have you been shot, miss?" asked the blue-and-gold-armored soldier, as the other two Omkem mechs turned and began lumbering back toward the Assembly Chambers. Or Ingray thought that was what she saw; she was having trouble concentrating on anything but the pain in her arm. "We need to get you to a doctor and get you looked at."

"Don't worry about me!" exclaimed Ingray, heart racing. "You should take care of Nicale Tai first! And the prolocutor."

"No question, miss." A medimech trundled up. "The prolocutor is fine, and Miss Tai's already on a medimech and she'll be with a doctor in just a few seconds. Here's your ride."

"I can walk!" Ingray insisted. Though she wasn't actually sure she could.

"I'm sure you can," agreed the soldier as Specialist Nakal lowered her to sit on the medimech. "The question is, *should* you. I'm thinking not."

There was blood all over her sleeve, and her skirts. But

the medimech would scan her and take her to a doctor. With a lurch it started into motion.

"Wait!" cried the soldier. "Don't forget your shoes, miss." And he bent to pick them up and ran to set them in her lap.

"They're not my shoes!" she protested. But faintly, and the medimech had moved away, and if anyone answered she didn't hear.

19

A neman in a lungi and a loose, long shirt met the medi-mech as it trundled into the Assembly corridor. "Miss Aughskold," e said as e walked alongside. "Let's get you checked out and get correctives on that knee and that arm."

"Nicale?" asked Ingray. She sniffled, finding herself suddenly teary again, and wiped her eyes.

"She's headed to surgery now. Lie back. I'll bring the headrest up if you like."

"Please," said Ingray. A blue-and-gold-uniformed soldier came from somewhere ahead and set a cup of serbat in her good hand. "Thank you."

"You're welcome, miss," said the soldier, and turned and left.

"Lean back, now," said the doctor, and she did, and tried raising the cup to her mouth. Her hand shook, but she managed it. She caught the warm, spicy smell of the serbat. Took a sip and closed her eyes. "You're a little dehydrated," said the doctor. "Blood sugar's low. The knee is sprained, which I'm sure you already know. The bullet didn't hit anything vital, thank the almighty powers, it's basically a graze, though I'm sure it hurts quite a lot. You'll be up and around in no time."

"And Prolocutor Dicat? Is e all right?" She opened her eyes. Took another sip of serbat. It was obviously instant, and it was the best serbat she'd ever tasted.

"Our prolocutor's a tough old bird," said the doctor, approvingly. "It'd take more than a few soldiers to ruffle em."

"Yes," agreed Ingray.

They exited into the wide station corridor outside the First Assembly Chambers. The space was full of people. Not visiting children or officials or representatives' staff, but soldiers in the blue-and-gold uniform of Hwae System Defense, with here and there a few civilians. Or at least they wore civilian clothes.

"Ingray!" Netano, striding toward where Ingray lay on the medimech. Almost running, the closest to disarray that Ingray had ever seen her mother. Which was to say her jacket was slightly askew and her expression was one of clear distress. "Ingray, dear, are you all right?"

Ingray knew a performance when she saw one. But then, Netano lived a life that meant her every public move had to be carefully considered, sincere or not. Ingray had to some extent been living that life herself. And she couldn't stop a fresh spate of tears. "I'm fine, Mama."

Someone died. People got shot because of me. But she couldn't bring herself to say it. "I want to go home."

"You're going to the infirmary first," said the doctor, brusquely but not unkindly. "And I suspect Over Captain Utury is eager to speak with you." The doctor raised eir eyebrow as e said that but didn't comment further. "Representative Aughskold, as far as I can see your daughter has a sprained knee, and her arm is injured but not badly. She could probably use some rest and quiet, though she likely won't get it for a while yet. I'm going to set the medimech moving again; you're welcome to walk alongside if you like."

Netano took Ingray's good elbow. "Yes. Yes, of course I'm coming along."

A dark gray Omkem mech loomed up out of the crowd of soldiers, two beige cardboard rectangles in one appendage, a brush in another. "Wait! Miss, it's me, Specialist Nakal."

"I thought you couldn't walk," said Ingray. "Or your mech anyway."

"It still can't. I'm borrowing this one. If you don't mind, miss, would it be too much trouble to ask you to sign an entry ticket for me?"

"Um," said Ingray. She was already weeping again.

"Miss Aughskold has other things to worry about, Specialist," the doctor said sternly.

"It's all right," said Ingray. "I don't mind." She handed the cup of scrbat to Netano, who took one of the Assembly entry tickets and held it steady on top of one of the shoes on Ingray's lap, and the mech handed her the brush.

401

She had only ever done this for the personal sort of vestige that was of no value to anyone but herself and maybe a few friends. This was like those, in a way. There was no vestige more trivial than the entry card from some famous tourist stop. But in another way it was very, very different.

Ingray Aughskold, she wrote. Surprisingly legibly, considering her hand was still shaking. And then, on reflection, *thanks for the rescue*. She handed the card and brush to the mech. "Now you."

As the mech was signing its own entry card, the doctor said, scowling at the mech, "Thinking about your vestige collection, at a time like this."

"Vestiges are important," Netano said.

"Speaking of vestiges," ventured Ingray. "What happened to the Assembly Bell? And the *Rejection of Obligations*?"

"That's a good question, miss," said the mech, as it handed her the signed entry card. "Thank you so much." And it turned and lumbered away. Ingray looked at the card. It said, *Nice work with that shoe, Mech-Pilot Specialist Char Nakal*.

The medimech brought Ingray to the infirmary, and within ten minutes her knee and her arm were cased in the clear, hard shells of correctives.

"Can I leave now?" she asked the doctor who had applied the correctives, and who had also, like the doctor in front of the Assembly Chambers, looked her over and declared her otherwise uninjured.

"You can't leave," said this doctor. Bored and even. "Over Captain Utury has ordered you held here until she has a chance to talk to you."

An hour later a mech woke Ingray from a doze as it tottered in with a box of noodles and a cup of serbat, set them on a table beside the medimech Ingray still lay on, and tottered out.

Ingray closed her eyes and tried to send a message to her mother, but found she couldn't connect to the system's communications. All she got was a message saying her account had been suspended for security reasons. She sighed, and started in on the noodles.

She was halfway through them when, of all people, Danach came into the cubicle. "Hello, Ingray," he said. Perfectly polite and pleasant. And then, "Mama came by to see you before but you were asleep. She's stuck with the news services right now."

Mama came by to see you before. For a moment Ingray wasn't quite able to comprehend what Danach had said. "Oh," she managed after a moment. Something was wrong, but she couldn't quite place what it was, until she realized that something about the way he was standing, or talking, struck her as unfamiliar, but having seen that, she still couldn't say quite why or how. She continued. "I'm surprised you're on the station. Last I heard you were at home."

"How could I stay home when Mama was being held hostage?" Indignant. His manner instantly more familiar to her. No doubt he felt she'd all but accused him of not caring about Netano. Or, worse, of not mattering. He would certainly make some sort of jab in retaliation. But instead he turned inexplicably more subdued. "Look, Nuncle Lak is right. We're better off if we treat each other as allies, not adversaries."

That wasn't quite what Nuncle Lak had said. *If I've thought of you as an adversary*, she thought, *it was because you made yourself one from the moment you met me.* But then, it had come as a shock to Ingray that Nuncle Lak had ever even said such a thing to Danach to begin with, and a shock, now, that Danach would refer to it, even in a form that minimized his own responsibility.

And it didn't matter. For years it had seemed to Ingray as though she had no future without Netano's approval, that if she didn't manage the impossible task of unseating Danach, she would be a failure. Now, whether it was exhaustion and relief after the past few days, or whether it was something else, she found she didn't feel that way anymore. Didn't care if Danach thought he'd triumphed over her, didn't care who Netano named her heir. Whatever happened next, it couldn't possibly be more difficult than what she'd just been through, and she'd come through that more or less all right. Now she just wanted to go home, and have some peace and quiet.

Still, she couldn't quite bring herself to reply to him. "Mmm," she said, and took another mouthful of noodles.

"You were always Nuncle Lak's favorite." Resentful. "It's always been obvious."

Why would that matter? Why would Danach resent it, if it were true?

And then Ingray realized. Netano would almost certainly name her heir very soon. All Danach's anxieties about his future would be shortly relieved. He would be Netano, as he had always wanted.

And Nuncle Lak would be his chief of staff. Nuncle Lak worked very, very closely with Netano. And even if Danach wanted to remove em from eir position at some point, there would still be the problem of who to put in eir place who might be even half as good at the job, even half as trustworthy.

You were always Nuncle Lak's favorite. Did Danach think Nuncle Lak wanted to make Ingray eir successor?

Ingray almost laughed at the thought. Nuncle Lak had never even given the slightest hint that e might give eir name to Ingray. Besides, she couldn't do Nuncle Lak's job. She didn't want to even try. But it would explain why Danach might feel he had to make some attempt to get along with her, even if it was difficult for him.

Or did he think Netano might actually choose Ingray now? That he was about to lose the one thing that had always mattered most to him?

But that was ridiculous. Netano had always favored Danach. And even if the news services' reports about this incident made Ingray look good, well, that would be valuable to Netano whether or not Ingray was her heir. The only thing that had really changed was that Netano had every reason now to end the supposed competition between her children and name Danach heir quite soon.

It didn't matter to Ingray, not anymore. After the last few days she was certain her mother would never send her away. She would always be Netano's daughter. And sister, soon enough. As long as Nuncle Lak let her keep her job, she would have her own income, and if she lost that job, she could go somewhere else. Or she could even go somewhere else right now. For a dizzying moment she imagined asking the Geck ambassador if she could go along to the Conclave. They'd have to come back through Tyr on their way home, so she'd have a way back. What would that be like?

Or maybe she could work for Planetary Safety, like Taucris. Thinking of Taucris, she wasn't so sure she wanted to leave Hwae just now. At any rate, there were quite a lot of things to choose from.

"I don't think it matters," she said to Danach. "The important thing is, Mama is safe, and so is the station, and whether or not there's fighting first, the Federacy is going to have to turn around and go home."

"You're right," agreed Danach, managing not to sound grudging. "That's what matters."

"Look," Ingray said, "I want to go home." Or even a lodging room on the station would be better than this. Over Captain Utury could find her there, if she wanted. "I'd just get up, but…" With her good arm she gestured to her knee, then realized that the corrective was under her skirts and Danach couldn't see it. "There's a corrective on my knee and I can't bend my leg and I don't know what would happen if I tried to walk without a crutch or something. But now you're here, you can help me. Does Mama have rooms somewhere?" Ingray was certain she did. She must.

All of Danach's accustomed smugness returned in full

force. "Sorry, sis. I would, but I can't. There's a System Defense guard standing just outside to make sure you don't leave, and, as it happens, to keep any unauthorized visitors out."

As he spoke, he moved over to make room for Over Captain Utury, who had appeared in the doorway. "You are not on the list of authorized visitors, Mr Aughskold," she said. And before Danach could answer, "I'd have been here before, but urgent matters have required my attention. They still do, in fact, but I have a bit of time right now, while I'm waiting for something else."

"Have the Omkem not come into the system?" Ingray asked.

"Oh, they have," replied Over Captain Utury. "But I'm only responsible for what happens here on this station. Actually I'm waiting for orders regarding the disposition of the troops we captured, along with Commander Hatqueban. Those orders, I'm sure you realize, depend heavily on what's happening out by the Enthen gate just now. Not my responsibility, as I said. Mr Aughskold, I don't mean to keep you from your business."

"Of course, Over Captain," said Danach pleasantly, with a little bow of his head. "I'll see you later, Ingray."

"So, Miss Aughskold," said Over Captain Utury, when he was gone, "I already have Prolocutor Dicat's account of what happened. Miss Tai is still unconscious. She's out of surgery, by the way, and she'll be fine."

"It was my fault she got shot," said Ingray, with a sudden, overwhelming rush of guilt, and relief at the news that Nicale would be all right. "I messed up."

"That would be an understatement," replied Over Captain Utury. "You disobeyed my direct order to go to a civilian shelter and *stay there*. Do you know what the penalty is for not seeking shelter when ordered, and remaining there until given permission to leave? It's much higher here on the station than on the planet. For very good reasons, I might add." Ingray frowned but didn't answer. "What the hell did you think you were doing?"

"I told you what I was doing," Ingray replied.

"Infernal powers protect us," said Over Captain Utury. "Do you realize what could have happened? You could all three of you have ended up dead, yes. But many more would have died if Commander Hatqueban had ever become desperate enough to order her troops to attack the station structure directly. Just three deaths to prevent that—that would have been an entirely acceptable trade. I'd say as much to Representative Aughskold's face. I don't have to say it to Prolocutor Dicat. E already knows."

"And those children?" asked Ingray.

"This isn't a party game," Over Captain Utury replied. "If it were up to me you'd be looking at public censure and years of punitive labor, no matter who your mother is, no matter how many Geck friends you have. No matter who you know from Tyr Siilas."

Ingray blinked, alarmed and bewildered. "I don't know anyone from Tyr Siilas." Well, that wasn't strictly true. After spending so much time there recently she had quite a few acquaintances there, but not friends. Not anyone who could bring any influence to bear in a situation like this.

"Captain Uisine approached me while you were standing in front of the lareum," Over Captain Utury said, coldly. "He had a plan. Or rather, he insisted that once inside the lareum, *you* would have a plan. Once you'd had a few minutes to panic and then taken a look around you, he said. He would be there to look after you, and help you if he could."

"That's why you didn't stop me," Ingray realized. "That's why that cleaning mech didn't actually drag me away."

"I confess I was dubious. But Captain Uisine also had those mechs, which he offered to use in our interest. Not as many as we'd have liked—if he'd had a half dozen more we could have ended the whole mess in a few hours. The Geck likely had enough to help us out, but of course we couldn't ask them without potentially violating the treaty."

The Geck. "Wait. The Omkem already think they've violated the treaty. They didn't know the Geck ambassador was just a mech."

"Yes," agreed the over captain blandly. "Ambassador Tibanvori seemed unhappy that the Omkem have apparently come away with the impression that it was the Geck ambassador herself they shot. Apparently Mx Ket wasn't entirely clear when e spoke to Commander Hatqueban about it. Still, even shooting her mech is likely to cause some sort of diplomatic incident, unless the Geck decide to be understanding about it."

"But..." began Ingray.

"It would be extremely unfortunate," Over Captain Utury broke in, sharp and deliberate, "if the Omkem were to get the impression that the Geck had intervened to retrieve a mech that actually belonged to a citizen of Tyr. That might open the door to suspicions that the whole thing had been contrived for some other purpose, like allowing Captain Uisine to attempt to send in another, hopefully better camouflaged mech. Because that would be a blatant violation of the treaty."

Ingray remembered Commander Hatqueban asking, *Is there another one with you? We can't see any, but I'm sure it's here.* And Garal saying there hadn't been. That if they'd sent another, the commander would have detected it. "Did they...but they couldn't have! The Geck ambassador would never have agreed to do that." Would Garal have? But clearly e had.

"Of course she wouldn't," said Over Captain Utury. "But if we'd known they were going to go in to fetch their mech, we might have been able to take advantage of that. Without their knowing, of course. If it were to come out it would look very bad and cause quite a few problems, so we didn't do that. What Captain Uisine might have done on his own, though, well, we're not responsible for that."

Ingray frowned. The over captain continued. "Captain Uisine is one of the best mech-pilots I've ever had the honor to meet. We couldn't have taken control of the Omkem freighters so easily without his help. Even with that help it was going to be tricky to do it without alerting

410

Commander Hatqueban that we were up to something, and endangering you and the other hostages. We were still considering our options when you set off the alarm and gave us the opportunity to cut off communications to the Assembly Chambers and make it look like it was just part of the security system. And once we'd taken control of the freighters, it was simple enough—for certain values of 'simple'—to break into their mechs' controls and use them ourselves, with Commander Hatqueban none the wiser. Well, for a little while anyway."

"But what happened to the vestiges? What happened to the *Rejection of Obligations*, and the Assembly Bell?"

"We have them, don't worry," said the over captain.

"But how…"

"The *Rejection* and the Assembly Bell were both inside the mech that Specialist Nakal was piloting. It's a mystery how they got there. Frankly I can't help but notice that you've spent quite a lot of time with a notorious thief lately. I'm not prepared to guess what skills you might have picked up."

"But I…" Ingray was aghast. There was no way she could have done anything to either the *Rejection* or the Assembly Bell. "I didn't do anything. And Garal's not a thief."

But Tic was. He had stolen three ships right out from under the noses of the Geck. Or, she didn't think the Geck actually had noses, but. He'd been there, in the Assembly Chambers, even though she'd thought she was alone. But Over Captain Utury wasn't going to admit that he'd been there.

"So," said Ingray after a few moments of thought, "you must be grateful that I kept Commander Hatqueban from threatening or destroying such valuable vestiges."

"Don't push your luck, Miss Aughskold. Right now the only reason you are going to be able to walk out of here—and not straight into a holding cell—is that Captain Uisine is a friend of yours, and my superiors are hoping there's some way to get access to his mechs without violating the treaty. And having said that, I will now warn you that the events inside the lareum and the Assembly Chambers, and our conversation here, are to be kept absolutely secret. There's an official version that has already appeared on the news services. Don't worry—it's not really all that different from what actually happened, and you come off very heroically"—with no change of expression that Ingray could see, or change of her voice, Over Captain Utury managed to convey her distaste at saying that—"as do Prolocutor Dicat and Miss Tai. Once you've become acquainted with the official account you'll have access to communications again. If anyone asks you, just confirm that official version. But for the moment you're better off just claiming exhaustion and not speaking to any of the news services."

"I...I suppose I can do that." The whole conversation had seemed surreal. This part of it wasn't much stranger than the rest.

"It's not a question of whether you can," replied Over Captain Utury. "You don't have any choice in the matter. You do understand that?"

"I do," Ingray acknowledged.

"Good. And lest I seem ungrateful, I acknowledge that you risked your life, and in so doing you allowed us to resolve this with a good deal less bloodshed and damage to the station than might otherwise have been the case. And I'm sure the Tyr Executory and the Peoples of Byeit will consider themselves indebted."

"I..." Ingray didn't know what to say, whether to cry or laugh. "I want to go home now."

The station's various transport services were all running again, which meant Ingray only had to walk a short distance supported by her blue-and-gold-uniformed guard, and then board a tram that stopped just across from the hostelry where Netano was staying. One of Nuncle Lak's aides met her, supported her to the rooms her mother had taken, sent Ingray to a bath while her clothes were laundered, and then installed her in a bed with a thick, fluffy blanket and cushions tucked all around, one under her injured arm. "Representative Aughskold is still in meetings," the aide said. "She'll be with you as soon as she can. I'll bring you some water. Would you like some serbat?"

Ingray remembered lying on the bench in the Assembly Chambers, wishing for just this—maybe not this exactly, because she'd wanted her own bedroom at home, but still—her bed, a cup of serbat, and maybe some food, and she realized she was quite hungry. "Is it possible to get some fruit and cheese?"

"Of course it is," said the aide. "I'll take care of that right now."

Ingray lay back against the cushions and closed her eyes. The correctives would probably be off in a few hours. She wasn't entirely sure what she would do once they came off anyway, and in the meantime this was wonderful, lying here comfortably, knowing she was safe and could go wherever she wanted once she could walk on her own again.

Time to check her messages. Top priority, a note from Nuncle Lak saying e'd assigned an aide to deal with messages that might be an annoyance or didn't need Ingray's personal attention. The aide e named was someone Ingray had known for years, and a quick look at the unfiltered mass of waiting messages told her Nuncle Lak had done her a favor.

The aide had already marked a few messages for Ingray's attention. The first was from one of the children from the lareum, and it read, *Dear Miss Ingray, thank you for saving my life. When I grow up I will work for you. I am good at math and I know how to cook noodles.* There were more, similar messages where that one came from, the aide indicated.

Next, a message from Taucris. Ingray spent some time over that one, and then some time over a reply. That done, she took a look at the station news services.

The version of events Over Captain Utury had given the news services was nearly unrecognizable, but as the over captain had suggested, from a certain angle it bore at least a superficial resemblance to what Ingray had actually gone through. The three of them did indeed come off as heroic, facing down the menacing Commander

Hatqueban and her huge and terrifying military mechs. Daringly rescuing the *Rejection of Obligations* and the Assembly Bell. The portrayal of Prolocutor Dicat seemed the most like emself in all the versions Ingray found, though still not quite right. Nicale might as well have been someone else entirely, and Ingray herself—well. Ingray didn't know who it was the "official sources" who'd supplied the information were talking about, but it couldn't have been her.

Ingray sighed. Blinked away the news, looked at her personal messages again, but Taucris hadn't replied yet. Thought of sending a message to Tic, but she didn't know how to address it. And Garal—would she need to send that to the Geck ship? How would she do that? Nuncle Lak would know. She sent the question to em. Heard the aide come in with food and serbat but discovered that she didn't want to open her eyes. And then she must have slept, because the next thing she knew the pieces of the spent corrective on her knee were a scratchy annoyance under her skirts and the aide was standing in the doorway saying, quietly, "Miss Aughskold? The infirmary sent along a pair of shoes they say is yours, and Officer Taucris Ithesta is here to see you."

20

Ingray had been hoping that Taucris would come, but once they were settled on the bed, leaning shoulder to shoulder—on Ingray's uninjured side, of course—on a bank of cushions, the pieces of corrective handed off to Nuncle Lak's aide, Ingray wasn't sure what to say. She couldn't talk about what she'd been through for the past few days, not in any truthful way, and talking about it in terms of what she'd seen in the news services felt not only useless but dishonest.

But as soon as the aide had left, with the promise of a fresh decanter of serbat, Taucris said, "I know you can't talk about what happened, and we're all just supposed to believe what's on the news, so I won't ask you about it. Unless you want me to." She looked sidelong at Ingray. "Maybe you'd rather watch an entertainment."

Which Ingray thought sounded like a nice idea, but they

began the process of choosing one—something light, something funny, something new—which turned somehow into a conversation. About Taucris's work, about Ingray's uncertainties in her own job, about parents and siblings, and each other, and hours later, the entertainment unchosen, Ingray and Taucris still sitting close up against each other, an empty tray on the bed with a scattering of seeds and bits of cheese, the aide came back into the room and told them that Tic and Garal had come.

"We didn't mean to interrupt anything," said Tic, with a barely noticeable glance at the bed they were sitting on. "I'd have sent a message but apparently I won't get access to system messaging unless I take a job with Hwae System Defense."

"You're not going to take it?" Ingray asked, gesturing Tic and Garal an invitation to sit on the bed.

He sat, and Garal beside him. "What, and sign away my mechs? That's what they want, you know."

"You were there," said Ingray. "You followed Garal and Ambassador Tibanvori and got back in. You put the vestiges in the mech somehow, without anyone seeing you."

"I have no idea what you mean," said Tic, seriously.

"Don't look at *me*," said Garal. "I certainly wouldn't know anything about it."

"And I'd have had to figure out how to hide from the mechs that spotted me the first time," added Tic.

"Over Captain Utury said you were the best mechpilot she'd ever met," Ingray said, and with a blink sent a request for more food and serbat.

"Of course she did," agreed Garal. "Because he is."

"Are you safe?" asked Taucris. "I mean, I know the Geck have acknowledged you as Geck, but that doesn't mean everything's forgotten. Are you actually allowed to leave the Geck ship?"

"I wouldn't say forgotten," said Garal, with a very small smile. "But considering the ambassador herself is clearly able to come and go as she pleases, permission or not, and considering how much System Defense would like to convince the Geck to maybe sell them some mechs..." E shrugged. "Yes, I have permission to be here, and unless I do something very foolish no one will bother me."

"So..." Tic hesitated then. "I promised I wouldn't talk about this." He glanced at Taucris. "The whole point of my getting involved was to avoid Ingray getting killed. Well, and doing what I could to prevent the Omkem from getting one step closer to being able to threaten Tyr. But someone did almost get killed."

Someone did get killed, Ingray thought, *and it was my fault.* But Tic obviously meant Nicale. She wondered what Tic had been doing in those few seconds when the light had gone out, when she'd heard gunshots. When Nicale had been shot. "She's going to be all right."

"Yes," agreed Tic. "I'm relieved. But people getting killed—that's basically what the military is about. And I don't want to do that. And besides, it's the mechs that they really want. I have them locked up right now, and I'm keeping a close eye on them. I'm sure the over captain is as honest as it's possible for an over captain to be, but I'm not taking any chances. I paid good money for my Tyr citizenship, and I'm still enjoying my shipping route. I might change my mind someday, but..." He waved away that future uncertainty.

"And the Geck?" asked Taucris. "Do you think they're really going to leave you alone now?"

"They will," said Garal. E pulled a cushion over from the other end of the bed and leaned eir elbow on it. "Certainly for however long the Conclave takes, and I'm sure they're going right home after that." Tic leaned his own elbow companionably on the same cushion.

"I read the Geck ambassador's message," said Tic. "And I'm...I haven't replied. I don't think I'm going to. I think it's better if I don't." Calm and serious, as though the contents of that message had not upset him at all, which Ingray was sure had not been the case. "I'm... I almost wish she hadn't sent it. But then again..." He hesitated. "I think it's going to be a while before I quite know how to think about it."

"She did send over some sea worms, though," said Garal.

"I almost sent them back," acknowledged Tic. "But damn, I miss sea worms."

Ingray imagined Tic eating worms, cold and wriggling, and managed not to grimace. And was struck by the thought that when Tic wanted that feeling of being home and safe, he doubtless thought of live sea worms and room-temperature algae paste, and lukewarm, salty poick rather than fruit and cheese and serbat. "Did the ambassador send some poick, too?" she asked.

Tic gave a laugh that somehow seemed both genuine and strained. "She did. Don't tell me you have a taste for it? I'm sure Garal can get you some if you want it."

"I tried it." She made a face.

"I've already said it's an acquired taste," said Garal. Tic laughed again, much less tense this time. Garal continued. "I was thinking about going to the Conclave, but I've decided I want some quiet and routine for a while."

"Are you going with Captain Uisine, then?" asked Taucris. She had evinced no surprise at Tic and Garal arriving together, or sitting so close.

"With the ambassador's permission, yes. Though I am under orders to memorize the treaty by the time the Geck ship returns to Tyr Siilas, and I have a list of restrictions I have to observe. Most of them obvious things like not breaking laws in the systems I visit. Which I wouldn't want to anyway. And some that didn't make much sense to me when I read them, so I assume they're based on Geck biology."

"They are," Tic confirmed. "And fortunately culturing sea worms won't break the treaty, unless we dump some in a non-Geck ocean. Which I know enough not to do to begin with."

"You can have them all," said Garal, equably. "Ingray, you could probably go to the Conclave if you asked. You'd have to ask very soon, but I'm sure the ambassador would let you come along."

Go along to the Conclave! There would be aliens there—the Rrrrrr, the Presger. And, chilling thought, the artificial intelligences that had broken away from the

Radch and demanded recognition as a Significant species in their own right. No matter the actual result of that conclave, it would be a historic occasion. She might well be the only Hwaean to go. She was fairly sure no Hwaeans had been at any of the others.

It would be an adventure, that was certain. And sitting here, safe, snuggled up against Taucris, she realized that, like Garal, she didn't want any more adventures. Not for a while. "No," she said. "I just want to go home. I want to go down to the planet, back to the house in Arsamol." And do her job in Nuncle Lak's office, have everything back to normal for a while. Except, having Taucris here wasn't normal, not just yet, but that was more than all right. "It'll be years, won't it? I heard it will be years just for everyone to get there, and this is a complicated issue, they might be more years debating it."

"That's true," said Garal. "It might be better to go visit some time, instead of committing to spend the next five or six years of your life with the Geck."

"You sell yourself short, you know," Tic said to Ingray then. "If your mother is somehow unimpressed with you, that's her problem, not yours. And actually, as a mother she may not be all cuddles and hugs, and it's possible you'll be happier at some distance from her—I think that's likely, actually—but from what I can see I'm pretty sure she does care about you. And that nuncle of yours certainly knows what you're worth."

"Danach will likely be easier to live with once the inheritance thing is settled," added Garal. "Still, I couldn't blame you if you wanted to be away from all of them for a while."

"You could come with us," suggested Tic.

"No," said Ingray. "No, I want to stay home for a while."

At that point, the aide came back into the room with a tray of bread and cheese and said, "Miss Ingray, your mother would like a few minutes with you. She's in the room just across."

The room was nearly identical to the one Ingray had just left, except the bed was rolled up and where it would have been, Netano sat on a cushioned bench, and the wall to her right showed Nuncle Lak, sitting in a single chair, in a nondescript pale blue room. "You wanted to see me, Mama?" asked Ingray.

"Ingray, dear. Sit down." Netano gestured at the space on the bench beside her. Ingray sat. "Have you seen the news services?" Netano continued. "You're a hero."

She didn't feel like a hero. "Apparently."

"I feel like I need to apologize to you," said Netano. And then, with a glance at Nuncle Lak, though e had said nothing, hadn't moved at all, "Your nuncle tells me I need to apologize to you. I've always told you children that any of you could be my heir, and I would choose the best one."

"It's all right," said Ingray. Almost feeling as though she was telling the truth. "I've always known it was going to be Danach. Everyone knows."

Netano gave a sardonic half-smile. "Even when he was small, Danach always had a . . . a certain something. And when he decides on a project, he is absolutely ruthless in carrying it out. And he's always understood that the family's interests are his interests. Even this business with the dirt mover—once he realized he had to change course, he did so immediately."

A certain something, thought Ingray. Of course Danach had that certain something. He was from a good family, with old names and a history. He wasn't some nobody out of a public crèche. But, no. Ingray wouldn't be angry or bitter. She had her own life to make, and she could do that whether she had *a certain something* or not. *You sell yourself short*, Tic had just said, and she wasn't going to do that anymore. She didn't need to worry about Netano, or Danach.

"Your mother considers herself to be very egalitarian, very democratic," said Nuncle Lak. "She was determined to give her public crèche fosters—that would be you, and Vaor before e left—every chance at inheriting. But somehow they never had that *certain something*."

Ingray managed to keep her face more or less impassive, despite her surprise. She had never, ever heard Nuncle Lak speak about Netano in quite that way, in Netano's presence or not. Certainly not on that topic.

"Now's not the time, Lak," Netano said sharply.

"Maybe not," conceded Nuncle Lak. "But that time is fast approaching."

Netano sighed. "I got a message from Prolocutor Dicat, not an hour ago, saying that if the gossip e'd heard was correct, I was choosing the wrong heir. I think e is probably correct. I think I should give my name to you, Ingray."

It was as though the solid ground she had been

standing on, steady and secure, had suddenly yawned open beneath her feet. "I...what?"

"Your mother wants to name you her heir," said Nuncle Lak drily.

"I...but..."

"You're thinking you can't do it," said Nuncle Lak. "But you can. And you wouldn't be doing any of it on your own. Not at first. Not for a very long while, I hope."

"And you're a hero," said Netano. "I'm quite sure the version of events I'm seeing in the news services isn't... entirely accurate. That's how the news services are, and besides, I don't doubt there are things System Defense would rather keep quiet. But you walked into that situation willingly, and you did it to save those children, and to save Hwae. And what's more, you succeeded. The details don't matter."

"And you've managed to acquire the good opinion of Prolocutor Dicat," added Nuncle Lak. "I'm sure you realize that's not easily done. That may well be extremely helpful, quite soon. Prolocutor Budrakim has managed to put himself in a remarkably difficult position this close to elections. There's every chance you would be Third Prolocutor this time next year."

Danach. Danach had known or suspected that this was coming. That was why he'd tried so hard to be pleasant, back in the infirmary. Why even so he'd said, resentfully, *You were always Nuncle Lak's favorite.*

"The Tyr Executory is fully aware of the debt they owe you," continued Netano. "They've sent to offer you indefinite residency documents, if you want them. No fees."

"Though not free lodging or citizenship," Nuncle Lak put in. "The Tyr are still the Tyr, after all."

"And the Peoples of Byeit have also expressed their thanks," Netano continued. "And there's your personal connection with the Geck ambassador."

"In short," said Nuncle Lak, "at this point your mother would be a fool to name anyone but you her heir."

She'd done it. She'd bested Danach. In the most undeniable, final way possible. This was a victory she had barely ever allowed herself to imagine, even as a private, grandiose fantasy. She'd done it.

She would be Representative Aughskold. Maybe Prolocutor Aughskold. The house in Arsamol, with the beautiful colored-glass front, the flower-lined courtyard, would always be hers. Of course she would be generous and gracious and let Danach live there.

She took a deep breath, opened her mouth, and found herself saying, "No. No, Danach's always been your heir."

"Are you worried I don't mean it?" asked Netano. "Or that I don't really want you as my heir? I do mean it, and I do want you to be the next Netano."

"No, I just don't want it," said Ingray. And the free-falling fear that had been growing ever since Netano had made her offer dissipated. Mostly. "I'm not your best choice. I wouldn't be good at it. Whatever the news services are saying about me now, it won't last, and I'm not good at the politics. No, you should give it to Danach." And then she braced herself for the inevitable result of having thwarted Netano.

To Ingray's distressed astonishment, Nuncle Lak

laughed. "I warned you, sis. Way back when." Amazingly, Netano only sighed again. Nuncle Lak continued. "I suppose it's useless for me to make the same offer and ask you to be *my* heir? Not that I don't want to very much, but it would mean you'd have to work closely with Danach, and, well, I know how that's bound to turn out. I'd have offered long since, otherwise."

"Ingray, dear," began Netano, into Ingray's inability to answer this. "I really think..."

"Don't argue with her, sis," said Nuncle Lak. "She knows what she wants. If that's not what *you* want, well, that's how it is to have children. And I imagine it's the better choice for her, if not for you."

"No," protested Ingray. "No, Danach will be much better. He's wanted it all his life."

"Which isn't the same as being suited to it," pointed out Nuncle Lak. "But no matter his deficiencies—no, we're not discussing that right now," he said as Netano sighed again. "But no matter the question of how suited he is, I do think he'll work very hard to be worthy of it."

"Yes," agreed Netano. "I think he will."

"But, Nuncle," asked Ingray, "do I still have my job?"

As Ingray stepped back into her own room, Garal was just finishing saying something, and Taucris and Tic both laughed. They all fell silent when they saw Ingray standing there, tense, managing to look as though nothing had happened, or so she thought, but Taucris immediately said, concerned, "What happened?" and they all turned to stare at her.

She tried to swallow and found she couldn't. "Mama said she wanted to give me her name."

"Congratulations," Tic said. "I know that's an important thing here, and quite something when the name you're getting is Netano Aughskold's."

Taucris frowned, still concerned. Garal said, "I was wrong, you *will* be in a position to do something about the situation in Compassionate Removal. Or at least to try."

Ingray opened her mouth to answer, and burst into tears. Taucris leapt off the bed and put her arms around Ingray, who gratefully laid her head on Taucris's shoulder. After a few moments Ingray managed to say, "I said no."

A moment of silence. Ingray could see nothing but the green silk of Taucris's shirt, which Ingray hoped wouldn't be damaged by the tears soaking it. Then Tic said, "Oh, thank goodness. I was having trouble imagining you as Representative Aughskold, but I wasn't going to say anything if that was what you wanted."

"I thought it was," admitted Ingray, still into Taucris's shoulder. "And when she said it, I don't know, I meant to say *yes* or *thank you* or something but instead I said no."

"Here, sit down," said Taucris. "I'll pour you some serbat."

"I'm sorry," said Garal, when she'd sat down and Taucris was reaching for a cup.

"For what?" asked Ingray.

"You started crying right when I said that about reforming Compassionate Removal. I didn't mean to

make you feel like you were responsible for that. Because
you're not. It's very important to me, and I would love to
have your help, but you're not the only help I have. The
important thing is you didn't say yes to something that
would have made you unhappy."

"Oh." Ingray wiped her eyes and took the cup of serbat
Taucris offered. "I'm not sure I even heard that. I just…"
Fresh tears threatened. No, no, she had heard it, and she
had felt, at that moment, that she had failed em. And that
had been as much as her self-control could take.

"Do you still have your job?" Taucris asked.

"Yes. Yes, and even if I get my own place I'll always
have my room at home, Mama said."

"Parents always say that," said Taucris.

"Do they?" asked Tic. "Mine didn't."

"Nor mine," Garal said, voice dry.

"Well," observed Ingray, with a small hiccup, "but I
didn't get any sea worms."

"Not everyone can be as lucky as I am," Tic agreed.

The next morning Ingray met briefly with Nuncle Lak.
"Well, I'll be sorry to lose you in the office," e said, from
the wall of Ingray's room, as she and Taucris sat cross-
legged on her bed. "But I think it's the right choice. Any
sort of reform of Compassionate Removal will need
more than just Netano's support, so it's better if you do
that on your own, officially. And of course any charity
work you do, especially with the district's public crèches,
will be good for everyone, whether or not you're doing
it in Netano's name." E sighed. "I do wish you'd stay to

talk to the major news services. But I can't blame you for wanting to go straight home. I would, in your place."

"The *Arsamol District Voice* will be very happy with their exclusive, though," Taucris pointed out.

"They will," agreed Nuncle Lak, with a smile. "And Netano can only benefit from that as well, which I will certainly point out to her when she wakes up. We talked to Danach last night, and of course he's very happy, though he was certainly surprised. He's too smart not to realize that you probably turned it down, Ingray, but also too smart to say anything about it. We're delaying the announcement, though. We don't want to give anyone the impression that you've been slighted. So actually the fact that you've got some plans of your own is very helpful to us."

"It's better to do it that way," agreed Ingray. She'd had confidence that Nuncle Lak would have reached the same conclusions she had, but she still felt relief. If Danach were to be announced as Netano's heir immediately, Ingray would have to stay here a few days, to be seen congratulating him, and to avoid giving the impression that she resented the choice. "You'll have time to plan the announcement, and make sure there's a big party." Danach would like that.

"Yes," Nuncle Lak agreed. "And Danach won't have to share the spotlight the whole time. You'll come, though, yes? It won't be for a few months, at the very least."

"Yes, of course," said Ingray.

As soon as Nuncle Lak signed off, Ingray and Taucris left the lodging via a service entrance, in an attempt to avoid the news service mechs, and took a series of crowded lifts and trams to the elevator shuttle. GECK DELEGATION DEPARTING DAY AFTER TOMORROW, one of the news services said in Ingray's vision as she stood next to Taucris on the first tram ride. Garal got only a brief mention, far, far into the article, and Tic wasn't mentioned at all, let alone his spider mechs. FIGHTING AT THE ENTHEN GATE said another news service announcement. FEDERACY SHIP CAPTURED; THREE FLED. She glanced closer, to discover that Commander Hatqueban was still in the custody of Hwae System Defense. Excellency Chenns wasn't mentioned at all. Prolocutor Dicat, along with the rest of the First Assembly, had met with ambassadors from Tyr and Byeit. The younger Prolocutor Dicat. "We don't want a war," he'd told the news services. "But we'll be happy to oblige the Federacy if they're determined to have one." The Omkem Chancery had not responded to the news services' requests for a statement.

News services based in Third Assembly districts were already speculating on the chances of Ethiat Budrakim resigning, or even facing litigation. Neither he nor his daughter were answering questions.

Ingray blinked the news away. Pulled up a draft of a message she was thinking of sending to the younger Ethiat Budrakim. Garal had seemed to trust eir sister somewhat, and Ingray was fairly sure she'd had nothing to do with either what had happened to Garal or the events of the last week. Likely her political career was over, at least for the foreseeable future, but that wasn't her fault, and Ingray thought she might be sympathetic to an attempt to rethink Compassionate Removal.

In the seat next to her on the second tram, Taucris said, "Danach's awake. I've just had a message from him."

"I have, too," Ingray admitted. "I don't think I want to answer him right now."

They got off at the shuttle dock. Detoured to get a change of clothes—all Ingray had was what she'd been wearing ever since she'd gotten on the elevator, days and days ago it seemed like. It had been all right while she was still in the rooms Netano had taken, and she could make the trip from the station to Arsamol with just the clothes she was wearing—she'd done it just a week or two ago. But this time she didn't have to. She grabbed a set of clothes in a soft, comfortable synthetic, blue and orange, and then, thinking of the hairpins she'd never gotten back, she added a blue scarf for her hair; she knew any pins she got would likely be gone before she set foot on Hwae, and her hair wouldn't stay in braids any better than it would hold hairpins.

Walking into the shuttle lobby, she felt as though the last week or so had never happened, or worse, that she was about to repeat it. The whole thing was so familiar— even down to the children in crèche uniforms waiting for the shuttle. And high on the walls, the shifting images from the history of Hwae. As Ingray watched, the picture changed to the archprolocutor making the last payment on the debt to Tyr, the *Rejection of Obligations* ready to be unrolled behind him. That image, one every Hwaean had seen at one time or another, felt different now. Was it because she'd seen the *Rejection* rolled up, torn, folded over to be shoved into the compartment of a mech, as though it were any piece of cloth, instead of awesome and untouchable in its case? Or was it because she knew, now, that the *Rejection* this image depicted wasn't genuine? Or maybe it was just that she'd been through so much in one week that she still had to sort through that she didn't have the emotional energy to spend contemplating this image, which was even now shifting to another one?

"Danach is here," said Taucris.

He was. Walking toward them from the middle of the lobby. "Ingray," he said, voice accusing. "I wanted to talk to you."

"I'm sorry," she said. Though she wasn't, not really. "I wanted to catch the shuttle to the elevator." Taucris, standing beside her, said nothing.

"I don't understand," said Danach. Still sounding aggrieved. "You said no. I know you did, I asked, because I was sure Mama was going to give it to you. Then I thought Nuncle Lak must have named you eir heir, but e hasn't."

"You don't want me as Lak Aughskold," Ingray said.

"No," Danach said. "I don't. But I'm going to need *someone* as Lak, someone I can trust." He looked for a moment at the images on the wall, and then back at Ingray. "E said if you won't be Lak, it's my fault and I'll just have to deal with that. I don't think e's being fair. E always favored you."

"Maybe e has." Ingray had begun to realize that Danach was probably right about that. "But it doesn't matter. Mama offered me her name, and I told her I didn't want it. Because I don't. I don't want to be an Assembly representative. I don't want to be a prolocutor." But maybe she wanted Danach to remember that she could have been. If she'd wanted it. "And I don't want to be the chief of staff for a representative or a prolocutor. I just want to be Ingray Aughskold." He stared at her, plainly disbelieving.

"They're boarding the shuttle," said Taucris, as uniformed children began filing by.

"Here, wait," said Ingray. Walked over to a kiosk and got an *A Visit to Hwae Station* card. Walked back to where Danach stood, Taucris watching him warily. "Do you have a brush?" He produced one from somewhere in his jacket. Ingray's arm was still in its corrective, so Taucris held the card steady as Ingray wrote, *Congratulations to the new Netano, from your sister Ingray*, and the date. She handed the brush back to Danach, and then the card. "There. I could have had it, but I turned it down. So now you know for certain that I don't want it, and I'm no threat to you."

"Ascended saints, Ingray, I'm not here to start a fight!"

"Then why are you here, Danach?" asked Taucris.

"Because..." He stopped. Frowned even more intently than he already was. "What are you going to demand in return?"

Taucris gave an incredulous *hah*. But Ingray said, "No, it's a good question. And the answer is, I don't want anything. But if it makes you feel better, if you get to be prolocutor, I want you to investigate conditions in Compassionate Removal."

"That won't be very popular," Danach pointed out. "They're criminals."

"Suit yourself," said Ingray, and turned to go.

"Look, Ingray." He sounded almost angry. "When I thought—when I knew that Mama was going to pick you, I was...that was hard. I was upset. It wasn't fair. It was just luck, you being in the right place at the right time. But I knew I was going to have to work with you. I decided that I would, that I was going to make it work. And then...look, just...It's the one thing I wanted most in my whole life. If it had been me, I would never have turned it down for you."

"I know," said Ingray. If he hadn't been family, if he had been some political opponent of Mama's, Ingray would have given him her sweetest smile right now. But he knew where that smile had come from, had his own version he could deploy when he needed it. And besides, he was trying. He had almost thanked her, even though it had obviously cost him to even come close to it. Even though he couldn't resist protesting as he did so. "I didn't do it for you. But you're welcome." He didn't move. "You're probably awfully busy right now. I appreciate your coming to talk to me. But I have to board the shuttle."

"Changing anything about Compassionate Removal will be tricky," he said. "I'll probably have better luck if the issue is raised by district voters, instead of me just bringing it to the Assembly. Better yet if it came from the voters of more than one district."

"Yes," agreed Ingray. "I'm already starting on that

part. It would be nice to have your help, though. Or at least nice to have you consider helping."

He nodded. "Yes. Yes, you're right. You'll know how to do that." He sounded as though the words didn't want to leave his mouth. "Let me know if you need anything. I have to go now, I have a lot of things I need to take care of. Have a good trip." And he turned and left.

"*Just luck*, he said!" Taucris's voice was disbelieving. "*In the right place at the right time!*"

"Well, it kind of was."

"It wasn't, either!" insisted Taucris. "But I suppose it's good he knows how much he owes you."

"I suppose it is," agreed Ingray. She turned toward the shuttle entrance and saw a knot of children in blue-and-yellow tunics and trousers staring at her, two Station Safety officers standing behind them.

"Miss Ingray!" cried one child. "Are you going on the elevator with us?"

"It looks like I am," said Ingray. "But where's your caretaker?"

"He ran away and left us in the lareum," said another child, to the evident distress of several other of the children. "He has to find a new job now."

"Shh!" said another child. "You're not supposed to say that!"

"We're escorting the children down the elevator, miss," said one of the Station Safety officers.

"Well, it looks like we're traveling together," said Ingray.

"We were interviewed by the news service!" exclaimed one of the children.

"Miss Ingray has been interviewed *millions* of times," said the first child, clearly trying to chart a course between knowledgeably bored, and excited by the idea of such celebrity.

"It's been an adventure, hasn't it," Ingray said. "But I'm ready to go home and rest and just be safe. Aren't you?" The children noisily agreed. "This is my friend Planetary Safety Officer Taucris Ithesta."

"Hello, Officer Ithesta," the children chorused.

"We need to board the shuttle, kids," said one of the Station Safety officers.

"If they leave without us," cried a child, "Miss Ingray will hit them with her shoe!" The children laughed, and the Station Safety officers tried not to.

"It wasn't *my* shoe!" protested Ingray.

"It's better not to threaten the shuttle staff, though," said Taucris as the Station Safety officers herded the children away.

"Officer Ithesta is right," said one of the Station Safety officers. "Come on, Miss Ingray will be on the shuttle with us."

"We'll try not to let them bother you too much," said the other officer. "But..." She waved vaguely toward the children, chattering now as they made their way to the shuttle entrance.

"Well," observed Taucris as the last of the children boarded, "it won't be a boring trip, anyway. Do we have everything?"

Ingray looked behind her, at the emptying lobby, the shifting images on the wall above; the image of the archprolocutor making the last payment to the Tyr Executory had come around again. "I'm pretty sure we do." She took Taucris's hand, and they walked together away from the noise and crowd of the station, toward the shuttle bound for the elevator, and home.

Acknowledgments

I'd like to thank my fabulous editors Will Hinton (Orbit US) and Jenni Hill (Orbit UK) for all their help turning my manuscript into a much better book. Thanks also to my wonderful agent, Seth Fishman.

Thanks to Crystal Huff, Margo-Lea Hurwicz, Ada Palmer, Anna and Kurt Schwind, Rachel and Mike Swirsky, Juliette Wade, and Jo Walton for incredibly helpful advice, comments, and discussion while I was writing the book.

I will always have a grateful shout-out for my local libraries: St. Louis County Library, St. Louis County Library Consortium, St. Louis Public Library, the Webster University Library, and University of Missouri St. Louis's Thomas Jefferson Library. And to all the inter-library loans librarians out there—you rule. Libraries are a public good. They make the world a better place. Please support your local libraries whatever way you can, even if it's just checking out books.

And as always, thanks to my husband, Dave, and my children, Aidan and Gawain. They've always been a hundred percent behind this writing thing, and I am grateful and fortunate to have their help and support.

About the author

The record-breaking winner of the Hugo, Nebula, Arthur C. Clarke and British Science Fiction Association awards for her debut novel, **Ann Leckie** lives in St Louis, Missouri, with her husband, children and cats. You can find her website at www.annleckie.com or chat to her on Twitter at @Ann_Leckie.

Find out more about Ann Leckie and other Orbit authors by registering for the free monthly newsletter at www.orbitbooks.net.